# DEATH OF
# AN EX

## Also by Delia Pitts

### Vandy Myrick Mysteries

*Trouble in Queenstown*

### Ross Agency Mysteries

*Murder Take Two*

*Murder My Past*

*Pauper and Prince in Harlem*

*Black and Blue in Harlem*

*Practice the Jealous Arts*

*Lost and Found in Harlem*

### Short Stories

"Midnight Confidential"
—*Midnight Hour: A Chilling Anthology of Crime Fiction
from 20 Authors of Color*

"The Killer"
—*The Best American Mystery and Suspense 2021*

"Talladega 1925"
—*Chicago Quarterly Review Vol. 33:
An Anthology of Black American Literature*

"Swanetta's Way"
—*Chicago Quarterly Review Vol. 40:
The Thirtieth Anniversary Issue*

"Yuletide Clean-Up"
—*Festive Mayhem 4 Fall 2024*

# DEATH OF
# AN EX

A Vandy Myrick Mystery

## Delia Pitts

MINOTAUR BOOKS
NEW YORK

First published in the United States by Minotaur Books, an imprint of St. Martin's Publishing Group

*EU Representative:* Macmillan Publishers Ireland Ltd, 1st Floor, The Liffey Trust Centre, 117–126 Sheriff Street Upper, Dublin 1, DO1 YC43

www.minotaurbooks.com

Design by Meryl Sussman Levavi

The Library of Congress Cataloging-in-Publication Data is available upon request.

ISBN 978-1-250-90424-9 (hardcover)
ISBN 978-1-250-90425-6 (ebook)

Our books may be purchased in bulk for specialty retail/ wholesale, literacy, corporate/premium, educational, and subscription box use. Please contact MacmillanSpecialMarkets@macmillan.com.

First Edition: 2025

1 3 5 7 9 10 8 6 4 2

To my husband, John W. Vincent
Together every step of the way
Forever

# HOMECOMING

# CHAPTER **ONE**

My guilt was a precious anchor, pulling me to the cemetery. This overdue date with my dead daughter clawed at my gut as the threat of October's early sunsets spurred my footsteps. I needed to reach her gravesite before night collapsed over Queenstown.

I shoved the glass door of the First Federal Bank. A cold fist of air jabbed back. Second heave and I staggered into the dusk. It had taken only ten minutes to deposit the fraternity's repulsive check in my bank account. Despite my worries, I'd managed to complete the transaction without questions from the teller. Or tears from me.

I turned off my cell phone, no interruptions allowed. Trotting between sluggish cars on Center Street, I stepped into the Queenstown Pharmacy to grab my tool for this expedition, a cheap plastic cigarette lighter. Then around to the parking lot behind the pharmacy. My office was on the second floor above the drugstore. With luck and speed, I could reach my car and escape to the cemetery before my boss spotted me.

I glanced up at Elissa Adesanya's office window. Sleet dropped a curtain of stinging rain over the yellow rectangle. Fingers crossed she was buried under a stack of law books, grinding on a new case. I was the lawyer's pet private investigator. In-house talent on a short leash. When Elissa snapped, I jumped. Usually. Insurance frauds, process serving, divorces. My portfolio was anything lucrative and low-grade sleazy. Restarting a career in middle age meant I was always short on money. Pride never bought groceries.

As I fumbled to turn the key in the car's lock, remorse stung like the icy needles pelting my face. Not the usual guilt I blew through every week: piles of filthy dishes, neglected expense reports, and wayward men were shrug-worthy faults. Only Elissa cared about those infractions. Ignoring her protests was my favorite parlor trick. Scrubbing her out of my hair kept our friendship stable. Elissa and I were the same age, forty-eight. Friends since college. Two Black women trying to make coin in a small New Jersey town that questioned our competence, challenged our integrity, and sometimes doubted our right to exist. But Elissa and I were not equals. I was obliged by the monthly retainer, slim expense account, and rent-free office space next to the supply closet. Only on that distant glory morning when I inscribed EVANDER MYRICK, INVESTIGATIONS on the door could I skip without answering the boss.

But now my conscience hurt for real. Today, a big check from the fraternity settlement landed in my mailbox. This blood money paid to forget my daughter's death burned a hole in my pocket. And my heart. Monica had died almost three years ago, drowning in her own vomit in a fraternity house on the Rutgers University campus. Now my punctured conscience demanded speed. Five months absence from her grave was long enough. To soothe my guilt and cool that money, I wanted to reach the cemetery before sunset.

With a bitten fingernail, I scraped grime off the flame-red numbers on my dashboard clock: 4:35. My window of opportunity for the cemetery visit was short. I had to attend a homecoming gala at the Rome School this evening. The can't-miss, blowout event of the season. The Rome School was the glittering jewel in the tiara of our small community. Queenstown's nine thousand residents had few bullets on the brag sheet: immaculate soy and corn fields; windowless warehouses; proximity to Princeton; whiffs of ocean breezes from the fabled Jersey Shore.

And the Rome School. The annual forty-thousand-dollar tuition allowed parents of Rome's ninth to twelfth graders to brag that their darlings attended an elite academy. First rank nationwide among private boarding schools. Not my people, not my worry. But I knew a few students at Rome, local kids whose grit and brains had earned scholarships to the exclusive high school. One of those stars had tapped me to be her guest at the annual homecoming banquet. So I was on the hook for Rome's big party tonight.

I revved the Jeep's engine, waiting for heat to sift through the vents.

Bare hands gripping the wheel, I studied the brick wall of the Queenstown Pharmacy. Flaking white paint, crumbling red blocks, a one-hundred-year-old building standing on pride. Though the drugstore's newest owners had gussied up the entrance with green paint on the moldings and door, the rear wall remained an unchic antique. Wind teased a dead leaf until it fell from its mortar perch.

As I stared at the engulfing gloom, a sly voice invaded my mind. *Long time, no see, Mom.* Monica's snarky tone was coated with sweet promises of giggles to come. *You can't hold out on me forever, Mom. I know where you live.* I shifted beneath the steering wheel. Against my will a laugh bubbled in my throat. My baby could always make me grin. Another voice, stern with maternal disdain, soaped the laughter from my mouth. *I raised you better than this, Vandy Myrick.* My mother's words stung, like always. *How you call yourself a good child when you been gone so long?*

Guilty tears I'd suppressed in the bank sprang to my eyes now. I'd let hours and weeks slip until almost half a year had passed since my last visit. Stupid with hope, I'd trusted that work would mortar my life together. Stitch the seams, cement the gaps. I'd done plenty since my return to Queenstown. Those hard jobs had helped. The mortar held, until it didn't. For all my effort, my dead never returned. After a while, distraction stopped working and memory reclaimed its time.

As a PI, I'd perfected my sneer and eye roll. But sarcasm wouldn't repair this lapse. Seven years since my mother died. My daughter gone twenty-nine months. Now, the arrival of the big check from the fraternity settlement propelled me into action. I owed a visit to Bethel Cemetery.

# CHAPTER **TWO**

The rain subsided before I parked my Jeep at the graveyard's black iron gate. The entrance to Bethel Cemetery was a spindly structure, fragile spikes dividing the uneven path from the sidewalk. Now, bars of late October sun slanted through the fence, shedding stripes of brass and copper on the lawns and gravestones.

The Flats was the Black section of Q-Town, and Bethel Cemetery, five blocks from my childhood home, was the pride of our neighborhood. The gold-and-red canopy of oak trees, the curving paths, fat squirrels, and brazen deer made the park seem like an enchanted empire when I was young. Bethel African Methodist Episcopal Church was my mother's favorite retreat. My father, also Evander Myrick, never attended with us, which diminished Bethel's value in my eyes. My father claimed my Saturdays for baseball or football games, museum visits, and chess tournaments. Now retired after twenty-seven years on the Queenstown police force, Evander lived in a nursing home. He was the robust, cheerful, and eternally oblivious victim of advanced Alzheimer's.

I stepped onto the cement track winding through the cemetery. Water glinted like lost coins in the chips and crevices of the path. My family's graves occupied a plot of balding turf in the northeast quadrant of the cemetery. As I dawdled, I studied the older graves, flattened mounds barely discernible in the grass, their headstones buffed smooth by decades of caresses.

When I reached my goal, I sat on a stone bench beneath an

oak tree before the double-wide family plot. Splashes of sun turned the marble headstone from gray to ocean white; chiseled script announced the precious names below the square blocks forming our shared plot:

*MYRICK*

*ALMA MARIE, LOVING WIFE DEVOTED MOTHER*

*MONICA ALMA, BELOVED DAUGHTER*

I pictured them lying side by side, arms entwined, my daughter resting her head on my mother's breast. Alma smoothing Monica's fuzzy hairline the way she used to stroke mine. The dimple flashing in my baby's cheek as my mother's hand flexed. I knew Monica's entire life from lonely beginning to ugly end. But I wished I'd known more of my mother's life. Her drives and desires, her creations and conquests. As a certified daddy's girl, I'd never tried to know my mother. This visit to her grave made me want to learn about that Alma. The one I'd ignored for so many decades. Now, before our time burned to cinders.

"I've been away too long," I whispered. Settling elbows on knees, I spoke louder. "But I've been thinking about you. Always." I meant them both, but Monica most of all. I touched a thin gold chain around my throat. I adjusted the dangling letter *M* so it nestled within the notch of my collarbone. Monica's necklace, now mine. Inheritance inverted.

As often happened, visiting Monica here summoned thoughts of her father. My ex-husband, Philip Bolden, had quit me before our baby was born. Did he ever visit her grave? Did Phil even mourn her loss? Was I gone from his life and forgotten, too? Reconstructing our split, I felt the decision was all mine. Philandering Phil was more than a catchy nickname for an ex. But sometimes I worried he'd wanted the divorce just as much as I did. Where did that balance teeter in my heart? That tilt between pride and desire that kept Phil's image scratching at my memories even twenty years after the death of our marriage.

I tugged from my coat pocket a folded white envelope. Shaking it helped scatter unruly thoughts of Phil. I read the return address out loud. "That's the name of the fraternity, Mama. And Monica, that's their national headquarters."

I pulled out the crumpled stub and ran a finger along the edge where the check had hung. Two hundred and fifty thousand dollars. I tried the "two," but didn't get further. I wouldn't recite the numbers out loud. No point. Alma and Monica already knew. Overhead, a squirrel scolded. I looked up at the orange quilt of leaves when he repeated the chatter. Of course, they knew the fraternity had paid me two hundred and fifty thousand dollars to forget Monica had drowned in her own vomit on a chintz-covered sofa in the parlor at a party in the campus house they owned. The fraternity bought a quarter million dollars of my forgetfulness. Blood money settled on my blood kin. I felt filthy. Dirty and rich.

I stood from the bench. "I can do this much." The squirrel yipped in reply, but I was talking to my family. "Not enough. But I'll make this money mean something. Watch me." I clawed a hole in the bare soil on Monica's side of the grave.

From the back pocket of my jeans I pulled the green Bic lighter, then knelt. The lighter's flame leaped to the stub in my hand. When it was well torched, I dropped the sheet into the hole. As fire consumed the papers, wind caught a plume of smoke, carrying its gray feathers toward the church.

After the fire guttered, I patted dirt into a mound over the ashes. The scent of burnt paper drifted around my head as I walked to the car.

When I reached the end of the path, I saw a Black woman standing at the gate. Her posture was stiff, like a sentry. She wore a navy blue pantsuit, her fists buried in the lapels to pull the jacket tight across her chest. No coat or gloves, a fuchsia blouse buttoned to her throat, as if she'd run from inside the church to intercept me.

I hitched my shoulders, then offered a semi-cringe. I had every right to visit the cemetery; but still I felt like an invader.

The woman said, "You shouldn't start fires here, you know." She cinched her lips. When I didn't reply she added, "Any spark could set off the grass."

"It was a small one." I thinned my voice. "I smothered it before I left."

She raised her eyes to the sky, as if she could see smoke scrawled on the clouds. Then she looked straight to my face. "I know you." Thrust lip, no smile. "You're a Myrick, right?"

Nailed, but how did this newcomer know my business?

## CHAPTER **THREE**

A burst of frosted air rustled the maple tree next to the cemetery gate. Orange leaves tapped the shoulders of my peacoat, sending tremors up my neck.

"Myrick, aren't you?" the stranger repeated. I closed in on her. She gasped then backed away until her hip touched the headlight of my Jeep. How'd this spy know me? Did she recognize my face or car? Had she noted the gravesite I'd visited?

I extended my hand. "Yes, I'm Vandy Myrick. And you are?"

"Nadine Burriss. I'm Bethel's treasurer." She tilted her head toward the church, then puffed her chest like I was supposed to be awestruck. I wasn't, but I smiled as if her title mattered.

I wanted to know more, not about church finances or hierarchy. I hadn't been inside Bethel AME in the two years since I'd returned to Queenstown. I wasn't inclined to break my clean streak now. And I needed to hustle to get ready for the Rome School's homecoming party. But PI curiosity reined me. A few questions would satisfy my itch; I wanted to learn what she had on me, so I pretended I was cold. I chafed my palms in the universal sign of freezing.

"I could sure use a cup of coffee, if you've got one." Eyebrows lifted, I made puppy eyes at the church.

She bit. "Sure, I can fix some instant in my office."

Her Sanka offer chucked a stone in my stomach. But I puffed on clenched fists and gritted out, "Wonderful. Thanks, Nadine."

As we scooted across the street, I catalogued. She was younger than me. If her silk-pressed black hair was real, I pegged her at thirty-seven, maybe less. Soft rump, thick waist: she never hit a gym or passed a buffet. Short neck and muscular legs maxed her at five-three, but four-inch heels brought her eye level with me. And young sister worked those black pumps like Naomi Campbell on the runway. I scampered to keep up.

We passed below the window of stained glass that bulged in the redbrick façade above double doors. I remembered gazing at this ten-foot-wide circle with infant awe. But now, with its thick black grout dividing chunks of blue, red, and green glass, the window looked garish. Growing up was cruel to childhood fantasies.

Nadine led me through the foyer to a metal door with a push-bar safety handle. She shoved; we entered the new wing of the church. The mood shift jolted me. Light streamed through glass panels lining the hallway. Underfoot, the green carpet was squishy as pancakes.

Nadine raised her voice to sweep us down the corridor. "Classrooms for Sunday School and infant care, choir practice, youth club." A stubby finger pointed at each door. "Pastor's office suite at the end of the hall.

"The elders' money allowed us to move from our first home in Trenton to plant our new church here in 1891." Nadine's phrasing suggested she'd supervised the nineteenth-century construction herself. Stepping to the wall, she tapped a black-and-white photo in a gold frame. A row of sharp-dressed Black men in top hats hoisted shovels. Though I guessed she was mid-thirties, Nadine's diction and vocabulary gave creaky church-lady vibes. She spent far too much time with the congregation elders. Nadine needed to stretch her wings.

I nodded, hoping my silence would cut short the recital. When Nadine squeezed her eyes and lips shut, my memories galloped into the gap.

By the time I reached middle school, Alma had given me chapter and verse on the history of her precious Mother Bethel. The church dominated the four square miles of Queenstown called the Flats. For over three hundred years, Black people had jammed into this neighborhood on Lake Trask's eastern shore.

In the 1970s, when the town's boundaries expanded to embrace subdivided farmland, few of us moved into the new developments. Integration wasn't a magnet for most. In my mother's words, *Bethel AME remained our rock, our solace, and our refuge. Why would we move any-where else?* I wondered what Alma would say about the four-bedroom Victorian I'd bought on Main Street, a white folks' mansion several blocks beyond the Flats' old borders.

At the end of the hallway, Nadine and I passed a color photo from the current century. Scanning the picture, I faltered. Prominent in his sober suit and crisp hair was Philip Bolden. My ex-husband. A flutter, like fallen oak leaves, jostled my heart. Phil had been gone twenty-plus years. When I returned to Queenstown after our daughter's death, I didn't know if Phil was still in the area, or even in the state. I made no effort to find out. I convinced myself I didn't care. Seeing this photo now unraveled those convictions. I studied his strong jaw and plush lips. Handsome brown eyes radiant with a joke just told. Chest thrust, elbows wide, he sat at the middle of a table stacked with beaming men. Phil burned brighter than them all. Claiming the spotlight, the space, and every sip of air. Nadine, unsmiling, was the only woman in the group. Against my wishes, my eyes flew to Phil's face. Teak-brown skin still smooth across his cheekbones and broad nose. Neat ears with that hint of gremlin's point to their upper ridges. Why did he shave his beard? When did he go gray? Why did I care? I flexed my fingers, hoping to shed the spell Phil had cast over me. Again. Didn't work.

Nadine noted my stumble. "This is the committee which launched our Sutton Hill rehabilitation project three years ago."

"Deacons?" She couldn't have detected the hunger in my gaze, could she?

"Yes, plus Reverend Fields"—she pointed at the gaunt pastor—"other church elders, and two representatives from Trenton. We wanted the neighborhood to have a say in shaping our plans."

Unless he'd found religion since exiting our marriage, I figured Phil wasn't a church leader. He must have joined the committee in his role as a Trenton native son. I studied the cashew-shaped dimple denting his right cheek. Still there, still alluring. Damn him. Damn me.

My stomach unknotted when Nadine steered me from my disorderly memories. I followed her toward the end of the sun-filled corridor, down two flights of stairs to the basement, then along a cramped passage.

"Here I am, cozy and quiet," she said. She swept her arm in an arc as we entered her office.

A belowground space, the office was dank and dim. The prison-chic décor was softened by paintings mounted on hooks drilled into the cement-block walls: primary-color flowers in majolica jars; a pastel spray of feathers in a crystal vase. I saw a stack of hardback books, a fan unfurled to showcase a red pagoda. Red had been Phil's favorite color; I shook my head but intrusive thoughts of my ex tramped on. Primary colors like those in the majolica jar painting sparked his imagination. Anything bold. And loud, like the music he preferred. Memories cascaded, warming my back. I didn't want Phil in my head, but here he was. Again. I brushed perspiration from my upper lip and resumed cataloguing the treasurer's office. Maybe the dull metals and muted lighting would push Phil's vibrancy from my mind.

A row of transom windows brushed the ceiling above one wall. Leaves piled against the glass blocked what little light they might have transmitted. The brown furniture—desk, credenza, metal file cabinets, floor lamps—was nicked, chipped, or dented. Castoffs looking for a garage sale.

While my host retreated to a hidden bathroom to fill an electric kettle, I continued to inspect her office. A conference table was covered with architectural blueprints. Cardboard packing tubes balanced on a combination safe to the left of the desk. To the right, I saw a black metal door below an oversize EXIT sign. Everything was dull and dingy. Eyes rolling, I snickered at Nadine's limited taste. A smooth baritone poured through my head: *Give the girl a break, Vandy. Phil's voice, chuckling at my snobbery. She's doing the best she can.* I scrubbed palms over my ears. I wanted Phil out of my head. Banished to the ex ranks where I'd kept him for so long. I shuddered. Exile violated, thanks to that damn photo. The armchair, upholstered in squirrel-gray chenille, looked more inviting, so as Nadine reentered the room, I sat.

Her back to me, she plugged the kettle into a wall socket. She rummaged in the lower shelf of a credenza for mugs, powdered coffee, sugar packets, and a jar of fake creamer.

Setting a mug and spoon on the desk in front of me, she said, "You've been good."

"What?"

"You're dying to ask how I knew your name." Her smile thinned. "But you're good. Controlled. I like that. Restraint is such a rare quality these days. Especially among us. You have it."

"So reward me," I said, grabbing the spoon. "How did you know my name?"

# CHAPTER **FOUR**

Nadine Burriss made me wait twenty seconds while she simpered at a secret joke. "Your mother was a longtime member of the church. One of our cherished elders. And Alma was the first woman to hold the position of chief usher."

Swiveling, Nadine stirred creamer into her brew. Gold bands decked both ring fingers, the slender wires digging into her puffy flesh.

A smile twitched; she drowned it with her first sip. "An important part of Alma's job was leading our weekly collection."

Nadine's eyes sharpened, like a cat prowling. "Here in my office, we'd count the morning's collection. Between the nine o'clock and eleven o'clock services, we'd often take in four or five hundred dollars each Sunday."

I hummed to mute my surprise. "Healthy sums, Nadine." For a striving community, I knew these amounts were considerable.

I remembered making my own childish contributions to Bethel's coffers. Each Sunday, after my mother fastened plastic barrettes to my freshly brushed plaits, she would press a dollar bill into my hand. "When the collection basket reaches you, take an envelope and put your dollar inside. Then drop the envelope in the basket and watch as it shuffles on down the aisle. That's how you know your bitty little dollar is on its way to doing the Good Lord's good work."

Once, when I was nine, I asked Alma if I could have a five-dollar bill to put in the collection basket. She always put in ten, so I figured five was a reasonable amount to request. Her brow tensed, the same look she had when I sassed her and she took a boar's hair brush to my rear end. Thrusting her face to mine, she thundered: "Don't you be asking that, Vandy Myrick. You talking 'bout adult money now. You ain't hardly earned the right to be putting your hands on no adult money."

Nadine's chuckle interrupted my memories. "Yes, those were impressive sums your mother collected."

I blew on the coffee although it was tepid now. "So, you remembered me as Alma's daughter?"

"You look just like her, don't you?" Nadine shook her head. "As soon as you walked through the cemetery gate, I said to myself, that woman's got Alma Myrick's face down to the last detail. Same coloring, eyes, teeth, everything."

"We used to get that a lot." The first real smile warmed my face. "Sometimes, Alma'd joke we were sisters." I didn't say my daughter also looked like us. As if we three had been molded from a single block of rich brown clay.

I returned to safer ground. "With Alma not in charge, are you still gathering big bucks from the congregation?"

"We do all right." A sheen glossed Nadine's cheeks and nose. "More than all right." Eyes sparkling, teeth bright. She arched her back until the cloth of her blouse tugged tight over heavy breasts. "In fact, at the homecoming gala tonight, I'm getting a community service award from the Rome School."

"Rome? What's your connection?" I tried to picture her among the polished crowd of future titans and world-beaters. I drew blanks.

"Class of 2008. We like to say 'the Great '08' 'cause so many of us hit it big."

"Nice."

Nadine dipped her head, accepting my feeble cheer like a beauty pageant queen. "Tonight's award is in recognition of my accomplishments as a fund-raiser. I generated ten thousand dollars last year for Rome's scholarship fund."

She fluttered her lashes. Gasping, I jiggled the mug. As I swabbed spilt drops from the desk, she continued, "And over the past three years, I've led the church's sponsorship of a major new housing initiative in Trenton." She thumped a fist into her palm. Her voice rose over the last words, "Mother Bethel is building back its home city, one block at a time."

I swiped my thumb over the wet ring on the desk. I felt like a miserable piker. A skinflint who had complained when the Olde Towne Diner raised the price of cherry pie by thirty cents. What had I built? Or fostered? Or planted? I heard Alma's voice, dripping with scorn. *You talking 'bout adult money now, Vandy Myrick.* But if I acted now, I could turn Monica's blood money to a finer purpose.

"Nadine, let me make a contribution to your fund," I said. "A healthy sum." *Adult money at last,* I told Alma.

Her turn to gasp. Game, set, match: Myrick.

I said, "I don't have my checkbook on me." A lip twist to tease her greed. "I don't usually bring it to the graveyard."

"Of course not." She was panting. "Could we meet here tomorrow? Say, two thirty?" She wouldn't let the weekend swallow my charitable impulse.

"Tomorrow would be fine."

I stood as she scrambled toward the exit and pushed on the crossbar. I noticed the door's safety lock was disengaged and a small wood wedge held it open. We stepped into the brisk darkness.

Nadine followed me to the top of the stairs. "I'll see you tomorrow then," she said. We shook hands. Hers were icy.

I buttoned my jacket and raised the collar against my neck.

"But I'll see you this evening, Nadine." I wanted the last word.

"What?" In the gloom, I could see her lips gape. Lamplight slicked yellow on her teeth.

"I'll be at the Rome party, too."

If she replied, the thump of my boots on the pavement covered her squeak.

As I revved the Jeep's engine, I scrolled through a parade of text messages from a single source:

Where r u? Late!
Waiting on your porch

Don't do me like this!
Ass froze Face next
Remind me why I invited u
Cold af Not playing Where r u

My date for the Rome homecoming gala, girl boss Ingrid Ramírez, was pissed.

# CHAPTER **FIVE**

When I bundled Ingrid Ramírez into my kitchen, hot cocoa and two pumpkin spice doughnuts soothed her temper tantrum. But they didn't extinguish the fire.

"Man, you know we got a shitload to do before the party tonight." In the months since I'd met her, the squeak in Ingrid's voice had smoothed into a charming mezzo. "How you plan on getting shit done arriving late like that?"

"Cool your jets, babe." I leaned across the counter to spear the last doughnut from the carton. Summoning Monica's voice, I added, "We got this like pros."

"Yeah, right. Like pros with plenty of lip and no game." The smirk below her brown eyes warmed the room.

I brushed doughnut crumbs from my shirtfront onto the white marble countertop. Her exasperated tone made me grin. I recognized sarcasm was Ingrid's love language because my daughter had strummed the same chords. I cherished Monica's mouthy attitude reborn in this new girl. Made me feel I could be a mother again, even if I didn't have a child anymore.

"Then hustle up, chica," I said, clapping hands. "Haul your ass to my bedroom so we can set this show on fire."

I watched Ingrid collect her backpack and mount the stairs to my bedroom. She was short, brown-skinned, and almost eighteen. She had the figure I'd wanted when I was in high school: lush curves, narrow waist. Huge eyes in a heart-shaped face. Bushy hair boiling like a black waterfall past her shoulders. I bet the Rome School boys hadn't met lots of girls like Ingrid. If they continued along the white-bread-crumb trail laid by their parents, they might never meet another Ingrid Ramírez for the rest of their born days. Big loss.

By the time I crossed the doorjamb, she'd thrown herself in the armchair next to my window. I plopped on the bed to remove my socks. "First dibs on the shower," I said.

"Already clean and polished." Ingrid rolled her eyes then pushed up sweater sleeves to reveal oiled elbows. "But do *not* take your sweet time. I want you to fix my hair. And you're slow as the last toothpaste in the tube."

On the regular, Ingrid alternated between treating me like an employee and like a substitute mother. Eighteen months ago, she'd hired me to investigate a case involving her brother. Now, still devastated by loss, she ping-ponged between clingy gratitude and brittle anger at the whole world, me included. I cut the girl slack; I fought the same tug-of-war most days. Tough breaks, tender recovery. That was the path we were on together.

After my shower, I settled in the armchair to attend to Ingrid's head. We made quick work of a fancy braided style copied from a fan magazine.

Fifteen minutes later, Ingrid looked gorgeous in a black poet's blouse with sequins outlining its low neckline. The black vegan leather pencil skirt touched below her knees, but its side slit snaked a dangerous path up her thigh.

"You're a star, chica. They won't know what hit 'em."

"I know, right?" She sashayed in front of the full-length mirror. "Fancy as fuck."

"You told me Rome doesn't have a homecoming queen, but they might elect you anyway."

"That's okay. I don't need that lame BS. This recognition is for academics anyway."

Ingrid's GPA topped her class the previous year, winning her the school's award for highest scholarly achievement. But pink rising in her cheeks said she was proud to blend sexy with brainy.

"Do you get a medal or a certificate?" I flashed my paltry knowledge of classical traditions. "Or maybe a crown of laurels?"

"Medal on a ribbon *and* a framed certificate. Mama can hang that in her bedroom."

A veil shimmied across Ingrid's eyes. Her mother couldn't attend the ceremony because she worked the late shift cleaning wards in Princeton-Plainsboro Hospital. When Carmen Ramírez asked me to escort her daughter to the gala, I'd felt humble and honored. Ingrid didn't need two mothers. And I knew replacing my daughter was a never-never dream. But this felt good.

Before tears prickled my eyes, too, I switched gears. "I need your advice. Which dress do I wear as your fairy glam-mother?" I'd selected two candidates in my go-to colors, black and maroon. Now, I tossed the dresses on the bed and stepped aside for the expert's appraisal.

Ingrid was ruthless. "This black Morticia drag, nope." She dropped the loose midi dress on the floor. She held the second by its shoulder pads. "Now this could get you action. Let's see it on."

I slipped the sweater dress over my head and shimmied the cables past my hips. "You think I'm on the prowl tonight?"

I glared at Ingrid in the mirror, then studied my reflection. Turtleneck framing my jawline, long sleeves, hem below the knees. A nun could wear this dress with confidence. Maybe not. It was a tad too tight. But this was a gala, wasn't it?

"Aren't you?" Ingrid's gaze dragged over my frame. "How long's it been since your last . . . um, date night?"

"Not your business." I could have sounded firmer, but I was distracted by the count thumping through my brain. One week, ten days, three weeks. A month gone already. Maybe Ingrid was onto something. I jerked open a dresser drawer of cosmetics and studied the jumble of pots, tubes, and compacts. And the square packets of condoms foil-wrapped like precious candy.

Ingrid wagged her head. "Trust me. This dress will do some damage with those Rome alums tonight. You could do worse." She left off, *And you have,* but I heard it. Ingrid knew too much about me.

But I knew a thing or two about her also. I struck back. "Who's Mr. Boo on your radar tonight?" Beat for the dig. "Or is Ethan home from Stanford this week?"

Ethan Cho had been Ingrid's ride-or-die sidekick since her freshman year at Queenstown High. When he transferred to the Rome School, their bond deepened. Following his example, Ingrid had transferred to Rome and they both flourished. Ethan had capped a brilliant senior campaign with admission to Stanford.

Now, her tone was brittle. "He's back, yeah."

"But out of the picture?"

"You could say that." End of story.

For her, not me. Had California jammed the spokes of their bicycle built for two?

As if reading my mind, Ingrid said, "Drop it, Vandy. I don't need your messing."

Dropping a clue wasn't in my private-eye tool kit. But I could ease up when the tactic served. "Sure, you got it."

Ingrid shoved a mascara tube toward my face. "Fix your own self."

I blinked and unsheathed the sticky wand. Did she mean repair my eye makeup? Or my love life?

After our silent walk to the Jeep, I helped Ingrid hoist her bicycle into the trunk. I slammed the gate shut, almost missing her words, "His name is Tariq. The one I'm seeing now."

I pulled the lapels of my leather jacket. "Okay." Cold slithered from my patent pumps up my bare legs. I wondered where her ex-boyfriend fit in. I got the answer immediately.

"Tariq'll be there tonight. I'll introduce you. But you peep one freaking word about Ethan and I'll hate you forever."

# CHAPTER **SIX**

Ingrid and I parked in front of Rome School's administration building. In the dark, the structure's gray arches and turrets listed like an ocean-going freighter. Vines clung to the stone blocks with black windows breaking the matted pelt of ivy. We teetered around the building on our high heels, entwining elbows for support, clutching coats to our throats for warmth.

Beyond the stone hulk, we found our goal, the gleaming new gymnasium. Strings of fairy lights draped from metal struts two stories in the air made the building's foyer twinkle like a dream palace as Ingrid and I entered the grand space.

We scanned the lobby. Twenty round tables transformed the space into a fantasy ballroom. Four-foot-high fronds of emerald and bronze feathers spurted from alabaster vases at the center of each table. Rome School's staid green and brown colors gussied up for the occasion. Between the plumage were metal stakes holding cards with numbers. Roman numerals, natch.

Ingrid cocked her head, gaze darting by my shoulder. She said, "We're at table one with Mr. Dumont." A chin jut indicated the north end of the vast room where we would sit with Rome's headmaster, Charles Dumont. "Catch you there." She flung her puffer jacket into my arms and swiveled toward a lean shadow in an alcove. Must be the new boy.

Alone and dazzled, I bumped into a black-uniformed server as I caromed through the crowd. Two-fifty, maybe three hundred people in the room. Well-cut tuxedoes, even on pimply faced youngsters; short cocktail dresses in jingle-bell colors. Lots of Ferragamo shoes and pearl button earrings. I slunk toward the coat station where I exchanged our jackets for plastic markers. The other coats on the rack were mink or fox. The Rome empire showed major for homecoming.

After a broken-field trot, I arrived at table one. A lone white woman was seated among the eight places. I took the chair next to the woman.

"Laurel Vaughn," she said over a sturdy handshake. Her fingers were slender with carbon-gray nail polish highlighting four carved silver rings. "I teach art. Who are you?"

I gave the cut-rate version of my relationship to Ingrid Ramírez. My name hadn't made social media or the local paper in connection with the murder case, so I figured if Laurel wasn't a dedicated gossip, I was in the clear.

"Ingrid's a terrific girl. I wasn't sure they'd give her the top prize, though." Laurel raked russet curls above her right ear. "It was a close thing."

"Close thing? How do you mean?"

"I sit on the committee that approves these annual academic awards. Ingrid's case pitched us into a donnybrook."

"Why? I thought she had the highest GPA in her class last year."

Laurel hiked her shoulders. The braided trim on her red silk jacket rippled. "She did. But some on the committee argued that as a transfer student she hadn't earned enough credits at Rome to qualify for the top award." She wrinkled the skin over her nose like she smelled the same rat I did.

I kept my opinion simple: "Not enough credits? Or too much melanin?"

"Of course, the credits argument was bogus. A flimsy cover for racism." Laurel tipped her head from side to side. "I've taught here nine years. Rome's a great place to work, even better now Charles Dumont is headmaster. But bigotry runs deep here. Ingrid is our first student of color to win this award. That was a hard pill for some people to swallow."

"People with small minds and tiny hearts."

Laurel snickered. "You've met our English faculty, I see."

"Are you here to present her the award?"

"Oh, no, Charles reserves that ceremonial flourish for himself." Warm chuckles gurgled from her chest. With the creases around her amber eyes, I'd first put her at early forties. But now, laughing, she seemed a decade younger. "One thing I learned is never to stand between Charles Dumont and the spotlight. He'd trample his own grandmother to claim the money and attention."

"So, you're here on your own account?"

"Bingo. You are looking at Rome's teacher of the year."

"Congratulations. That's a high honor."

"It is. I'm proud of the recognition." A quiver rippled her lips.

Before I could pose another question, a tall Black man in a trim navy suit leaned over Laurel's right shoulder to deposit two lowball glasses on the table. "If I'd known you'd be here, Vandy, I'd have juggled a third drink."

Keyshawn Sayre was a familiar figure around town and a former fixture in my life. I wanted him to be a friend. Maybe once I'd wanted more. I wasn't sure where he fit now, so I kept my greeting to a tight hello.

Laurel swung her gaze between us. "No intros needed, hum? You two know each other, I take it." Her tone was clipped, the warmth of her earlier comments stowed for now. Not yet suspicious, but ready to leap there.

If Key was her boyfriend, he could lead the explanations so I smiled and fluttered eyelashes.

"Yeah, Vandy and I been knowing each other since, what? Grade school?" He slid the glass with brown liquid toward Laurel. She stabbed the orange slice with a cherry-festooned toothpick. As she took a first sip, he sat beside her.

I said, "I had you beat by a couple of years, Key, but yes, it's been a minute."

He looked good; outdoor work as the head of Rome's buildings and grounds department suited him. Wind had burnished his face to a ruddy glow and squinting into the sun had engraved handsome creases around his eyes. Maybe this artsy-fartsy love affair with Laurel had buffed him, too. Key looked happy. I wanted to feel happy for him, he deserved this.

"How's Evander doing these days?" he asked. Old habits of concern for my father blew mist across Key's brown eyes. "I need to get over for a visit before the holidays."

I turned toward Laurel. "My dad is a patient in the Alzheimer's wing at Glendale."

Wincing, she asked Keyshawn, "And he was one of your charges?" I figured she'd met Key at Rome and knew his job history. Key had worked for several years as an attendant at the Glendale Memory Care Center. My father was a resident under his care, until sixteen months ago when Key landed the position as head of buildings and grounds at the Rome School.

"My favorite." Keyshawn took a long pull of his drink and studied my face. "Your dad was—is—a good man."

Key had been a daily attendant since the first months of my father's tenure at Glendale. Disease had robbed Evander Myrick of all memories of his twenty-seven-year career as a Q-Town cop. He couldn't remember his wife or granddaughter. Since he'd already lost them, I imagined he didn't mourn their deaths. He didn't remember his namesake, either, despite my thrice-weekly visits. But he kept the physical vigor and movie-star looks that had been the hallmark of his eighty-two years. Now, Evander was strong, loud, mostly cheerful, utterly oblivious. Not the worst way to wander through this sorry world.

I poured water into a wineglass. "Thanks, Key. I bet he'd love a visit from you." Doubtful, but I couldn't drop the habit of speaking about Evander as if he were the dad I'd known before. The dad I wanted again. I tilted the glass for a loud gulp.

Key slid a hand over Laurel's and squeezed. She dipped her head. Sweet smiles flickered between them. Brown eyes igniting amber. I felt like an intruder. Keyshawn and I had grown close during his years of service to my father. Last year, we'd missed the chance to convert that friendship into romance. Probably for the better, though every so often I wondered about the road not taken. Now, seeing him with Laurel, I wanted this path for him. He was the good man my father should have been. Key deserved this joy.

He stood, leaning over us, hands on our shoulders. "Ladies, I'll catch you later." When I frowned, he added: "I'm sitting at table double *X*." His eyebrows flew toward the rear of the hall. "Gotta hang with my boys from the B and G crew in the back of the house."

Drink in hand, Key disappeared into the crowd, his blue suit like a meteor slicing across the tuxedo-dark sky. When he vanished, I spotted other Black people in the throng, raisins scattered among oatmeal lumps. My boss/friend Elissa Adesanya and her wife, Belle Ames, rocked complementary gowns of amethyst and daffodil silk. Lots of cleavage and leg; braids and wigs. The A-Team looked killer. I waved, but they didn't see me. We'd do our after-party analysis tomorrow in the office.

I saw Nadine Burriss claim a chair at a distant table. Before sitting, she smoothed the sequined lapels of her glacier-white pant-suit. Then she patted the fresh crimped waves above her ears. She looked around, as if waiting for applause. A white man approached, smiled, got the stink eye, and moved on. Nadine resumed scanning the room, looking for someone else. During our meeting this after-noon, she'd given the impression that her generosity had won her a prime place in the gala program. Maybe she'd exaggerated her im-portance. Or the size of her donation. If I had time after the awards ceremony, I'd scoot over to tease needy Nadine.

Looking at empty seats around the table, I asked Laurel, "If Key-shawn isn't sitting with us, who else are we expecting?"

"Melinda Terrence will be along soon. I saw her in the bathroom a few minutes ago."

"And she is?"

"The school guidance counselor." Laurel sucked the cherry off its toothpick and chomped twice. "Melinda shepherds our little darlings into the college careers their parents always dreamed of."

"She won an award, too?"

"No, Melinda's the mother of the other student honoree." Laurel chewed a meatball, then peered into my face, as if I were pulling a joke. "I thought you'd met Tariq. He's a brilliant artist. One of my best students." Her eyes glittered with excitement. "Almost as important, Tariq is the Rome School athlete of the year, long-distance runner who powered the Falcons to the championship at the Middle States Independent School track meet last May." Emotion flushed her breast as if she'd run the race. With dramatic flourish, she finished: "And Tariq's the boyfriend of your girl Ingrid Ramírez."

Slam dunk for Laurel Vaughn. And a three-pointer at the buzzer for Ingrid. Heat prickled my throat. I ran a finger inside the turtleneck, hoping to release the warmth. I wanted an explanation—maybe an apology—from Ingrid. I harrumphed and touched the cool glass to my temple.

Four minutes later, Ingrid and Tariq glided to our table, the sheen of youth and beauty radiating from their perfect bodies. Hands clasped, they sat beside me, bronze divinities playing with us mortals. Judging from Ingrid's cat-in-the-cream grin, apology was far from her mind.

# CHAPTER **SEVEN**

Ingrid Ramírez shimmied into a seat at my table, stationing her handsome escort next to me. A grin split her face; a puzzled pout graced his. To our right, classical ensemble music swelled from a corner of the giant gymnasium, then dribbled to a flute solo that drowned in the babble of the giddy homecoming crowd. Muscles around my mouth twitched into a smile as Ingrid giggled at her beau.

"Yo, Vandy, this is Tariq," she said, trills dancing in her voice. "So great you get to meet him, right?"

"Nice to meet you, Tariq," I said, honey dripping.

His handshake was solid. "Yes, ma'am." Dumping me in the old lady bin. "Same here."

A well-tailored charcoal suit wrapped his runner's limbs. His jaw squared into an imposing frame around the solo dimple in his cheek. Stubble flecked the light brown skin. He'd fluffed his soft black curls into a corona.

The kid squirmed under my review. I said, "I hear you're quite the athlete. Track, I gather."

Ingrid jumped in. "Tariq anchors the four-by-four-hundred-meter relay. And he was the top marathoner last season. Nobody's better than T in distance races." She gushed like a Hollywood flack. "You oughta see him, Vandy. He's great."

I swallowed the last of my water and reached to pour a second glass. I didn't often regret my vow to shun liquor. Most days, the promise to honor Monica's memory with sobriety sat easy with me. But now, with this mini-betrayal by Ingrid, I felt the old tingle, that desire for a splash of something strong, preferably brown, in my glass. I poured water to the rim and clutched the stem. The bourbon urge drowned with my next gulp.

Laurel Vaughn leaned across me to ask after the champion's missing parent. "What happened to your mother, Tariq?" She dragged her gaze from his face to scan the crowd beyond our table. "I ran into Melinda a few minutes ago, then we got separated at the bar. I thought she was right behind me. But I haven't seen her since."

"I saw Mom at the front door." Tariq turned toward the entrance. The view was blocked by the surging crowd. His voice dwindled so low I had to bump shoulders to hear him. "She was on the phone. Maybe Dad called her. He texted me he was running late. Maybe he told her the same thing."

Laurel cackled. "We can't raise the curtain on this show without the guest of honor, can we?"

My turn for confusion. "I thought you three were the honorees." I looked to Ingrid. "There's *more* award winners?"

Laurel plopped the orange slice on her tongue. Sour made her squint. Probably tainted her words, too. "This school's crawling with honor, don't you know." A smart-mouth myself, I recognized the sarcasm. What was the art teacher's beef?

I'd raised my eyebrows to toss the new question when a reedy tenor piped above my head.

"Ms. Myrick, I see you're well situated amidst Rome's finest tonight." Charles Dumont, school headmaster, fluttered with excitement. His hand hovered near my shoulder like a giant wasp. When I craned my neck to greet him, his breath washed sweet over my face. Altoids masking the harsh of gin and tonic. A left side razor's-edge part divided black hair above matching black eyes. His cheeks glistened like hard-boiled egg whites. "Our guest of honor has arrived at last. Let me introduce you, then we can launch the proceedings."

Dumont stepped aside. I scooted my seat back and stood. Before I could turn, a tingle caressed hairs along my neck. Instinct, gale-force premonition, skin memory. Something ancient flickered before

I saw the newcomer. His brown face glowed, the body, firm and familiar, loomed over me.

"This is Philip Bolden. Perhaps you've heard of him." Dumont bubbled like shook champagne.

Overhead lights dipped and twined inside my skull, buzzing. My husband that was. The father of my child. My only love. That Philip Bolden. The buzz churned to a roar.

The headmaster's babbling introduction flooded my ears: *Phil Bolden, chair of the school's trustees; CEO of Philmel Enterprises; president of Mason County Black Brothers United.* Accolades slithered like silver-finned fish, too swift to grasp, too slick to comprehend. Would Dumont never stop the praise song? *Founder of Move Up Trenton; a shooting star in the state political firmament; father of champion athlete Tariq Bolden.*

This paragon, familiar yet alien, shot his hand toward me. "What a fantastic surprise, Vandy. Great to see you," Phil Bolden boomed. "It's been too long."

A gasp wafted between us. My lungs burned, grabbing oxygen. Had my ex-husband always had this effect on me? *Yes,* my gut said. *Yes.*

Again, my large hand felt small in his. As always, my stomach clutched when I met his gaze. "The surprise is all mine, Phil." Pathetic. But better than the shout or curse or swoon welling inside.

The lone dimple in his cheek winked at me. The dimple I'd seen on Tariq, Phil's son. The dimple that dented the curve of our daughter, Monica's, face. My phantom family popped into my mind, then vanished when Phil burst into laughter.

"You're gawking at me like you've seen a ghost, Vandy. Don't tell me I've changed that much." Phil Bolden played to the audience at the table. He looked around, smoothed a palm over his moustache, then grabbed his chest, shaking with mirth. "A man's pride can only take so much damage."

I croaked, "It's good to see you. The best."

Swerve in the road, meet cliff.

# CHAPTER **EIGHT**

Plaintive wails from a violin shimmered over the homecoming crowd, the thin mewl cutting through the din, tempered by the viola's darker sound. After a moment's hush to note the mournful chords, the throng resumed laughing. At me? Flat-footed and agog, as my ex-husband, Phil Bolden, took a scalpel to my open heart?

Ingrid Ramírez stretched a hand toward my waist, as if to catch me. Was I trembling? I angled my hip to avoid the contact and beamed at her. She patted my wrist and sat. I saw eyes and mouth widen to my left: Laurel Vaughn on drama alert. Was she hoping a cat fight would break the formal tedium of the gala?

The white woman standing between Philip Bolden and Charles Dumont glared at me. Had to be Melinda Terrence, Tariq's mother, Phil's wife. My successor. Pink glaze on her forehead deepened to strawberry when no one offered introductions. She puffed to cool her face; her honey-blond bangs wafted on the breeze. Blue-gray sequins on her sheath dress rippled as she stalked to the seat next to Laurel. When Melinda's knee snagged the cloth as she sat, a tremor scampered across the tablescape. I flattened my hand on the rim of my water glass to stop its trembling. And to curb my own shudders.

What can you do when your heart's one desire reappears, churning through the dregs of your new life like a tornado? Do you whimper and take the hit? Or fight like a junkyard dog? I'd married Phil Bolden a few months after we graduated from college. Against my mother's pleas and my father's warnings. They both pegged Phil as unreliable. My father called him a snake in tight pants; my mother said he was too pretty to be trusted. Believing in my own talents as a reformer, I'd clung to Phil until I couldn't take the cheating anymore. We'd separated when I was four months pregnant. The day we divorced I loved him as much as I had the day we married. Our daughter, Monica, grew up without Phil's involvement. My choice. When she died, I thought he might attend the funeral. But I refused to smother my shame to reach out, so the moment passed without contact or resolution.

Seeing Phil again now unearthed shock waves of memory. Chagrin mixed with unsettling desire flooded through me. My first instinct was to fight. A few sharp words, a snide jab. Mellow was never my style. But the setting called for silence, so I slumped in my chair, quiet and fuming.

"You okay?" Ingrid whispered. "You know Tariq's dad?"

I shrugged. "It's complicated." When I figured it out, I'd share the good news with her, first thing. "We'll talk." *In a million years, kid.*

A line sliced between her eyebrows. "Sure?"

"This weekend." I squeezed her hand. "One hundred percent."

Now his chief guest was in the house, Charles Dumont called the celebration to order. Lights dimmed, but waiters flowed between the tables, distributing plates of filet mignon and seared tuna.

Phil consumed four glasses of wine with his steak. Each time a waiter poured a refill, he tipped his glass toward me with a wink. I returned the salute with a chin bob. In our college days, the Bolden booze capacity was legendary; I wondered if Phil still had the iron stomach and hard head of old.

After the second private toast, Phil's wife leaned in with a question. His black hair pressed against her blond bangs. He whispered, she nodded, her lips disappearing into a magenta line.

Sharp eyes caught the exchange. Tariq leaned toward me. "You know my dad?"

Between us, Ingrid tilted until her curls brushed my cheek.

"Yeah, sort of." I took a swig of water to cover the bobble. "Back in the day."

Ingrid's phone buzzed. She hopped from the table, tapping the cell's screen as she moved.

Tariq whispered to me, "That's the fifth text she's got tonight. Like, what's up with that? Rude, hunh?"

I agreed. "Rude. But when it's an ex you take the call."

"Ex? Like who?"

"So close," I snickered. "It's Cho, not who. You know, Ingrid's ex. Ethan Cho." Knives out.

Ingrid returned to her seat in time to catch the end of my sentence. "You talking about Ethan? Why?" She glared daggers at me.

My answer was simplicity itself: "It's *Night of the Living Ex,* right, Tariq?"

Tariq chugged the end of his Coke and reached for Ingrid's glass. He swallowed half of hers, wiping his mouth with a soiled cuff.

The arrival of trays with coin-size spice cookies and raspberry tarts blocked more poisonous exchanges. I piled four of each on my plate and watched as Tariq did the same. Her shoulder hiked as a wall against me, Ingrid waved off the sweets.

Dessert served, Dumont returned to the mic. As MC, he lobbed dad jokes to propel the ceremony. Chuckles and groans cascaded. My table mates, Laurel, Ingrid, and Tariq, accepted their awards with muted grace. Framed certificates for the art teacher and the honors student; a saucer-size medallion on a brown-and-green ribbon for the athlete. When her name was called, Nadine Burriss floated to the front of the room, index cards clutched in her hand. Her shining eyes meant she intended to deliver prepared remarks in appreciation for her community service award. Instead, after a quick handshake from the headmaster, his assistant hustled Nadine to her seat. The church treasurer got a framed sheet of paper.

Following the formal introduction, Philip Bolden strode to the microphone, accepting Dumont's hand grab and shoulder squeeze. As Phil squared to speak, I studied the minute changes imposed by the twenty years since we'd married. Under the tux, he was thicker through the chest but still trim at the waist. Covered by the table-cloth folds, I patted my stomach. Was my torso as taut as it had been in those wild days when we'd spend entire weekends in bed?

Phil's jawline sagged where it used to slash; I prodded the fugitive folds where my throat drooped. I missed his full beard, but this new salt-and-pepper moustache forced attention to his mouth. Full lips, great teeth, check and double check.

Fogged by reverie, I snagged only a few of his first words. When I caught up, Phil was in full throat. Giving back was his theme.

His baritone spread like syrup over the hushed crowd. "So, you're wondering, what is this jacked-up fool going to ask of us now." Anxious laughter confirmed his guess. Phil's eyes glittered. "Rest assured, my brothers and sisters. I'm not coming after your purses tonight. I'm here to tell you a story about my own ambitions."

A loud sigh echoed off the glass walls at the rear. When Phil laughed in reply, the crowd's relief rumbled. He had them in his palm.

"I came to Rome School as a scholarship student. Tuition, room, books, and board paid in full. Some of you know I grew up in Sutton Hill, one of Trenton's toughest neighborhoods."

I heard murmurs of approval, tongues clucking in empathy. Phil was good at this. Great, even.

When we first dated, I teased him about the baby-bottom smoothness of his cheeks. Now I saw luck, genes, or vats of lotion had preserved the satin of his brown skin. When Monica was young, I'd sworn she was the spitting image of me and my mother. But seeing Phil Bolden again, I knew that was wishful thinking. My daughter was her father's perfect double from toe to crown. Warmth zapped through my stomach. With Phil out of the picture, Monica'd missed a lot in her short life. Maybe I had, too.

He continued with a moving tribute to the librarians whose generosity had shaped his academic success at Rome. "As sure as I'm standing here, I tell you that old library saved me."

The people cheered, pounding their hands on their thighs.

Mouth loose, eyes dancing, Phil turned toward the headmaster.

"So, Dr. Dumont, here's my pledge to you: I will plant the seed with a donation of one million dollars to fund the construction of a twenty-first-century library complex for the Rome School campus."

While the audience hooted, Dumont's eyes boggled, his ears

turning brick red. I could see the quiver of pleats on his white tuxedo shirt. He tipped his head toward Phil. Greenish lips gaped for air as he raised clasped hands in salute. Dumont looked sick, not satisfied.

Phil continued, rocking from foot to foot. He grinned until his incisors showed. He was drunk, for sure, with equal portions of booze and power.

"Hear me," he shouted. "Athletics is a blot on the name of Rome. Football, soccer, lacrosse, basketball. Yes, even track and field." Pounding fist into palm, he finished, "We have no business—no *business*—rewarding young men whose chief accomplishment is leaping over hurdles. Tossing a steel ball. Or running circles on a filthy dirt track."

The Phil Bolden I remembered, equal parts generosity and cruelty, was on full display now.

I heard groans to my left: maybe Melinda Terrence. I knew Laurel Vaughn hissed. When I turned, she'd clamped her hand over her gaping mouth.

Chairs screeched to my right. I saw fire leap from Ingrid's eyes. "*Pendejo*. Fucking asshole." She growled at me, "You too, bitch."

Beside her, gray draped Tariq's cheeks. Lips trembling, he rose from his seat. He vomited a stream of brown liquid onto the cookie crumbs in his plate. Ingrid jerked the tablecloth. Plates crashed, glasses tumbled. I jumped to dodge the muddy flood. Tariq charged toward the exit, shoving guests in his path.

I reached for Ingrid. "Oh, baby, please . . ."

She boxed my hands with tight fists. "Don't touch me." Then she spit on a plate of cookies. Howling, "Tariq, no. Wait . . ." she tore after him, clutching the braids I had woven.

The gala broke into pieces then. Without goodbyes, I rushed for the door, clearing my way with elbows jammed into ribs.

Around me, the crowd shambled and bounced, laughter quickly replacing gripes. Alumni loved the evening's drama, especially the whopper finish. The disruption at the head table was sheer entertainment. *Best homecoming gala in years. Can't wait to tell Tad and Susan. They'll be sorry they missed the fun.*

As I waited for the swarm to part at the coat-check alcove, I thought about the havoc wrought by Phil's speech. I understood some of the reverberations. His son Tariq had been wounded by Phil's harsh comments. A father disparaging a son's accomplishments would hurt in private. But this way, in public, ranked as the cruelest of humiliations. Tariq's mother, Melinda, and girlfriend, Ingrid, had witnessed the boy's shaming. They shared in his torment and experienced his fury.

I was less certain about other reactions I'd witnessed at our table. Tears sprang to the eyes of art teacher Laurel Vaughn. She'd swiped at her nose then clamped a fist to her gaping mouth. Was she horrified at the insult to Tariq? Or maybe the humiliation of her friend Melinda Terrence shocked the most. Whatever its source, emotion ran deep in Laurel Vaughn. And why did Headmaster Dumont turn a sickly green during Phil's speech? Wasn't he thrilled with the sudden infusion of major cash into the school's capital campaign? I remembered how Phil's forehead smoothed as he finished his speech. The way his eyes glittered and the lines around his mouth deepened as he gazed over the commotion before him. Not a smile, but close. Satisfaction for sure. Was Phil so drunk he was oblivious to the damage he'd inflicted? Or had his purpose been to disrupt and display power? If so, mission accomplished.

The coat-check attendant was swamped, so when I reached the front of the crowd, I shoved a ten in his pocket, dragged our jackets from the rack, and fled the building.

# CHAPTER **NINE**

I crept into work at noon the next day. My head rang, my stomach sloshed with acid, aches rattled my knees and ankles. Middle age was a horror show. Late nights filled with tension and distress were tough to handle in the homestretch toward fifty. Extra-bold coffee helped. A plate of Elissa Adesanya's jollof rice absorbed the misery.

The lunchtime analysis in our office was boisterous. Because they liked her, Belle and Elissa sided with Ingrid Ramírez, picking her as the victim over the unfamiliar boyfriend, Tariq Bolden. Of course, they knew Phil Bolden's name. He was an artifact from my buried history, my ex restored to life like the pharaoh's mummy in the movies. *So, what* was *Phil,* they asked, eyebrows bobbing. *A curse or a blessing?* I sipped, munched, and offered no insights. I wasn't holding out; if I had any ideas, I'd have shared with my friends. But I came up empty.

In the afternoon, I slunk to Bethel AME to drop my check in the hands of the church treasurer, as promised. I was prepared to play twenty questions with Nadine Burriss. I figured she'd be as interested in the gala blowup as my colleagues. But Nadine surprised me. She didn't ask a single question.

After I scrawled my signature on the check for one thousand dollars, her thank-yous were gracious and prolonged. She swiveled in her chair then bent to spin the lock on the safe. I watched as she lifted a small revolver, then withdrew a square canvas satchel trimmed with tan leather bindings and handle. She unzipped the bag and dropped the gun and my check inside.

"This is the same money bag your mother used to transport our Sunday collection to the bank back in the day." She patted the worn fabric, then resealed the satchel. "I still follow Alma's routine. Every Monday afternoon I carry our weekly intake to the bank. I work with the same banker she did, too. Jackson Peel. Old guy, fruity but sharp as a pickax."

After replacing the lumpy satchel in the safe, Nadine asked if I wanted to see where my money would go. When I said yes, she grabbed two of the cardboard tubes stacked on her safe. She moved to the conference table, where she unfurled sheets of heavy paper with an architect's renderings.

"These are the latest drawings, delivered last week." Nadine stroked the edge of a sheet. When it refused to lie flat, she anchored it with a coffee mug. "You get a good look at what we hope the development will become."

Sketches of low-rise townhouses in the Sutton Hill section of Trenton featured pastel sidewalks and open porches. Hazy faces in taupe, brown, and vanilla represented the idealized residents of the new development. One stick figure walked a stick dog. Another pushed a carriage, stick baby hidden.

I played along. "What's your timeline? When will residents move in?"

A sheen of perspiration rose on her temples. "This is the second phase. We've already got twenty homes occupied and another two families will move in just after Christmas." She pulled from the stack a page with floor plans. "Our Woodbridge model: three bedrooms, two baths, and an eat-in kitchen. Nice, hunh?"

"More than nice." Compliments "R" Me. As a smile burst over her face, I added, "Great."

When I left a few minutes later, Nadine was poking a pencil at the stick figures on the streets of her paper city.


Sunday was slow, Monday morning the same. Lunch was a frigid picnic of peanut butter sandwiches on the park bench next to the town library.

When I returned, menthol fumes of forbidden cigarettes floated past the conference room from my office. I looked a question at our assistant, Belle Ames.

Her blond pixie wig tipped to the side, its fringe tangling with her false eyelashes. "I couldn't stop him from busting in." The pink bow on her blouse flounced in double time, barely contained by the lapels of her suede blazer.

"Who?" I knew, of course. The odor of Salem menthols was a dead giveaway. But the delay gave me a moment to hope my intuition was wrong.

"That man, your husband. The drunk from the gala. He's here." Belle pointed to the hallway. "He barged into your office."

I rushed by her station, unzipping my jacket as I ran.

Phil Bolden was planted in the guest chair facing my desk, neck bent, body coiled. When I entered, he jerked a cigarette from his lips. A scowl etched his forehead.

As I sat behind the desk, I clenched my right hand until nail stabs stung the palm. No greeting, smile, or banter. "What are you doing here?"

Eyes averted, he double swallowed. "I'm desperate, Vandy. I need your help."

# CHAPTER **TEN**

I chucked my leather jacket on the back of my chair and stalked to the window. Phil Bolden had invaded my office, claimed my space, and polluted my air with his goddamn cigarettes. I was set to reject his application for help, no matter how heartfelt. But I was curious about his troubles.

"Desperate about what?" I cranked open the jalousie windowpane. Cool jets ruffled the smoke over my desk.

Phil straightened the lapels on his navy wool blazer. He was tieless, his throat exposed in the *V* of his white button-down shirt. He looked at his fingers clutched in his lap, then tore a shred from a chewed cuticle. Anxiety radiating from him infected me. He'd always been good at that. Pushing me to experience what he felt, making me absorb the shocks, joys, and ambitions he held.

This was going nowhere. "Look, Phil," I buffed the edge from my voice. "You came here. You've got something to say. Say it. Or find your own way out."

"Vandy, I need your help." Repeating his plea made my neck stiffen.

"For what?"

He dragged on the cigarette, then whispered, "I screwed up. Everything is batshit crazy now."

A moan crept through his lips. He ran a hand over his mouth as if to snuff the sound. Then he covered his eyes. Tears trickled through his fingers. He wasn't wearing a wedding band. Had he worn one at the gala? I couldn't remember; maybe it meant nothing sinister. Everyday adornment forgotten in the rush to my office? Somehow, the absence of the ring comforted me. Twisted, sure, but that's what I felt.

"Start from the beginning," I said. "What's screwed up?" I could think of several options, starting with me.

Phil said, "You were there. At the homecoming. You saw what happened."

"Lots happened that night. Headmaster sucker-punched, staff confused, alumni shocked, your wife mortified." I didn't know that for certain but I pulled a pad and pen from the desk drawer like I intended to list his errors. "Or are you thinking of the public humiliation of your son? Is that what you mean?"

Phil puffed a sharp burst. "Yeah, Tariq hasn't spoken to me since then. Not a single word. I phone, text. Nothing. Not a fucking word." Smoke fogged the air.

"And this surprises you? How?" Snippy tone to create distance between us. I didn't want to be swept into Phil's drama. Been there, collected the damage stamps.

Phil said, "When he ran out of the gala last Thursday night, Melinda . . ." Mouth sagged left. "We haven't spoken since then, either." He moved toward the windows. A last drag on the cigarette, then he tossed it through the slanted blades of the blinds.

I stepped beside Phil to look out the window. I could see a chocolate-brown Infiniti—sleek, shiny, new; must be Phil's—parked next to my Jeep in the slots below my office. "Is it usual for Tariq to be in touch?"

My experience was only with teen girls. Monica used to text me three or four times a day. Checking in was our regular breakfast and dinner routine. Even now, more than two years after her death, I kept my cell by my plate in hopes she'd text one more time. Maybe boys asserted their independence with radio silence.

Phil shifted, then plucked a shirt cuff. "He's on again, off again. Some weeks he'll check in every day. Then he'll go five days without a peep."

"Maybe this is one of those peep-less periods." I straightened from the window. "How am I supposed to help? I barely know your son."

Phil frowned, stymied.

I fled behind my desk barricade. "Maybe the ghosting is Tariq's form of self-care." I pointed my pen at Phil. "You wounded him with that outburst at the gala last week. You shamed him in front of hundreds of people. Maybe Tariq is taking a few days to cool down, lick his wounds."

Phil pressed his left hand to his temple, then raked the crown of his head. "Yeah, I fucked up. I got that."

I let the admission freeze for twenty seconds. My instinct was to stay the hell out of Phil Bolden's problems. His plea sounded theatrical. I wasn't buying the disappearing son angle. My gut said Phil had ginned up this problem as an excuse to talk to me.

Curiosity—okay, call it prying—pushed me to go along. If the request had come from anyone else, I'd have turned him down. But I wanted to get inside Phil Bolden's orbit again. Under his skin, too. Revenge? Maybe. Consolation? No doubt. I wanted assurance I'd made the right decision in divorcing him all those years ago. That ditching my baby's father had been the right choice for me and for my daughter.

"That's not what you really came for, is it?" I leaned on both elbows.

Phil slouched in the chair, chest caved, eyes on fire, their warmth pulsing toward me. "You get me, Vandy. You always did."

Tears pricked behind my eyes. This acknowledgment was tiny. But enough. Our connection was still there. And he wanted to test it. I made no promises about repairing things with his son. Phil dropped the pretext for this visit. He wanted to see me. And that was enough for now.

Minutes later, I walked Phil to the parking lot behind our building. Sleet pelted my leather jacket and his overcoat as we moved toward our cars. Dusk wrapped a frigid blanket over the town, and lamplight glimmered on tablets of ice dotting the lot's uneven asphalt. Phil's wool coat matched the chocolate of his fancy car. And complemented the rich color of his skin. My stomach flipped. *Traitor*.

As we neared the Infiniti, I skidded on a slick patch and fell to one knee. Phil grabbed my elbow, hoisting me to my feet. "Go back inside, Vandy," he whispered. He touched my bare hand. "You're cold."

My rebel fingers curved against his warm palm. Covering embarrassment, I tugged the hem of my jacket. A wet spot froze on my thigh. I brushed pebbles from my jeans. "Th-thanks, Phil. I'm okay." Stammering like a fool on a first date.

Phil's eyes dropped to my throat. "You're wearing Monica's necklace." Wet glistened on his cheeks. Sleet probably, not tears.

"I always do." I grazed the gold chain. The dangling *M* had drifted left. I moved the links until our baby's initial nuzzled the skin below my collarbone.

Phil's breath sprayed heat near my cheek. "I want to visit her grave, Vandy. I want to see where you buried her."

He'd never visited the cemetery. Never absorbed the meager comfort of seeing Monica resting in such beauty. The discovery stabbed, twisting until I gasped. "Of course. I'll take you." I gripped his hand. "Whenever you want. I'll show you."

"Soon." His mouth crumpled. Not sleet, real tears. His chest rose and fell. "Tomorrow. Can we go tomorrow?"

My heart stuttered until all I could manage was, "Yes. That's good."

"When do I meet you?"

I looked at the sky where the last embers of sunset struggled through the clouds. "The cemetery's beautiful at dusk." I lifted my cheeks, a tiny gesture, but he returned the smile. His dimple—Monica's and Tariq's dimple—flickered.

I drew my thumb along his jaw, wiping wet from the bristles. His sorrow scraped crusts of doubt from my heart. I'd never known if he'd suffered as much as I had in these years since Monica died. "Meet me here at four thirty," I said. "We'll drive in my car." I tilted my head toward the Jeep beside us.

Phil nodded and dragged a hand over his face. Before he could say more, I raced around my car and jumped in. I waited for him to pull from the parking lot and take the right onto Center Street.

When he vanished, I drove home. My heart felt sore, as if I'd been kicked. Why did I agree to escort Phil to the cemetery? Had he won me with a few tears? Why were invented images of a reunited family dazzling my thoughts? Guiding the Jeep over rain-slick streets, I tried to outrun these questions, to focus on immediate needs: a hot shower and my down comforter. My gut rumbled as visions of cheddar cheese sandwiches sizzled in the skillet of my mind. But when I parked in my driveway, the old question returned with gale force: What did I want from Phil Bolden?

# CHAPTER **ELEVEN**

"You know what Phil Bolden wants," Elissa Adesanya snapped at me the next morning. My legal eagle partner consumed all the air in my office, pacing before my desk with her mouth flared and her eyes snatched tight. "The same thing he's always wanted."

I tried to derail her lecture. "If I beg you don't tell me what that is, will you cease and desist?"

For breakfast, I'd only had one cup of coffee with the leftover grilled cheese sandwich, so my voice retained early-morning grit. My hoped-for second cup had been blocked by Elissa's arrival in my office five minutes ago.

She halted. "You better believe and trust I won't." Stamping both fists on the edge of my desk, she delivered the verdict. "He wants to get in your pants."

As usual, Elissa was dressed to convict. Orange silk pantsuit, fire-opal stud earrings, and an aquamarine turtleneck. With her micro-braids pulled into a topknot, she looked sharp and fast. I didn't stand a chance of evading her opinions.

Meek was my best option. I gave in: "So what's got you raging this morning?"

She nudged the yellow envelope she'd deposited on my desk four minutes ago. It skidded to a halt, sealed edge facing me. "Go ahead, open it. Like I told you, Phil dropped this on me as I walked through the door."

"Did he say anything?" Middle-schooler crush coated my voice with syrup. "About me?"

"He tossed that grin he has, dimples flying like poker chips. Like he knows he's holding all the cards. He said the envelope was an appreciation package for you." She glared at the bulging packet. "You know it's a big-ass wad of money. Only thing makes Phil Bolden grin like that is cash . . ." A beat to make me flinch. "And snatch."

"Gross much?" I puckered my mouth; Victorian-auntie style replaced seventh-grade goo.

Elissa squared her hips. I weighed the envelope on my palm. She crossed her arms, twin gold cuffs blinging from her wrists like Yoruba warrior armor. She wasn't moving. I slit the envelope with my fingernail. She was right, of course. The stack of bills was an inch thick. I riffled the edge with my thumb.

"You gonna count that?" Keeping her eyes on the money, Elissa backed up three steps and dropped into a guest chair. She wasn't leaving.

Trapped, I tallied the stash. The hell. I hadn't asked Phil for money. I'd refused to help repair his rift with Tariq. What was this cash for?

Elissa harrumphed, a snort of disapproval. "Grins and cash. That's Phil's MO in a nutshell."

"He asked for my help patching up things with his son. And I'm glad to assist. That's all." Lying to Elissa stung, but only a bit. She didn't need to know every shred of my private life. I stuffed the bills into the envelope and widened my eyes for innocence.

Spine straight, she leaned forward. "Tell me you're never seeing that asshole again."

I stood, shoving my chair into the wall. Finger aimed at Elissa, I fired bullet points: "I'll return the money to Phil. Not your order. My choice." Unsaid: *What happened in my pants was my business.*

PowerPoint presentation over, I dodged from my own office. Elissa sputtered as I crossed into the corridor.

\*   \*   \*

At four thirty sharp, Phil guided the Infiniti into a parking slot five spaces from where I was waiting. He slipped into my Jeep with a short greeting. I handed him the yellow envelope of cash.

"You didn't owe me anything," I said. Cool to mask the dryness in my throat.

"Probably more than that." He unzipped his hunter-green parka and stowed the packet.

"This isn't work."

"I know that. But I wanted you to take the money, make me happy." His dimple jumped for a fledgling smile.

A hint of moss and warm spices flew as he tugged at his sweater. This was not the cologne he'd worn last night. Picked for me? Or his usual daytime scent?

From inside the jacket, he pulled out a gray cloth figure. "I brought this . . . for Monica." A stuffed elephant with ears lined in pink satin, white tusks beside a floppy trunk, and black button eyes.

"That's Harvey," I blurted. "How did you find him?" This toy was identical to the velveteen elephant Monica had cherished as a child.

"I've kept him for a while. Looking for the right time to give him." He stared through the windshield at crinkled leaves skittering over the glass.

I rubbed my eyes. "My dad gave her Harvey for her second birthday." I petted the elephant's velveteen head. "She played with him all day and slept with him under her arm every night until he disintegrated. By the end, the poor thing was a mess: eyes dangling by a thread, tusk torn off, ear split. My mother restuffed and sewed Harvey many times. Finally, when Monica was seven, we held a ceremony and buried Harvey's raggedy remains in a shoebox in the backyard."

Phil's eyes glimmered. "Sounds like Harvey was loved to bits."

"He was. But how did you know Monica had a toy like this?"

"I gave it to her."

"What? No, that's not right. Harvey was a gift from my dad."

Phil studied the toy, stroking the fat belly. "I picked the elephant and sent it to your father. I asked him to give it to Monica for her birthday."

"And Daddy never said a word," I mumbled.

Phil nodded. "That was our agreement. Evander insisted I stay out of your life. Permanently." Swallowed to contain the bile. "He said I'd done enough harm already. He told me you never wanted to see me again. When I brought the gift, he said he'd deliver it. A year later, he told me she'd named the toy Harvey. I never knew if he told Monica where it came from."

"No, he never said." I fired the ignition. Then dialed the heat to max. Warm air brushed our faces. My father's recall was chewed by dementia now. I couldn't ask for his side of the story.

Ten minutes of silent driving took us deep into the Flats. Phil kept his face toward the passenger window, as the sun's silky gold draped the neighborhood.

As I'd promised, these simple bungalows and curving streets looked beautiful at dusk. I saw Phil's cheekbones rise. His eyes closed as if he couldn't fill them with beauty anymore. Phil pressed his skull against the headrest, eyes burning holes in the car roof. His wet lashes shone like patent leather.

As we pulled to a spot opposite the hulk of Bethel AME Church, Phil spoke. "I've got two stone elephant statues guarding the door at my house." He lifted the toy, dancing it on his chest. "I put them there for Monica. They mean delight, strength, confidence." He looked straight at me. "Every day I think of our baby when I pass those elephants."

The admission I'd waited almost three years to hear. My heart cracked open and let him in again.

I pointed at the iron picket fence guarding the cemetery. "Come on. I'll show you Monica's grave. You can give her Harvey. She'll like seeing him again."

After forty minutes, we returned to the car. I released Phil's hand when I retrieved my keys to open the Jeep. As I gripped the door handle, a dark shape congealed before the church door. Nadine Burriss stepped from the shadows into the last sliver of sunlight on the top step. The church treasurer wore a pastel blue overcoat and black boots with low heels. Her head was bare, as were her hands. She waved. I returned the salute. But her eyes were on Phil, not me.

Without a word, he trotted across the street and up the flight of stone steps. He towered over Nadine, his body curving to bring his face near hers. They spoke; after two minutes, he spread his arms, then he reached inside his coat and gave her a yellow envelope. The one I'd returned to him an hour ago.

Nadine took the envelope and slid it into her right pocket. Their jaws worked as they talked over each other. Were they arguing? Or bursting with news and fond cheer? Night shadows and distance blurred their faces. I couldn't read them clearly, only the head tilts, the flash of eyes. I wanted Nadine to vanish and yield Phil to me. This was my moment, not hers. Jaw grinding, I got into the Jeep and lit the engine. After another minute, Nadine turned her body. I thought her mouth was pursed as she peered in my direction. She nodded at Phil. He clapped her arm, buddy-style, then brushed a kiss close to her ear. I hated that fleeting intimacy. Hated my pang of jealousy more. This night was mine. As he loped across the street, Nadine disappeared inside the church.

"You know her?" I asked. "I didn't think you attended Bethel." My voice scratched a little, probably husky from the cemetery's chilly air. Or suspicion.

"Sure, I know her." Phil's tone was brisk. "Nadine and me go way back. To Trenton. Always try to boost my home girl when I can." I figured this was his explanation for the money he'd given Nadine. Was she a relic from Phil's past like me? Could I make a claim to press further? Into his future? Not yet, so I dropped the questions.

We drove toward Q-Town center. I knew what I wanted now. Harvey the elephant had convinced me. I wanted Phil Bolden in my bed. In my life, where he belonged. *Bad choices, no strings. My brand. My way.* Messy consistency was my hallmark.

I murmured, "I could share photos of Monica with you. If you want to see them."

He bit his lower lip. "Yes, I'd love that." Chin tucked, he blew into the collar of his parka.

"I warn you, though: my cooking skills haven't improved in twenty years. I still burn water."

Chuckling, he asked, "You keep a carton of eggs, don't you?"

"Yes."

"And fresh milk?"

"From Elsie the cow this morning."

"Then we won't starve tonight."

"Promise?" I asked. I wanted food and much more.

He nodded. "Promise."

# CHAPTER **TWELVE**

While I assembled the tools and ingredients for Phil's omelet, he toured my house. My fingers jitterbugged as I scoured the refrigerator for blocks of cheese and pots of week-old yogurt. I wanted Phil to like my house, to understand the choices I'd made when remodeling it. His opinion mattered.

The open plan of the first floor allowed me to bustle at the kitchen island and watch Phil move through the living room. I saw him skirt the four brass coffee tables to touch the fawn leather sectional sofa. He sat to stroke the long guard hairs of the faux fur throw—Arctic fox—re-draping it over the sofa arm after a minute. I knew Phil favored rich shades. I wondered what he made of my pale color scheme: couscous-and-raisin rug, upholstered chairs in creamy wool with yellow accents, brass floor lamps, ivory moldings. Too neutral? Boredom overdrive?

I pointed to a woven grass basket on the ledge before the fireplace. "You can use the controller to light the fire, if you want. It's gas. No wood chopping for this girl."

"You always were the smart one." He aimed the electronic wand, tapping with his thumb until the flames leaped. I was too far away to feel the warmth, but I liked the way light gleamed on Phil's forehead and nose as he gazed into the fire.

A cell phone buzzed. Phil slapped his pants pocket then pulled out the phone. The conversation was muffled; I heard him say *Mel* three times, his voice rising with the repetition. I thought I heard

*Main Street*, my address, but the words were garbled. Had he told his second wife he was visiting the home of his first wife? Doubtful, but possible. Maybe Phil shared his itinerary out of malice, caution, loyalty, or exasperation. Was he that mean? Or that honest?

I waited for a bolt of guilt to jab me. Or at least a remorseful pang. I wanted to sleep with another woman's man. A pinch did strike then, regret as a feathery tickle on the conscience. Not enough to derail me. Was I a monster? Or just greedy? Yes, and yes.

Call over, Phil walked around the chairs that divided the living room from the dining room. "I told Melinda I was here. Giving you the money we owed for your help." He tilted his head for the little lie. A smile darted across his face. "She was cool with it. Said to say hi to you."

I didn't believe him. No way the conversation went like that. Nothing about Monica or photos or dinner? I wondered if he'd told Melinda he'd paid me to pretend I was an employee, instead of something more intimate. A lie, but I dodged the fight. "Okay. 'Hey' back at her."

As Phil crossed into the dining room, I set white porcelain plates on the island. My kitchen was white, too. Not ivory, cream, or taupe. Avalanche white. Marble island like the Titanic's iceberg; stainless steel appliances with white knobs.

I balanced a saucer in my hand, thinking of its cruel purchase price. When I left my campus police job after Monica's death, the university settled a breathtaking sum on me. Deprived of breath, of life, I used that money to buy my dream house. I'd stocked the place with every luxury I could find. I bought bold paintings and a custom glass table for the dining room, a high-end stereo system I never used, a glass-enclosed sunroom I shunned. Now, thanks to the new check from the fraternity, I had more of Monica's money to spend. What would I buy next? An in-ground Olympic pool? Three Bentleys and a Mercedes? Money couldn't buy what I wanted.

Phil tapped my forearm, breaking my reverie.

I startled. "Sorry, I was woolgathering."

He shook his head. "Your house is stunning." Wonder softened his tone. "It's like walking through your mind, seeing the world as you do."

I rubbed my mouth. "Or as I wish it were."

"Yeah, I get that. It's your dream house."

I shook my head to clear the blues. "Yeah, sure." I glanced across the space, then wriggled to restore warmth to my shoulders. And to switch subjects. "I'm starving. But that's no excuse for bad hospitality. What can I get you to drink?"

"Jim Beam, like always." He chuckled. "Brown heat on the rocks."

I reached for the bottle stowed above the microwave. Dust on its neck coated my fingers as I unscrewed the top. I launched into an explanation of how I'd given up booze after Monica's death by alcohol-fueled asphyxiation. Except for a one-night bender months ago, I hadn't touched the stuff in two years. A recital of my favorite mocktails was interrupted by buzzes of Phil's cell phone. He stared at its face, then poked it into silence.

"Damn him."

"Who's bugging you?" I asked.

"That fucking headmaster, Dumont. Sent me four texts in one hour." He shoved the phone until it clattered against his glass. "Goddamn him."

"Must be urgent."

Phil snorted. "Melinda said he'd called twice to the house this evening."

"Sounds serious. What does Dumont want?"

"He's trying to get me to sign some letter." Double gulps of bourbon to ease the next words. "A stupid apology message to Rome donors."

"Apology for what?" I guessed the grit in the headmaster's engine might be related to Phil's speech at the homecoming gala.

"That's what I asked, 'What for?'" Eyes wide, long lashes batting his brows. "*No* way I'm sending *no* apology to *nobody* for *nothing*." A knuckle rap on the counter for each negative. Pissed, Phil swallowed the end of his first round and lifted the glass for a refill. I poured and the tirade continued. "That man's a rat on stilts. That's what I call Dumont to his face. Beady eyes, pointy nose, and all. Rat on stilts wants to kiss up to fat cats."

Phil laughed, his chest pumping with glee. He reached for the carton of eggs and cracked one into an aluminum bowl. He cracked a second, then a third, using one hand like a TV chef. He wasn't done with Charles Dumont: "The rat wants me to sign this letter he's written. Tonight. That's why he's texting me like a crackhead jonesing for a score."

"You going to meet him?" I sliced cheddar from an unyielding brick, eyes on the task.

"Tonight? Not a chance." Phil reached for the wire whisk. "I'm here. Period."

Fueled by a steady flow of bourbon and my best private-eye jokes, Phil created a beautiful dinner. The omelet was lacy perfection, golden and oozing with cheddar. I tore enough lettuce to convert the sole beefsteak tomato into an entire salad. I only had whole wheat bread, but toasted slices worked fine in place of a baguette.

As I sipped my third glass of sparkling water, I asked Phil one of the least fiery questions burning on my agenda: "You think I should bring more color into the house? Is the whole place too beige?"

Phil looked toward the living room's picture windows from our seats at the dining table. "Yeah, I know what you mean." He paused, searching for praise to avoid insult. "I think you got a cool vibe going on." He pointed with his lips toward the wall above the table. "Especially these big paintings. They bring the heat for sure."

He was right. I'd picked two audacious canvases, abstract human figures outlined in emerald and garnet, splashed with sunset colors. "Thanks, I'm glad you like them." I wanted to pay Phil a compliment, offer praise to his new family. "I wonder what Tariq would think of these. He's sure an accomplished artist."

He frowned. "Tariq messes with that shit. No good reason for it, killing time is all."

"Maybe he's got real talent."

Cords on his neck bulged. "You saw Tariq's paintings?"

"No, but I'd like to. Laurel Vaughn told me he has major artistic gifts."

"When did you talk with her?"

"At the Rome homecoming. Before the blowup." I raised a palm as a peace sign.

Phil growled, "That snake needs to keep away from my family." He ripped a corner of bread and crushed it in his fist. "She's a troublemaker."

"She seemed sweet to me." I intended to needle. "And super supportive of Tariq."

Phil jumped from the table. Snatching both plates, he moved toward the kitchen. Forks rattled when he collided with the edge of the island. I stood, hoping to stop him from throwing the dishes into the sink.

He wasn't that destructive. The plates landed on a folded cloth next to the paper towel dispenser. He snarled, "Laurel Vaughn poisoned our family with her nasty ways last summer." When I stepped to his side, he turned to face me. "Like the serpent in the Garden of fucking Eden."

His nostrils flared. I didn't duck his glower. "What in the world did she do, Phil?"

He dragged a hand from hairline to chin, erasing the scowl. "She moved on me, at my own party, in my own house." His voice lashed. "That bitch cornered me in the garage. Tried to jump my bones. Kissing on me in front of my own damn son."

I laid my hand over Phil's. His fingers, still trembling with emotion, stiffened on the counter. I took a deep breath; he followed suit. Another breath; he rotated his hand so our palms touched.

"Okay?" I asked.

"Yeah. Sorry. You didn't deserve to hear that."

"No worries," I whispered. "No apology needed." I squeezed his hand. "I want to hear about you. From you. Always."

He sighed, the tension rippling away. Eyes brightening, it was his turn to switch subjects. "You promised me pictures, lots of Monica pictures. Where do you keep them?"

I pointed to a door beyond the dining table. "Come to my cave."

Cradling a bottle of Perrier and two stemmed glasses, I bumped the door with my hip. When it eased open, I beckoned to Phil.

The side room was my haven. In it, I kept magazines, photos, and books. I stowed my laptop and iPad on the small desk here. Not grand or elegant, this retreat's midnight-blue walls and furnishings brought me solace. After a day of dogging clients or interviewing informants, I came here to quiet the rush of thoughts. This was my home inside home. I'd filled the space with spongy sofas, oriental rugs, ceiling-tall bookshelves, a sound system, and a flat screen. Sapphire velvet curtains over the window blocked the outside world.

"Here's my kick-back-and-chill spot," I said, tugging Phil's hand.

When we'd settled on the sofa, I pulled a picture frame from the bookcase behind us. The photo was of Monica in her gold-and-black high school graduation gown. She'd tilted the mortarboard at a jaunty angle above her smiling face. Her hair, silk-pressed for the occasion, draped around her neck in soft waves.

"Check out this newfangled photo album," I said. I tapped a button on the frame and the image dissolved. In its place emerged a shot of baby Monica, her first tooth erupting between chubby brown cheeks.

Phil's eyes sparked. "Oh, wow, that's something."

"Yeah, it's great, isn't it?" I flipped the frame to indicate a row of buttons on one edge. "I sent five hundred photos to this company and they created a digital file, uploaded to the cloud." I stroked the mahogany wood, then set the frame on Phil's lap. "Go ahead, explore."

Under his fingers the memories exploded. Pictures of Monica from every year of her life danced across the screen.

I poured Perrier in both glasses. As the bubbles tickled our noses, we talked. About her first ice skates and video game obsessions. About her braces and skinned knees. About her sticker collection, piano recitals, debate prizes, and performance as the Stage Manager in *Our Town*.

Phil stopped the cascade of photos to cradle the frame in both hands. He studied a seventh-grade class portrait of Monica then kissed the frame above her lovely face. "This right here, Vandy, *this* is my homecoming."

I leaned my head on his shoulder, a sigh whispering against his neck. I showed him photos of our trip to France: Eiffel Tower, Arc de Triomphe, Notre-Dame Cathedral, the island castle at Mont St. Michel. Our trip was a gift from my dad for Monica's high school graduation. Three weeks of bliss before Rutgers freshman orientation.

"Too fast," Phil said. "Back up. I want to see that one of you two in front of the glass pyramid."

"That's the Louvre," I said. Monica was wearing black leggings, lug-soled sneakers, and a giant red sweater. For our day at the art museum, I'd chosen gray slacks and a mauve cardigan over a mariner-striped T-shirt.

Phil leaned his shoulder into mine. "You both look great." He shook his head. "Beautiful and happy."

"We were that day." I swallowed a gulp of fizz. The warmth of his body flowed into mine. "Each day of that trip, we were happy in a different way."

"That means so much to hear you say that." Phil scrubbed a finger across his upper lip. "I thought about that trip to France a lot."

"You knew about our vacation?" When I stiffened, cool air rushed between our shoulders.

"Yes, your dad gave me a few details. No pictures, though. This is the first time I've seen what Monica looked like in France."

"Why did Evander tell you about that trip?" Unease snipped my words. "What did our vacation have to do with you?"

Phil drained his flute, then set the glass on a side table. He stared for thirty seconds at a stack of magazines tottering on the edge of my desk. He licked his lips as if the water had left them dry.

"You know something, but you won't say it?" I asked, shifting to face him.

"Yeah. It was a secret."

"Spill it. We're past hiding now, Phil."

He narrowed his eyes, but met mine straight. "I paid for your trip to France."

"What?" I squeezed the sofa's cushion. "No, that's not possible. Daddy paid."

"It is, Vandy. I gave the money to Evander so Monica could have a blowout graduation gift."

I whispered, "And he never said a word."

"That was our deal. I was the money man. A silent partner." He snarled through clenched teeth: "A silent parent."

"Because Evander wanted it that way?"

"Because he said *you* wanted it that way."

"No." Heat surged from my chest to my throat. Words rattled like pebbles flung at a screen door. "He—he never asked me. He never told me. Daddy never let me make my own choice." I never realized Phil had made these overtures. Perhaps I might have taken a different approach if I'd known of his interest. I brushed her necklace, touching Monica's scrolled initial. The gold cooled my burning fingers. I threw my head against the sofa back. "I don't know what to think anymore." I closed my eyes. As if that would shutter the revelations. Or cage my newborn guilt.

"I'm sorry." His breath shot through open lips. "I didn't mean to upset you."

"It's not you. It's Daddy." I ran an index finger along the delicate chain, rolling the links over my skin. The grit of an idea scratched my mind. As I turned it, thoughts layered like nacre over the idea until the pearl formed.

I whooshed. "And this necklace, his present to Monica for her nineteenth birthday. It wasn't from him, was it?"

Phil studied a fingernail, then coughed. "No. I picked it out at a jewelry store in Princeton."

He gasped, as if speaking the truth aloud violated the pact with my absent father. When I squeezed his hand, he continued, words flowing in a torrent, "I chose the design and the style of links. Italian gold. From Florence. Just after New Year's, I visited Evander. I asked him to give Monica the necklace. He said he would. I never knew what happened after that. Next thing I heard, she was dead. On her birthday. No details. Just gone." He swallowed hard. "I wondered if she ever knew I loved her. If she even got my gift. I didn't know for sure until I saw the necklace on you yesterday." Tears ran in twin streams beside his mouth.

I stroked the wet crevasses with my thumb. "You didn't know. How could you have known?" My father was the one who'd denied vital information to Phil. My father had sliced the wound. But with my silence I'd deepened the cut.

"I'm sorry, Vandy." A muscle twitched near his eye. Then another fluttered in his cheek. Turmoil contained in these small flickers made my heart ache to ease his pain. My father would never be able to undo the damage he'd done, but I could make an effort.

"This isn't on you." I hoped repetition would soothe. "You didn't know." Was this guilt talking? Or lust spiced with affection and a dollop of nostalgia? Yes. Even hope blended in the mix of sensations. Everything I felt for Phil welled up in that moment. I kissed a teardrop in the dip of his dimple. Then another at the corner of his mouth. "You couldn't have known."

I ran my hand over the back of his neck, pulling him to me for a deeper kiss. His lips were warm and soft under mine, the way they'd always been. His mouth tasted smoky from the bourbon and sweet from all the past we shared. My tongue stroked his, sending sparks from my ears to my gut. I leaned, he reclined. My shirt rustled against his sweater, a gentle counterpoint to our sighs. I angled, he relaxed. Heat rising from his chest smelled of burnt leaves. Sensations of our cemetery visit flickered in my mind. Smooth stone, lacy trees, plush moss. When he shifted under me, the scent of earthy metals enveloped me. I raised my hand to angle his face in the old style. Familiar and warm, his legs, hips, stomach all fit me, as always. Any objections I had, any thoughts pleading for consideration, everything reasonable or safe, evaporated in the rush of remembrance. Kissing Phil promised everything: returning home, restoring family. I wanted more. More of everything we'd created. Everything I'd lost. The sofa wasn't broad enough to contain everything I wanted. My bed offered a new chance. We took the risk.

Water splashing in my bathroom awakened me. I rolled over until my knee touched the trench on Phil's side of the bed. Empty but still warm. I heard more splashes, then a drawer scraped open. Scrabbling sounds, then scrubbing and gargling. Was he going away? Too soon. Red lights of the bedside clock gleamed 1:35. I wanted him to stay another hour, even two. Why not until dawn? *Snick.* He turned off the light.

He tiptoed across the carpet, arms extended to navigate the unfamiliar terrain of my bedroom. I switched on the table lamp beside me. When its glow bathed him in pink light, he straightened. He'd buckled his trousers, but was still bare-chested. The crisp hair there was flecked with gray. Soft flesh folded over his belt.

"You're going?" *Casual, avoid desperate or bossy.* "It's not late."

"Yeah, babe. It's late. Or early. Depends on how you're counting." A crooked smile to soothe the rebuke. When he sat on the corner of the bed, it sagged. He bent to lace his shoes. I wanted more minutes. More years.

I stretched until my toes touched a bundle of cotton crammed under the quilt. With clever pincer moves, I fished out his T-shirt. I leaned to dangle the black cloth over his back. "If you want this, I'm charging a finder's fee."

He knelt over me, raining kisses on my neck and shoulders. "This enough to claim my shirt?"

I chuckled. "Not enough. But I'll collect soon."

"Deal," he said. He slipped into the T-shirt. "My favorite kind of debt."

I tied the pink chenille robe around me, scrounged in vain for my scuffs, then, still barefoot, I hurried down the stairs after him. We found his sweater in the blue study and his scarf on the leather couch in the living room.

As he zipped up his parka, I chirped like a dutiful host, "Don't you want a lift to your car?" I was still naked under my robe, so I added, "Give me thirty seconds to dress and I'll drive you."

Phil snuffled doubt through a bent smile. "I'm a big boy. I know how to get to your office from here. You go back to bed."

"Straight north on Main to Center Street. Turn right . . ."

"Then four blocks to the pharmacy at the corner of Abbott Street. Your parking lot is behind the drugstore, right?"

"Right." I stuffed a fist into my mouth to cork a yawn. "You got it."

Phil kissed my forehead, nose, then both eyebrows. Minty freshness floated over my face. "Go back to bed, babe."

I yawned, unblocked this time. "Yeah, I'll call you tomorrow . . ." I scrubbed my eyes. "I mean today, I'll call this afternoon."

"Good, catch you then," he said. Out the door on a *whoosh* of frosty air. I heard shoes tramping the wooden porch then crunching leaves I'd failed to sweep from my front walk.

I glided through the living room. Refold the fur throw. Straighten the Ibeji statue on the mantel. Extinguish the fire. Up the stairs to our bed. Still warm from us.

At seven thirty that morning, my second bowl of oatmeal tasted even better than the first. I blew on the second cup of coffee, waiting for the double-dose brew to cool.

I'd come to the kitchen in a gray sweatshirt and pants, with pink socks to protect against the cold tiles. Balanced on a stool at the island, I spooned a glob of cereal and studied the dinner plates piled in the sink. Cleanup was on the agenda. Showering, too, later. I refused to rush this day. I rubbed my cuff over my nose then sniffed my wrist. My skin smelled of Phil and me. The unique blend of us two. I wanted to bask in the warmth of this new direction for a while.

My shower could wait another forty minutes.

The front door buzzed, short, then long. Had Phil returned so soon? Another buzz. Long, short, short. I scrambled to unbolt the lock.

Two white Queenstown police officers blocked the weak sunlight. I couldn't see their faces. Their necks and arms were rigid inside dark uniforms. I stepped back. They surged into my house.

The man squared his bulk to claim the space. He was a few inches taller than me, thick through the neck and chest. A scowl cut his face into quadrants of anger, resentment, fear, and distrust. The woman was shorter, with a large head on a bony neck. She'd cropped her brown hair into an ugly shag whose loose strands curled over her forehead and nape. The uniform, gathered in stiff folds around her wiry frame, looked scratchy. I scrubbed my neck in reflex sympathy and tried a mild opening.

"What is it, Officer? Can I help you?" I stared at her, ignoring the male to needle him because I didn't like his bully-boy stance.

She glowered then pushed up the plastic bill of her cap. Rain-drops danced from the rim. "You're the private dick, right?"

My reputation reached more sections of Q-Town than I'd imag-ined. My hometown felt big when you needed help, small when you wanted privacy.

She scraped her gaze down my body. When I crossed my arms, she frowned at the speck of oatmeal on my sweatshirt front. Or maybe she intended to enforce a town ordinance against going bra-less in your own home.

"Yes, I'm Vandy Myrick." Still cool, but firmer. "What can I do for you?"

The cop coughed; pink stained her throat. She looked at my socks. Rain puddles swelling around her boots crept toward my toes.

The other cop elbowed past her. "We're canvassing the neighbor-hood," he said. "There's been a murder."

# CHAPTER **THIRTEEN**

The entrance hall's shadows contracted around my head, dark bands tightening until my ears rang. *Murder.* Heat from the floor vent clutched my ankles. *Impossible.* The woman cop pushed the door shut, dripping gloom into the vestibule. *Wrong house, wrong morning.* Dawn's rain shone on the black epaulets and brass buttons of her slate-blue QPD uniform.

Her partner stepped toward me, his arms clamped across his chest. "We're going door to door. Talking to everyone in the neighborhood. Trying to collect data on this murder." His lips were gray lines. "The more, the better. The faster, the better."

Dread pushed me toward the leather sofa in my living room. When my thighs collided against the back of the couch, I croaked, "Who's dead, Officer," still addressing the woman.

The man's eyes squeezed when I spoke to her. I didn't care who was the senior officer. I shot my questions at her. "How do you know it's a murder?"

She removed her cap, holding it at her waist like a shield. Squaring on me, she said, "The body was discovered at six-oh-five this morning. The pharmacist called in the report." Sweat darked the curls on her brow. She licked her lips. "I'm Officer Lola Conte. I was the first responder on the scene—"

"What pharmacist?" I interrupted. If they were canvassing this area, the incident must have been nearby, not more than two or three miles away.

Conte said, "The doc who owns the Queenstown Pharmacy. He's the one called nine-one-one."

My office was located above that store. Phil had been headed to the parking lot behind that building when he left me last night. *This morning.* I repeated, "How do you know it was a murder?"

The male cop barked, "We ask the questions here, lady. Not you." He pulled a notepad from his pocket to bolster his authority.

Conte snapped her head. Her voice rumbled from her belt. "All right, Baker. I got this." She was in charge. She eyed me; her chin bobbed once. Decision made. She was for me. For now. "We know it was a murder because of the two gunshot wounds to the victim's chest."

My mouth dried. "And you know the victim's identity?" I wanted my jaw to steady, but it slid from side to side.

"We do," Conte said.

Baker growled, his nose red, eyes glassy with anger. "You shouldn't share that information, Lola."

He wanted to diminish her with the first-name ploy. Didn't work. Her chest expanded under the navy wool. Her shoulders squared.

"I decide what to share here." She stepped close to me. "Like I said, I was first on the scene. I identified the body. The victim was Philip Bolden."

Orange sparks shot into my eyes. I sat hard, hands gripping the sofa cushion. My stomach leaped, then clenched. Heat, like an enflamed iron rod, jabbed my gut. Crushing the leather with slow beats, I timed my breathing to the pulse of my fists. I blinked to clear my eyes. The lids felt hot and tight; no tears, only the grit of charred cinders. My lungs filled with dry heat. I coughed; the vibrations singed my throat.

I said, "Thank you for letting me know." Even and low. Like the news was a police-blotter update. Not a bulletin from hell.

Baker wasn't the clod he appeared. Sensing my anguish, he drilled, "You knew the vic, Bolden?"

I rose, speaking to Baker for the first time. "Yes, Mr. Bolden contacted me this week for help with reaching their son." A distortion, but the plain phrases cooled my distress. I could do this. I could make it through the next minute. Then the one after that.

"And you found the kid?" Baker took my meager words to be about a runaway. About a phantom case I'd worked as a private eye. I let him ride the misdirection.

"Yes, I did." I fell into the age-old script of people of color. When confronted by police, speak little, offer nothing. Guard your family, save your neck. Now I had more reasons to practice safe talk. I wanted to protect my privacy. Unless my final hours with Phil Bolden proved relevant to his murder, I wanted to keep our renewed relationship secret. Protecting his wife and son was my priority now. And shielding myself. That mattered, too.

Baker barged on. "We're gonna need you to give details on that incident."

I shivered. What "incident"? Did he mean Tariq's brief retreat or my even briefer interlude with Phil? The cop couldn't have guessed, could he? Was sex draped like a shroud over my face and body this morning?

I stiffened my spine and kept my lie scant. "There was no formal missing person's report filed by the Boldens."

Baker wasn't satisfied. "Yeah, but you still might have inside facts. Details about the family that can help the murder investigation."

The bulldog was right. But that didn't make me sing. A still, cold voice rattled from my throat. "I'm sure you know, as a private investigator, my contacts with the Bolden family are confidential. I won't share information about them unless they give me specific permission to do so." Lips icy, I clamped my mouth shut. I stared at Baker, daring him to challenge me.

He swallowed and pulled at his right earlobe. When he ducked his eyes, the round was mine. I knew he'd swing for me again. QPD cops were low-imagination, high-tenacity workers. I wasn't off the hook.

Conte shifted from left to right foot. She steered us toward the core question of the canvass. "Did you hear or see anything out of the ordinary last night?"

Relieved, I answered in a rush, "No, nothing different. Car traffic on Main Street was light as usual. Until around twelve thirty, when it shut down altogether." I tried a weak smile. "You know how Q-Town sidewalks roll up by midnight." I wanted the old joke to ease tension, but the cops' mouths tightened.

"And you were awake past midnight?" Conte caught the clue, but had no way to tease out the underlying details. "That how you know about the traffic?"

"I was in my study, Officer." I poked a thumb toward the side room. "Catching up on Netflix."

I remembered how my sapphire-blue retreat had warmed when Phil entered it last night. The way he cradled the framed portrait of our dead daughter. *This right here, Vandy, this is my homecoming.* How he'd kissed the frame above Monica's beautiful face.

"What show?" Conte said. She was pushy.

"*The Crown,*" I lied.

She shot her eyes across the open space. "You were in a room toward the back of the house. But you know when traffic stopped out front. Good ears." Her brows flew in skepticism.

"Private-eye tool kit, Officer." Frosty smile. I wanted this interview ended. "You'll excuse me now." Not a question, an order. I walked to the narrow bench in the hall and sat. I pulled on my shearling boots and lifted the parka from its hook.

As I sealed the zipper, Baker snapped, "Where do you think you're going?"

"To my office." I jerked open the door and stood aside. "I've got work to do."

I followed the cops down the porch steps. From my Jeep I watched the pair push the doorbell of my neighbors' house. I fumbled inserting the key into the ignition. I pulled the sweatshirt cuffs over my cold knuckles then punched the dashboard. When I lifted my wrist, a plume of earthy green—our scent—brushed my face. I shook my head to block the tears. No room for soft sentiment now. I wanted a fire-tempered heart of steel. I needed to solve Phil's murder. I jammed the key home and stamped the pedal.

# PHIL'S CASE

# CHAPTER **FOURTEEN**

The death scene engulfed my little corner of Queenstown. I wanted to get to my office, but policemen stood in blue clumps on the curb before the pharmacy; others lined the sidewalk beside the Heinz Photography Studio across the street.

Two squad cars, lights blazing, were parked bumper-to-bumper across Abbott. They intended to block the street, but I turned anyway. I drove thirty yards with right front and rear wheels on the curb. I angled into the incline for the entrance to the parking lot behind the pharmacy, nudging my front bumper against the wooden horse that blocked access. I saw crime scene experts in white jumpsuits bent in clutches around the parking lot. Rain piddled in the creases of their clothing and slicked the folds of their pale faces.

Officers ran from each end of the barricade to bracket me when I hopped from my car. "No access, lady. You can't go any farther."

"I work here." I pointed toward the second floor, then the parking lot. "That's my name on the brick wall."

The cops were unimpressed. "Stand back, ma'am," the blond ordered. "You can park your vehicle behind the photo studio," said the buzz-cut one, thumb jutting across the street.

The arrival of a new figure saved my bacon. Robert Sayre said, "I'll handle this." Tall and barrel-chested, with a voice as dark and commanding as his face, the Queenstown police chief glared at the two junior officers. I saw necks bow and shoulders shrink until their uniforms looked three sizes too big.

"Sure, Chief," Buzz Cut said. "We're just trying to keep the crime scene clear."

"Understood," Sayre said. "Resume your posts. I've got this." Glancing at each other, the sentries scurried to their places next to the wooden barrier.

With his subordinates still in earshot, Sayre bellowed, "What the hell are you doing here, Myrick?" The rebuke landed as intended. I could see smiles flicker as cheeks reddened. The junior cops were pleased to hear a Black man give a Black woman her comeuppance. The chief took my elbow and marched me ten paces away. He'd zipped a black puffer vest over the regulation blues, which made him seem larger than usual. He stroked raindrops from his salt-and-pepper beard.

Bending to wrap me within his force field, he whispered, "Don't get mixed up in this, Vandy. Any more than you have to." Behind thick lenses, his black eyes glowed with what I hoped was fondness.

I'd known Robert Sayre since eighth grade. I watched Bobby morph from a chubby Pop Warner wannabe into an agile quarterback, Bobby the Beast. As center fielder and home-run champ, Bobby was the linchpin of Q High's state championship baseball team. In between cheerleaders and glam girls, Bobby dated me for a sweaty half year when we were sixteen. I never figured out what drew him to me then. Afraid to ask that question, I was grateful for the attention and prestige of dating the Beast. Those weren't the goals I had when I triggered our brief affair several months ago. Coming off a brutal murder case, I wanted commitment-free solace. *Bad moves, no strings. My brand, my way.* Bobby, determined to hang on to his third marriage, was the perfect comforter. We lasted three weeks. That was enough. I'd grown some since then, but messy was still my call sign.

I jammed my hands into the pockets of my parka. "I *am* mixed up in this." I studied my stained boots, wriggling my toes until the fleece warmed them. "I was helping the Boldens and their son earlier this week." I didn't want to weave full-blown lies for Bobby, just bend the truth a bit.

I sighed, then chanced a glimpse into his face. Hard jaw, wide nose, skin the color of sun-drenched maple wood. Bobby and his younger brother, Keyshawn, looked so much alike they were often mistaken for twins. Seeing Key at the Rome gala last week had underlined the brothers' resemblance in my mind. Although Keyshawn had a minor criminal record, I'd always found Bobby the more dangerous of the two. And the more alluring.

"I helped fix things with the Boldens' son." I offered a smile with the fib to ease the conversation. And to avoid the detour I feared.

Bobby wasn't buying. "If you say so," he growled. "But that's not what I'm talking about. You understand me?" He punched his fists into his hips. Drizzle made the neon blue of the plastic gloves scream against the black trousers.

Bobby knew I'd married Philip Bolden and divorced him when I was four months pregnant. He didn't know I'd slept with Phil last night. I wanted to keep my secret. I figured the QPD chief's business didn't extend to my private choices. Even in a murder investigation.

"I'm clear, Bobby," I said. "My contact with the Boldens ended when they got back with their son." I hoped that sounded professional and definitive enough to get me off the hook. Private eye wrangling private business. Nothing to see. Move along.

Bobby angled his face, sliding his hat back on the dome of his shaved head. Skepticism tangled with concern on his features. Had he detected my lie? His eyes ranged over my mouth, down to my slapdash clothing. Baggy sweat pants stuffed in scratched boots. No hat, gloves, or scarf. No earrings, makeup, or perfume. I looked rough.

Bobby wanted to know why. "You feeling okay?" He raised a blue finger toward my chin, but didn't touch. "You look gray."

"Gray?" I coughed a chuckle. "You mean, like a fish? Mackerel? Or perch?"

He didn't laugh. "Your eyes, something don't look right." He knew me too well; old-school ties constricting as he combed my face.

"We're at a murder scene, what am I supposed to look like?" I scrubbed the skin beside my left eye. "Can you show me what you've got so far?" I gestured toward the parking lot.

He squinted at me, then at the crime scene behind us. A grunt framed a reluctant "Follow me. But don't open your mouth. Understand?"

I was glad to dodge his scrutiny. "Aye, aye, Chief."

As we walked across the tarmac, following Bobby Sayre's order was easy. I didn't dare open my mouth for fear of vomiting. Phil's body had been removed. His chocolate-brown Infiniti remained, driver's window lowered two inches. Had he been accosted after he entered the car? Did he stand from the vehicle to confront the assailant? Why not drive away? Did he know the attacker? Or was he moved by a stranger's appeal for help?

I stood beside Bobby at the taillight of the Infiniti and glanced around. I'd walked through this lot hundreds of times. The place always seemed tidy. But now I noted the cement was cracked in a dozen places. Overnight rain hadn't washed away the stains of a broken liquor bottle or ink from discarded crates. I saw trash bins and an old ladder propped against the brick wall next to the pharmacy's rear entrance. The anonymous space I crossed every day now seemed sinister. These mundane items were the last things Phil saw as he died.

Now, crime scene technicians added their own official litter. Bent like field hands, the forensic team placed little plastic tents at spots around the damp lot. Each white tent had a number marking a station on Phil's final journey. Number sixteen was where he'd sunk to his knees. Seventeen where his hip had nestled in a puddle of mud. Eighteen and nineteen were where his outflung arms had embraced the asphalt.

Bobby asked questions; his techs answered. I heard someone say they'd found a driver who remembered spotting Phil walking on Center Street around 1:45 that morning. The other exchanges seeped into my head in a blur. The fog receded when two uniformed officers trotted to Bobby's side. Conte and Baker had returned from their canvass of my block.

Conte handed Bobby a sealed plastic bag. She jerked her eyes at her partner. "Baker found this on Main Street. Under bushes in front of one-fifteen." Three blocks from my home. I said nothing. Bobby knew where I lived, had visited there several times during our brief affair. Would he connect the addresses now?

Bobby extracted a black leather wallet from the bag. He opened it, eyes searching the plastic ID window. He held the billfold toward me. I saw Phil's New Jersey driver's license. His picture, an ugly image, stared into the distance.

I asked Conte, "Any cash?"

Looking at Bobby, Baker answered, "Cleaned out. Credit cards untouched. Couple of receipts from a dry cleaner's and a shop, the Curious Cat."

This was a children's bookstore on Center Street. Yesterday Phil said he'd bought the stuffed elephant for Monica years ago. Now I wondered if he'd purchased the toy in the bookstore yesterday before meeting me for the trip to the cemetery. My fingers burned in my coat pockets, then my stomach flared. Grief melded with anxiety to demand a weird etiquette. I wanted to retrieve his gift from Monica's grave. I didn't want the toy rotting in the rain. I wanted to bring Harvey home to stay. I could make a quick run to the cemetery before the end of the day.

Sparkling dots swam before my eyes. I swayed, shuffling my feet to catch my balance. Every inch of my body hurt, like I'd been swatted with a baseball bat. Bobby bent his neck to watch me. He leaned in my direction, but our shoulders didn't touch.

He said, "If the money's gone, this could be simple robbery. A stickup gone sideways. The perp follows Bolden to his vehicle, induces him to exit the car with some sob story, pulls a pistol, asks for money. When Bolden resists, the skel shoots him. Rifles his pockets, runs with the wallet. Dumps it a few blocks away."

Conte nodded. "That's how I make it, Chief. But the perp could have been on a bicycle."

Baker blurted, "We found deep bike tracks in mud next to the bushes. Deep enough last night's rain was still pooled in the grooves." Smugness flushed his cheeks and lower lip.

"Agreed," Bobby said. "The stickup artist could be some fool kid. Clown gets spooked by hard words from Bolden. Shoots in reflex."

"And boom, instead of armed assault, the thug's facing a murder rap," Conte said.

Bobby folded the consultation. "Conte, you're in charge of this investigation. I want this sewed up quick and tight. Philip Bolden's an important man in our community. Noise about this murder is going to get loud in a hurry. City hall, Rome School, county prosecutor, governor's office. Everybody's going to jump our necks hard. I want this solved fast. Understand?"

"Yes, sir," Conte said. She looked at me, eyebrows raised.

Bobby answered the silent question. "Myrick is a solid investigator. She has connections to the family. She may have leads you can use." Baker grunted in disbelief. Bobby scowled, raising his voice. "So, Conte, you work with Myrick. I want this seamless, understand?"

"Yes, sir," Conte repeated. I thought amusement glimmered across her eyes as she clocked Baker's disgust. "We'll get on it, pronto."

If I'd been in a mood to gloat, I'd have enjoyed Conte's small victory. But I left the cops to their rivalries and repositioned my car across the street in the lot behind Heinz Photography Studio. My stomach rocked with increasing ferocity as I climbed the stairs to my office. Would I make it to the top without hurling?

Elissa Adesanya and Belle Ames were in their familiar spots when I entered the suite. Elissa loomed over the reception desk, armored in an onyx velvet pantsuit. No blouse visible, her collar was filled with a bib of turquoise beads. Belle sprawled in her revolving chair, arms crossed over a baby-blue sweater. Her blond pageboy wig and claret lips were quirked off-kilter. Both women straightened to stare at me. I figured they'd learned of Phil's murder when they arrived earlier. As their mouths gaped, I rushed past them to my office, where I dropped my coat on a chair.

Elissa stepped in as I sank into my seat. "You doing all right, honey?" Soft voice, mild black eyes. Pity blunted her lawyer thorns. "We heard the news. Awful any way you cut it. Just horrible."

"I'm okay," I said, pressing a throbby spot on my temple. My gut rumbled disagreement.

As she revved to deliver more sympathy, I jumped toward the door. I undercut my assertion by dashing to the bathroom at the end of the hall. Vomiting engaged every muscle and pore in my body. Twice I tried to stand from the porcelain bowl, twice I sank to my knees for a new round of retching. At the end of the final bout, I rinsed my mouth and splashed my face with cold water. According to the mirror, the skin around my eyes was gray, just as Bobby Sayre had observed. Now I'd added a blue tinge on the lips. My hair was flattened on the right side and spiked like hobnails on the left. Ruffling a palm over my scalp couldn't rescue the hairdo, but my headache returned with a vengeance.

When I emerged ten minutes later, Elissa was standing outside the bathroom door. "You need to lie down in my office," she said.

Her office overlooked the parking lot. When I walked in, Elissa rushed to close the venetian blinds so I couldn't see the ongoing police investigation. She'd stacked two pillows against the arm of her leather couch, making the invitation irresistible. I thought she'd leave me to my misery. But she sat on the edge of her desk, legs extended, breathing hard as she watched over me. I lay flat, hands folded over my aching belly. I closed my eyes, but I could sense Elissa noting my sweat clothes, missing bra, and grungy boots.

In the quiet, cop voices wafted to the window. I couldn't make out their words, but I knew they were working. Rest wasn't on my agenda, either. I knew my next steps and I wanted to hit the road. After three minutes, I swung upright.

As if she'd been watching from the hall, Belle swooped in with a mug of hot herbal tea. "You been through a shock, baby girl. This peppermint'll settle your stomach," she said. "And your nerves." She handed me the cup and used the wet warmth on her fingers to plaster the wig's curls against her cheek.

Both women gazed at me with calf eyes. They knew of my long-ago marriage to Phil Bolden. No way they'd clocked our renewed relationship. Too soon for the story to leak; too outlandish for the news to be believed. I sipped, wondering if I should test their knowledge. I wanted to understand where I stood with my partners.

I said, "Yeah, it was a shock when the cops rousted me in my house this morning. All the questions about if I'd heard or seen anything last night." I blew, the steam floating a veil before my eyes. "Took me a while to get my bearings, figure out it was Phil they were talking about."

Belle clucked. "And to think, you saw the man here only yesterday. Awful, just dreadful." I nodded to confirm her inaccurate timeline. "And a young man, too, right?" She was fifty-six and acted like the mother of us all.

"Forty-eight," I said. "My age." Belle sucked her teeth at the tragedy of shattered potential.

Elissa was the practical boss. "You need to go home, girl. Get some rest. You look whipped."

"I'm working this case," I said, reaching to set the mug on her desk.

"You what?" they squawked in chorus.

"No argument. It's settled." I smiled, a small twist devoid of triumph. "I work for him now."

"That's ridiculous, Vandy." Elissa stood, her chest bumping mine. She repeated, louder: "You don't owe him anything."

I shook my head. Argument over, I turned for the door. At the threshold I pointed at Elissa. "You're wrong. Phil Bolden is my client now. I'm going to solve his murder."

Taking the long way home, I stopped at the cemetery to retrieve Harvey the stuffed elephant. He was heavy with rain. I wrung the toy, spurting water into the grass next to Monica's side of the grave. I placed the toy on the rubber floor guard of the Jeep and ran across the street. I wanted to question church treasurer Nadine Burriss. Aside from me, Nadine was among the last people to see Phil Bolden the evening before his death. I wanted to know why he'd given her the envelope of money. Of course, she might ask that question of me, if she learned he had tried to give me the same cash. I wouldn't let that happen.

I walked along the sidewalk separating the church's renovated wing from the parking lot. I knocked on the door that led to Nadine's basement office. No answer. I rattled the door. Even if I couldn't talk with Nadine, her office might contain information I could use. Letters, receipts, memos, photos. Documents that could illuminate her ties with Phil Bolden. The bolt slipped when I turned the knob. I stepped inside. The room was dark. My chance to explore.

## CHAPTER **FIFTEEN**

Darkness cloaked Nadine Burriss's office. Reedy light played through the transom windows near the ceiling of the long wall. Shadows stroked the framed watercolor bouquet above the desk, turning the bizarre fronds from baby pinks and blues to lead. I eased the door behind me, further dimming the space. Hands outstretched, I stepped from the terrazzo to the thin carpet. I bumped into the stiff guest chair near the desk.

The corner of the conference table butted my hip. I saw sheets of paper unfurled on the long table. These were the architectural drawings and interior design sketches Nadine had shown me when I visited the previous week. Her ambitious plans for redevelopment of Trenton's Sutton Hill neighborhood. Anchoring one edge of the sheets was a new feature: a three-dimensional display of the proposed project. This maquette was made of white construction paper and cardboard fixed to a plywood board, maybe three feet square. The district's name, Sutton Hill, was etched in black colonial script on one edge of the wooden platform. The white buildings were two and three inches high. I flicked the crowns of lacy trees glued at intervals in front of the townhouses. Where were the residents of this wonderland? In their absence, I walked my fingers along a street, climbed pretend steps, knocked on a make-believe front door. Where were the cut-out dolls who inhabited Nadine's city of paper?

Overhead lights flashed. I jumped from the table, upsetting the display.

"What are you doing here?" If Nadine Burriss was surprised, she contained her feelings well. Her voice was low, any urgency well slathered with honey. "How did you get in here?"

"I knocked on your door." I jerked a thumb toward the back entrance. "It was open, so I let myself in." I inhaled twice to slow my heartbeats.

Nadine wore a charcoal dress whose princess seams squeezed her curves. The white collar made her resemble a Puritan maid. I looked like a tramp, which fit the break-in I'd committed.

She stooped to pick up the mock neighborhood. With mini-towers and curving sidewalks, the district looked like a frothy wedding cake in her hands. The gold rings I'd noticed during our first conversation were gone, replaced by dents in the swollen skin of her fingers.

"I was meeting with Reverend Fields," she said. "We discussed a memorial celebration of the life of Philip Bolden." Her voice was firm, like a church elder scolding an unruly child. "He was one of Bethel's major donors. You've heard of his death, haven't you? So tragic."

"Yes, I heard." I stepped forward. "That's why I came to see you, Nadine."

"Oh? About what?" She replaced the maquette on the table, then smoothed invisible wrinkles in her dress. The fabric stretched over her stomach where her belly button popped.

"He gave you money last night."

She clasped her hands before her waist. "Did he?" Lilting, like I was delusional. Two slow blinks over a sweet smile.

"I saw you talking with him."

"Ah, was that you in the car? I couldn't tell from across the street." She raised her eyebrows and sniffed. A finger grazed her nose. Something foul—me—polluted the air. She grimaced.

Insult wouldn't distract me. "Why did he give you that cash?"

"It was a donation to the church." Her voice rose. "Not that it's any of *your* business."

"I'm making it my business." I clenched my fists. I wouldn't punch her, but I wanted my urgency to strike fear in her heart.

Fear, doubt, exhaustion, sorrow. Some combination squeezed a sigh from Nadine's breast. She looked at me, then at the miniature cityscape on the table. She raised a hand, stroking the palm over the cardboard buildings as if offering a blessing.

"This has been a dream project for me." Her breath jetted like she was sprinting. "I want to use church funds for something import-ant, for work that will make a permanent difference in this stressed neighborhood."

"Looks like you're well on your way to that goal." I dialed down the growl. "What's next?" I remembered the church committee members in the photo Nadine had showed me. Phil Bolden, promi-nent as a sunburst in their midst. I wanted to know more about this project my ex was involved with. Anything I learned might point to clues about his murder.

Nadine continued, "There's plenty more I want to do to bring Sutton Hill back. So far, we've focused on rehabbing existing prop-erties. But I want the third phase of the project to include new high-rise construction."

"Like the old-school housing projects? Vertical concrete prisons?"

Nadine sighed, shaking her head. "No, not like those ugly hulks from the 1960s. That was urban underdevelopment, designed by outsiders to keep us corralled and controlled. White people dreams of Black folks' heaven."

Lifting, her voice grew strident. She raised two fists, then popped the fingers free. "I want fresh, open, people-focused spaces. I see high-rise structures with retail and community services on the ground floor. I'll build health and child care facilities. A business training center. I want reception and club meeting rooms." She caught her breath. "Sutton Hill deserves a better future. With Mother Bethel's support, I will deliver that future."

My heart pounded in rhythm with her words. Lots of self-references in her declaration. I, I, me, I. But still it landed. "Nadine, you've got a mission and a message."

I wanted to learn more about the young woman behind the proj-ect. So I invented a cough that I dramatized by clutching my throat. Nadine extracted a box of cough drops from a side drawer. Settling in the chair, I took my time unwrapping the lozenge. I wanted background and I refused to move.

Fake raspy, I asked, "Did you grow up in Sutton Hill?" I remembered that neighborhood was Phil Bolden's home turf. He was several years older than Nadine; doubtful she'd met my ex back in the day. I figured service on the church committee was their only connection.

Nadine eyed me, lashes flickering. Was she making up her mind about me? I must have passed her test. As my coughing subsided, she sighed then reached for a large glass jar near the lamp at the edge of her desk. The brass-topped container was half-filled with quarters.

She said, "My father worked in an upholstery shop. My mother ran a laundromat. Daddy was also a janitor, so we lived rent-free in the basement of a Sutton Hill high-rise. Mama's two sisters shared the apartment with us."

I low-whistled. "How many did that make?"

She ticked the census on her fingers. "My parents, me, and my younger sister. My two aunts and their three sons. Nine in two bedrooms, one bathroom."

My eyes bugged, but I was all about the platitudes. "Nice to have a big family like that."

"Sure, if you're sardines. My parents had one bedroom; my sister and I bunked in the second bedroom with my aunts. The boys were all younger than me. Each night they tossed coins for the sofa in the living room."

Growing up a singleton made me wary of so much forced intimacy. How did Nadine's crowd dodge daily combat?

"Were you close with your aunts? Aside from sharing a bedroom?"

Her hoot was harsh. "Rochelle and Juanita were strict on us girls. Hairbrush spankings were doled out on the regular. My sister, Toni, got lickings with a belt every so often."

Raising my eyes heavenward, I said, "And the boys could do no wrong?"

"How'd you guess." Flat, without a smile. "Aunt Rochelle did have one practice I liked. She was strict about swearing. Anybody swore in her presence, they had to deposit coins in her big mason jar." Nadine tipped her chin toward the glass container next to her desk lamp. A handwritten label—*Unstoppable*—was taped to the jar.

"Quarter from an adult; nickel from a child. Rochelle kept a tally sheet of all the cussing. And at the end of the month, the kid with the fewest marks got all the money in the jar."

"Sweet."

"It was." Nadine's eyes lit up at last.

"You win often?"

"Got so I could take the prize at least every other month. Used to drive my sister and the boys crazy. But I was unstoppable. Determined to get that money, so I learned to hold my tongue."

"Money management paid off. Your career path was set early."

"For sure." She rotated the glass jar, then tipped it so the coins rattled into a silver slope.

"Not so bad, then."

"Things were all right. If we kept out of each other's way. Hard to do, but we managed. We could have gone on like that forever, I guess. Until everything changed the year I turned twelve."

"Middle school is tough."

"Not middle school. Learning the truth about adult arrangements at home."

"Arrangements?" I sat forward, chin thrust.

She shrugged as if this were old news, but sweat popped at the part in her hair. "The boys I thought were my cousins? Turned out they were my brothers. My dad had a thing for years with my aunt Juanita. Gave her two sons. My half brothers. The third boy was Rochelle's by her ex. So Quincy was my only for-real cousin."

I whooshed a stiff breath. "That's a tough one."

Nadine grunted. "I had to get out as soon as I could. I scraped and studied my way out. Maybe my mother was willing to put up with that mess. But I wasn't going to stay if I had a choice."

"And the scholarship from Rome School gave you that way out."

"Yes, it did."

"And still, you want to help your old neighborhood."

Nadine blinked then shook her head. Maybe the gesture would

jog the clouds from my brain. Her breath spewed a mix of patience with exasperation. Couldn't I see the picture she painted? "The sorrows in our family had echoes on each block of Sutton Hill. I know that now. Each family was different, but each was the same: hungry for safety, respect, and a chance to do better." She rubbed her arms to generate warmth against the icy memories.

I leaned forward. "And now you hope to make a difference."

"Just like Rome School did for me." She nodded. "I can do for others."

She settled her rear against the desk edge, fists jammed at her hips. "Why am I dumping this on you? Sounds ghetto cliché. Like a Spike Lee Joint, doesn't it?" Mouth twisted with the sour taste.

"Everybody's story is different. No formula. Just truth."

Her sniff subbed for a thank-you. She sat to jerk open the shallow center drawer of the desk. Pulling out a stack of index cards bound by red rubber bands, she slammed the deck against the wood surface. "Here's why I'm blubbering now. I meant to tell my family story at the homecoming gala. Had it outlined in neat chapters, see." She jabbed the cards with her pointer finger. "I wanted to tell those rich people at Rome about Sutton Hill and Trenton. Where I came from and where I plan to take my old neighborhood." She inhaled, snapping the rubber band for punctuation. "But I never got the chance. They shoved the certificate at me and hustled me to my seat."

Nadine wailed, "You saw how they did me," voice spiraling in a shriek. "Like they smelled shit in my fucking pants." Another laugh, her tirade subsiding to hiccups.

She slid her left hand into the desk drawer, extracting two quarters. She dropped the coins into the mason jar labeled *Unstoppable*.

She said, "Adding to Rochelle's curse word collection."

"Fuck, yeah." I tugged a stray quarter from my pants pocket. I deposited the coin and watched it roll down the slope, clinking against its swear sisters.

Nadine thunked the jar on the blotter next to the lamp. "Each morning when I sit at my desk, I pray before starting work." She raised her hands, mimicking those daily devotions. "Then I write a word on a note card. I prop that card against my lamp so I can read my inspiration as I work."

"And the word is?"

She turned to retrieve a stack of index cards from beside a water glass. "Unstoppable."

"The same word every day?"

"Every day the same." She handed me the top card. "Unstoppable. With God under my wings, I am unstoppable." Her lips glistened with passion.

She fanned the deck, maybe forty deep, identical bold letters on each card.

Tipping her chin toward the card in my hand, she said, "Keep it, if you want." She patted the proof of her obsession until the stack squared in her grip.

I slotted the card she'd given me into the deck. "That's all right. Your word, your motto."

Shaking her head, Nadine said, "Phil Bolden's death has affected me. I've babbled too much." She swiped a pinkie into the corner of her right eye, then pointed toward the rear entrance. "Now, please leave the way you came." She sniffed, then turned her back, dismissing me.


At home, I stripped the sheets from my bed. In front of the washing machine, I pulled the sweatshirt over my head and unknotted the drawstring holding the pants. I threw them into the machine's barrel on top of the sheets. Next, I dropped in the soggy toy elephant. When I sprinkled detergent onto the gray pile, I began to cry. I didn't stop until I fell asleep on the bare mattress under my quilt.


The next morning, I paid a lightning visit to my father. I wanted to tell him about Phil's death. And to question him about Phil's role in my life. I figured the quickest way to solving the murder was to develop a 3-D picture of Phil, his character, contacts, and disputes. My father had known Phil Bolden for over twenty years. Evander's

insight, however impaired by disease, could help my work. To su-
garcoat this trip to Glendale Memory Care Center, I brought a jar of
honey-roasted peanuts and boxes of yogurt-coated raisins. I hated
both snacks, but Evander loved them.

When I entered his apartment, my father was seated as always
on the lumpy couch opposite the wall-mounted TV. The set was
dark, but Evander stared at its screen, his eyes darting as if watching a fabulous show. He was dressed in purple-and-white athletic
pants with elastic waist and cuffs. A matching pullover opened at
the collar to reveal his powerful neck and shoulders. He looked like
a slumming Hollywood god.

"Daddy, I'm here," I boomed, walking toward him. Evander
always liked a smart-dressed woman; when I was tiny, I'd often
seen him wolf-whistle at pretty girls when we drove for Saturday
ice cream outings. I never stopped trying to meet his high mark, so
after throwing my jacket on a chair, I tucked the hem of my ivory
crewneck into my jeans. Years ago he'd complimented me on the
black snake-embossed belt, so I hoped he'd notice it now.

But he just grunted and swung his gaze to the vacant TV. I saw
his white hair was brushed in neat waves. His light brown cheeks
were shiny with a fresh shave. When I leaned close, I smelled
almond-cherry lotion on his neck and chest. I brushed stray clip-
pings of white bristles from his military-style moustache. He looked
handsome and robust, as always.

Evander had been at the nursing home for over three years, his
strong body shackled by a devastated mind. Alzheimer's had crept
into our lives slowly, then with ferocious swiftness. Looking back, I
could discern hints of decline for at least ten years before the final
blow. Now, I tried to visit three times a week and I always brought
snacks. Maybe food was my apology for locking my father away
from his home, his neighborhood, and his town. I felt guilty, though
he never griped about the apartment or staff. Never asked me for
anything. Never recognized me at all. But he loved those snacks.

When I sat on the sofa, he turned his head, scowling. I held out
my offering. He lunged for the plastic bag as if he'd been starved for
a hundred years. I knew the Glendale schedule; he ate three-course

meals at eight o'clock, noon, and five thirty. And I knew my father's appetite: Evander Myrick maintained the muscular frame of a Queenstown police officer by eating well at every session.

"Take it easy, Daddy." I dumped the bag's contents on a cushion between us. "There's plenty to go around."

Politeness was not Evander's strong suit. As a twenty-eight-year QPD veteran, he'd learned to never apologize, concede, or withdraw. The lone Black cop on the force, he had no room for compromise. That rule applied on the job and at home. But this time, the sweetness on his tongue must have gone to his head.

Gobbling a third handful of raisins, he said, "Thank you, Monica. I never can get my fill of these." He pointed at the jar of peanuts. "Open that for me, will you, sweetie." He thought I was my daughter, Monica.

I cranked the lid, then mounded nuts in his upturned palm. "Here you go, Daddy."

He munched with passion, smacking sounds filling the room. He grinned at me. "You know you're my favorite grandbaby, don't you?" He patted my head.

"Your *only* grandbaby," I said, forcing a smile.

He chuckled at the slender joke.

I never corrected him. Sometimes Evander believed I was Alma, his wife, dead almost seven years. Other days, he preferred to be visited by his granddaughter, Monica, also dead. I was his daughter, namesake, and guardian, his only living relative. But he didn't know me. I wanted more: *Evander, meet Evander; Evander, see Evander*. Not in the cards. Sometimes I imagined my father was punishing me with his indifference. He'd done it often enough before he fell sick. Or maybe these were the natural swerves of this cruel disease. Nothing I could do but grit my teeth and accept the slights.

Now, I wanted to turn this quirk of Evander's mind to my purpose. If he thought I was Monica, I wanted to see what the masquerade might uncover. I reached behind my neck to unfasten my gold chain.

"Do you remember this?" I asked, draping the necklace over his honey-dusted fingers. "Remember when I got this?" My voice drifted into singsong tones, like a young girl's.

When he held the chain high, the dangling letter *M* twirled before our faces. Sunlight streamed through the picture window, gold washing gold to elegant effect.

"Of course, sweetie. You think I'd forget a beautiful thing like this?" He smiled and tapped a finger against her initial. "I remember when your father brought it to me. He asked me to give it to you for your birthday." The gold letter *M* revolved. "I figured you'd love it. But you never said a word."

I shook my head. Was this recollection false or true? Phil had reported he purchased the necklace for Monica. He said Evander had insisted on keeping Phil's involvement secret. Now was this confirmation in a drop of diluted memory?

I pressed on. "But I *love* this necklace." I squeezed my voice higher, channeling Monica. "I've worn it every day since you gave it to me."

"That's wonderful to know, Monica, honey. I'm so happy to hear you like it. All this time I been afraid you hated the necklace." Two lines puckered between Evander's eyebrows. "Why didn't you say anything about it for so long?"

No way could I tell him—again—that she was dead. I had Monica chirp: "You mean, my dad bought this necklace for me? I didn't know it came from him."

"Sure did." Evander popped peanuts into his mouth. "You know, your daddy bought you all kinds of gifts. Big and small. Phil was always rolling in money. And he wasn't shy about spending it on you." *Chew, chomp, smack.* "I liked that about him. Say what you want about the man, but he spent big money on his baby girl."

"I like hearing this," I said in my own voice. Turning my head, I bit my lip.

Evander let the chain dribble into his palm, like a trickle of golden sherry. I watched him close then open his fingers. He handed the necklace to me. "You put it on now. I like seeing this pretty thing on you, sweetie girl."

I fastened the clasp, adjusting the charm to nestle in the notch of my throat. I touched the *M*, then laid my hand over Evander's knuckles. "Thank you," I said.

He leaned close to whisper, "Now, don't go telling your mother about this present. I won't have her troubled. She finished with Phil Bolden long ago and she's better off without him. Fact is: That man's a junkyard dog, no two ways around it. I don't mean to hurt you, baby girl, speaking ill of your father like this. But, as your grandmama would say, that's the gospel truth."

I hugged his broad shoulders, pressing my nose against his neck. Now I knew for sure: Phil had spoken the truth. Whether to protect me or for spite, Evander had kept Phil from my life. I'd never know my father's motives. They were shrouded forever by his damaged memory. But another truth was tangled in this story, one I could know for certain. I bore responsibility for the separation, too. I could have pushed to bring Phil into Monica's life. I might have overridden my father's unkind devices and remade our family. I'd failed. Now, with Phil's murder, that chance was gone forever.

Guilty tears pricked the corners of my eyes. I jumped from the sofa to hide them. Should I tell my father about Phil's death? Would his murder make Evander regret having manipulated our lives? Or would the ex-cop figure Phil the villain had met a deserved end? I scrounged in the kitchenette's refrigerator for two cans of 7UP. I decided Evander had no need to know about this newest death. He'd erased the other losses in our family; why add new grief to the ledger?

I set the sodas on the table, popping open both cans. Evander guzzled his drink, crushed the empty container, then reached for my can. Bubbles twinkled on his moustache as he gulped my portion.

"Thanks, Alma," he said. My mother had arrived now. "I needed that. I was thirsty as a pig in sawdust." With a burp and a sigh, he smashed the second can.

I turned on the TV to fill the silence between us. Commentators yakked about the Rutgers football game tomorrow and the Eagles match on Sunday. Delight sparkled in my father's eyes as boys in scarlet or green uniforms dashed across the screen.

After thirty minutes, an attendant arrived to take Evander to lunch. "Will you be joining us, Ms. Myrick? It's meatloaf and roast chicken today."

As she talked, she flipped the footrests on a wheelchair. Although Evander was mobile, Glendale staff often preferred to transport residents around the facility by wheelchair. My father sat without being asked and crossed his hands on his lap. Lips smacking, his eyes glittered with anticipation. Lunch, not my visit, was the highlight of his day.

"Thanks, Pilar," I said. "Not this time, but it sounds delicious." I'd had enough of Evander for now.

I rode with them in the elevator to the first floor and gave my father a hug in the lobby. When I reached the revolving doors, I turned to see Pilar roll him into the dining room. I waved, Evander didn't.

Driving home, I thought about what I'd learned at Glendale. I already knew my father had despised Phil Bolden. Now I realized how deep that hostility ran. For almost twenty years, Evander kept Phil separated from Monica. He'd thwarted Phil's parental affection, then used those hopes to take significant amounts of money. Phil's adultery may have given Evander reason to hate him, but this loathing was harsh. Hypocritical, too, given Evander's own infidelities. However, my father was locked in a fortress. Though he detested Phil, there was no way Evander could have escaped Glendale to commit the murder.

But were there others who hated Phil as deeply as my father did? I knew from Melinda Terrence's side-eye daggers at the homecoming gala that Phil's wife had distrusted him and resented his former connection to me. That party also revealed tensions between father and son. Could shame have driven Tariq to kill? Maybe I'd thrown more fuel on the Bolden family pyre by sleeping with Phil. Had either the wife or the son learned about Phil's latest infidelity? Was adultery worse if the third party was an ex-wife? Perhaps I'd launched the murder assault with my selfish indulgence. Another reason to pursue this investigation: find the killer, erase my guilt.

Heat poured into my chest. Thumping heart shot stars before my eyes. I veered to a halt behind a parked station wagon. I unclamped my hands from the steering wheel and blew hard to release these dizzying thoughts. A kid barreling on a skateboard waved at me. I lifted my chin in salute. He executed a neat spin and rolled on. Heart slowing, I edged into the street and resumed my trip home.

My route took me past the Rome School. Redbrick pillars supported iron pickets to gird the campus perimeter. Beyond the wall, swaths of green rolled toward residence halls clustered in quadrangles. Monks would feel at home in these somber cloisters. The gothic architecture was contradicted by six tennis courts and a sandy volleyball pitch beyond the dormitories. Wimbledon and Wildwood recreated for the kids' delight. Phil Bolden's connections to Rome were tangled. I remembered the odd reaction of Headmaster Charles Dumont to Phil's disruption at the gala. I'd written off Phil's behavior as drunken excess, but maybe Dumont felt otherwise. How many Dumont initiatives had Phil stymied as chairman of the board of trustees? No doubt the headmaster cared deeply about the success of his beloved school. Could administrative defeat be a motive for murder?

A turn onto Academy Street at the southern corner of campus took me past a newly planted stand of yew trees. I saw the creative hand of Rome's chief grounds man, Keyshawn Sayre, in every landscaping initiative. I wondered about Key's girlfriend, art teacher Laurel Vaughn. The angry lightning she hurled at Phil during his gala speech had startled me. Maybe it shouldn't have. Laurel was Melinda's friend. She admired Tariq's talent. Naturally, the art teacher would dislike the man who inflicted misery on people she cared about. Phil had told me Laurel had made crude advances during a party last spring. If he'd rejected her moves, that put-down would have deepened Laurel's loathing of him. The I Hate Phil Bolden club overflowed with members. And the clubhouse was Rome School. That posh enclave had to be the focus of my investigations.

When I pulled into the driveway beside my house, I lowered the window. Chilly air buffed my face as I leaned against the headrest. I closed my eyes. The damp fumes of moldering rhododendron leaves invaded the car.

The police had their theory of the crime: a simple mugging gone wrong. Let them pursue details in support of that idea: tire tracks, missing murder weapon; round up the usual suspects. I wanted to look in another direction: to dig into Phil's life and the people he'd harmed. Instinct told me that way led to the killer. If I was wrong, I'd be relieved that no one I knew was responsible for Phil's murder. Sure, I'd be thrilled if a street thug turned out to be the evildoer. I wanted to wriggle off the hook as possible instigator. Shattering a marriage might be mean; prompting a murder was horrific. But I doubted a rando villain accounted for this crime. The Rome School was the key. As I walked the cement path to my porch, I brushed the rhododendron bushes; their rotting leaves mocked me.

Inside, from a perch at my kitchen island, I phoned Ingrid Ramírez. I wanted to know how the Bolden family was coping with Phil's murder. I had no standing to make a direct inquiry, but I could use Ingrid's connection to Tariq as an entrée. And I wanted an excuse to repair my relationship with her.

"Jesus, what is wrong with you?" she screeched. "Phoning like you're my mother or something."

Laughter tinkled in the background, dishes clattered. Was she at work? Lunch hour ran late at the Forum Sandwich Shop. "You weren't answering," I said.

She growled, "You got no manners? Shit. Hang up and text like a decent person." When the connection broke, I sent a text, with adult punctuation.

> You know about Phil Bolden?

Yeah I heard

> Let's talk.

Cant Im at work

> When does your shift end?

Four thirty

> I'll come to you there.

What for

> Talk. About Tariq. How's he doing?

...

> Have you seen him?

No

Let's talk.

Yeah OK

I'll be there soon.

OK

Deal done, I rinsed my face at the kitchen sink. After gulping a glass of tap water, I phoned the Queenstown Police Department to check in with Lola Conte. She sounded harried. Could the high-profile Bolden case be working her last nerve after just one day? She said she was too busy for me. "Chief Sayre's orders," I reminded her. She groused, but set the meet: coffee at headquarters in fifteen minutes. That was enough. I wanted to divide our labor and establish boundaries, not paint each other's nails. Crossing wires with Conte at the beginning of my investigation would only create confusion and expose information I wanted to keep private. I needed the cop on my side. And out of my business.

# CHAPTER **SIXTEEN**

Police headquarters occupied the first floor and basement of the town's municipal building. A revolving door and bilge-beige lobby gave 1990s chain motel vibes. The effect was reinforced by the spindly trees and flickering safety lights scattered in the parking lot.

From the front desk, Officer Lola Conte escorted me to the basement break room. Two minutes complaining about lousy vending machine fare, three minutes exchanging résumés. Then Conte tried to grill me about my ties to her boss, police chief Bobby Sayre.

I smiled, fluttering my lashes sweetly. "You got a need to know, Officer Conte? Or you fishing for gossip?"

"I like to look before I leap, Ms. Myrick."

"I'm not asking for a date." Mean-girl snarky. "I'm trying to help solve a murder."

Conte plucked the waxen skin on one knuckle. When she looked up, her eyes softened. "Yeah, it's a tough one. The county prosecutor's been on the horn all morning with Chief. We need answers fast. Or at least ideas."

"I understand the way it goes." I smoothed the edges. "I was on the job in New Brunswick a while back."

She nodded. Strain eased from the cords behind her ears. "We're looking first at the family. Any tensions or conflicts between Mr. and Mrs.—that kind of thing. Also checking Bolden's ties in Trenton." She rubbed her clavicle inside the uniform's navy collar.

"Grit in the marriage engine. It happens." I kept my voice cool, like a wise older sister. She couldn't scan the legend reading MAN-STEALING BITCH etched inside my skull, could she? I looked toward the vending machines to veil my eyes, in case Conte was a mind reader.

"Tell me about it," she groaned. "My husband says I take advantage of his schedule as a prof at MCC. Says I push off all the child care on him." Her eyebrows bobbed as she chuckled. "Maybe I do. Gotta get something out of the deal, don't I?"

Neat combo: a cop hitched to a Mason County College professor. "Did you think the Boldens' tension centered around their son?" I rushed to pick up on Conte's reference to kids as a source of marital strife. Safer territory for me than adultery hints.

"Maybe. When I asked the names of the boy's friends, Mom seemed clueless. I asked who his favorite teachers were, zero."

"And the mother works at Rome School," I said. "You'd think she'd have ideas about Tariq's life there."

"You'd think, right?"

"Have you talked with the boy yet?" I asked.

Conte dipped her chin until it folded into her throat. "No joy. Not at home with the mom. Not at his dorm." She peered at me. "You got any leads on him?"

This was the edge I wanted. "I'll take a run finding him. Talk with people I know at the Rome School. See what they have on the Bolden family."

Conte shrugged. "Works for me. You want to tackle the snobs at that fancy-pants joint, be my guest."

I added, "Lots of possibilities there. The kid's a star athlete, a bang-up good artist, too. The mom works as a college counselor. Phil Bolden was a big-time donor and chairman of the trustee board."

"Knock yourself out." Conte drained her cup then licked a drop from the rim. Her eyes, black as the coffee, drilled into me. "You gonna tell me about your own connection to the late Mr. Bolden?"

So she knew. At least part of the story, the part she could dig from public records about Phil's life. No good would come from playing coy.

"College sweethearts. We were hitched for a minute two decades ago. We had one daughter. She died two years ago. An accidental suffocation." Straight and clean was my path out of this conversation. I hoped the mother connection might smooth my way into Lola Conte's good graces.

The mom card worked. She mumbled, "Sorry for your loss."

I exhaled. My eyes were wet, but I resisted touching the scratchy napkin to my nose. I figured Conte's children were still young, toddlers her husband could wrangle with one hand. Now she viewed kids as distractions or amusements. Permanent threads in the fabric of her days. She'd change her tune in a few years when the borders of parenthood expanded beyond the playpen and the sandbox. I hoped she'd never learn how ephemeral those gossamer stitches could be. Was I still a parent, even without a child? Working on the answer, I sighed, then rubbed under my lower lip to hide the tremble there.

She coughed to curb the misery. "You dig into the boy's friends, classmates, teachers."

Brisk, back to business suited me. "That's my next stop."

Conte nodded approval, a tiny smile ruffling her mouth. With our tasks outlined, we agreed to check in, but didn't set a timetable. I figured she was as satisfied as I was with the informality. This was how I'd hoped we would draw our collaboration: neat like cornrowed hair. The cop had no need to know of the newest twist in my connection to Phil Bolden.

After quitting Conte on the front steps of the municipal building, I headed toward my meet-up with Ingrid Ramírez at the Forum, a sandwich shop near the Rome campus. I had questions about her boyfriend, Tariq Bolden. And since the gala, she'd thrown me an ice-cold shoulder I wanted to thaw.

# CHAPTER SEVENTEEN

When I loped into the Forum Sandwich Shop, Ingrid Ramírez was crouched beneath a table, sweeping crumbs into a dustpan with a whisk. Her back bent, she didn't see me. We'd texted to fix the meet-up, so my arrival wouldn't be a surprise. But I didn't know how welcome I'd be. Was Ingrid still bent out of shape about my errors of sarcasm at the gala? How had Phil Bolden's death landed for her? I wanted to contact his son Tariq and hoped Ingrid would be my way to reach him. Thaw and connect were my twin goals for this meeting.

I took a laminated menu from a stack near the cash register and mounted the stairs. The Forum was designed after a Hollywood image of imperial Rome: *Ben-Hur* boffs *Spartacus*, spawns *Gladiator*. Tables sat on three rings, the risers curving Colosseum-style around a glass-walled kitchen. Customers could watch their sandwiches being assembled by chefs wearing pleated togas. Maybe some came to the Forum for subs and Philly cheesesteaks, but for most people, the kitchen theatrics were the lure.

Three thirty was between rush hours, so the restaurant was empty except for a knob-kneed cook lounging inside the glass enclosure.

When I reached the top row, I flopped into a chair and slapped the menu on the table. Ingrid looked up, startled. Russet flowed from her throat to her ears. She dabbed her damp forehead then swiped her palms on her khaki pants. No smile, no greeting.

"You got a minute," I asked, looking around. "Not too busy?"

Snide was a dumb opening move. So I studied the menu like I wanted a Pompeii burger.

"Yeah, I got time," she mumbled. "Thanks for bringing over my bike last Sunday." She shifted from right to left foot, then pointed at the menu. "You ordering something? Palladium salad was pretty good today."

I shook my head. "I want to apologize for my behavior last week at the Rome homecoming gala."

Ingrid's eyes popped at my direct appeal. She bit her lower lip.

I continued, "I know you got a beef with me because I wasn't candid about having been married to Tariq's dad back in the day."

Silent, she snatched the menu and held it against her green polo shirt like a shield.

I mumbled, "Okay, I blew it. Didn't handle that the right way."

"You didn't handle it. Period," she growled. "Then, because *you* fucked up, you dropped the Ethan bomb to try and smash everything for me and Tariq. Rude to the max. Even for you."

Spilling about the return of Ingrid's ex-boyfriend Ethan to her new flame, Tariq, was not my finest moment. "My bad. I was hit with an avalanche of surprises that night." She was raw. I was, too. But somebody had to be the adult. My turn. So I extended my hand, palm open. "I'm sorry for the screw-up."

"Okay, yeah." Ingrid ignored the offered handshake, but her pout softened as she pushed a stray curl from her forehead. "Now everything's wrecked anyway. With Tariq's father dying and all."

Murdered. But she avoided the ugly word, so I would, too. I leaned forward, chest pressing the table. "You talk with Tariq since it happened?"

"No." She toed the dustpan and broom with her boot. The metal clatter echoed in the empty restaurant.

"I figured you would reach out. Touch base."

"I told you, no." Her eyes roved across the table between us, as if searching for a breadcrumb to sweep. "Homecoming was the last time I saw Tariq." She bent to grab the broom handle.

I didn't believe her. Throat and ears dusky red, eyes darting like poked hornets. These were Ingrid's tells. She was lying about something. I pushed, "Isn't he supposed to be your boyfriend?"

"Boyfriend, not cellmate." She dug the edge of the plastic menu into her chin. Her voice grew stronger, her eyes harder. "We're not shackled together like a chain gang. I see him when I see him."

"Not handcuffed. In a relationship, like ordinary people."

"You mean like you and Tariq's dad?" Her mouth twisted sideways, sour tastes tracking ugly thoughts.

I didn't buy it. She was hiding something about Tariq. The tapping foot and clenched fists read like deceit plus anger. I remembered monumental fights I'd had with Monica during her high school years. About boundaries and boys. About the difference between reins and joysticks. I knew the more I pushed Ingrid, the harder she'd resist. I wanted her cooperation. I needed her friendship.

I yielded. "Okay. Got it. Since Thursday, you never saw Tariq." Standing, I uncrossed my arms. "You see him, give him a message from me, okay?"

"Yeah, maybe."

"Tell Tariq I'm worried about him." I remembered the anguish on his face when the Rome gala blew up, the way Phil's nasty darts had wounded him. Now Tariq had to deal with the murder. "I want to talk with him. To know he's all right."

"Yeah, if I see him, I'll pass the message." She flapped the menu, cooling the heated air. "You done here?"

"You tell him I'm working for his dad now. I want to solve his murder."

Ingrid's eyes bulged, her mouth round with astonishment. She dropped the menu. As it fluttered to the floor she whispered, "Why?"

"I'm a private eye. It's what I do." I shoved the chair. "I'm doing this for my baby's father. I'll find his killer."

Hand pressed to throat, Ingrid murmured, "I'll tell Tariq."

I'd come to the Forum hoping I'd get Ingrid to thaw. Judging by her reaction to my pledge, I'd succeeded.

I descended the stairs two at a time. When I hit the door, I swiveled to nod at Ingrid. Stooping to whisk crumbs into her dustpan,

\

she missed my salute. First my dad, now Ingrid. I was disconnected from the ones I wanted to pull closest.

I paused on the limestone steps at the entrance to the Rome School's main building. An arc of ivy embraced the doorway, the dark green extending like a shaggy cape across the three-story façade. The foliage made the structure seem alive. I almost expected the building to shrug its stony shoulders to release the rain pelting its flanks. I shivered then wiped drops from my nose and mounted the top step. Two hundred years of foot traffic had worn gentle valleys in the treads; the stone appeared pliable, like molded flesh. If I stomped, would I bounce? Rain dribbled from my boots down the curved stairs to the slate-paved patio that surrounded a flagpole. I noted the banners—American flag and Rome's brown-and-green pennant—flew at full mast. Wind whipped the ropes against the pole, snarling the flags so they deflated instead of soaring free. No one had thought to lower these flags in honor of Phil Bolden's death. Did the murder of a school trustee matter so little? Would another donor—someone more docile and whiter—have rated more appreciation? I swallowed my resentment and hauled open the door.

As I entered the reception room guarding the office of Rome's headmaster, I felt like a Barbarian invader. My garments were all wrong—tight denims, cream pullover, stained boots paired with a scarred leather jacket. My matted hair needed a trim around the ears. Cherry lip balm was my only cosmetic.

The two white assistants who smiled in greeting modeled the Rome way to dress: the male wore knife-pleated slacks in charcoal with a lichen-green button-down shirt. No tie, but the rigid angle of his neck implied one. The woman's ivory cardigan and turtleneck twin set were striped with margarine yellow. Her sleek pencil skirt was cocoa brown.

I hoped they imagined I was a slumming hip-hop heiress intent on donating Daddy's fortune to Rome.

"I'm here to meet with Dr. Dumont," I said, nose in the air.

The woman chirped, "Do you have an appointment?" When my eyes widened in faux shock, she hurried on. "If not, I'd be happy to make one for you. He has room in his schedule tomorrow afternoon."

The man rotated to his computer, ready to set up the delayed meeting.

"He'll see me now," I said. I thrust a business card at the woman. EVANDER MYRICK, INVESTIGATIONS. Black script popped off heavy white stock; uncomplicated power, like a left jab. "Take this in. He'll rearrange his calendar."

Twenty seconds to crack the two-inch-thick oak door. Another ten to deliver the message. Charles Dumont flung wide the door, shooed his assistant away, and beckoned me with flexing fingers.

"So glad you could stop by, Vandy." A cheerful boom like we were old tennis pals. "Edward, please bring us fresh coffee. And a plate of those vanilla wafers, thank you."

Dumont gripped my biceps to steer me into the office. He wore the black-over-black suit I'd seen him in before. Maybe, like a comic book superhero, his closet was stocked with seasonal variations on his uniform, ranging from summer-weight wool to worsted blends. All blackity-black-black. Perhaps parents took comfort in the familiar sobriety of Dumont's garb. The suit worked as mourning dress, too. No need to shuffle outfits for the death of Phil Bolden, school trustee. How thick did the headmaster's sorrow lie?

As soon as the door closed, Dumont released my arm. "I suppose you're here about the Bolden matter, correct?" He tightened the knot of his platinum-striped tie. Matter, not death or murder. The Bolden matter, as if Phil's passing were a calculus problem to be solved, graded, and filed.

He herded me to a conference table beside his ocean-liner desk. The table, desk, chairs, and bookcases were carved of black oak and built to withstand an earthquake. Chenille fabric striped in brown, green, and pearl upholstered the chairs and seven-foot sofa. He'd picked the oversize furnishings to accommodate his lanky frame. Two moss-colored pillows lay dented at one end of the couch. Had

Dumont been napping when I arrived? As we sat at the table, I saw fog clouded his pupils. Sleep, perhaps, or drugs or pain.

I said, "Yes, I'm here as an adjunct to the official investigation into Philip Bolden's murder." An exaggeration, but one the status-conscious headmaster would respect. I shed my jacket and dropped it over the chair arm. "When I conferred with QPD this morning, I said I would take the Rome side of the inquiry."

He peered at me as if ink was smudged on my nose. "Isn't that somewhat irregular? I was under the impression you and Phil were old friends." His sniff suggested something foul wafted from my pullover.

To rile him, I leaned back and shot the cuffs of my sweater. "Old, but not close." I sealed my mouth with a smack. Dumont didn't need to know about my new connection to Phil Bolden. Now or ever.

I scanned the room. A luster like the sheen of a spider's web spread over every surface: desk, oblong conference table, book-cases, carved chairs. The gleam was dark, nonreflective. Dumont's decorative choices played up school history: sepia photographs of leather-helmeted football teams on the wall above the bookcases, all the players white and bowlegged; over the sofa were cracked oil paintings of Rome's medieval buildings, the stone walls draped with ivy and gravitas; a quartet of handsome white gents in World War I khakis grinned from horseback in a photo near the printer; beside a closet door were portraits of two sandy-haired men with dark suits, stiff white collars, and red radishes for lips. I thought the old boys looked constipated. Tarnish on the brass plate below the painting obscured the inscription, except for the date, 1823.

Dumont caught me staring. "Those are the founders of the school: the Burtons, Carl and Clarence. Twin brothers and Princeton graduates." He puffed his chest, ready to lecture.

I didn't care. "You have any thoughts about the murder of Philip Bolden? Any ideas you can share could cast light on the identity of his killer."

Dumont pulled his left index finger until the knuckle cracked. "If

I had to say where to start, I'd look to the Bolden boy." Black eye-brows bobbed in his milky forehead.

I swallowed a gasp. This turn startled me. Unvarnished targeting of the most vulnerable person in the circle around Phil Bolden. Dumont's move reminded me of Phil's description of him during our last night at my house: *a rat on stilts.*

I asked, "You don't mind, do you? I'm not recording this conversation." I reached for a pad of paper from a stack in the center of the table. Grabbing a green ballpoint from the spray of pens in a Rome mug, I scratched at the pad. "I'll take notes. Keep my ideas clear." I curved my right hand to block his view of the page as I scribbled three words: *T under bus.*

Dumont tipped a tight smile toward me, the good pupil. "Tariq was humiliated by his father's performance at the gala, no doubt." Two more joints snapped. If he pulled on the pinkie, I'd slug him. Lucky for us both, the headmaster jabbed his cuticles instead. "But then, Tariq was hardly the only embarrassed party that night."

"What do you mean?"

"Bolden's surprise announcement threw my entire administration off-balance." Lips scraped from pink gums as he concluded, "It was horrendous."

"Reeling in millions of dollars in a single night is horrific? How?"

"Phil knew our plans. We'd spent Thursday morning in meetings with our development team. With Phil in the chair, the trustees had approved our proposal for a five-year, thirty-five-million-dollar capital campaign."

I puffed a low whistle. "So Phil's announcement at the gala was his way of boosting the campaign. Kicking it off with a bang, right?"

"Hardly," Dumont growled. "Bolden screwed us. Royally."

"How? He's giving you a wad of dough. You ought to be thrilled." I'd worked at Rutgers for over a decade. But campus cops don't play in the same pen as deep-pocket donors. I wanted to hear how Phil had wrecked Dumont's pretty plans.

The headmaster walked to his desk and drew a brochure from the center drawer. He skated the pamphlet across the table to me. Its olive-green title read: ROME: CAMPAIGN FOR OUR THIRD CENTURY.

"The centerpiece of our campaign is construction of a major residential complex." As he resumed his seat, Dumont's voice sharpened into lecture mode. "We launched the quiet phase of the campaign last year. Already we have secured over two million dollars. Our plan was to launch the public phase next spring. Bolden had agreed to chair the campaign. He was to kick off the public phase in a big ceremony next April. The focal point of the event was to have been the announcement of Bolden's foundational contribution of three million dollars."

I opened the brochure. Dreamy renderings of a glass-fronted building flanked a pastel sketch of the proposed quadrangle. Two paragraphs of bold-type prose documented the project. "So he jumped the gun, big-time."

Dumont's hand flew to the nape of his neck. He rubbed circles until the skin reddened.

"Worse," he snapped. "By designating his donation to build a new library, Bolden derailed our development efforts. Now we're blocked." He leaned to retrieve the brochure. "We were planning to mail three hundred of these today. Under cover of a letter signed by me and Phil. The first stage of our campaign."

He tore the pamphlet in half then in strips. "Now we can't approach potential donors to ask for major contributions. The development goals of our campaign are hopelessly muddied. What are the school's priorities? Are we raising funds to build residence halls or this new library Phil announced?" Dumont crumpled the shredded paper and tossed it into a wire basket beside the desk.

He clenched both fists. Then ground them as if drilling holes into the wooden surface. "Thanks to Bolden's selfish gesture, donors will believe we're rudderless. That we don't know our priorities." His lips retracted, baring piano-key teeth. "They'll think *I'm* confused and impotent. He made *me* look like a fool. A fucking idiot." Dumont turned the crisis into his personal calamity, shunting aside the brutal murder of his trustee. Weird, even creepy.

Jolted by the headmaster's fury, I jerked my eyes toward the picture window behind his desk. Satiny gray sidewalks crisscrossed the tranquil lawns. In the afternoon drizzle, students scurried in brown overcoats and puffer jackets. Knit beanies pulled low made it hard to distinguish boys from girls. Dumont wanted to be master of this campus he surveyed. Now Phil Bolden's outburst at the gala undermined that control. I thought about the headmaster's barrage of text messages to Phil the night before he was killed. At my house, Phil had mentioned Dumont wanted him to sign a letter. Was this letter drafted to correct the damage of Phil's homecoming pledge? In the wake of his murder, had the letter been mailed to donors without Phil's signature?

A tap on the outer door relieved the tension.

When Dumont barked, "Come in," Edward entered with a tray. The assistant arranged a coffee pot, two mugs, silver bowls with cream and sugar, and a plate of wafers in the center of the table. As Edward poured, Dumont rummaged in the lower drawer of his desk. He took his seat, fist tight. The assistant left; the headmaster unfurled his fingers and downed two Tylenol tablets with a gulp of hot coffee. The headache must have been killing him if he'd risk a scalded tongue.

After I wolfed a wafer, I stayed on topic: "How do you hope to correct the implications of Phil Bolden's gala speech? Are you planning a new campaign target? Perhaps a letter to donors announcing the new direction?" My eyes goggling to fake innocence, I pressed the pen against pursed lips.

"No, you can't know about that new letter." Dumont grasped the edge of the table. "Who told you about that?" Bafflement, maybe worry, washed in ashen waves across his face and settled in trenches around his mouth.

"I'm a private investigator. Confidential sources are the stock in my soup." I wanted to throw a triumphant grin at the anxious headmaster. But thinking of that last conversation with Phil drove snarky gladness from my heart. "Did you get Bolden to sign your letter to donors?"

Dumont lowered his head. "No. He was dead before I could show him the draft."

I couldn't read his hooded eyes. His assertion was technically true. Death intervened and Phil never signed the letter. But had a

quarrel with Dumont ended in the headmaster shooting his disruptive and unrepentant trustee?

I wanted to dig further into Dumont's interactions with Phil.
But if I pushed on that front now, he'd boot me from his office. I
could revisit those questions in a second interview. I switched gears.
"What can you tell me about Tariq's relationships with his parents?"
Open-ended question, but I hoped Dumont would drop his anger
with Phil and focus on the student in his care.

Smoothing the scowl from his forehead, Dumont said, "The boy
is a middling student, but a superb athlete, as you know." He retrieved a manila folder from his desk then angled the flaps so I
couldn't read the papers inside. "No major disciplinary issues."

"But some minor ones?"

"Two outbursts in the cafeteria; one fistfight with a boy in the
dormitory; a shouting match with a teacher." He read from a report:
"'Anger and impulse-control issues.'"

"Strung together they sound major."

"After Tariq switched into a single room first semester last year,
the issues eased." Dumont dragged a finger over a paragraph, then
smiled. "Evidently, the threat of removing him from the residence
hall was effective in correcting his behavior."

"Tariq didn't want to be forced to return home?"

"Exactly."

"You said he was a middling student. Was he college-bound?"

Dumont shrugged. "There are three thousand universities and
colleges in the United States. I'm sure Tariq will find his place in one
of them." Sighing, he picked at invisible lint on his lapel. "With help
from his mother, of course."

"Momma guidance counselor as miracle worker?"

The headmaster spoke with frosty precision. "Melinda Terrence
has a remarkable track record of college placements. I'm sure she'll
do her best for Tariq." An odd endorsement of the mother and a
solid condemnation of the son. It seemed every member of the
Bolden family scraped Dumont's hide one way or another. What
was behind the strain?

Peering at me over the rim of his mug, Dumont rushed to amend the negative portrait of his student. "Aside from his excellence in track and field, Tariq is also a fine artist. I hear wonderful accolades about his work from Laurel Vaughn. You may recall meeting her at the gala last week. Perhaps you could visit with her if you want more insight into Tariq." He shifted on his haunches and stole a glance at his wristwatch.

"Before you go," Dumont said. Yep, my time was up. "I want to outline a few expectations for your work here." As if I was a rookie teacher and this was the first day of orientation.

"I take my brief from the police." I crunched a final cookie and slurped coffee. I wanted to say, *And my client, Phil Bolden.*

"Yes, of course. But you are investigating on *my* campus. Among *my* students and staff."

I wanted to learn what his boundaries were, so I jogged my head as if conceding the point.

Dumont continued: "So far, the Rome connection to Bolden's death has been kept out of the media."

"Except for that TikTok clip about the homecoming disaster." I couldn't help the dig.

He frowned. "Yes, well, the *real* media haven't gotten wind of the issue yet. I want you to keep it that way."

I ducked his gaze and tugged at the collar of my sweater. Did he know how much I had to be discreet about?

"You understand subtlety and restraint. I am sure you will exercise similar discretion in the current circumstances." Again with the euphemisms. Like Phil's murder was a social faux pas, not a tragedy.

"I'll try." Weak, but I wasn't making grand promises.

Dumont escorted me through the front office, a hand hovering at my waist as if I might escape. Edward and the female assistant grinned as I passed.

In the hallway, Dumont beckoned to a pair of girls slouching near a water fountain. He swung an arm leftward. "The art studios are in the adjacent building. Out the door at the end of the corridor, then across the patio." He raised his voice. "Jenny and Becca, will you please escort our visitor to Ms. Vaughn's classroom? Thank you."

As he shook my hand, the girls quick-stepped to my side. They dropped their obedient beams as soon as Dumont vanished into his suite.

Laurel Vaughn's studio was shaped like a double-height Quonset hut: iron struts supported an arched roof made of corrugated metal panels; windows encased by oxidized steel frames sported oversize bolts. Peacock blue was splashed on the long walls, balanced by tiger-lily orange paint on the cement floors. Closet doors at the far end of the studio were enameled in high-gloss black. No reference to the brown and green school colors. The place felt contemporary and unorthodox, like Laurel Vaughn defied Rome traditions every time she called a class session to order.

Seven students were working before easels when I entered the studio. Their backs were to the door, so it was the live subject—a freckled brunette girl dressed in a yellow flapper costume—who signaled my arrival to the teacher. Laurel turned, her face brightening when she saw me.

"I've been expecting you, Vandy." Arms extended, she took my hand in both of hers. My fingers tingled, still cold after the open-air trot to the art studio.

Laurel fixed my jacket on wall hooks next to the door and waved me toward an alcove containing a desk and computer table. As we threaded through the rows of easels, Laurel paused by several students. "Lovely line there." "That chartreuse works for the shadow, yes." "You've captured the glow on her shoulder perfectly." The artists nodded, lips twitching to contain relief or joy. Klutz that I was, even I might have been good at this if I'd had a teacher like Laurel.

We sat on fuchsia satin tufted chairs facing the desk. Her knee pressed to mine, Laurel leaned toward me. "Are you helping the police?"

"I hope so." Small school, small town. Her boyfriend, Keyshawn Sayre, was the brother of the police chief, after all. I shouldn't have been surprised that news of my involvement in the Bolden murder investigation had spread like measles in a convention of anti-vaxxers. Still, I was shaken. I hoped the energy dancing in flashes of red across Laurel's face meant she would collaborate with me.

She whispered, "I'm worried about Melinda and Tariq."

Cold ran from my wrists to shoulders. "Are you?" Curbing the shudder, I pulled my sweater cuffs over my knuckles.

She shook her head. "Melinda more than anyone."

# CHAPTER **EIGHTEEN**

Laurel Vaughn's eyes widened, as if she'd spilled a great secret. She glanced over her shoulder at the students busy at their easels. One boy bent forward to dab a rag against his canvas, smearing blue he'd used to capture highlights in the model's dark hair. The other six artists stared at their creations. The flapper model sighed, twitched her buckled shoe, but held her pose. No one seemed to have registered our conversation.

"I don't know how well you know the Boldens," Laurel continued. Pink lifted under the freckles on her nose. "I mean, of course you know them . . . Phil, in particular . . ." She ruffled her red curls.

I assumed Melinda Terrence had told the bare history to her friend the art teacher after the sudden return of Phil's first wife at the homecoming gala. "Why do you say Melinda is in trouble?"

"She's seemed so despondent these past few days."

"Of course she's sad, her husband has been murdered."

Laurel jerked as if I'd jabbed her with a cattle prod. "I meant before this horror."

"What did she tell you? Did anything she say give you ideas about why Phil was killed?"

I wanted to know more about the family. A PI operates on details. Opinions from sources count as valuable data. I couched my questions in terms of the murder. But I wanted insight into Phil's marriage, too. Maybe I was a bitch, self-involved and nosy. But I figured, if I kept the intel for my own use, I couldn't be accused of gossiping, right? Wasn't looking to lift my unease natural? Professional, even? The quicker I switched from home-wrecker to investigator, the faster I'd solve this case. I hoped.

"Nothing so concrete as that," Laurel said. "Melinda and I meet almost every day for lunch in the faculty lounge. Hard to have deep conversations there. But these past few months, Mel seemed upset, anxious, stressed."

"Anxious about anything in particular? Home or work?"

Laurel slid her eyes left. Light from the rain-streaked windows overhead turned her hazel pupils green. "I'm not sure Mel draws a sharp distinction between home and work anymore."

"Why not?"

"During the past three years she's shifted her schedule to take on more clients at home."

"I thought she was the school's guidance counselor. How does she advise students from home? Does she make appointments on-line?"

"Nothing like that. Mel meets students and their parents in her home office. Three or four afternoons a week."

"That's a lot of time off campus. What does Dumont say about a key staffer playing hooky like that? He can't be thrilled."

Laurel frowned. "Never heard him complain. Mel keeps her clients happy and places them in the best universities in the country. Happy parents keep Charles Dumont happy."

"But not Melinda?"

"When I first met her, six years ago, she loved the work. She used to rave about how motivated her students were, how engaged they were in learning and exploring. She felt she was contributing as much as any teacher to the intellectual and personal development of the students she worked with." Laurel's mouth turned down.

"Then things changed?"

"Now she gripes about the demands of parents, their expectations of quality placements in Ivy League schools. Everything is bottom line for the families now."

I let my cynicism fly: "It's all grub, grab, and brag."

"Exactly." Laurel stood, a finger sealing her lips. She glanced toward her students. "Little ears."

She raised her voice to a shout. "Hour's up, people. You've done marvelous work this session." She clapped and the students joined the self-applause. "Now a round of appreciation for our patient and beautiful Kristen." Applause chattered as the model stretched on her platform and bowed to each corner of the room. She whipped the goldenrod shift over her head, rolled it into a burrito-size bundle, and stuffed the costume into a backpack. No one seemed to care that the girl was dressed in sheer navy panties and bra that revealed her whole world.

Laurel's instructions continued. "You know the drill: clean your workspace, clean your brushes." Her lilt made the chores seem fun. "And Steven, I've got my eye on you. Last Wednesday I spent fifteen minutes soaking the brushes you failed to clean." Reprimand delivered with a grin made the culprit blush.

For five minutes, turpentine's acrid scent wafted toward the skylights. When the last student bustled from the studio, Laurel resumed her seat next to me. "They're a focused bunch, but I didn't want to risk them overhearing our conversation." She pulled two bottles of water from the lowest shelf of a bookcase beside her desk.

Starving as four thirty loomed, I'd hoped she'd offer a triple-decker BLT but settled for the minimum. I took a swig of tepid water. "You told me Tariq Bolden is one of your students. Have you seen him since his father died?"

Slow headshake. "No. The last time I saw Tariq was at that horrid gala. Before that, in my Wednesday morning drawing class."

"Is he any good?"

"He's quite good." She closed her eyes as a smile painted rose petals on her pale lips. "Superb. Strongest in charcoal and pencil. He loves hyperrealistic drawings of inanimate objects. He balks at painting from live models. So I've encouraged him to make portraits from photographs. His work is brilliant. Let me show you a few."

Laurel retrieved a portfolio from a worktable. I flipped through the pages of Tariq's work: grayscale sketches of fruit; detailed studies of human eyes, mouths, and ears. "Not into tackling the whole face, I guess."

"Keep going. He'll surprise you." Smugness warmed her voice as she bragged on her star pupil.

I flipped more sheets. Under a dozen still-life drawings of pears and cantaloupe, I found portraits of dead musicians rendered with painstaking care. "These are great. But I wouldn't have figured him for a fan of Jimmy Cliff, Janis Joplin, or Bob Marley."

"He's working on a large portrait of Jimi Hendrix right now. His best yet. Simply stunning."

I lobbed platitudes to keep her talking. "Modern classics. Music is Tariq's refuge?"

"Absolutely. Last month he was wild about this new place he'd found. A sort of club. He called it the Barge. A place kids could dance, hang, chill."

"Did he say where this club was?" Maybe I could find the boy through this lead.

"Only that it floated around Mason County. The Barge, get it?" She chuckled. "So I said, 'Beyond the adult gaze?' Like the uncool art teacher that I am. And he laughed and said, 'One hundred percent.'"

"Sounds perfect." I could have used a place like the Barge, growing up. Somewhere to dodge the "cop's daughter" label, to skip the grind of a responsible life. "A place to get away. Be yourself."

"Yes, like I told you: Tariq is sensitive and extremely talented."

"Not just a long-distance runner."

"And not at all like his father."

"You weren't a fan of Phil Bolden?" No stretch to interpret the lowered voice and pursed mouth as disapproval. "Did you know him as well as Melinda and Tariq?"

"No." Narrowed eyelids didn't block the flashes of anger. "And I was happy to keep the distance."

I wanted to get to the root of this conflict. "Did you and Phil clash?" Maybe the father didn't approve of his son's artistic bent. Phil Bolden wouldn't be the first macho man to consider painting a sissy pastime unfit for his heir. "Over Tariq and his love of art?"

Laurel laughed, a dry rattle high in her throat. "Over art? Hardly."

She inhaled then blew a long spurt. "I doubt Phil even knows Tariq can sketch."

I remembered Phil telling me he believed Tariq was wasting his time on art. The father knew about the son's passion, but resented it. I wanted to hear the art teacher's side: "Then what was it?"

Biting her lower lip, she focused on a sprig of dried herbs nestled in a ceramic bottle on her desk. A sigh then a shoulder hike seemed to clear her course.

She squared on me. "Last May, I attended a Memorial Day party at the Boldens' house. I'd been there before, tea or lunch with Mel on several occasions. But this was a big affair, maybe one hundred guests or more. They went all out. Four barbecue grills in the backyard, self-serve bar in the garage, horseshoe pitch, badminton. A live band under a tent, and wooden planks laid on the lawn for a dance floor."

"Sounds fun."

"It was." Corners of her mouth drooped. Furrows deepened between her brows.

"Until?"

"Until I went to the garage for a soda. Phil followed me, helped me choose between Diet Coke and root beer. Then he pushed me against the bar and squeezed my ass. He said he knew I liked 'dark meat.' He asked if I wanted a taste of something better than I'd ever had before. I said no. He kissed me. I pushed. He kissed me again. I slapped his face. He laughed. He said he could wait for me to come around. He knew I would, he said. I ran from the garage. I left the party without saying goodbye to Mel."

I winced. This wasn't at all how Phil Bolden described their encounter at the party last spring. During our night together, he told me Laurel Vaughn had made a crude pass at him. Had he lied to me about this ugly incident? I knew Phil liked women, pursued them with relentless focus. I understood this about him before we married. Foolishly, I thought he'd improve when we exchanged rings. My father had seen through Phil from the outset. His scolding words rumbled in my brain even now: *Bad move, Vandy. Marrying that dog is never going to turn out right. Even Stevie Wonder can see he's big trouble.* Phil's infidelities had ended our marriage. However, I had never suspected him of brutalizing women. Could he have changed so much in the years since our divorce?

But I always believed a woman's account. Always. And I believed Laurel's story now. I had to accept that on the last night of his life, Phil Bolden had lied to me.

Through a painful gulp, I said, "I'm so sorry to hear this. I'm sorry you had to go through that. It must have been horrible." I stammered, "Did it, this—this incident taint your friendship with Melinda?"

She shook her head. "I never mentioned it to Mel." She sighed, scratching at the lifeline in her left palm. "I couldn't find the right time or words to tell her."

"Maybe she guessed anyway," I said. "Maybe that's the source of the distress you'd noticed in her recently."

Laurel's jaw dropped. "You could be right. That would be awful." Digging into her palm sped up. "I'd hate to think I'm the cause of her troubles."

"You're not the cause. Never believe that." My statement slid through clenched teeth. "Phil was."

I seized her fingers to stop the clawing. Three tears slipped over her cheeks. "Thank you," she said. I blinked hard to stop the water in my eyes from falling.

Five minutes later I scuttled across the patio to the main building.

# CHAPTER **NINETEEN**

Rain had lifted by the time I quit the Rome School administration building. Golden lances of sunlight played hide-and-seek with the mist-draped spires as I crossed the parking lot. Shadows tinted the ivy vines blue as they tangled across the arches. In a slate-paved circle near the front door, two boys in brown sweatshirts worked the pulleys of the flagpole, lowering the Stars and Stripes and Rome flag for the evening.

As I trudged to the parking lot, I thought over my conversations with Headmaster Dumont and Laurel Vaughn, the art teacher. Both had given me insights into tensions roiling the school: fund-raising worries; stifled artistic creativity; physical harassment and emotional assault. But how much had high passions and conjecture curdled their accounts? I'd wanted to learn about Phil Bolden's connections to the Rome School and this visit had delivered plenty of information. What was it all worth? To gain perspective, I needed to speak directly with Phil's son and widow.

I'd stationed the Jeep beside an oak sapling sprouting from a decorative grill. Ten identical clusters were dotted across the asphalt. I wondered if this was my friend Keyshawn Sayre's work, his gardener's sensibilities infused with a yen for order, color, and permanence. As I approached, the trees shivered when frigid gusts stroked their orange leaves.

I wanted to locate Tariq Bolden. Offer condolences, of course. But also question him about Phil. Ingrid's stubbornness had blocked me. Maybe she was protecting him. Or perhaps she was still miffed at me. Either way, she didn't want to help me contact Tariq. Now I hoped the art teacher's hint about the teen hangout, the Barge, could point me to another way to reach him.

Twenty minutes later, I parked in the lot behind the Kings Cross Tavern.

I glanced across the street toward our second-floor offices as I locked the Jeep. Lights off in the break room and the corridor. Elissa might be pulling a late shift in her own office at the front of the suite. But I didn't intend to search. Six thirty was quitting time. And long past my missed lunch hour, according to my empty stomach. A day of coffee, wafers, and bottled water didn't cut it. I wanted a blue cheese burger—medium rare—sweet potato fries, and an icy glass of my favorite virgin Tom Collins. The best—the only—place to get these treats done right was the Kings Cross Tavern. I also wanted to follow up on ideas I'd developed about Tariq's location. If I could find the floating dance club, the Barge, maybe I could find him. To learn more, I needed to tap the oracle of local intel, tavern owner Mavis Jenkins.

Beside the tavern's green door a garland of tiny plastic pumpkins draped across the plate-glass window above the bar's name. On either side of the entrance, jack-o'-lanterns lit by electric candles celebrated the season.

The tavern had commanded this choice location in Queenstown's commercial district for more than two hundred years, since George Washington and his troops roamed the region.

Inside the tavern, I scanned the room. Maybe twenty-five customers, mostly men. Half clung to stools at the bar, staring into their drinks with gritted jaws. Others occupied tables against the long wall, clustered in twos or threes, grinning and joshing, much happier than their brothers at the bar.

I unzipped my jacket and waggled my arms to shed the night chill. My wriggle caught the attention of the bartender, who popped me a crisp salute.

To the chagrin of Q-Town's old guard, Kings Cross Tavern was bought seven years ago by a Black woman, my friend Mavis Jenkins. Serving as chief bartender, Mavis kept the fare hearty, the drinks substantial, and the atmosphere warm. She hiked the prices and held her breath. After initial hesitation, customers flocked to the tavern from all quarters of town.

Every visit, I'd conduct a census of the crowd. I'd see tables of Black and white financial wolves fresh from their Manhattan commutes or clusters of civil servants beating the rush from Trenton. Latinos came in all flavors: mixed batches of tech bros and teachers, gym rats and busboys. Women were plentiful, too. From yoga moms and church ladies to housekeepers and book club babes. Historic but not outmoded, everyone came to Kings Cross Tavern.

I hit the tavern each Thursday night and many Tuesdays and Wednesdays as well. Through ties with my mother's church, Mavis Jenkins had known me half my life.

She was about ten years older, but acted as if she owned me. My dress style, drinks selection, work ethic, sex partners—everything was fair game for Mavis's surgical comments. I griped about her meddling, though she was often right. At forty-eight, I didn't need a second mother, especially one with a hall monitor's rigid moral code.

Now, Mavis beckoned me to a stool at the foot of the horseshoe bar. "I saved you a choice spot."

Sweat beads played among the rusty freckles on her nose. Mavis was light-skinned and olive-eyed with a thick waist and short legs. My polar opposite in each category. She kept her hair auburn with monthly trips to the beauty parlor. No lipstick, powder, or nail polish. The only makeup that stayed on for a long night of bartending was waterproof mascara, so Mavis layered the black stuff with a rake.

"Next to the kitchen is *not* prime real estate." I eased a hip onto the seat. "Noisy, smelly. Overheated. This is the low-rent district." I grinned to show I didn't mind the slight. Savory odors made my stomach rumble in happy anticipation.

"Close to the kitchen, close to heaven." Mavis swiped water rings from the wood surface and slapped a coaster between my elbows. "Plus that twisty smile on your face says you got something sneaky on your mind."

A whistle from the other end of the bar drew Mavis away. When she returned, she deposited a tall glass of my special drink. We called our invention Clean Tom Collins. Simple syrup laced with ground black pepper; a jigger of lemon juice, topped with club soda. No gin, no vodka, nothing but clear sparkle.

Mavis set the sweating tumbler on the coaster between my forearms. "What's on your mind?"

"I need a blue cheese burger from Pepé. And some information from you."

Mavis leaned through the kitchen's swinging doors to yell my order. Turning to me, she added, "Info will cost you."

I mumbled, "It always does."

Fizz tickled my nose as I sipped the virgin drink. I'd quit cold turkey two and a half years ago. Four months after Monica died. Sometimes I still tasted bourbon's smoky-sweet ghost dancing at the root of my tongue. The urge came late at night, when my joints ached and I knew a sip would banish the desire twisting in my gut. I wanted that release, that oblivion. But I'd made a promise to my daughter. I refused to retreat. Sticking to that pledge was hard. I'd fallen once. But images of Monica's gray face, liquored vomit dribbling from her lips, stopped me from backsliding. I remembered gripping her limp body to my chest. Smelling the bile she'd inhaled in the seconds before she choked to death. Those memories chained my life now. I was going to keep my promise to Monica.

As she often did, Mavis caught the downbeat shift in my mood. "You need something—news, gossip, a job—anything, you ask. You know I got you, baby girl." She patted my hand and dragged a bowl of mixed nuts from a customer two seats away. "You eat this while you waiting for your dinner."

I plucked two almonds from the heap. My spirits lifted. "Bowl of nuts. The bartender's true friend."

"You got that right," Mavis said. Raised voices from a table called.

She hustled to take a refill order. When she returned, she asked, "What you want to know?"

"I'm working a new case. The murder of Phil Bolden." Mavis's lips gaped around an objection, but I barreled on. "I need to know about a nightclub called the Barge." I hoped Laurel Vaughn's tip about the floating dance party being a favorite hangout of Tariq Bolden might lead to a breakthrough.

Mavis's face reddened. Her eyes popped. She squeaked, "You punking me or what?"

"No punk, no game." What fueled her fierce reaction?

She whispered, "You know the Barge is owned by my man, right?"

Lucky I'd emptied my mouth, or I'd have spit. I never imagined anyone was tight with Mavis Jenkins. Much less the owner of a hip club. I pried the shell off a peanut, dropped the meat on my tongue, then chomped twice before answering, "Tell me more, Mavis."

# CHAPTER **TWENTY**

The amiable hum of barroom chatter washed over me as I swiveled on my stool waiting for my friend Mavis Jenkins to drop a text message to her boyfriend. When I'd asked the bartender if she knew the Barge club, she'd stared at me like I had ice tongs sprouting from my forehead. Of course she knew it, she sputtered, the owner was her boyfriend.

I wanted to find Tariq Bolden because he could give me new information about his father, Phil. I hoped the man who ran the kid's favorite hangout could give me a lead on his whereabouts. What I didn't expect was news on my friend's love life. I hunched to cover my astonishment. Mavis Jenkins, the queen of snap and snide? With a boyfriend? Five minutes after she texted, the man himself walked into Kings Cross Tavern.

"He was around the corner, taking care of bank business," Mavis said, beaming like a magician pulling the rabbit from a top hat. "I told him Alma Myrick's little girl needed help. And here he comes."

The idea of my fifty-something friend with a white lover felt surreal. Both words—*white* and *lover*—sounded weird in my head. How had I missed this development in her life? Was Mavis pulling my leg? Stunting to rile me or teach me some new life lesson?

Her lower lip quivered as she tracked the man's movements across the room. Warmth rolled in red waves from her cheeks to her ears. Mavis was gobsmacked. If I found out this guy didn't return the sentiment, I'd kill him.

Lean as a telephone pole, the man wore his Canadian tuxedo with grave style. Faded denim jacket, dark jeans, lug-soled boots, silver bangles as icing on both wrists. A black motorcycle helmet bobbed against his thigh as he walked. He carried a leather messenger bag slanted across his body. He tipped his chin at Mavis and took a two-seater table in the front. I followed her to the table. He'd tied the steel threads of his long ponytail with a leather cord. Willie Nelson with a ration of Sam Elliott's generous moustache and rustic charm. I could sense—barely—the appeal.

Mavis pulled out the empty seat and thumped my shoulder until I sat. "Joe Kidd, meet Vandy Myrick."

I raised my hand, but Joe lifted the messenger bag's strap over his head, setting it and his helmet on the floor. Then he shot a hand across the table. Knobby and cold, with ropes for veins. I squeezed as hard as he did.

Mavis finished the introduction. "She's a private detective. Needs your help with a case."

Joe jerked his hand from my grip. Frowning, he repeated his name, "Joe Kidd." He rubbed his right ear. The pale lobe was divided, like a wedge had been sliced from the flesh.

I wondered if Mavis would touch her boyfriend. Even kiss him? I prepared to squirm, but the bartender got to business. "You want your Monday usual, Joe?"

"That'll be fine. And another round for Vandy. On my tab." No smile yet, but the moustache quivered. "So, you're Alma's girl? Hard to believe you're grown like this." The scan flowed over my body until I cringed. Maybe I didn't measure up to expectations. "I can see where you favor Alma, especially in the face."

"You knew my mother?"

"We were tight—in a friendly-like manner—back in the day." His eyes, black in the tavern's dim light, glowed as lines deepened around his mouth.

Glad he cleared that up first thing. I did *not* want to find an old boyfriend of my mother's. Especially one who was now screwing my bestie. I stuck to the distant past: "How did you meet Alma?"

Joe settled into his chair. "I wanted someone who could spark my stage outfits with unique details. Something special to make my jeans stand out. The lead guitarist in my band said Alma Myrick was the best needlework artist on the East Coast. Turns out he was underselling her talent." A wide smile at last. "Your mother was the best in the whole fucking country."

The tops of my ears tingled. "I didn't know that about her." I remembered my graveside pledge to learn more about Alma. Now, with this sudden connection from her past, I could push forward on that quest.

My heart raced with pleasure at the sudden insight. I knew my mother sewed, of course. I'd always hated that Alma had made most of my dresses and shirts when I was in grade school. On the schoolyard runway, I stood out. In a bad way.

"Your mother was a genius with a needle," Joe continued. "She'd deck my Levi's with sequins, studs, and jewels. Her specialty was embroidering peacocks or eagles." He shook his head, moustache twitching. "I had a fondness for her patchwork. Alma'd make us look like top-of-the-charts rockers with her velvet-and-calico collages."

I squeezed a dollop of sour down my throat. When I reached middle school, I had begged my father to give me an allowance, which I usually spent at the mall on new sweaters or blouses. Now, seven years after her death, I wanted to apologize to Alma. Another fugitive visit to the cemetery was in order.

"Thank you for sharing." I dodged his direct gaze. "I guess I missed a lot about my mother."

He reached behind his neck and grabbed the jacket's collar. He slipped his arms from the sleeves. I saw oily stains on the cuffs of his pink chambray shirt. As he moved his hands, I smelled an acrid tang on the cotton. Holding the jacket by the shoulders, he displayed its reverse. "Still wear this every day."

An embroidered phoenix raised its wings across the denim. Gold, bronze, silver, and scarlet threads shone in fiery feathers. The bird's sapphire head faced right, flames bursting from the platinum beak.

Joe said, "Your mother had style. And vision." He caressed the bird's head then folded the garment across his lap. "We were so young. Never hit the big time. But her designs made us look like we belonged there. Alma believed in us."

Regrets, Joe's and mine, swept across the table. I'd wanted to learn more about my mother. Now I had. I longed to trace the embroidered creature on his jacket, feel the silky slip of threads and the sequin's sharp facets. I'd gained an important insight about her: she saved people back then, just like I did now. Mavis arrived with our drinks. She set the highball glasses on coasters, something amber for him, another virgin Collins for me. Patting both our necks, Mavis departed.

After a sip, I spoke. "I want to ask you about your current club, the Barge."

Joe sucked a swig of his drink. "What about it?"

"I understand lots of kids visit every week."

He huffed, hearing an accusation. "We check IDs at the door. No one under sixteen gets inside. And nobody under twenty-one gets served alcohol."

The policy sounded good, but I doubted his operation was that tight. Not if he wanted to attract young patrons as his core clientele. Easy access to the Barge would draw crowds. Hassles were a turnoff.

I raised an open hand. "I'm not charging you with anything. I'm looking to find one kid. I understand you might have seen him."

"Name?"

"Tariq Bolden."

Squinting, eyes on the barflies to our left. "Nope. Nobody I know."

Looked like lying to me. I pressed on: "Tall, slim, but well-built. Mixed race with light complexion." I saw Joe's brows hike. I added, "Could go by Terrence." Mother's name would make a simple alias.

Chin jut. "Maybe I know him, maybe not." Lying for sure.

"He's an artist. Likes to paint classic rock stars. You know him?"

"Why do you figure I know a kid like that?"

I gestured with my lips. "Your shirt is stained with oil paint and you've recently used turpentine to clean your hands."

He looked at the splotches on his cuffs and chuckled. "You're good at this." His moustache bobbed, flashing the white of his teeth.

"I may know a kid like that. Goes by the handle 'T.' Hangs with a little Latina beauty, big hair and a sweetheart face."

Ingrid had accompanied Tariq to the Barge. I nodded. "That's him. You seen T lately?"

His answer detoured: "The Barge is my side gig. A way to stay in the music game. My main line is an art gallery I run out of that old warehouse on Glenhurst Drive."

"The one past Tidwell Park?" I remembered the park's lacy gazebo, floating in a manicured square five blocks from the historic heart of Q-Town. The warehouse seven miles north of the park looked like a listing aircraft carrier with its windows punched out. "I thought that place was derelict."

Joe laughed. "That's what it's supposed to look like, abandoned. I bought it years ago when the old Gleason battery factory went bankrupt. Call the gallery Spark. Nod to history, see."

When I smiled, he continued, "I show contemporary work for clients with lots of bread. People sick of the insipid crap hawked in those galleries in the Meatpacking District. I mount three shows a year at Spark. The art I sell is challenging, heart-stopping; guaranteed to make your eyes water and your bowels loosen. Collectors on my mailing list know where to find me."

"How come I've never heard of you?" Dumb question, but that was my info-unearthing technique.

Joe snorted like a bull. He raised his right hand, rubbing thumb over middle finger. "Adult money, sister. I'm guessing you don't have it." Amused eyes rambled over my clothes. "At Spark, we play in deep pockets."

"Exclusive and elusive, right?"

"Exactly."

"And T fits in how?"

"The boy's been a Barge regular for months. Always grilling me about the old days of rock and roll. Pretty knowledgeable for a kid. One night, T showed me sketches he'd done of Jimi and Janis. I liked his touch, hyperrealism with flair and mystery. I asked him if he'd be interested in making something for me."

"You commissioned a painting?"

"I wanted a mural, a monumental work on canvas I could move from place to place, a distinctive piece to fix the vibe for the Barge. Old-school meets Gen-Z edgy. The kid had the chops. I set him up in a studio in one wing of the Spark warehouse. Bought brushes, paints, canvas. Ladders and platforms. Even a winch to hoist the canvas. Kid's been charging hard for months. His shit is blow-your-mind gorgeous." Joe squeezed his eyes shut as if to capture the glory of Tariq's art.

My heart jumped. I wiped my thumb across my mouth, too eager perhaps. "Is T working at your place tonight?"

"Why're you looking for him?" Joe's eyes narrowed to flinty shards. "What's he to you?"

Tariq was my dead daughter's brother. A dangling tie to my own shredded family. I gargled the truth with a sip of soda. I wanted to find this boy, help him deal with his father's death. Did I see Tariq as kin? Almost. Did he have useful information for my case? Maybe. Could solving Phil's murder help repair my past? Yes, I wanted that chance. Tariq was my way forward.

# CHAPTER **TWENTY-ONE**

Horselaughs burst above the dinnertime racket of Kings Cross Tavern. Noise rattled off the windowpanes and brass light fixtures as the evening sank into night. Though smoking was forbidden, the air thickened with musk and mischief. People were eating, drinking, connecting. At the bar, two men in tracksuits smacked high fives. Near them, a pair of women in turtlenecks and power blazers simpered over a shared cell phone.

I shifted on my haunches and examined the man sitting opposite me. Chin bristling with gray, mouth a pink crease below the long upper lip, shrewd eyes raking my face. Joe Kidd's question hung between us: *Why are you looking for Tariq Bolden?* Detective work demanded privacy: sometimes for clients, sometimes for myself. I needed Joe's help to close this case and ease my scoured conscience. So I gave him half the true answer.

"I'm on a job. Tariq's father was murdered earlier this week."

"I heard. Tough break for the kid."

"I'm working with QPD to investigate the circumstances that led to that killing." When Joe nodded, I expanded. "I want to speak with Tariq. Learn what he knows. Help him if I can." I looked around the tavern, hoping Mavis would deliver my hamburger. Now. Before I spilled about my convoluted link to Phil Bolden. And Tariq's connection to my daughter.

Joe said, "Okay. Not sure T will speak with you, though. From what he's said, the dad was a sorry-ass sonovabitch." Joe paused, eyelids at half-mast as he studied me.

Skin on my neck prickled. Had he scanned Phil Bolden's chapter in my heart? Below the table, I clawed my palm.

Joe finished: "Let's give T the last say. He's grown. He can choose his own path."

"Fair enough." I exhaled. Private stayed private.

Joe stood to shrug into his jacket. "Let's ride. I'll take you to him." Stooping, he retrieved his leather satchel. He gestured toward the bar with his helmet. "Mavis can lend you hers."

After three sentences to my friend explaining our hasty exit, I plunged through the tavern door, clutching her white helmet. Joe Kidd was six strides ahead. He'd stowed his Harley in the parking lot of the First Federal Bank of Queenstown, around the corner from the tavern. Gusts tormented leaves piled below the walk-up ATM's shelf. Mini-cyclones of receipts, cigarette butts, and movie tickets buffeted my jeans. I lifted my jacket collar, but raindrops writhed along my neck. The helmet helped against the cold, but I wished for gloves.

As Joe tightened the strap under my chin, he said, "Today's banking day. Drop weekend receipts from the Barge." He patted the leather bag, sliding it around his body to rest against his stomach. "Chat with my good buddy Jackson Peel." An overhead streetlamp lit Joe's grin. "He keeps my cash tidy for the tax man."

Jackson Peel. The name rang a bell. Someone had mentioned the banker to me recently. But the clang was too muffled for me to make any connections.

Joe slung his leg over the hog's saddle. "You ridden before?" Glare from his black helmet struck my eyes.

"Been a minute." A college boyfriend's puny red Honda scooter almost counted. "But I remember the basics." I straddled the bike and inched forward until my knees gripped his hips.

Maybe Joe doubted my expertise. "No leaning, squeezing, or steering," he shouted over his shoulder. "Hold on if you need to. We'll reach Spark before you catch your breath."

We flew over slick roads; down Center Street, around the black hole of Lake Trask, under the highway bypass, beside cornfields shorn to stubble. Most of Queenstown was stowed at home for the night. Headlights from the few cars dazzled my eyes so I lowered my nose to Joe's collar. Smells of sweat, flesh, paint, and turpentine nestled in the fabric of his jacket.

The ride gave me a chance to study Alma's stitchery like I'd wanted. I couldn't see the colors, except as shocking flashes revealed by rare streetlamps. I touched the threads of the phoenix's wings and the sequined spray of its coxcomb. I marveled that her silk stitches remained taut. I wished I'd known about her artistry, appreciated her imagination and drive. Maybe it was the rain, or maybe lost chances pricked my eyes.

As we shifted lanes near a construction site, I lifted from the seat. Unbalanced, I clasped Joe's waist. I touched metal. My fingers slid over the crosshatching of a gun handle, then along the trigger's curve. The weapon nestled tight in the waistband of his jeans. Protection for the bank run. The gun's grip burned my palm. I released the weapon and, against orders, squeezed his torso as we pitched around traffic cones near the new municipal water tower. After the old structure's collapse last year, the town had built a shiny reservoir whose metal legs gleamed like lightning bolts planted in the turf.

After twenty minutes, Joe veered into a rutted path. We lurched by overgrown forsythia bushes, bare branches scraping my sleeves. Soon, the path widened into a square clotted with spiky weeds and concrete chunks. I saw a four-story brick building, its windows as black as the puddles dotting the gravel courtyard. Joe steered the bike into the maw of a garage and dismounted. My knees felt like jelly, still jiggling from the ride. When I faltered, he grabbed my elbow and guided me to a door at the rear of the hangar. We skirted a silver Prius, a white Mustang ragtop, and a Chevy Suburban.

"Welcome to Spark." Joe pointed up the staircase beyond the door. "Pardon the back entrance."

Still gripping my arm, Joe led me through four barnlike rooms on the second floor. I figured these were exhibit and party spaces. Long benches were pushed against walls in each room. Aluminum legs, white leather, stiff with buttons and black cord. I wondered if his fancy clients appreciated the rough comfort of the metal camp chairs stacked beside each door. Maybe, at Spark, coarse and crude were the point. In the near darkness, the walls glowed like oil slicks on a sullied ocean. Rain rattled corrugated tin panels overhead.

Down a corridor, flipping lights as he marched, Joe reached a closed door. "My office. He'll be here." He shouted, maybe to be heard over the rain racket from the ceiling. Or perhaps to alert Tariq to our arrival.

Stepping across the threshold, I saw the boy stretched on a sofa, arms in the air, thumbs tapping a cell phone. He wore a faded red sweatshirt and baggy jeans. He turned his head, saw me, and jerked upright.

"You," he squawked. He kicked a pizza box, skidding it toward a desk. The box thumped against the casters of an old-fashioned library chair, spilling gnawed crusts on the floor. "How'd you find me?"

We weren't doing greetings. "Questions, digging, help from friends." I sat in the wooden chair and rotated to face the kid.

Tariq glared at Joe. "Not cool, man. You ratted me out." He threw the phone onto a pillow scrunched at one end of the couch. Pout in bloom, he stabbed hands into the kangaroo pouch of his sweatshirt.

Joe hoisted brows over round eyes, an innocent gawp spreading his mouth. "Listen to her. That's all you gotta do." He thrust his chin at me. "If she makes sense, talk. If not, kick her out. Choice is yours, T."

Joe pulled the bottom drawer of his metal desk. He removed a tumbler and a half-full bottle of Maker's Mark, sitting both on the desk next to a lamp shaped like an iceberg. A finger flick lit the plastic ice floe, sending beams through the bourbon's golden juice. Joe stuffed his pistol inside the messenger bag and placed the roll in the drawer.

"I'm outta here," he said. He grabbed the glass and bottle with one hand and pointed at two brooms leaning against a doorway. "Talk or don't, kid. Leave or don't. But clean up while you're deciding."

After Joe disappeared, I picked up the pizza carton at my feet. Would I look weak if I ate the scraps? Maybe, but I was starved beyond caring. Chewing was my contribution to the cleanup. Tariq snorted at me, but ridicule was better than rage. As I munched a second crust, the kid grabbed a broom.

While he swept, I pitched. "I'm here because I'm trying to find out who killed your dad." I flicked crumbs from my chin.

"You talk to my mom? She paying you?"

Leaden stains embossed hollows below Tariq's eyes. Their almond shape and heavy lashes reminded me of Monica's best features. The solo dimple in Tariq's right cheek winked as he spoke. The same one Monica had. *An angel's kiss,* my mother called it. Sister and brother inherited this dimple from their father.

I swallowed to cover sighs welling inside. Tariq shuddered under my examination. The lustrous cheeks I'd seen at the homecoming banquet were veiled with gray. My heart squeezed in surprise. I'd expected Tariq to look sad. His father had been murdered a few days ago. Grief was normal, even for the death of a despised parent. But Tariq's fragility shook me. Seeing him now, I wanted to wrap my arms around him, siphon the sorrow from his chest into mine.

Instead, I curbed my impulse and stuck to the bare facts. "No. I'm working with the cops. Nobody's paying me. This is on my own nut."

He harrumphed then scraped dust from behind the couch. "Not getting paid makes you a sap."

"Makes me a freelance. No strings."

The broom's dry scrabbling grated. To counter the irritating noise, I seized the second broom and attacked the bun feet of a short bookcase. We worked side by side for a minute.

Eyes on bent bristles, Tariq spewed scorn. "I don't believe you. How much did they pay you to say shit like that."

"This isn't about money." I stopped sweeping.

He stabbed his broom into the floor, splaying the bristles. "Of course it's about money. With them, everything's about money." Brushing a new spot, he piled debris into a pyramid.

"That how you see your parents?"

His face crumpled. He touched his mouth to the tip of the broom handle.

I pressed. "On the last day of his life, your father was trying to reach out. To apologize to you for how he screwed up at the gala."

He looked at me with blazing eyes. "I wanted him to suffer. Not her."

"Your father?"

"Yes. The great Philip Bolden. I wanted him to hurt, the way he hurt my mom, the way he hurt me." Knuckles yellow, he choked the broomstick with both hands. Didn't take imagination to picture whose neck he was throttling.

"You wanted to hurt your father?"

"You know what they called him?" Off my headshake, he continued, "King Philanthropy."

"You blamed your father for making money?"

He rolled his eyes, as if my questions proved I was dumber than he'd feared. "When I was twelve, I overheard two dinner guests at our house, Black dudes, ragging on him. I was hiding on the staircase when one said, 'Who the fuck he think he is? Just some no-account Trenton trash. A skel from Sutton Hill.' The other one said, 'Yeah, Phil got big bucks, but he got balls to match.'"

That was hearsay, not details. I wanted more from the kid's direct knowledge. "How'd he hurt you?"

"Not me, my mother. That money he tosses around? It's not his."

"What do you mean?"

"My mom earns that money. My dad spends it. That's how it works in our house." He used present tense. Still digesting the dynamics of the vanished family. "That's how it's been for ages. He squeezes her dry, then struts like it's down to him. Calls his company Philmel Enterprises. Like they got even dibs in it. But Phil Bolden ain't worth shit."

"That's a serious charge."

"Serious as a heart attack." His nostrils flared with fury. "Then how you think he behaves? He cheats on her with any female crosses his path."

My gut sank. I blinked away guilty tears. I knew Phil had been an unfaithful husband; I had participated in his most recent infidelity.

Seeing the wounded boy's lips tremble, I didn't offer any defense for Phil. There was none.

But maybe Tariq read skepticism in my eyes.

"You don't believe me? You check with Laurel Vaughn. You met her. My mom's friend. I saw Laurel with my dad last Memorial Day at a party at our house."

"You saw them?" I remembered the art teacher's story of her nasty encounter with Phil at the holiday party.

He coughed, eyes shifting. "Yeah, in the garage. They were kissing and all. Sloppy, like in some porno."

Doubt strained my words. "You saw that?"

A wetter hack this time. Teeth gnawing lower lip. Eyes left toward a low bookcase, Tariq mumbled, "Yeah. That's the kind of man my dad is. Was."

He covered his mouth as choking racked his chest. The teeth and eye moves were tells. He was lying. About a detail or a core event, I couldn't be sure yet. This story jibed with what Laurel Vaughn had told me in her classroom. I believed her then. But I didn't believe Tariq. Not all the way. His account smacked of anger-fueled exaggeration, not plain truth. There was more to this story. If he was lying about Laurel and Phil, I wanted to know why.

I leaned my broom against the bookcase. "I hear you. I get it: Your dad was an asshole. He's dead now. I'm not here to defend him. But I do want to find out who ended his life. You're an adult. How you square your feelings for him is up to you." I stepped closer, lowered my voice. "But think about your mother. Have you seen her since your father died?"

Tariq shook his head, flames licking the ridges of his ears to a dusky red. "I stayed here."

This rift was deeper than I'd first realized. "How is she feeling?" I squared so he could see my face. "Do you even know?"

He gulped, eyes fogging.

I had my angle so I plunged the knife. "I'm a mother. I know how it feels to miss your child. All she wants is you home." When he sipped to contain a bobbling Adam's apple, I thrust for the target.

"Your mother needs you. She wants to see you. Go home. You're her family. Deal with this together."

Tariq threw his broom to the floor. As it clattered, he lunged at the bookcase, pulling paperbacks from the shelves. I'd sliced him, even sprinkled guilt into the cut. But he was thinking, so I counted that a victory.

I handed the fallen broom to Tariq. My instinct told me he was the key. Uncovering what he knew would lead me to Phil's killer. Maybe my hunch was driven by vague fantasy, my desire to regrow family ties, the need to replace the lives I'd lost with new ones. Perhaps the cops would uncover other threats to account for Phil's violent end. But this boy and the people laced around him held the answers I wanted. To the murder puzzle. To my life. I wanted to rebuild a family. Rejoin the human race. Maybe Tariq could be my new start.

Tariq angled the broom like a sword across his body then thrust it toward the shelf, poking books until their spines stood in a neat line.

Softening my voice, I turned the questioning. "I get why you stayed clear of your parents after the gala blowup. But why have you kept Ingrid at arm's length?"

"Embarrassed, mostly." He chewed his lower lip and exhaled. "My family is a shitstorm. Been that way for a while. And my dad's death underlined that." His shoulders and neck eased. "Ingrid, she's amazing. Straight-up good. Better than I deserve." His brown eyes widened in wonder. "I don't want her soiled in the dirty muck of my family. Ingrid is ride or die. I don't want to mess up with her." Lines disappeared from his forehead. A ripple of a smile said he was in a good place at last.

His lifting mood made this decision time. "What's it going to be, Tariq? You heading home tonight?"

With a heavy sigh, he said, "All right. You talking about my mom like that was rough. You dealt truths, though."

"I ride with you to your parents' house." No room for debate. I swept my dust pile onto a sheet of paper and dumped it into a wastebasket beside the desk.

Tariq mumbled under his breath. His gaze scraped the corners of the room then the junk-strewn landscape on the desk.

He folded a blanket into a neat bundle that he squared on the pillow.

"I'm ready," he said. "Let's go."

# T FOR TARIQ

# CHAPTER **TWENTY-TWO**

Tariq Bolden kept his car in good condition. I'd been expecting a bumpy ride in a clunker. Wouldn't he scorn the Mustang as a hand-me-down gift from a detested parent? But our drive from the Spark gallery to his home on Allentown Road was smooth. Despite its convertible top, the Mustang stayed warm and dry. I only shivered once, when a doe scampered from a soy field into the yellow headlights revealing our path. Tariq braked, turned into the skid, and jogged us into a grassy trench. Twenty seconds to catch our breaths, then we resumed the trip in silence.

I lost track of time and direction. It was my suggestion that we stop at the Bolden home before dropping me off. Now that I'd convinced Tariq to see his mother, I wanted to witness the reunion. I knew the Boldens lived on the road leading from Queenstown to Allentown. But I'd only driven these winding country miles once when accompanying my friends Elissa and Belle to a nursery to buy a Christmas tree. So I was startled when we lurched around a blond brick post holding a mailbox. White wooden railing extended on either side of the postbox, marking the boundary of the Boldens' estate. We drove on a straight road between rows of pines. Two minutes, four minutes. How far from the world was Phil's house?

We charged onto a circle of white gravel, frosted by spotlights lining the roof of the building. Tariq nosed to a stop before a double-height door painted black. Pale bricks formed the façade, broken by picture windows on both sides of the entrance. Living room to the right, dining room to the left. I couldn't see it from the car, but I guessed a foyer divided the first floor. I wondered if Tariq would ring the door to announce his return. Or maybe he'd sneak in and run up the grand staircase to his bedroom as if he'd been absent only a few hours.

"Come in for a minute. Then I'll drive you to town," Tariq said, climbing from the car. "I bet Mom would love to see you."

Sure, like a snowball loves hellfire. Melinda Terrence would never forget I was Phil's ex-wife. "That's okay. I'll stay here. You go on."

I watched Tariq trot to the door. Two carved stone elephants flanked the door with trunks raised. Just as Phil had described them the afternoon before he died. These were the statues he'd placed here to remind him of our daughter, Monica. Granite figures a yard tall, uplifted feet balanced on spheres, like relics of a shrunken circus. He told me during our visit to Monica's grave, *They mean delight, strength, confidence. Every day I think of our baby when I pass those elephants.* As his deep voice receded, I swiveled my head, searching the darkness. Nothing. Only rain splattering on gravel. A distant rustle of trees. When the illusion passed, I resumed watching Phil's other child silhouetted against the black door.

Lit by a gigantic overhead lantern, Tariq worked a key in the brass lock and slipped inside. I turned my collar against my neck and slouched in the bucket seat to wait. I hoped after the reunion the kid would remember to drive me to town. Even saviors need rescuing sometimes.

As the Mustang cooled, I dropped my chin against my chest to guard the remaining body warmth. I touched my right temple to the windowpane, studying the house. Tariq and his mother were in the living room. The room seemed ablaze. Lamps, chandeliers, or fire? The duo squeezed until no light slipped between their bodies, arms tangled, faces pressed together. Blond head against dark one. I could see Melinda's hand clasped over her son's scalp; Tariq's arm circled his mother's waist then fell away. They separated. Tariq gestured with a raised hand. Melinda's head whipped toward the picture window. She looked at me. Darkness cloaked me, but I slumped anyway. Shadows swallowed her eyes as the mouth gaped in the porcelain surface. Stiff-necked, she turned to her son, clutched his shoulder. He twisted until her hand slid off. They were arguing. About me, probably.

I puffed; a white cloud condensed against the windshield. This cold was fierce. I wanted Tariq to return for my ride home. My stomach rumbled, the scavenged pizza crusts long gone. Five more minutes of arguing, then I'd break up the family gathering. I cupped my hands over my mouth, blowing for warmth.

Three minutes later, Tariq slipped beneath the Mustang's steering wheel. With the hoodie pulled over his hair, I could see only his soft profile against the side window.

"Everything okay?" I asked, though I knew nothing was okay inside his wrecked family.

"Yeah, fine." He pounded the accelerator, jutted chin daring me to challenge him. "Perfect."

Pebbles sputtered from wrenched tires as the Mustang rotated in the driveway. I accepted the challenge: "How's your mom?"

"Don't jerk me around. I know you watched. You saw us arguing."

"I don't read lips. Or minds. You want to tell me what the argument was about?"

"No." Tariq floored the gas.

"About me?" I was as persistent as a wart.

"No."

The car rumbled over the gravel path to the brick mailbox then leaped onto the asphalt road heading toward Queenstown.

The Mustang ate the miles. I didn't talk. Tariq needed room to stew. He'd open when he was ready. I stared at the fields rippling like a dark river beside the road. I thought of what I'd learned about Phil's selfishness, his infidelities. How he'd alienated his wife and son. Even in death he seemed to have driven a wedge between them. By the time we stopped at the red light on Academy Street my hands had chilled again.

But Tariq had warmed. "We were fighting about me staying at the house. My mom and me."

"You're not returning after you drop me?"

"I told her I'm spending the night in my dorm room."

I gasped. "But she needs you."

"I guess. Maybe." When he tightened his grip on the steering wheel, his knuckles glowed red. "But I've got a trig midterm tomorrow morning. I need to study." He gulped air. "And I need rest, sleep. I can't do that with her around."

"Okay." My croak faint, like a plea.

"We're not in a good place right now." Facing me, his eyes shone with tears.

I nodded. Reaching over the gear shift, I squeezed his forearm.

The traffic signal turned green. He sighed; a faint whistle through sagging lips. We didn't move. Sharp honks from the car behind startled Tariq into action. The Mustang leaped through the intersection taking the diagonal into Center Street.

When we reached the corner of Abbott Street, opposite the Q-Town Pharmacy, I told Tariq to pull over. I'd get out in front of the Kings Cross Tavern, I said. No way I'd let him see the parking lot behind the pharmacy. I remembered walking with police officers around the spot where Phil died three days ago. I wanted to spare his son the sight of those details. Tire grooves, scuff marks, fabric shreds, bloodstains. The ghastly mosaic of Phil's final moments. Fewer gruesome facts, less vivid dreams. I had enough nightmares for the both of us.

I stood under the tavern's green awning to watch Tariq pull into traffic.

Peering into the recesses of the tavern, I saw three women in yoga gear at a table in a dark corner. My stomach growled when one woman chomped on a french fry. I wondered if my friend Mavis Jenkins had preserved the blue cheese burger I'd ordered hours ago. Before my jaunt to the Spark gallery with her squeeze, Joe Kidd. Before my talk with Tariq Bolden and our ride to and then from his home on Allentown Road. In that time, I'd eaten exactly two pizza crusts. Another gut grumble sealed the deal. I pushed through the tavern door in search of my lost burger.

# CHAPTER **TWENTY-THREE**

I slept late the next morning and phoned my bosses with notice I'd work from home. I could hear Elissa Adesanya tapping her keyboard in search of excuses to require my presence in the office. Some little Friday tasks she could concoct to prevent me from working on Phil Bolden's murder. Despite a flurry of hissing and teeth sucking, she came up empty. I was off the clock and on the case.

After my usual coffee and oatmeal, I filled the morning with phone calls to Rome School administrators, staff, and trustees. I'd hoped for a 3-D picture of Phil from the Rome people who'd worked with him. What I got was a textbook description of a paragon. To put my informants at ease, I scrubbed my voice for maximum sweetness. I parboiled my phrases, subduing every slang term and corralling each Black inflection. I knew the vocal ruse of code-switching worked when the first trustee slipped a reference to "those people" into her comments.

The trustees agreed Phil Bolden was a wizard with money. His super-talent was erecting a golden façade. Now I wanted to discover what secrets he had kept hidden all these years. I hoped a talk with his wife, Melinda Terrence, would put a crack in the Bolden wall.

By three thirty I was exhausted by the playacting. Starving for real food and authentic company, I fired multiple texts to Ingrid Ramírez.

I told her I'd met with Tariq Bolden and promised to share what I knew. I invited her to bring sandwiches from the Forum at the end of her shift. A solid girls' night in on my dime. How could she resist? I had no intention of spilling Tariq's family troubles. But I figured the vague promise of learning more about her boyfriend would be enough to entice Ingrid into visiting me. I wanted to speak with her, continue the process to rebuild our friendship.

And I needed another way into the Bolden house. I wanted to speak with Melinda Terrence. She had known Phil Bolden better than anyone. Not counting me. I hoped information she might share could point me toward his killer. Tariq wouldn't work as my ambassador; the rift between mother and son might be temporary, but I couldn't count on him for help. I hoped Ingrid would be the ticket.

When she bicycled to my house at five, Ingrid brought the Forum's Jersey Shore special for me: stacks of ham, salami, prosciutto, and Romano on a cheesy Italian loaf. She chose a sprout-filled vegan combo for herself. We spread wax paper sheets on the kitchen counter and ate our sandwiches hunkered on stools at the island. No dishes or utensils needed. Ditching glasses, we drank club soda and root beer from cans.

Ingrid looked drained. Bags under her eyes twitched like moth's wings. Thanks to the bareheaded bicycle ride, her hair sprang in a halo of coils. But the exertion hadn't raised color to her cheeks; the green shirt of her Forum uniform cast a sickly gloss on her face. Between bites, I gave Ingrid a condensed version of my conversation with Tariq last night. No beef with Dad, no argument with Mom.

Sandwich done, I got to the point: "You said you hadn't been in touch with Tariq since his dad's death?" Wednesday to Friday. Not long, but an eternity in teen relationships.

"Yeah." She crumpled a corner of the wrapping paper. "I didn't know what to say. It's just so fucking awful."

"I bet he'd appreciate hearing from you." Old-people advice, but I offered anyway. "You could text a few words. Let him take the lead."

I wanted to get into the Bolden house to interview the mother. I hoped Ingrid would assist, but I kept that goal out of my first suggestions. "I guess phoning would be a moron move, hunh?" Remembering her rebuke on the ancient adult practice of phone contact, I smiled.

She nodded, face sallow with fatigue. "Yeah. A text might work, though. I'll try in a while." She rubbed her forehead and sighed. "I haven't slept much since . . ."

"Since when?"

"Tuesday night."

That was the evening Phil and I visited the cemetery. The night he made me dinner and spent a few hours in my bed. The last night of his life. Ingrid knew nothing of that, I hoped. What happened Tuesday to disrupt her sleep?

I took an oblique angle into the subject. "Where were you Tuesday?"

"Tariq and I visited Spark." She captured crumbs in the folds of wax paper, forming a compact square.

"Spark? The art gallery?" My daredevil ride to the gallery clinging to Joe Kidd's motorcycle last night roared through my memories. "What were you doing there?"

"Tariq wanted to work a few hours on his mural. He's painting this giant-ass thing for Joe, the owner. Like, massive. And Joe's paying him a buttload of money. I brought my physics textbook to review for an exam."

"How long did you stay Tuesday night?" When we'd talked at the sandwich shop yesterday, Ingrid claimed she hadn't seen Tariq since the homecoming gala. Why had she lied?

"We drove there around eight thirty. Joe fixed a pot of chili, so Tariq ate some of that. *Con carne*, yuck." Mask of disgust, thumb down. "I made a cheese sandwich. We had a few beers, nothing much." She stared at the floor, her mouth twisted left. An undersell on the booze, for sure.

"Did you watch Tariq paint?"

"Yeah. There's an old couch in one corner of the studio. So I hang out there, reading or listening to music while Tariq's up on the scaffold with his paints." She lifted her eyes to the space above the refrigerator, as if watching her boyfriend work. "I love seeing him paint. He's so into it, you know? Like, in a zone. And the mural is freaking awesome. You gotta see it sometime."

"I'd love to." I remembered how Laurel Vaughn, Tariq's art

teacher, had raved about his talent, though not about this mural. Had Laurel ever seen her favorite student's masterwork?

Ingrid's eyes brightened, pleasure flushing exhaustion from her face. "You'd get a kick out of all the OG musicians he's put in. Artists from the eighties and nineties. Like, super old but cool."

"Ancient." I winked. "How long did you work?"

"Tariq was on the ladder for maybe two hours. I remember, because he always says he never really gets into his groove until he's been painting for an hour. But then . . ." A gulp captured by bitten lips.

"Something happened?"

"He got a call."

"Rude."

She rolled her eyes. "No kidding. But he answered anyway. I figured it had to be his mom or dad. Anyone else, he'd have let the call go to voice mail."

"You don't know who was on the line?"

"No. Like I said, he was up on the ladder. I could see him speaking but I couldn't hear anything." Her eyes narrowed as memories collided in her mind. "I knew it was something bad, though."

"How could you tell?"

"Because of how Tariq's face went stiff. First, he got scary pale, then red. He swayed then tightened his fist on the rung. I thought he was going to fall, so I stood up. I couldn't run fast enough to catch him. But I was ready to try."

Was Ingrid right? Had Tariq been speaking with his parents? "What happened next?"

"He climbed down the ladder. He was mad. Pissed off like I've never seen him. I asked what was the matter. He stalled and blocked me. He didn't want to talk."

"Did you two drive to town?"

She fiddled a coil of black hair beside her jaw. "No, Tariq went by himself. I went to the bathroom to give him some space to cool off. When I got back to the studio, he was gone. I heard the Mustang engine and looked out the window to see him tear off."

This story upended my ideas about the night Phil was murdered.

I'd never considered his son a suspect. But now I remembered how agitated Tariq had seemed when I confronted him at Spark. I'd believed his distress was related to Phil's death. But now a grimmer prospect percolated through my mind. Had Tariq shot his father? That would account for the tension I'd witnessed between mother and son last night.

I glanced at Ingrid, worrying a flake of gray skin from her lower lip as she thought about her boyfriend. I wondered if Tariq had taken the pistol Joe Kidd kept in his desk drawer. Had there been enough time while Ingrid was in the bathroom for Tariq to go to the office, grab the gun, then get to the garage? I couldn't ask her that, not yet.

I went in another direction. "He left you alone?" I wanted to say *abandoned*.

"Yeah. I mean, not *alone* alone. Joe Kidd was there. He gave me a lift home after Tariq split."

"At midnight?" I put on my toughest mother-scowl. The grimace I had used when Monica waltzed in late from a date. "That's not good boyfriend behavior."

Ingrid stood from the island, a frown squeezing her face. I figured she wanted to change the subject, away from Tariq's movements on the night of Phil's murder. I let her. We could revisit Tariq's actions at the gallery later. She gathered the remnants of our dinner and tossed the bundle in the trash. Over her shoulder, she said, "He's not my longtime, for-real boyfriend, you know."

This was news to me. I'd assumed they were sexually intimate and exclusive. Color me mind-blown. "Not for real? How's that work?"

"It's complicated."

"Educate me."

Ingrid huffed, like an indulgent teacher with a slow pupil. "Can I make some tea first, before the birds-and-bees talk?"

I heated mugs of water in the microwave while she rummaged in the pantry for the box of herbal teas. Chamomile for two. We moved to the living room to sit on the rug, legs crossed butterfly style so we could face each other. The setting sun flowed over my shoulder, gilding Ingrid's lovely features. Bronzed light turned her eyes amber. Steam from the tea pinkened her lips as she talked.

She described the history of her relationship with Tariq Bolden. She'd met him the week she arrived at Rome as a transfer student. He became her first friend. And they'd stayed in the friend zone for ten months. Ingrid was smitten from the start. She detected hints he was interested in her "that way." Kisses here, cuddles there. Plenty of heat, nothing definitive. But he made no moves to deepen their involvement. Maybe Tariq was gay? Cool. Could he be involved with another girl? Okay, but when she asked, he denied. She tunneled into the Rome chatter heap, but even the savviest gossip girls offered no insight. So she settled for best-pal status. Until last summer, when Tariq revved his engines and leveled up. The romance, sex included, launched last July when they celebrated his eighteenth birthday in grand style.

Since we were being frank, I asked, "What happened to change his mind?"

"You mean, beyond the fascination of my charms?" Brows bobbing, she slurped tea to drown her cat grin.

"Which are many and mighty. But what opened his eyes last summer?" I asked.

I dragged a thumb over the mug's handle. Something had flipped for Tariq around that time. I remembered he had received the cast-off Mustang from his father to mark his transition into adulthood. Ingrid was an even better birthday present. I wanted to learn what had triggered the switch in his affections.

"Honest? No clue." Ingrid chuckled. "Alls I know is, after Memorial Day, the boy wised up." Did she inspect her good fortune? Nah, only fools analyzed when bounty arrived. "I'm not worrying about that. Just enjoying what we've got right now." She shrugged, the mantle of youth light on her shoulders.

Memorial Day was when the Boldens' holiday party shattered in disaster. When Phil moved on Laurel the art teacher. Was there a connection between the party's nasty fallout and the shift in Tariq's relationship with Ingrid?

Ingrid rotated her mug on the brass table. Maybe talking about her intensified relationship with Tariq had cleared her mind. She returned to the earliest element of our dinner conversation.

"I think I know how to text him now." She jumped to her feet. Thumbs flying over the cell, she sat on the sofa opposite me. Spine curved, shoulders hunched. This exchange was private.

I cleared both mugs and retreated to the kitchen. Washing dishes twice in three days was extra. Usually, I let the stack accumulate for a week. But extreme times called for extreme measures. As I squirted dishwashing liquid in the sink, I imagined tactics to get Ingrid to invite me to the Bolden house. She knew I was the ex-wife. Close to the family, but in the most awkward way possible. I was the long-lost relative everyone avoided. I dunked one mug and swirled it below the soapsuds. Maybe I could remind Ingrid of my conversation with Tariq. I thought I'd earned some credibility with him. And perhaps Ingrid would see the role I had played in bringing him home might soften Melinda's grieving heart. I wanted to meet Melinda and dig for insights into Phil. I wanted to know where his wife and son had been the night he was killed. How could I convince Ingrid to make this happen?

I needn't have worried. My girl had it all worked out.

When she returned to the kitchen, she stepped to the sink. Leaning her head against my shoulder, she said, "Will you drive me to the Boldens' house? I don't want to go there alone." Her breath hitched. "I'm kinda in the family. But not really. You know, like a stepkid or something. I figure with you there, the convo will go easier. You can be the focus, not me."

She'd assigned me that long-lost-relative role: Auntie Pernicia arrived from back-of-beyond with fruitcake and bad breath. Ingrid calculated with me there to absorb any resentment, heat would be off her. Smart girl. We could work that action, each to our own purposes.

"Of course I'll drive you." I wiped my hands on a dish towel. "When do you want to go?"

"Tariq said to come over tomorrow afternoon. Maybe two or three."

"That's fine," I said. "Pick you up at your place at two thirty?" I opened my arms and she stepped into their circle.

"Great, I'll be ready." Before she nuzzled her face into my chest, I saw her eyes glowing. She mumbled, "I guess I should have said something earlier."

"What, baby?" I pressed my lips into her hair.

"I'm sorry for your loss, Vandy." Her words were muffled by my shirt. "I know you were longtime divorced and all. But still, with Phil's death, you gotta feel some kind of way."

I squeezed until she gasped for breath. Brushing my eyes against her curls, I murmured, "Thank you for that." I hugged hard, then turned away so she wouldn't see my tears.

# CHAPTER **TWENTY-FOUR**

Saturday morning brought the season's first wintry mix. Sudden ice glazed the trees and lampposts. All at once, pumpkins on porches seemed out of season with their stems wreathed in snow. I liked seeing my little community this way. Trimmed in white, Queenstown looked pretty, like the girl skating on a pond in a Currier and Ives print, her rosy cheeks framed in rabbit fur.

At three o'clock, when Ingrid and I arrived at the Bolden residence, rain had washed the asphalt clean of snow. But white froth still clung to the lawns bordering the long private street leading to the house. Ingrid wore a dark green sweater and black jeans, the most somber outfit in her wardrobe. She'd ditched her usual combat boots in favor of black ballet flats, dressy but too thin for the weather. I'd chosen a black wool pantsuit and a white button-down shirt. I looked like an undertaker's assistant, but it was my best outfit. My courthouse-and-church suit. I'd thought about leaving the gold necklace at home. But I figured neither Melinda nor Tariq would notice the chain, or understand its significance if they did. And now, at her father's house, touching Monica's initial strengthened me. I needed all my daughter's energy and grit to pursue the questions I had for the Boldens: I wanted to ask Melinda and Tariq their whereabouts on the night of Phil's murder.

"Right on time," Tariq said, opening the door for us.

As he stepped aside, I saw his eye sockets were ringed in gray, but the pupils were clear, the whites free of red. I wanted to ask about the math test, but before I could speak, Tariq bent to accept Ingrid's hug. He nodded at me over her shoulder. "My mom's waiting in her office. You can visit there."

I looked toward the staircase at the end of the hall. The entrance was double height, dominated by a vast chandelier like an upside-down crystal tree. Formality curbed the colors and décor, as if the house had been waiting for a funeral to highlight its reticent glamour. The space didn't look like Phil at all. Where were the vibrant colors and bold images he loved? This foyer was peach with wainscoting painted pewter. A carved rug in pastel shades of blue and pink covered most of the marble floor. A large floral display with the same soft colors branched from a crystal vase on a table to the right of the front door. Among the petals were spiky feathers in shades of mint and mauve. The arrangement seemed weird, but familiar somehow. Had I seen this spray before? The mirror behind the bouquet was five feet tall, making me feel insignificant. Which was the point, I supposed.

Though Ingrid and I murmured our first round of condolences, our phrases seemed to echo from the ceiling. To the right the hall opened into a living room, the space I'd glimpsed from the car when I brought Tariq home to his mother. Was that only two days ago? I remembered the six-foot-high fireplace, flashing heat then, now cold and dark. I glimpsed acres of mauve velvet covering sofas, love seats, chairs, and tufted footrests. An insipid rug anchored the room in dusty greens, aqua, and cream. Had Phil really lived in this bland igloo?

I looked to the left. Beyond French doors, I saw a dining room littered with brown furniture. Table for twelve, breakfront, sideboard, heavily carved chairs. Four police officers bent over the table, notebooks and photos spread across the polished surface. I assumed this was the squad assembled by Lola Conte to pursue leads on Phil's murder. When one young cop raised his head, spotting me, I nodded. He returned the chummy move, then shrugged as he talked with his partner. Maybe I should have checked in with Conte. But I skipped the introductions. If the cops wanted to find me, I was easy to track.

At that moment, Melinda Terrence floated into the hall. Maybe she'd opened a door to the hidden kitchen, because scents of cinnamon and butter wafted around her as she moved. When I delivered condolences, she squeezed my arm. Not a hug, but an unexpected embrace all the same. Hand in hand, Tariq and Ingrid disappeared toward the rear of the house.

I followed Melinda into the living room. She was dressed to match the furniture: lavender silk blouse, slacks and cardigan in dove-gray wool. Fashion magazines tagged the look "soft suiting." My grandmother would have called these mourning clothes "fool frippery."

I dropped my overcoat on a chair and settled into a sofa next to her.

Melinda said, "I've asked the housekeeper to bring some sandwiches with our coffee." Mellow tones, like we'd convened to plan the Junior League's annual holiday party. "I hope you don't mind."

"Coffee sounds good," I said, blinking. My murder etiquette book left out this chapter.

Her eyes were clear; no sign of tears or swelling. Powder on her nose covered shine, not redness. She'd applied black mascara and eyeliner plus peach blush and lipstick. Scent of Bulgarian roses drifted from her ears. Was this dress-up party for me or was she expecting other visitors?

As if I'd spoken out loud, Melinda explained, "With these policemen all over the house, we keep the coffee pot running in high gear day and night." Stiff smile at the inconvenience. "And we've made enough sandwiches to feed an army."

"Have the cops said how long they intend to stay?" Dumb question, but conversation with a widow was tough.

"No clear indication yet. The lead officer, Lola Conte, has been polite, but firm." Melinda's blue eyes clouded.

"Of course." Mentioning I was supposed to cooperate with QPD's murder investigation might end our talk, so I asked another question. "Did Officer Conte give you any idea what they were looking for?"

"Nothing specific." Eyes drifted toward the fireplace. "They fingerprinted us. They asked for the names of our employees."

"Household staff?"

"Yes, and the names of our cleaning service, lawn service, pool company, and caterers."

"Of course," I said.

"We hire drivers from a car service, too. But naturally, that's not every day."

"Naturally," I said.

Armed with those names, I figured QPD would spend the next week rounding up every person in Abbott's Landing. The neighborhood was home to the Latino community that stretched along the streets bordering Lake Trask. Most residents, whether native-born or immigrant, worked in the service industries of Queenstown. I imagined the Boldens employed a battalion from Abbott's Landing.

The cops believed a botched holdup resulted in Phil's death. In this scenario, anyone working for the Boldens might have coveted their wealth. A Bolden employee could have wrangled a few desperados for a late-night robbery on a deserted street. The fact that Phil was shot behind the Q-Town Pharmacy strengthened this hypothesis. The drugstore was on Center Street, at the border of Abbott's Landing. Now, every brown-skinned person in the district would be under suspicion for this high-profile murder. "Round up the usual suspects" was more than a line from *Casablanca*. Melinda's intel had thrown lots of people into the QPD dragnet.

Melinda continued her account of invasive police operations in her home. "And I know they went through Phil's den, including his desk. My desk, too. They asked for the combination to my safe." Another smile, broader this time. "Of course, I'm not stupid. I opened it for them rather than disclose the numbers. They took our wills, gun, and tax documents from our company, Philmel Enterprises. They inspected the jewelry and cash closely, so I stayed right at their shoulders, watching every move. No need to encourage sticky fingers, is there?"

"Smart. Got to stay on your toes around the boys in blue." I might have offered a more generous interpretation of police procedure, but the arrival of a slender woman with a tray interrupted. The housekeeper's somber uniform fit the occasion, though maybe the charcoal shirtwaist dress was her regular outfit.

"Thank you, Olivia. Just set it on the table. We'll pour for our-selves."

"Yes, ma'am."

The housekeeper deposited the tray then stepped toward the hall. Melinda raised her voice. "And Olivia, would you set us a fire, please. It's cold in here." She rubbed her arms like it was Antarctica.

"Yes, ma'am." Olivia made quick work of the task: loading logs and kindling from stacks beside the fireplace; lighting rolled news-papers, nudging the sparks until they burst into flames.

Melinda sounded almost gracious. "Thank you, Olivia. That will be all."

"Yes, ma'am."

This *Gone with the Wind* scene made my skin crawl. Except in-stead of Mammy, this servant had sallow coloring and a waist-length braid of black hair.

The housekeeper scurried from the room, wiping her hands on her pockets. The mistress poured two generous servings of coffee and lifted a mug toward me.

I wondered if Phil ate like this on the regular: silver coffee urn; white mugs tipped in gold; finger sandwiches piled beside two gold-trimmed plates. Another plate held a pyramid of cinnamon buns, dripping with white sugar glaze. The silver creamer and sugar bowl flanked by silver spoons seemed too fancy for a kid raised on the streets of Trenton. I took the mug offered by Melinda, shook off the cream and sugar, then reached for an egg salad sandwich. Creamy and tangy, just right. Maybe Phil enjoyed being pampered by a tony wife who hobnobbed with the rich and Botoxed. The man I remembered would have mocked this whole bougie setup. But those memories were two decades old. I'd changed; so had Phil.

Melinda sat her mug on the table. "Save room for the cinnamon rolls," she chirped. "I made them myself this morning."

"I sure will. They smell delicious." My exaggerated inhale caused her eyes to narrow.

She plucked at the crease in her trouser knee. Then straightened blond strands behind her ear. "They do, don't they." The pink tip of her tongue dabbed shine to her lips. "That's how I met Phil."

"Classic way to a man's heart." I erased the snark from my voice, barely.

"The selling point was the homey smell." When I blinked, she rattled on. "I grew up in Wilkes-Barre. My dad was a city trash collector. My mother cleaned office buildings. After graduating high school, I worked for an interior designer. Natasha's company staged homes for open houses. 'Cozy interiors, quick sales' was her motto." Melinda smiled for the first time. "My job was hanging pictures, stacking books, posing knickknacks, arranging potted plants." She glanced around her grand living room, perhaps reflecting on how far she'd come since those hard-scrabble days.

"And you baked delicious goodies to entice potential buyers?" Not much of a stretch.

"Yes, these cinnamon buns were my specialty, my mother's recipe. I'd fix a fresh batch in my own kitchen, then rush them to the house we were staging. Still hot, smelling like heaven. Worked like a dream, every time."

I inhaled the sweet fragrance. "And Phil came to an open house?"

She nodded, pink rushing across her chest and under the blond bangs. "He was a few years out of college. But already filled with such big ideas. He'd come to Wilkes-Barre to buy houses, renovate them, then resell for a profit. The first time he smelled my cinnamon rolls, he bought the whole plate from me on the spot." Laughter creased fine lines around her eyes. "And made an offer on the house the same evening." She raised a cinnamon roll to her face to breathe in its nostalgic fragrance. Then she bit off a large chunk.

I reached for a gooey bun. Buttery magic melted on my tongue. As I gobbled, the calculator in my mind churned over those dates. Phil and I married within a year of our college graduation. We split thirteen months after the wedding, when I was four months pregnant with Monica. Could he have been making house-hunting jaunts to Wilkes-Barre before we inked the divorce decree? Possible. Not a topic I'd ever raise with the Widow Bolden.

Melinda swiped the corner of her mouth, catching a stray crumb. She fiddled again with the knife pleat on her pants. A sigh then a swallow. Something was on her mind. Something awkward. With a tap to her cheek, she said: "Tariq tells me you're working for the police. On Phil's . . . on this case. Is that true?"

I set the remainder of my roll on the plate next to her mug. "I'm a consultant to QPD, yes. Is that a problem?" The arrangements were not so official, just a request from Chief Sayre, but I let the impression of formality stand. Maybe she'd spill more if she thought I was authorized to investigate. Or would my status as Phil's other wife carry more weight?

She grabbed her coffee. Puffs jetted from her pout, rippling the tawny surface. These stall tactics plucked my last nerve. I said, "I'd like your help as I investigate Phil's death."

She flinched. "*Investigate* seems such a clinical word." A frown for my faux pas. "But yes, I could help, I suppose." When I tightened my jaw, she added, "What do you want to know?"

"About Phil. About you and Tariq. Any insights that might generate clues as to who killed him." I said it rough to wound her. To draw tears. To sting her like I hurt.

Under the powder, she flushed cherry red. "I'm not sure I can offer much." *Alice in Wonderland*–blue eyes combed my face. No tears. Lots of imploring. "I would appreciate any friendly help you can give." She exhaled and sank into the sofa.

I said nothing. Because we weren't friends. Not even in-laws.

Against my silence, she said, "Thank you." Like I'd made a big concession. She ran a palm to lift her bangs. Another *whoosh*, then, "I know Tariq will be grateful, too. When will you start?"

"How about now." Cinnamon crystals felt gritty on my tongue so I washed them down with a swig of coffee. "Tell me where you were Tuesday night."

She sat forward. "The police asked me that, too." Chin cocked, the better to look down her nose at me, the hired help. "I was here at home, of course."

"All night?"

"Yes, all night."

"And Tariq was here with you?" I knew the truth from Ingrid's story. He had been at Spark until past midnight. I wanted to test Melinda.

She flunked. "Yes, he was upstairs in his room."

"All night?" To nail down the lie.

"Of course, all night. Where else would he be?"

"His dorm room on campus. Tuesday was a school night."

She shifted her eyes right, then left. Tarnish smeared her blue pupils. "Yes, you're right. He might have been on campus. But last Tuesday, he was here at home. Ask him yourself." She ground her fist into her left palm.

"I will." Had mother and son coordinated their stories already? Would they provide mutually supportive alibis for the night of Phil's murder?

I wanted to check another element of the Tuesday-night account. At my house, I'd heard Phil speak with someone before we ate dinner. He'd used the name Mel, but had he been talking with his wife or his son? Or to someone else?

I asked, "Did you receive any visits or phone calls that night? Is there anyone besides Tariq who can confirm you were here Tuesday?" Of course, I could never tell her why I asked.

Confusion streaked across her face like a comet. "No, no one called me that evening." Was she lying again? Her phrasing was careful. Not denying she'd made outgoing calls. Certainly to Phil. And then to Tariq at the gallery. She ran a shell-pink nail over the top button of her cardigan, twisting the pearl.

If she was discomfited by my questions, I'd pile on the stumpers. "Tell me about your finances."

She gasped, red blotches staining her face. "How dare you ask such a thing."

I trailed my gaze over the fireplace mantel with its array of family portraits. This house, these fine clothes and fancy cars, the massive tuition at Rome School. Where did they get the money to support the luxuries they enjoyed? Would Melinda open to me? If not, I could dig at Rome School to find how much she earned as a guidance counselor. Phil had been a real estate investor when she met him. Was that still his primary source of income? Could flipping houses haul in enough to support this extravagance?

I clamped my lips, refusing to retract my question. The money mattered.

Melinda's eyes narrowed. "I don't see how that's any of your business." Teeth-chattering cold. Cancel the Junior League meeting, call off the holiday party. Ma'am was pissed.

I said, "I'm putting together pieces of a puzzle. A puzzle that's been blown to smithereens. You don't see how they fit. Neither do I." Maybe she'd hoped engaging with me would show she wasn't involved in Phil's murder. Proof of innocence, OJ-style. Not gonna fly. "You asked for my help. That's what this question is about."

She flung her head against the sofa, blond hair fanning against the mauve cushion. A groan lifted the front of her cardigan. When she straightened, her eyes drilled my face. "Phil's a difficult man, as I'm sure you are aware." Present tense, as if he were still alive. She leaned forward, voice low, maybe threatening. "We've reached a treaty of sorts. A settlement which allows for the smooth running of our marriage. I'm not sharing those details with you. Just the outline."

A dry laugh, then she fiddled the top button of her lilac blouse. "I make a considerable income between my Rome salary and my private clients. Phil handles the money, but I keep a portion in a separate account. I don't need him to cover any costs." She stroked the silky collar, pressing invisible wrinkles as she stared at me.

"Phil's income stream was separate from yours?" I wanted to know how money moved in the Bolden family.

Silence, then a rustle of wool against wool. Her lips shrank in a scowl. Before I could repeat my question, a voice rang from the entry hall: "Melinda, I know we're a tad early. I hope we're not interrupting anything."

# CHAPTER **TWENTY-FIVE**

The entry hall of the Bolden house filled with trampling boots and swishing coats. I looked at the three newcomers. With their tan skin, white blond hair, and large teeth, the family resembled palomino horses. The man continued speaking, his voice bounding to where Melinda Terrence and I sat in the living room. "If we're barging in, just say the word."

Melinda stood from the sofa and stepped around my knees. To broaden my investigation of Phil Bolden's murder, I wanted details about his family finances. The idea of giving me that information made tendons surge like riptides over his widow's fists. I threw mental lightning bolts, hoping the visitors would disappear so I could continue questioning Melinda Terrence.

They didn't budge. The man blared, "Don't mean to intrude. We can come back in a half hour." He shifted a British tan leather attaché case from left to right hand. He glanced at his watch, then at the older of the two women. "All right with you, Eve?"

The woman dashed a hand across her face, brushing raindrops from transparent eyelashes. "Of course." She looked at her watch, then at Melinda. "I suppose we *are* a few minutes early."

The younger woman, a teenager with toffee-colored eyes and a sprinkle of acne, shifted from foot to foot. Her long face and bony figure were a perfect blend of her parents' features. She tugged her yellow ponytail from her parka collar and studied the rug's curlicues.

Melinda crossed to the threesome at the living room entrance. "No worries, Hugh." She shook hands with the man, then the woman. "You're *right* on time." Seizing their elbows, she angled the couple so their backs were to the dining room where the cops were still at work. Staring at me, she added, "I was *just* finishing."

"Of course," I said. I didn't offer my name. Melinda could play hostess if she wanted.

She didn't introduce me, but she did expand on the newcomers. Clipped tones, crisp smiles, no hugs. This was a business appointment, not a condolence call. "The Gaylords are here for an appointment to discuss college placement prospects for Morgan."

The girl blushed and rolled her eyes. She scuffed her feet on the rug, then heaved a tornado of sighs. Teen agony personified.

With pursed mouth, Melinda noted the girl's demonstration. Maybe the counselor was used to these mini-protests. Or perhaps she wanted to use the child's behavior to instruct the parents in the value of her services. Did she want to underline for me the professional nature of this Saturday afternoon meeting? For whatever reasons, her explanation ballooned: "I handle several private clients from my home office. I didn't want to cancel today's appointment, even though the Gaylords kindly offered to postpone. Application deadlines are so tight, I didn't want to lose momentum for Morgan." She shot a glance at the girl, who ignored the barb.

Widow or no, Melinda the college counselor was on the clock. My time was up.

I grabbed my overcoat from the side chair and edged toward the front door.

I didn't merit a formal farewell from Melinda, despite all we'd meant to each other: wives-in-law of a sort. Without a backward glance, Melinda left me standing in the hall as she escorted her visitors to a room beyond the staircase. The four turned right and disappeared through a closed door. Her office, no doubt.

I marched toward the rear of the house, calling Ingrid's name as I went. She and Tariq were huddled on a couch in a media room off the barnlike kitchen. I gave Ingrid the high sign. She kissed Tariq on the cheek and trotted after me. As we passed through the front door, I jiggled the lock to fix it open. I wanted to perform a little trick.

In the courtyard, while Ingrid climbed into my Jeep, I walked around a golden-beige BMW. White leather interior and dashboard, rocket ship instrument panel faced in mahogany with inlaid ebony. The Gaylords' vehicle for sure. As a pre-apology, I patted the aerodynamic front light crystal. Behind the wheel of my own car, I angled my tires and nudged the accelerator. I delivered a kiss to the front bumper of the Gaylords' BMW. The hairline crack in the dent looked angry but not serious.

Satisfied with the ding, I charged through the Boldens' unlocked front door and raced along the hall. Straight to Melinda's office. I knocked once, then barged in.

"Sorry to disturb you folks," I said, fake wheezing, "I think I bashed your car, Mr. Gaylord."

The three adults jumped from their chairs. Hugh Gaylord snapped shut his attaché case before I could glimpse its contents. Eve Gaylord screeched through clamped fingers. Melinda Terrence slammed the door of her wall safe, blocking my view inside. Melinda and Hugh exchanged glances. Guilty looks? Or were they embarrassed by whatever was hidden in the briefcase and safe? Only Morgan Gaylord seemed unaffected by my announcement. The teenager slumped lower in her armchair. She'd been sucking on the end of her ponytail; after watching her parents' reactions, she dragged the hair from her mouth. The damp strands looked like a paintbrush dipped in yellow mud.

Hugh Gaylord recovered first. "What in the world are you talking about?" His hazel eyes narrowed as he tried to place my face.

"I smashed your car. Accidently, of course." I clasped my palms in prayer position. "But I think you should come have a look."

He glanced at Melinda. She waved a hand, the one not clapped on the safe's rotary dial. "Go ahead. See what's the matter. We'll wait here."

Her brow smoothed and lines eased around her lips. She nodded to dismiss me. Before I turned to leave, I saw a photograph of Phil, smiling from a carved ebony frame on the corner of his wife's desk. I felt sick. With what? Rage? Desire? Guilt? Tick all of the above. I ran from the room.

Hugh Gaylord loped after me into the courtyard. Coatless, he shivered through our inspection of the damage to the BMW's bumper. I murmured apologies to him and to the car. He snuffled as he traced a finger over the fracture. I wrote my cell number on the back of my business card and asked for his contact information. His pockets were empty so I gave him a second card and my pen. With ivory fingers, he scribbled his address and phone number. I promised to be in touch. His eyes were streaming, his nose red, and his teeth chattering by the time he escaped into the house. Hugh Gaylord didn't seem as worried about the nicked-up BMW as I was. Maybe he had two more at home. Nice to be loaded.

Ingrid had watched the theater from the Jeep. When I buckled the seat belt, she said, "You did that on purpose." White teeth flashed in the gathering dusk. "Why'd you eff up the Gaylords' ride?"

"I want to talk with the Gaylords about Melinda's consulting business. I want to know why they meet at her home. Why doesn't Melinda work with the daughter in her office. Aboveboard, like with the other students?" I steered toward the end of the long driveway. "This business smells fishy. Like an off-the-books operation all parties want to hide."

Ingrid snorted. "Duh. Of course it stinks. That's how the deal works."

"You know about this?" My squeal was unbecoming for a forty-eight-year-old.

"Sure, some kids know about it. Not everybody. Just the ones with the most money."

"Everyone at Rome has money."

"Not me. Not the other scholarship kids. Obvi."

"Doesn't everyone have equal access to work with Ms. Terrence on college applications?"

"Sure. Equality's a big deal at Rome. One of the core values they keep shoveling. Like integrity, decency, industry. All that shit in the honor code. All Rome kids are equal. Anyone of us can go to her office, check out the catalogues. Sign up for counseling sessions. Meet recruiters. We're all equal at Rome."

"But some kids are more equal than others? Is that it?"

She tapped her forehead. "*Now* you get the picture. Some kids, the ones with superrich parents, get a special invitation. They get on Melinda's List. That's what we call them: Listies."

"Are you on her List?"

"Nah, I told you, the Listies are all big-bucks babies."

"But you know who's on the List."

"Sure, I know some of them. Like, Morgan Gaylord, I know she's a Listy. Her parents are loaded. You think Mr. Gaylord's going to repair that car you dinged back there? *Pfft.* Why bother? He'll buy a new one. No problemo."

"I want to talk with Morgan. Before I tackle her parents."

"I can hook you up."

"Can you set up a meeting with her?"

"Give me a day. Let me text her after she escapes her parents' clutches tonight. I'll see what I can do."

"Think she'll meet with me?"

"After I tell her how you dunked on her old man's ride? Sure. She'll *love* that." Fist daps sealed our deal.

I dropped Ingrid at the steps of her apartment. She promised to text later with plans for our visit with Morgan Gaylord. My ambitions for the end of Saturday night were simple: canned New England clam chowder, toast, and chocolate cake for dinner; hot shower; hit the sack under two quilts, dreamless sleep. Simple goals, well earned.

Three cranks of the can opener, the front door buzzed, short, then long. I recognized the QPD signature. Another buzz. Long, short, short. Cops for sure. I opened the door to Lola Conte, Saturday night goal destroyer. I let her in. What else could I do?

## CHAPTER **TWENTY-SIX**

When I pulled open the front door, Lola Conte looked as happy to see me as I was to see her. Stomping into my hall, she grimaced like I'd kicked her dog. And drowned her cat. She hung her puffer jacket and hat on hooks, easy as a permanent lodger.

The cop blew on her hands to warm them. I decided to needle her with sweetness. Maybe the sugar would cut short her visit. "Nice to see you. What brings Q-Town's finest out on an icy Saturday night?"

I pointed toward the living room sofa. When she sat, I took a cushion at a right angle to hers. For three seconds, I debated lighting the fire. *Nope. Not wasting gas on QPD.*

"I was in the neighborhood. Saw your light on," she lied. "Thought I'd check up on a report from my team."

That sounded like the truth. I figured she'd received notice of my visit to the Bolden house from the cop crew stationed there. I said, "Conte's Heroes don't miss a beat, do they?"

No smile for the weak quip. She tugged at the hem of her navy sweater, unlatching the buckle on her utility belt. I glimpsed red dents on her bare waist. Her forlorn glance toward the kitchen said, *Feed me.* I ignored the hint. With neither food nor drink in the offing, Lola drilled for business. "Yeah, I heard you dropped by the Bolden residence this afternoon. With your little Mexican sidekick in tow."

"Ingrid was born in Princeton. She's as American as me or you. And yes, we paid a condolence call on Melinda Terrence and her son. You surprised?"

"It's police business when a citizen is disturbed in their own home." She ruffled the brown curls at her nape, mimicking the disorder I'd caused.

"Melinda said I disturbed her?"

"She told my officers you damaged a car belonging to her client. A 2020 BMW, I understand." Did the make and model of the vehicle up my offense? But when her coffee-brown pupils glittered, I wondered if Lola enjoyed my tiny act of class warfare.

"It was an accident. I gave him my contact info." Melinda had only mentioned the collision. No report of my bursting into her office? Was she hiding details of her transactions with the Gaylords? More reason to pursue my interview with the daughter, Morgan, if Ingrid could make the arrangements.

Lola pushed to the main event. "Why were you really snooping over there?" She crossed her bony fingers before her chest.

"Simple: Phil Bolden's death matters."

She smirked at my generalization. "Because you're one of the family, right?"

"You know we were briefly married twenty years ago. If that old connection makes me part of the family, then yes."

"Nothing more recent? I saw how you reacted when we delivered the news of his death. You looked pretty broken up."

"You saying old wives can't have fresh emotions?" This conversation was spiraling toward places I wanted kept hidden. Lighting a fire might give me time to curb my feelings and cage my expressions. Grabbing the controller, I toyed with the buttons longer than necessary before setting the fake logs ablaze.

Lola cut past my feint. "I'm saying sometimes bygones are not so bygone." Her eyes crawled over my face, searching for clues. "Here's how I see it: You and your ex meet at that fancy school shindig. The reunion gets more intense than either party planned." She hefted an elaborate shrug, like we were actors in a sophisticated play. "One more round for old times' sake. What's past is past. You know how it goes."

"But that's not how it went." I swung to look her in the eyes. Dryness in my mouth tightened my jaw.

My lie writhed in the air. She nodded then dropped her gaze.

With my denial and no counter facts, she retreated to conjecture. "Yeah, but work with me here. Let's say it *did* go that way. Adultery could be a solid motive for murder."

The fire crackled and spit behind its glass shield. "And in your scenario, who does the murder?"

"I'm looking at either the missus or the son. Together. Independent. What d'ya think?"

I agreed. Melinda and Tariq were on my suspects list, too. But to salve my guilty conscience, I wanted to find a different motive for either one to murder Phil. I couldn't tell Lola that, so I said, "Yes, jealousy or anger might prompt killing."

"Happens all the time," she said, like a jaded cop chewing through a script from *Law & Order*. "On the other hand, jealousy and envy could point to you."

I snorted in derision. "You really going off base like that?"

Her stare pierced me. Sweat dripped along the canal of my spine. I swallowed, hoping she'd believe the heat thumping my cheeks was caused by the fire.

I needed water and a change of subject. Back to sweet mode: "Lola, forgive me. I know this is a professional call, but that's no excuse for being a bad hostess. What can I get you? Soft drink, water, juice?" Grinning, I stood and shuffled around her knees. At the edge of the kitchen, I yelled, "I've got bourbon or scotch, if you want to blow the whistle on the business portion of this visit."

She shouted, "Coke or Pepsi, thanks."

I returned to the living room with two glasses of Coke and a Triscuits box. We sipped in silence for a minute. Lola gobbled the crackers like she hadn't eaten in four days. I felt guilty for starving a public safety officer.

Since she'd turned down the booze, we were still working. My turn to ask questions. I wanted to learn more of the QPD investigation. "Melinda Terrence told me your boys did a thorough job on her office. What did you make of the gun in her safe? Mother and son both had access."

Munching crackers, Lola said, "No report from ballistics yet. So I can't rule the weapon in or out."

I wrinkled my nose. "Okay, but why kill, then return the murder weapon to the safe where your guys were sure to find it?"

"You're itching to tell me." She illustrated by scratching the crook of her arm.

I was. "The Boldens keep a stash of money in the house. Maybe they own several guns for protection. Could be Melinda or Tariq took one pistol, used it to shoot Phil, then disposed of it. That leaves the other gun in the safe for you to find."

"Good point. We'll check state records Monday to see how many weapons are registered to the Boldens." Lola pressed into the sofa cushion, cuddling the Triscuit box in her lap. "Got any more ideas?"

"Dredge Lake Trask for the missing weapon." The body of water behind Kings Cross Tavern was two miles long but only a quarter mile wide. I figured QPD could get the job done by the end of the week. "There's the creek behind Q High, too. But I'd start with the lake. Nearer to the crime scene."

"Of course." She didn't sound pissed with my how-to-suck-eggs suggestions. Maybe chewing Triscuits tamped her outrage.

With Lola at ease, I took my shot. "Melinda gave you a long list of people she employed for various household services. You plan to turn Abbott's Landing upside down looking for all those folks?"

Lola sucked her lower lip. "We have to follow plausible leads." Flat, like a bureaucratic manual. She plucked crumbs from her shirt.

"Sure. I was on the job, too. I know how police procedure goes."

"Then you know we can't skip steps. We got big shots gnawing our tails to find somebody to pin this murder on. The quicker it's solved, the better for everyone. I want my promotion off this case and I intend to get it."

Naked honesty; I liked that in a woman. "I get it. You make your bones with the case you got. Not some dream scenario." When she nodded, I dragged my hand over my chin. "But you know most people in Abbott's Landing have nothing to do with this stickup scenario." A flush spread across both cheeks as her throat bobbled. I pushed: "How I see it, you got a choice. You can go hard with this investigation. Flash metal. Break doors and heads. Maybe shoot up a few apartments executing a search warrant. Drag people from their shops or classrooms or beds. Impress the hell out of the big bosses with shock-and-awe stunts."

As I described the way the neighborhood raid could proceed, Lola winced.

"Or you can go easy," I said. "Make your inquiries, of course. Question the gangbangers on your list. But don't tear up the entire neighborhood in the process."

"And what do you want?"

"I'm asking you to go easy." I upended my glass, swallowed the dregs, then set it on the table.

After a pause, she shook her head. Her eyes were glazed. I thought she'd ditch my request for leniency in handling the Latino community. I read her wrong.

"No guarantees," she said, rubbing her right ear. "I won't soft-pedal this case. We'll do our due diligence. But I don't buy the random robbery theory. I'm guessing you don't, either. For my money, the real motive lies far from Abbott's Landing."

I nodded. We agreed on that. Relief broke like cool surf over my body. My heart slowed and my stomach unknotted. I tossed Lola a thin smile and stuffed my fingers between the cushions to hide their shaking. When she asked for the bathroom, I pointed to the corridor beyond the kitchen. I walked the empty glasses to the sink, dumping ice slivers before I rinsed them.

I hadn't been up-front with Lola Conte, not all the way. Not yet. I didn't want to tell her about my brief reunion with Phil. Not unless that secret became crucial to solving the case. I didn't mention Tariq had access to another gun in the office desk at Spark. I didn't say I'd seen Phil give money to Nadine Burriss, the church treasurer. And I didn't want to share with Lola my information about Melinda Terrence's off-the-books counseling gig. Not until I learned details about that operation and whether Phil Bolden's life was strangled in its processes. For now, my investigation required sidelining the police.

When Lola returned, she walked straight to the hall, where she retrieved her coat. I followed her onto the porch for a fast handshake.

"Don't forget to change your clocks tonight," she said. QPD never stopped serving the public.

"Fall back, yeah. Thanks for the reminder."

No promises to call or check in. No summary of action items for the week ahead. A simple sign-off for the night. I watched her amble to her squad car. We weren't friends, Lola and I. Not colleagues, certainly not pals. If we were lucky, we might become allies, unless this case chewed us to pieces first.

I was in bed forty minutes later when a new thought coasted in: I was keeping important information from Lola Conte. Could she be holding out on me, too? The idea of mutually assured deception rankled. Had she found something but declined to share it with me? I jittered my toes against the quilt. The sheets tangled my legs and sweat beaded between my breasts. A bathroom trip to splash cool water on my neck quieted the troubling notions.

Trickery on my mind, I burrowed into the pillow and sank into sleep.

Much later, my cell phone brayed on the night table. Ingrid's instructions were brief:

Meet Morgan + me tmrw

When?

330pm

Where?

Forum sandwich

Ok

No notes no recording

Ok

Nighty-night

# CHAPTER **TWENTY-SEVEN**

Sunday afternoon dawdled at the Forum Sandwich Shop when I arrived. I guessed Rome students were still in their beds after weekend ruckus. Churchgoers took their families to fancier restaurants. Setting the clocks back an hour Saturday night threw me for a loop. I felt groggy. And blue with the rapid onset of evening darkness. Long nights, long winter, and me without my burrow for hibernation. Thoughts of bed fired images of Phil—brown shoulders draped in ivory sheets, bare foot poking from my quilt. I dragged a hand across my face to dispel the impossible vision.

I looked around the sandwich shop. Only six customers lounged in couples. Good. I wanted as much privacy as possible. The questions I had for Morgan Gaylord might be tough, so I claimed a table on the upper rung of the Forum's circular auditorium. A freckled boy took my Coke order and brought the glass plus unopened can. As I poured, Ingrid and Morgan strutted into the shop. I sent brainwaves until they spotted me.

Arching an eyebrow, Ingrid the matchmaker led the way to my table. She and Morgan were dressed like opposing queens on a chessboard: Ingrid in black joggers and long vegan leather coat, blond Morgan in white puffer jacket and turtleneck over silver jeans. The effect was striking. Other customers stopped chewing to track the girls' procession to the top of the room. My bid for anonymity was shot.

Ingrid ordered a double dose of the Forum's signature milkshake:

the Vesuvius, a fire-red froth flecked with chocolate cookie crumbs. She and Morgan stuck green straws in the aluminum canister and sipped like lovebirds. They chatted about boys and bands, their scarlet-stained lips pursing in approval or disdain. I kept quiet after the first round of greetings; I wanted my approach to seem casual and unthreatening.

After five minutes, Morgan leaned toward Ingrid. "I thought you said she had questions about the List." Like I was in another galaxy.

"Yeah, that's how she works. Real slow." Ingrid's eye roll left me twisting in the wind. "Kinda cringe, but . . ."

More third-person sniping might reduce me to rubble. I jumped in: "Morgan, I want to learn about your college application process."

"Okay, what about it?" She picked flakes from her army-green nail polish.

Start easy. "How did you first get to know Ms. Terrence?"

"My parents made me go to her office before spring break of sophomore year. For a prelim convo, they said."

"Isn't that early?" I remembered Monica's college application journey starting around Halloween of junior year. She already had her heart set on Rutgers, so maybe she didn't feel the need to ramp up sooner. "Not even halfway through high school seems early to me."

"Yeah, that's what I thought, too." She sighed, a red milk bubble glimmering on her lip. She wiped her mouth, then her eyes, smearing liner into raccoon rings. "But my parents are hyper about college. They wanted to get a jump on the whole process. They've been talking at me about going to an Ivy League school since the day I started Rome. About how I needed to make top grades, join clubs, play sports, volunteer with poor people. You know, to make my application stand out."

I saw Ingrid's eyebrows jolt. How did she feel about Morgan's patronizing note on volunteering among the deprived wretches of Queenstown?

No diversion from the main subject. "Did you do that stuff?" I almost said "shit," but repping the adult end of the conversation carried responsibilities.

Morgan grimaced. "I did. For a while." She threw glassy eyes at Ingrid. "I tried Red Cross freshman year and debate sophomore. Gross. And after-school tutoring those underprivileged kids. Total wreckage." She rolled her eyes until the hazel pupils disappeared for a second. "Remember how I went out for chess club last year? Mega disaster."

Ingrid chirped, "Yeah, but at least we met at chess orientation, so something good came out of it, right?"

Morgan nodded, reaching to tighten the spiky knot on top of her head. "I'm not cut out for that joining, do-gooding shit. I screw up everything." Her sigh dwindled to a whine.

I guessed: "But your mom and dad kept pushing?"

"Of course, that's how they are. You'd think Dad would be satisfied getting Hubie—that's my big brother—into Yale." She hiked her shoulders. "And Mom was worse, poking at me every day. Ranting all crazy like they'd die if I didn't get into Harvard, or at least Columbia."

Ingrid patted her friend's fingers. I wondered what dynamic fueled the girls' *Odd Couple* friendship. Did they share a love of graphic novels, music, movies? Ingrid fished a crumpled tissue from her pants pocket and pressed it into Morgan's hand. The girl closed her eyes and wiped her nose. Maybe the protector/victim dynamic drew them together. I could relate; savior mode was my default, too. Morgan needed sympathy; Ingrid delivered, big-time.

Morgan blew a tornado into the Kleenex. Ingrid glowered at me. I figured she wanted me to stop the questions: I was harming her friend. But I needed more details. I ignored her to press Morgan. "And that's when you signed up with Ms. Terrence?"

"No, that was the crazy thing. It was *Melinda* who came to us."

"She contacted your parents?"

"Yeah, by phone. I remember because I was away that weekend, visiting my brother in New Haven. When I got home, Mom said we had an appointment with Melinda for the next Saturday."

"At her house?"

"Yeah. Way weird, right?" Eyes narrowed to golden slits.

"What did Melinda do for you at that first meeting?"

"She was super nice. Talking to me direct. Supportive, you know. Asking me where I wanted to go to college. Large campus or small? Big city or college town? Like she really cared about what I wanted."

"That's good, right?" I asked.

"Yeah, sure. But after two meetings with Melinda, I got the picture loud and clear."

"And that was?"

"This college thing was all about my parents, not me. Not ever. Once I made the List, I never had a private meeting with Melinda. Never went by myself to her office. Or talked one-on-one by phone or Zoom. We only met at her house. Not me. Always the three of us."

"College applications, didn't you fill them out yourself?"

"No, Melinda did that. She asked me questions. Typed the answers."

"Like, coaching? To help you?"

"No. More like writing the damned thing herself, then having me sign it."

"Even the essays?" My voice rose as I remembered how Monica had struggled to write her composition. The tears and hair pulling, the tons of chocolate bars and miles of red licorice. And how proud Monica had been when the battle was won. "Those are supposed to be personal expressions of the applicant's views and life."

"Yeah, sure." Morgan snickered without mirth. "Maybe *some* kids do it that way. But on Melinda's List, *she* did the heavy lifting."

"Do you know how many kids are on her List this year?"

"No, not exactly. I know two others for sure." Morgan raised bleary eyes to Ingrid. "You knew about Harris Jankowski, right? And Adrian Jones."

Ingrid chimed, "One hundred percent. And I think maybe Ellie Bartman, too."

"Yeah, true that." Morgan sniffed. "Ellie's grades are as rotten as mine."

A sob behind red-stained tissues. The truth hurt. Morgan knew she was getting shoved into a fancy college, despite her poor academic record and lousy extracurricular résumé. Maybe other kids on

Melinda's List enjoyed their status as the undeserving rich. But I saw the awareness chewed at Morgan's tender self-esteem.

Morgan whimpered, "We're not brilliant like you, Ingrid."

"Don't knock yourself. You're smart, too." Ingrid flashed teeth, hype-girl perky.

"Yeah, right," Morgan huffed, sarcasm at full blast. "You know it, we know it. We're capital-*L* losers. All us kids on Melinda's List are GPA clowns." She sobbed. "I know what they call us: trust-fund boobies."

Tears dribbled from her chin. Ingrid handed a paper napkin to her friend. Nothing pierced deeper than the taunts of teenage despots. Growing up a cop's kid, I'd been on the receiving end of jibes galore.

I swirled Coke dregs in my glass to give Morgan time to recover. My lungs tightened over a jagged gasp. I didn't want to buy the poor little rich girl mythology. But the ache pinching my heart said I did. I could have quit; I'd done Morgan's spirit enough damage for one afternoon. But I wanted the rest of her insight into the college placement scheme.

Her tears dried, time for the toughest ask: "Morgan, what do you know about the money aspect? What financial arrangements did Melinda make with your parents?"

She shrugged, twisting the soggy napkin in her lap. "They never tell me how much they pay Melinda. I mean, my dad brings money every time we visit her home. In that stupid tan briefcase. You saw it." When I nodded, she continued, "I don't know how much, probably a lot. One time I picked up the briefcase and man, it was heavy as fuck." Her eyes and lips popped in wonder. "You know, maybe a couple hundred dollars each visit."

"Uh-hmm . . . yeah." The number had to be thousands higher. Each session. Far more than a naïve and sheltered teenager could imagine. "Sure, hundreds. You could be right."

Eyes drilling into my forehead, Ingrid halted the interview. She swiveled to her friend. "Don't you have rehearsal this afternoon?" She tapped the cell phone on the table.

Morgan's face flushed with pleasure. "Is it time already?" She turned to me. "I sing with a retro rock band. All-girl group. We call ourselves the Jewels."

Loyal Ingrid added, "The Jewels are great. Your cover of 'Like a Virgin' is amazing."

Morgan blushed more. "I don't know if we're great. But it's tons of fun. That's what I really wanted to do. Sing. I mean, I was even pretty good at it." She frowned, clinching her fist around the green straw. "Going to college was always my parents' crazy dream. I was always going to be a useless fool in college. The joke played on me. Everybody laughing, except me. But singing, yeah, I could have made something with singing."

"Not past tense. Future," Ingrid corrected. "You *will* be amazing." She stood from the table, buttoning her black coat. "We're outta here."

At the shop's entrance, Morgan zipped her puffer jacket while I settled the bill. Small change for the important information I'd received about Melinda Terrence's scheme. In the parking lot, I hugged both girls.

After Morgan got into her sky-blue Triumph convertible, I pulled Ingrid aside for a stronger squeeze. "She going to be okay?" I whispered.

"That was rough." Ingrid twisted from my grasp. "I'll let you know."

As I drove home, I reviewed what I'd learned from Morgan Gaylord. The outline of Melinda Terrence's college scheme sharpened, though gaps remained. Now I knew the counselor collected off-the-books payments from Rome School parents for placing their kids in universities beyond their academic reach. How much money did Melinda make from each placement? How long had the operation been underway? Did she only serve Rome families or were students from other private schools on Melinda's List as well? Who helped her identify the target families? Someone with access to financial information about wealthy parents and the academic records of less-than-stellar students, for sure. A Rome insider had to be the source of those tips. I wanted to find out who.

Morgan's information clarified a second line of investigation.

Now that I knew more about the Bolden family's money source, I wanted to learn if Phil had been involved in the movement of these large sums of cash. Not *if*, but *how*. I remembered Melinda's scanty explanation at her house: "I make a considerable income between my Rome salary and my private clients. Phil handles the money." Phil was involved for certain. Cash in those quantities aroused suspicions. You might pay for a refrigerator in cash, or maybe a sofa. But too many cash transactions raised uncertainties. Doubts from the banks; questions from the taxman. To be functional, big money had to be translated—washed—into a usable form. Cleaning money was dirty business. Had someone knee-deep in this river of cash murdered Phil Bolden? I remembered Melinda's bitter words about Phil's control over the family finances. Could she have killed for her freedom?

# CHAPTER **TWENTY-EIGHT**

A lone white cop blocked entrance to our parking lot behind the Queenstown Pharmacy when I arrived Monday midmorning. I stared at him. Scowling, he touched the crime scene barricade, a hand stroking the wooden cross beam like it was his family pet.

I wanted to check in the office before returning to the Rome School for a second, tougher interview with Charles Dumont. I needed to review my files on the headmaster. I'd first met him when he hired me to recover the school's missing sports trophies eighteen months ago. Then we reconnected at the homecoming gala. Our previous talk had outlined Dumont's connections to the Boldens. But now, armed with Morgan Gaylord's information about a college placement scheme, I wanted to dig deeper with the headmaster.

I considered plowing around the wooden barricade to claim my designated parking spot. Instead I saluted the boy in blue and steered across the street to the lot behind the Heinz Photography Studio. As I got out of my car, Jeff Heinz, the studio owner, jumped from his.

"Q-Town's finest are still at it, I see," Jeff said. He was a big man with a tiny voice. I leaned close to understand him. "Think they'll give up the blockade by tomorrow?"

"No clue." I shrugged. "Only hope for the best." I smiled, raising a hand to shield my eyes from the sun's glare.

"You work with them, don't you? Seeing as you're a private detective and all."

"Sometimes, sure."

"Then you can use your inside connections, get them to lift the crime scene banners. All that black-and-yellow ribbon crimps business." Grinning plumped his cheeks. "Cop-blocks the mood, you might say."

Jeff's was the only formal photography studio in town—if you didn't count the cramped alcove in Target. I figured he enjoyed a monopoly on sweet-sixteen parties and quinceañeras, engagements, weddings, graduations, and family reunions. Every job applicant hoping a new headshot would do the trick; every couple looking for boudoir photos to spice up their limp marriage. Everybody came to Jeff Heinz. I doubted the QPD murder investigation halted traffic to his storefront.

But to be neighborly, I went along. "You finding visitors shy away from a murder scene?"

"Hah, no." Spurts of laughter jiggled his belly. "Opposite, in fact. My parking lot's jammed most afternoons with sightseers. Out-of-towners, mostly. I hear them re-creating the attack, playacting the events like they heard on the TV news. Guy that got shot was a big deal, you know."

"Yeah, I heard," I said, rushing to a new point. "I call them disaster tourists."

Jeff nodded, pulling his stocking cap from his head. "Kinda ghoulish, right?" Steam puffed in a pink aura from his bald scalp. He jabbed an elbow toward the rear entrance. "You want a cup of coffee? My sister gave me one of those pod coffee makers for my birthday last month. The contraption looks like a high school science project, but damned if it don't brew a first-rate cup in no time flat."

As I waited in the photo studio's reception area, I could hear Jeff fussing in the kitchenette. Smells were promising, so hope grew. I'd been in the space before; cheery reds and turquoise brightened the room. Jeff's photos decorated the walls, promising that if you held still and followed the artist's instructions, you, too, could be as airbrushed and windblown as the gorgeous people in these portraits.

One framed work stood out among the photographs: a watercolor painting of a bouquet of flowers. I walked closer. Jeff Heinz's cramped signature was scrawled in the lower right corner of the paper. As I studied it, the spray of pastel blooms interspersed with feathers snagged a memory. I'd seen this flower arrangement recently. Where? Not in a photo or book. The real thing. I bent for a new angle. The bouquet burst from a vase on a splintered wooden stool. Jeff had captured the shimmering glass with skill. Light reflecting from crystal facets jogged my mind. I recognized the source. This was a painting of the flower-and-feather arrangement I'd seen in the entrance hall of the Bolden house last Saturday. The same petals shaded soft blue and mauve. The same unnatural plumage tinted milky green and lavender. Did Jeff Heinz know the Boldens? How had he come to paint their strange bouquet?

Jeff crossed the room carrying two mugs. I took the one smelling of pumpkin spice and turned toward his painting. "This is wonderful, Jeff."

He beamed. "I told you my machine made good coffee."

"Yes, thank you, it's great," I said. "But I mean, this watercolor painting. It's beautiful."

"Oh, yeah. I'm pretty proud of that." His grin widened. "I've been a photographer since I was thirteen, but I always wanted to try my hand at painting."

"When did you do this?"

"Last April I took a class in watercolor painting at the community center. Tuesdays and Thursdays for six weeks. Each Tuesday the teacher would bring in a new subject."

"New subject?"

"You know, like, a model. Only we never did live people. Sometimes she'd bring in a bowl of fruit or a wood statue. Once she brought pottery candlesticks from Mexico. Another time a basket of acorn squash."

"And this bouquet. It's unusual." I tipped my mug at the lively painting.

"Yeah, that mix of flowers and feathers isn't something you see every day, is it? A friend of Laurel's brought it in for our class that day."

"Laurel?"

"Our teacher, Laurel Vaughn. Maybe you know her. That lady's got loads of talent. For her day job, she teaches art at the Rome School."

"Yes, I know Laurel Vaughn." My heart thumped in my throat.

"Like I said, she's a heckuva talented lady. And a good teacher, too. Well, one Tuesday, she arrives with a friend of hers toting this crystal vase filled with this bouquet." He gazed at his work. "Right away I loved the oddity."

"Yes, I can see that," I said. "Plucked from a fantasy garden."

He hummed. "The way the feathers seem like they're from outer space. Or a landscape in one of those video games."

"You captured that eccentricity perfectly." Laying it on thick. After he beamed, I added, "You said Laurel's friend brought the flowers. Do you remember who it was? Maybe I know them, too." I figured the art teacher had coaxed her chum Melinda Terrence to lend the fancy arrangement.

"I didn't catch the name." Jeff raised his eyes to a corner of the room, picturing his April class. "Tall, good-looking Black kid, sort of café au lait color." He shrugged.

Tariq Bolden, for sure. I said, "Probably a kid she knew from school." As excitement buzzed nerves along my forearm, the mug shook. Could this news complicate the puzzle I was fitting?

"Yeah, maybe a student. Anyway, that boy was strong as Superman. He struggled with that vase, though. It was heavy as all heck. Lead crystal is no joke, I tell you what."

"Jeff, you did a beautiful job of capturing the facets of the vase. Just stunning."

A few more compliments, another slurp of coffee, and I was out the door. I added Laurel Vaughn to my list of Rome School targets for the morning. I knew Tariq had taken classes with her. She admired his artistic talent. Was there more to the involvement of teacher and student?

The flag at the front entrance of the Rome School flew at half-mast. Wind whipped the banner as I darted inside the heavy doors. I was glad to see Phil's death acknowledged in this way. A token gesture, but the school knew its duty.

In the lobby, I stopped to inspect a large oil portrait of Phil that had been installed above the guard's station since my last visit. Another official obligation checked. The painting erased the gray from Phil's sideburns and moustache, rendering a perfect picture of the man I'd married twenty years ago. He looked handsome in a peacock-blue suit cut to display a bold chest and robust neck. Cheeks raised on the verge of smiling, shiny eyes poised to wink. A black swag covered the top of the frame and draped both sides.

As I walked below the painting, space around my heart shrank until my ribs ached. My jaw tensed, dry tongue stuck in my mouth. Everything hurt. Run away now. Interview Dumont and Vaughn another time, a day when Phil's death didn't stab with such ferocity. Maybe I'd return, a hundred years from now.

I wriggled my hands to disperse the tension. No ducking, no dodging. Phil was my client. I needed answers to quell the churning in my gut. In front of the closed door to the headmaster's suite, I clenched and released my fists, bobbing on flexed knees, ready to enter the boxing ring. I figured this second round with Dumont would be rougher than our first meeting. Then, we'd mimicked cordiality; now I was set to land real blows. I burst through the outer office. The assistants tried to catch my eye, grabbed my elbow. I jerked from their grasp. I'd discover for myself if Dr. Dumont was receiving visitors. Three raps on the boss's door pushed my politeness past the limit; I charged in before he had time to respond.

# CHAPTER **TWENTY-NINE**

When I burst into his office, Charles Dumont was seated at his boat-size desk, the admiral of his fleet. His cream-and-green-striped tie was knotted to choke. The rolled cuffs of his white shirtsleeves revealed muscular forearms. A wafer-thin gold watch floated on his left wrist. His black wool suit jacket was flung on the sofa.

To seize the moment, I sat next to the coat, smoothing razor-sharp lapels and folded sleeves.

"Charles," I said. "We need to talk. Now." Cool, hard, like I owned the show.

The boy assistant fluttered in, apologies tripping from his mouth. Dumont waved him off. "It's all right, Edward. Close the door."

Grimacing, the headmaster stood. I thought he'd join me on the couch, but he took a chair at the oval table. As he walked, I noticed physical anomalies I'd missed during our last visit. Irregularities camouflaged by his suit jacket. His left shoulder jutted two or three inches higher than his right. The left hand swung higher on his flank than the right hand. I guessed scoliosis. The tailoring of his suits disguised a congenital curvature of the spine. I had his life-altering costume in my grasp. I slipped a finger along the inside of the jacket's collar. His crisp scent of pine and orange flowers rose from the fabric. Expensive cologne. I saw a beige silk label with the purple embroidery of an exclusive London haberdashery. The man knew how to flash a bankroll: subtle luxury to avoid envy but convey power. Smart. These exquisite suits hid his torqued spine. Was he hiding more?

"What do you want, Vandy?"

I matched my sneer to his. "Straight answers, Charles." My perch on the sofa kept my head below Dumont's. Not good. I crossed to the table and sat opposite him, eyes level.

He met my stare. "I've never given you anything but the truth."

"As far as it goes." I squared an issue of *Ovid*, the school literary magazine, on the wood surface. "Now I want the rest."

"What do you want." Repeating without the inflection. He was angry. Red flecked the whites of his eyes. Under chalky skin, black bristled on his jawline. "I have an emergency virtual meeting with the board of trustees this afternoon. I can give you fifteen minutes."

I leaned forward. "You'll give me as much as I need. Understand?" When he gulped, I said, "Tell me about Melinda's List."

Dumont shifted on his haunches. "I don't know what that is."

"Yes, you do. You're head of this school. You know every detail of the curriculum and every corner of the physical plant. You know who scored touchdowns in last Friday's game. You know what every administrator and teacher does each hour of the day. You know what the janitor ate for lunch."

I sacrificed a fingernail to carve a divot in the table's polished surface. "So, here's what I know: Melinda Terrence picks a handful of students for special treatment each year."

He sputtered, "I—I don't think that's true. Melinda is a fine counselor. She gives excellent guidance to all our students." Composure regained, he delivered a canned speech. "We've had a college placement rate that exceeds ninety-eight percent for the past six years. That puts Rome in the top percentile of independent schools in the region. We rank with Hun and Peddie, just below Lawrenceville." Satisfaction shone from his eyes. Bragging about the place of his school among the leading prep academies in the region wound him up.

I wanted to cut him down. "As you told me, there are three thousand universities and colleges in the United States. I'm sure any Rome student who wants can find a place in one of them. Not in the most prestigious universities, of course. But somewhere."

He doubled down. "Melinda is an exemplary administrator."

Fingers on the oak surface sounded like startled roaches scrabbling for cover.

I said, "But she treats some students to a megadose of her superior skills. Each year she identifies a few students for special treatment. She gives them counseling during after-hours sessions at her home. She helps them complete their college applications. She goes above and beyond with this chosen handful."

"How do you know this?" Sweat stained his shirt collar. Wet crescents darkened his armpits. "Did she tell you?"

I shook my head. "How I learned this isn't important. Focus on what else I know: Melinda takes money directly from the families of students on her List. And she pays university admissions officers to admit the students she recommends." I didn't know that last part, not for sure. But bribes to admissions officers were the only way to make sense of the scheme. I'd dig for proof later if I needed it.

"That's an outrageous charge." Dumont's eyes bulged and the crests of his cheeks flashed red. "You're accusing her of criminal acts." I'd struck a bull's-eye.

"Your words, not mine, Mister Headmaster."

His panting increased. "You have no proof."

"I have eyewitnesses. This isn't a legal proceeding. Not yet."

Lower lip protruded like a second tongue. "Go on then. Why do you imagine I know anything about the operation?"

"Because Melinda needs a source of information. She can't pick students to target from thin air. She needs to know how much the parents can afford to pay before she makes the call."

I pushed from the table and walked to Dumont's desk. I stroked a finger along the top of his computer. "I want to know how she identifies those families."

He tracked my movements with twitches of lids and mouth, his head oscillating like a lizard's. As I caressed the monitor, his right fist curled and uncurled. I'd come to his office ready to fight. Now he'd joined the fray.

When he said nothing, I continued.

"No comment? Then I'll tell you: each spring you comb your databases looking for the perfect targets." I tapped the computer screen. "You want families who are filthy rich. Almost everyone at Rome has money. You can tag people who have more money than Daddy Applebucks." I scratched at a speck of dirt on the mouse, then puffed to lift dust from the keyboard.

Dumont gasped. He shook his head, blinking to a slow inner drumbeat. After a moment, his focus returned to me.

I pounded. "Then you sort for those super-loaded parents whose kids are underperforming. Students with weak academic records. Those are your marks. Parents who are most susceptible to this scheme. They fear that without Melinda's help, their children won't get into a top university. Or any university. They worry they'll be labeled 'losers' because they produced inferior children. Desperate people like that will pay hundreds of thousands of dollars to buy a place for their kid in a top college."

Dumont's voice gurgled from his throat. "Even if what you say is true, why would I participate in such a scheme?"

My tongue dabbed my lower lip. "Money. The simplest, dirtiest motive of all."

"Money? You think I take bribes?"

"I know you do." I strode to the sofa and hoisted his suit jacket by the collar. "This is custom tailoring. High-quality work." I ran a finger over the buttonhole in the lapel. "I know about sewing. My mother was a seamstress. I recognize the superior skills it takes to achieve this."

I turned the jacket inside out. Triangles of wadding nestled under the lining at the seams of the right shoulder. Discreet layers molded to a custom shape, each seedlike stitch laid by an expert hand. Aided by this art, Dumont's twisted body was refashioned into handsome symmetry.

"This takes superb talent." I prodded a tight pad. "And talent like this takes money. Lots of it."

Slumping in his chair, Dumont fiddled the brass tacks lining its leather arm. After a minute, he moaned then glanced out the window at the campus below. Breath rattled from his sunken chest. "All my life I wanted this—this deformity—to go away. Wished for it, prayed for it." He rubbed the knob of his offending left shoulder.

"In these suits, I can look like everyone else. Like a whole man." A gulp of air. "Instead of a monster."

His eyes reddened. Tears clung to the lower lids, refusing to fall. "This was a way to get the money I needed."

"How much did Melinda give you?"

"Ten percent of whatever the families paid." He looked up, lips thinned to a gray stripe. "But it wasn't Melinda who delivered the money." The line split, pink tongue flickering. "It was Phil Bolden."

# CHAPTER **THIRTY**

Dumont's strike about Phil Bolden jolted me. Phil was more than a financial adviser to his wife. If the headmaster was right, Phil was the linchpin of the college scheme.

My vision blurred, ten seconds at most. To halt my stagger, I gripped the edge of the conference table. I hoped he hadn't caught my stumble. I'd figured Phil was involved in the admissions racket somehow, but this new angle threw me. Was Phil's pivotal role the motive for his murder?

I glanced at Dumont. Sweat traced a pasty streak beside his left sideburn. I coughed, then mumbled his bombshell: "Phil Bolden was the bag man for your college application operation?"

Did the headmaster know I was Phil's ex-wife? Perhaps Melinda had told him. Or maybe Laurel Vaughn had spread the gossip. I wanted to keep Dumont's understanding to that minimum. Holding the upper hand in this exchange was my priority. Contain my emotions, win this round. The headmaster's eyes fixed on the darkening campus beyond his office window. With his mind rambling, I hoped my momentary lapse was covered.

Dumont swung his gaze to me. "You make it sound like the pitch for a heist movie." His lip curled. When he unrolled his shirtsleeves, I saw tiny initials, CDD, embroidered in green on the French cuffs. He drew gold cuff links from his pants pocket and fastened the doubled cuffs. "Who's your star? Jamie Foxx or Will Smith?"

I ignored the sneer. If I engaged, my advantage would crumble. "Were Phil's deliveries in cash?"

"Yes, that's the way we both preferred. They say money is dirty. But without a paper trail, cash is the cleanest way to turn a transaction."

No argument from me. "How often did Phil make deliveries?"

Dumont walked to the couch and lifted his prize garment. He examined the lapel, maybe searching for PI cooties. He scraped an invisible blot from the wool. "Deliveries were irregular. As you might imagine, parents paid Melinda at odd times. Upon completion of services."

I said, "How do you know you got your fair share? If you don't know how much the parents paid or when, you can't be sure you received your proper cut of what the Boldens collected."

"That is technically correct. I can't be certain." Dumont swung the jacket behind his crooked back, thrusting his arms into the sleeves in two graceful movements. "The arrangement was for ten percent. A reasonable share." As he pulled the garment forward, the fabric molded to his body. "But I retained leverage in our arrangement."

"How so?"

He tugged the jacket hem. White shirt cuffs jutted one inch from the sleeves, revealing a sliver of gold cuff links. Once more clad in his superhero costume, Dumont resumed, "I know enough of the Boldens' scheme to do great damage to them if I choose. On occasion, I reminded Phil of my insights. He understood if he attempted to deceive me, I could bring the whole operation crashing around their heads."

"But you'd be crushed, too. If it fell apart publicly, you'd be ruined."

"Perhaps. But I could tell a sad story of extortion and pressure tactics that compelled my compliance in a scheme I loathed." He widened his eyes and fluttered black lashes. "Who do you think the public would believe?" He extended both palms, weighing the options. "Me, the respected head of a distinguished academic institution?" Lips curled from pink gums as if tasting rancid milk. "Or the

Boldens, white trash from Wilkes-Barre and a mongrel hustler from the slums of Trenton?"

"You'd lie to destroy the Boldens?"

"If necessary, yes." Dumont adjusted a kelly-green display handkerchief in his breast pocket. "In fact, I stated this to Phil last week. He told me Melinda was pushing him to end the arrangement."

"She wanted out?" I rubbed a throbbing spot between my eyes. When Dumont clocked the gesture, I dropped my hand.

"Yes. He said she was weary of the work and wanted to quit. I reminded him we all made handsome profits from the operation. I told him if she tried to disentangle from our arrangements, I would expose them."

"What was Phil's answer?" I imagined he was furious, his anger directed at both the arrogant headmaster and his own unruly wife. Was this the context in which Phil had turned to me? Had my bed been his venue for revenge? My stomach vaulted at the idea. I smoothed perspiration into the curls at my hairline.

Dumont shrugged. "He said he would talk with Melinda. The way he ground his teeth indicated their discussion wouldn't be pleasant." A flicker of his tongue sealed a smile. He was enjoying my distress. "I've never married. But I imagine conflicts between spouses are so ferocious precisely because they are so intimate."

Straightening his tie, he walked to the desk. He shot his left arm to expose the gold watch. "Vandy, as lovely as our conversation has been, I must bring it to a close." His words were ice shards dipped in honey. "I told you I have a video conference with the board. We'll discuss establishing a scholarship in memory of Phil Bolden. One of Rome's most distinguished alumni, struck down in his prime. I'm sure it will be a tremendous fund-raiser for the school, don't you agree?"

I walked to the corner of the desk. "I have a few more questions, Charles." Return jab, land a punch. *What other families were on Melinda's List? How long had the college placement scheme been in operation?* I wanted to keep him on the ropes.

His block was swift. "And I have some advice for you." Dumont squared his shoulders and thrust his face close to mine. "If you pursue this line of inquiry, I will make sure your student friends at Rome pay a heavy price."

"My student friends?"

"Yes, I believe you are close to Ingrid Ramírez?" He smiled, mouth gaping black. "In fact, you met Ingrid and her dear friend Morgan Gaylord yesterday at the Forum, did you not?" He flashed canines when I gulped. "I understand you treated the girls to a round of that hideous red drink, Vesuvius. Correct?"

I sputtered, "W-what? . . . How?"

"You're not the only one with friends in the student body, Vandy. I have a cohort of young people who are happy to gather information for me. I assure you, I wouldn't be able to run Rome as efficiently as I do without the assistance of my legion of loyal followers."

Repulsive insect. I said, "You bribe students to snitch on other kids?"

"You make it seem so tawdry. But yes, that's the crude outline." He whisked his coat sleeve, chuckling. "Sounds like the pitch for another film, doesn't it? Who would you cast? Timothée Chalamet? Selena Gomez?"

My nasty reply was interrupted by a knock on the door. Dumont's girl assistant poked her head into the crack. "Sir, your meeting is about to start."

He beckoned her. "Thank you, Bethann. I'm ready." She rushed to his desk to poke at the computer keyboard.

"All set for you to sign in, sir," Bethann said, looking at the screen.

The headmaster glared at me through black lashes. "Will you escort out Ms. Myrick, thank you."

The assistant hesitated, maybe assessing how much resistance I'd offer. I gathered my coat, smiling. No civil disobedience today.

Dumont added, "Then, please check the class schedule of a student, Morgan Gaylord. I want Morgan in my office immediately after the conclusion of this meeting."

My stomach plunged. What did he intend to do to Morgan? Threaten disciplinary action? Contact her parents? Warn her to avoid me? Certainly, nothing the emotionally fragile teen would want to hear. Should I defy Dumont, stage a sit-in? But that would further harm Morgan and Ingrid, perhaps Tariq Bolden as well.

The assistant chirped, "Yes, sir," and stepped to my side. Pausing at the office door, I glanced at Dumont.

In command again, he leaned toward the computer, his profile lit by the screen's watery glow. His lips stiffened into a grimace. Satisfaction—no, triumph—shone from his hooded eyes. Dumont had shared details of the college admissions scheme with me to display his power. He did it as a dare. Challenging me to retaliate. He calculated I was paralyzed. That I wouldn't use the information I'd collected from him because I wanted to protect the students I cared about. He was right.

I trudged the corridor away from the headmaster's suite. In the hall bathroom, I stood at the bank of sinks between two white girls in bulky sweaters. As I washed my hands, they fished in makeup bags. My interview with Charles Dumont had not gone as I'd wanted. I'd learned plenty about the scheme run by Melinda Terrence. I'd discovered the depth of Phil Bolden's involvement in his wife's operation. But I'd endangered the kids whose information had opened the path.

I glanced at the girls beside me. Giggling, they dabbed rose or coral gloss on mouths and cheeks. I blinked as steel braces, strong brows, and purple bra straps swirled in the mirror. They seemed so young, so free. Thoughts fled to Morgan Gaylord. I wanted to text her a warning about Dumont, but I didn't know her number. I could contact Ingrid. Bad idea. I'd done enough damage for the day. I hoped Morgan possessed the strength to endure whatever pressure Headmaster Dumont might exert.

I wanted my next interview to yield more information. And no threats to people I cared for. Zipping my jacket against the sharp gusts, I crossed the courtyard in search of art teacher Laurel Vaughn.

# ART FOR
# HEART'S SAKE

# CHAPTER **THIRTY-ONE**

I dawdled across the slate pavers of the courtyard, kicking at pebbles lodged in the ribbons of ice. Slow steps evened the pitching that roiled my stomach. I wanted time to formulate my questions for Laurel Vaughn. And to disperse the foul odor from my disastrous meeting with Charles Dumont. The headmaster had staggered me, threatened my student friends and dealt unexpected information about Phil Bolden's large role in his wife's college placement scheme. I needed a win from this second interview with Laurel. And a new direction for my investigation.

As I neared the art studio, the door burst open. Kids spurted from the building in clumps of threes and fours. Faces shiny, voices shrill, plaid-flannel arms wrapped around backpacks and portfolios.

In our first meeting, I'd learned the art teacher was a friend of Melinda Terrence. Were they more than work mates? Laurel had defended Melinda, explained her behavior, lambasted Phil Bolden. The couple's son, Tariq, was a student in Laurel's class; she'd praised him for his artistic insight. Photographer Jeff Heinz told me Laurel had borrowed home décor from the Bolden family and enlisted Tariq as her porter. To learn more about her interactions with the Boldens, this second interview would have to be rougher. But Laurel would bolt unless delicacy guided my touch.

When I stepped inside the classroom, a girl with tiger-striped hair stood in front of the teacher's desk, flinging hands toward the windows. I waited near the door until the scowling student exited.

Laurel beckoned me, the loose sleeves of her smock flapping around her arms. "Another case of genius thwarted," she said. As I gained the desk, she rolled her eyes. "Kristy believes she deserves better than the C-plus I gave her on the most recent exercise." Laurel tilted a cardboard panel toward me. "You be the judge."

I glanced at the swirl of ochres and olive pocked with blue gravel and blotches of salmon. "You were generous," I said. "Grading on a curve?"

Laurel grunted through clenched teeth. "According to Kristy, if she gets anything lower than an A in this course, her GPA will tumble. So *I'm* the wicked witch, a direct threat to her chances of getting into a good university." A harsh laugh. "Sometimes I wonder if it's worth the grief teaching students at a college-prep school like Rome."

"On the lookout for easy As, right?" I said. "When I was in school, we took 'Rocks for Jocks' to boost weak averages."

Unsmiling, Laurel swiveled in her chair to flip the switch of the electric pot on the credenza behind her. Fishing in a flower-strewn wooden box, she dropped tea bags in two mugs, then turned to me. "You'd be surprised how violent some of these kids get. Three times last year I had to fend off attacks. One boy waved a box cutter in my face; a girl pulled a penknife. Another kid shoved me against the wall and ripped the collar on my blouse. Several sent texts threatening rape."

I'd worked law enforcement in a hard city and a tough university. Still, I was shocked. "Don't you report them?"

"To whom? The administration?" She snorted, a drop of bile at the corner of her mouth. "These darlings are the protected sources of Rome's income. Who will discipline them?"

"That's horrific."

"They take art because they've been told these are 'gut classes.' Then when their privilege is outraged, they come at me."

"I had no idea you faced that kind of danger." My voice quivered.

Laurel pointed at the bookcase. "You see that fruitcake tin?" I nodded. Gold with red and green ribbons across it. "Looks like sweets from Grandma, right? Well, I keep a Smith & Wesson revolver, just in case."

Her face hardened as she stared at the enameled box. "You carry a weapon, don't you? In your line of work, it's mandatory, right?"

I gulped. I didn't want to reveal too much. "I used to, when I was a police officer."

"And now?"

I'd never tell her how rage at my daughter's death had pushed me to pistol-whip a Rutgers student. That only brute restraint by fellow officers had stopped me from killing the boy. That, on the day I'd resigned, I vowed never to carry a gun again. For love of Monica, I'd locked the weapon in my office safe. I removed it only for periodic target practice. I hated the gun, feared its hold on me, the lure of its power. But every other week, I swallowed the nausea and logged forty-five minutes of target practice. By the time I finished each session at the firing range, the slime of sweat on the grip turned my stomach and greasy fumes snaking from its barrel drove water to my eyes. Since my return to Queenstown, I'd shared this story with only one person, Keyshawn Sayre. Had Key passed these details to Laurel, his new girlfriend?

I sketched the bare outline. "Now I have a license. But I stow the weapon in a safe at my office. I figure a gun is an invitation to violence. If I'm carrying, danger flows in both directions. I'm safer unarmed." My gut twisted over the second half of the equation: And so is everyone around me.

Laurel chewed flakes from her lower lip, eyes tightened to slits. Giving her this minimal answer now might earn me more information going forward. Unlike my slugging match with Headmaster Dumont, this interview with Laurel required finesse.

I redirected the conversation to glean the Bolden family insights I wanted. "But at least you find a few standout students, ones with real talent. Like Tariq Bolden."

Worked. Below her russet curls, rose bathed her face. "Yes, Tariq is special. Every once in a great while you click with someone and through them you view the world with a fresh perspective." Her fingers flew to her throat then her mouth as if to contain smiles skipping there.

Laurel's flush wasn't maternal, but I misunderstood her on purpose.

"For sure, Tariq is special. He's got such a bright, unusual mind. A kid like Tariq can change your outlook on life." I poked further. "Having a daughter gave me so many insights. Ones I'd never have discovered on my own." Images of eight-year-old Monica, sassy in her red snowsuit, collecting icicles to cool our after-school tea danced in my head. Then I dropped, "Do you have children?"

Laurel squinted, color draining from her cheeks. "No, that never happened for me. Marriage either. Not that the two must be connected these days." A twitch lifted the left side of her mouth. Steam bustled from the electric pot. Filling both mugs, she asked, "Sweet or savory with your tea?" She pointed toward cartons stacked on a bookcase shelf. "I've got gingersnaps, chocolate chip, or cheesy thins."

I took two ginger cookies plus the paper napkin she offered. Accepting the change of subject, I steered in a different direction. "This morning, I spoke with one of your most satisfied students, Jeff Heinz."

"Heinz? I'm not sure . . ." She shook her head.

"Jeff owns the photo studio on Abbott Street. He took an adult night class you taught last spring at the Q-Town community center. Watercolors."

As I spoke, images of Jeff's painting jarred loose another memory: I'd seen a different watercolor rendition of this same bouquet in the office of Bethel AME treasurer Nadine Burriss. Private-eye nature abhors coincidences. Making sense of flukes was my prime business. I knew the art connection between Burriss and Laurel had to be real. But was it important?

"Ah, yes. That class was an absolute hoot. Seniors are the best." Laurel's eyes glinted with pleasure. "Enthusiasm and dedication made up for failing sight and shaky hands."

"Aging is not for the fainthearted," I said, matching her grin.

I wanted to learn about Laurel's activities beyond the Rome School. "Do you teach many night classes there?"

"I teach outside classes each semester. And I work on commissions for private clients as opportunities arise." She sipped through pinched lips.

I cheered in working-class solidarity. "A girl's got to make ends meet. Who's your latest client?"

"Right now, I'm painting a large oil canvas commissioned by a new housing development in Trenton. It's an abstract cityscape celebrating the capital's history as an industrial force."

Could this be the neighborhood reclamation scheme so near and dear to Nadine Burriss's heart? I asked, "Is this new project in the Sutton Hill section of Trenton?"

"Why, yes, it is." Laurel's eyes popped. "You've heard of it?"

I said, "I have contacts all over Mason County." I studied my fingernails to ape modesty. How to probe Laurel's connection to Nadine?

Before I formed the question, the art teacher blurted her answer. "Funny thing is, I met the woman who is the dynamo behind the Sutton Hill restoration in my adult class last spring. She's a finance officer at one of the Black churches in Q-Town. Nadine Burriss. Maybe you know her." Embarrassment clogged her face. "I mean . . . not that you *must* know her. Of course, every Black person doesn't know every other Black person . . . I just . . ." She fumbled to the end of her thought.

I nodded, keeping my face neutral. "Nadine? Of Bethel AME? Yes, we've met."

Laurel gaped, big teeth flashing in relief. "Nadine wasn't the strongest student. Watercolor is difficult. Control was her toughest challenge." Headshake, sip, then a sigh. "But she was so determined. Nadine had such passion for the work, almost an obsession. So I suggested she take my pen-and-ink drawing class. We got to talking. I showed her my own work. And, next thing you know, she offered me a commission."

"Boom, just like that. And nice coin, too, I bet."

Laurel's eyebrows flew. She sniffed at my crass conjecture. "I do not sell my talent cheaply. Only amateurs undervalue their art. And I am not an amateur." Stiff, like she wanted to slap me. "So, yes, it's true. Nadine has been quite generous." She slipped her hand into the pocket of her smock. I watched the fabric flex as if she were stroking the adult money this commission would bring. "But my real satisfaction comes from contributing to community improvement."

"Certainly." I yielded the point. No arguing with people's purses.

Now that Laurel was pliable, I pushed for confirmation of her link to the Boldens. "Jeff Heinz showed me the watercolor he made of an unusual flower arrangement you brought for the class to paint. It was a bouquet of aqua and coral feathers and flowers in a crystal vase."

"Oh, of course. Such a bold, spectacular display," Laurel said. "I knew my students would adore it. I asked Melinda to lend the bouquet to me for the class."

"Jeff said Tariq Bolden delivered it."

"Well, yes . . . that's right." Laurel broke a chocolate cookie, furrows trembling between her eyes. "You keep mentioning Tariq. Why? What are you driving at?"

I chipped a crescent from my gingersnap. When Laurel shifted on her chair, I said, "Nothing. I'm driving at nothing at all."

"I don't believe you. You want to say something. Imply something." Finger jutting, cheeks concave around a sour taste. "Something nasty or untoward. You want me to stop seeing Tariq. Is that it?"

That threw me. I didn't know where she was headed. Soothing words bubbled up. "He's taking your class. How can you avoid seeing him?" I widened my lids to mimic innocence. "And he's a family friend, right?"

She leaned against the desk, rushing toward the solution I'd offered. "Yes, that's it. Exactly. Tariq is a family friend, the son of my best friend. Why shouldn't I look out for his welfare, guide him, worry about his future?" Insistence pointed toward intense emotions.

"You've told me how gifted he is." I launched a lie to push the issue. "I saw that talent for myself when I visited the Spark gallery last week. His giant canvas of those rock stars was magnificent." I hadn't seen Tariq's work, only heard descriptions of the painting from Ingrid Ramírez and the gallery's owner, Joe Kidd. They were enthusiastic. Did Laurel feel the same?

I struck fire. Laurel exploded. "That horror show is utter crap.

The worst kind of drivel." She slammed the desk; the cheese-cracker box jittered. "Tariq has so much to offer the world. A discerning eye expressed through a fine hand. But he squanders his gifts on that crass piece of shit. That hideous rock-and-roll canvas is his fuck-you to his father."

I raised a hand to staunch the rant, but she flowed. "Phil Bolden is to blame for that debacle. If he'd offer even a morsel of encouragement, Tariq would feel supported. He'd believe in himself. He'd be able to follow the arts career he truly wants. It's his calling, his dream, his destiny."

Why refer to Phil in the present tense? Did Laurel believe his malign power over Tariq's future continued despite his murder? I folded the corner of a napkin over the cookie scraps, then stamped them with my thumb.

"Phil's gone," I whispered. I studied murky ripples in my mug.

Laurel blinked, her tirade dammed. "Yeah, okay . . ." Slowly, peering through a fog. "I guess . . ." She looked at me, fire banked under stiff lids. "But Tariq still feels the pull of that repulsive canvas at Spark. He still works on it. I know he does. He won't quit it. He could come back. But he won't."

I coughed, soft, then ragged.

Laurel shook her head. "It's as if he's a prisoner. Captured by Phil. Obsessed by that horrid painting. Enchanted by some grotesque spell." Muttering, she stared across the studio to the forest of empty easels behind me.

Three seconds to gulp my cold tea, twenty seconds to apologize for interrupting her day, a minute to button my coat as Laurel escorted me the length of the room. Hustling my exit, she steered toward the door with a surprising grip on my elbow. She had hands like a railroad pile driver. I was as happy to leave as she was to see me go.

In the school's lobby, I stopped before Phil Bolden's portrait. In the afternoon sun, his eyes seemed burnished to cognac. I heard murmurs in the distance, but the entrance was empty. I smiled at the painting. *Not a week yet, Phil. Give me more time.* Like a superstitious fool, I hoped he felt satisfied with my work that afternoon. I grazed the humpback of an upholstered chair and looked around. Chatter from the hall grew louder.

I studied Phil's image. He was my client, so I assessed the day's work as he might have done. In contrast to the first interview with Charles Dumont, this intense second meeting was a net loss. I'd learned plenty of new details about Phil's role in the college placement scheme. But the headmaster had gained an advantage by exposing my connections to several Rome students. Dumont now saw me as a threat. What would he do to check me?

And what to make of my unsettling conversation with Laurel Vaughn? My stomach jittered as I raked over the twists the art teacher had tossed. I needed time to unravel these knots. According to Laurel, church treasurer Nadine Burriss was spreading big money around the Trenton redevelopment project. And what was behind Laurel's fierce defense of Tariq Bolden's artistry? She admired Tariq, pitied his mother, despised his father. Were these passions ferocious enough to fuel violence? *Your case is breaking me in places I never knew were cracked, Phil. I need a little more time.* A dust-laden sunbeam caught the portrait's right eye. I was sure Phil's face sparked with a familiar crease. I winked in return.

When two boys wielding hockey sticks slouched into the lobby, I pushed through the door and loped to my car.

# CHAPTER **THIRTY-TWO**

As I drove from the Rome campus, Nadine Burriss was on my mind.

She knew Phil Bolden, served on the Sutton Hill redevelopment committee with him. Last week, I'd glimpsed one encounter between them; the intensity of that exchange suggested more to discover there. And now, thanks to Laurel Vaughn, I'd picked up a new wrinkle in the church treasurer's complicated involvement with real estate ventures in Trenton. I wanted to learn more about these two entries in the Burriss portfolio: both the personal and the professional seemed to inspire her passionate attention. And all of it was connected by big money.

I steered the Jeep toward Bethel AME Church. Four in the afternoon wasn't too late to catch a diligent church officer at her desk, was it? As I rounded the southeast corner of the cemetery, I spotted a low-slung sedan slide from the lot next to the church. I sped closer. Nadine Burriss wheeled her fawn-colored Nissan Sentra into Quincy Street and pointed its nose north. I braked and slunk into an empty place near the cemetery gate. I hoped Nadine hadn't spotted me. When she took the corner, I zipped to catch her direction. I wanted to follow her. It seemed early to quit the office; maybe illness had forced her to call it a day. Or was she skipping out to run errands, maybe meet a church member?

The Sentra chugged through an empty intersection with a rolling acknowledgment of the stop sign. I hung back, hoping another car would arrive to join our train. Nadine knew my Jeep. Without intervening traffic to cover my movements, following her undetected was tough. Late afternoon on these side streets was quiet. Most residents of the Flats were still at work; school buses had already deposited their precious cargo; dogs had to wait until after supper for their last walk. When Nadine turned onto Center Street, I darted into the traffic stream aimed toward downtown. Safe at last, I followed with two cars between us.

Just beyond Kings Cross Tavern, Nadine took an abrupt left turn into the parking lot of the First Federal Bank of Queenstown. I plowed straight ahead, catching the Nissan dive into a slot two rows from the bank entrance. I guessed she was going into the bank, but I wanted to be sure. I continued by First Congregational Church, which loomed at the bend where Center curved into Mott Street. A break in traffic allowed me to turn into a gangway beside the church. I darted around the church to an alley that threaded along the edge of Lake Trask. The alley attended the rear doors of commercial buildings on Center Street. Snow hadn't been plowed on this service road, but I bumped along the ruts fast enough to catch Nadine Burriss as she slipped into First National. Her canvas money satchel was slung over one shoulder.

I wanted to learn her business in the bank. But jamming myself into a private transaction wouldn't work. Nadine would shut me down and the banker would reject my overtures on principle. I needed a personal connection to grease my inquiry. I knew tavern owner Mavis Jenkins, like most Center Street merchants, banked at First National. Could I tap my friend for assistance? I aimed for the parking lot flanking the tavern. I hoped a quick chat with Mavis before the dinner rush would get me squared.

As I rolled past the rear of the tavern, an even better grease jockey appeared, Joe Kidd. I slowed to watch the DJ slash gallery owner haul crates from the bar. Aided by a busboy, Joe piled the boxes into a white Chevy Suburban.

The cartons, like the truck, were unmarked. But I guessed liquor. Not a stretch: this was a bar, booze the prime currency.

When I found Mavis in her cramped office, I skipped chitchat.

"I saw Joe out back," I said. I'd taken the straight chair nearest her desk. As I edged forward, my knees bumped against the splintered corner.

She pushed the bulky computer monitor toward the wall. "Yeah, he's doing a job for me." Her eyes narrowed and she batted a drop of perspiration from the tip of her nose. The sweat was nerves, the slit eyes a warning. She swiveled the old library chair to face me. "Shut the door behind you."

I did as she asked then plowed ahead. "Whatever deal you and Joe got going on, can it. It's nothing but bad business for you. You already got cops breathing down your neck."

I knew Q-Town police surveilled customers leaving the tavern. The township hoped to press Mavis into lowering her voice as president of the Center Street Merchants' Association.

"Don't give them an excuse to bust you," I said.

"We're careful, Vandy. Don't need no warning from you." Mavis slapped a manila folder, two ballpoints skittered.

I said, "Joe wants to serve booze at the Barge, he needs to get his own liquor license. Not piggyback on yours." When Mavis rolled her eyes to the wall calendar pinned beside her head, I raised my voice. "That's a ticket to disaster. You could blow your license, lose the tavern, bag a big fine, even a stretch in jail. You figure Joe's worth all that?"

"None a that's happening." She pointed at me. "Unless you snitch." Her voice scratched like gravel. "You a rat, Vandy? You diming me to your cop friends?"

The door hinge whined. Joe Kidd stepped into the overheated room. "Who's dropping a dime?" He swept his dark gaze across our faces. His denim jacket was buttoned to the chin; cold tinged his nose and ears red.

I said, "Nobody, Joe." I watched him stride behind Mavis, frigid air swirling in his wake. "I got no beef with either of you."

He leaned against the wall, arms crossed. "Well, that's good then." The line of his lips blocked excess racket. But the tilt of his moustache hinted at a smile. "Because you know, a beef with Mavis is a beef with me. No warning, just fact."

He laid a gloved hand over my friend's shoulder. Mavis leaned into the touch, the way a cat nudges for an extra caress. Her smile at me was feline, too, suspicion mixed with superiority.

They had me cornered. I wanted help from them, not an argument. I raised my eyebrows to loosen my face. When my sweet pose caused both sets of shoulders to ease, I sailed toward warmer latitudes. "As long as we're not beefing, I got a favor to ask."

He wiped the curve of his moustache. "So, what's on your mind?" He leaned, torso parallel to Mavis, close as keys on a piano.

"I want to get into your bank," I said.

That left-field ask threw him. Joe's cheeks caved as his mouth fell. "Come again?" Eyes round, he retreated. Grabbing a straight chair from beside a file cabinet, he straddled it. "You looking to pull a robbery, some kind of heist?" Were the red splotches on his throat enthusiasm? Did dreams of outlaw rampage fire his imagination?

To bug him, I didn't smile as I doused his excitement. "I need to speak to someone at First National. Not a teller or clerk. You have an account there. Long-standing, right?"

Joe nodded, eyes glinting through narrowed lids. The tip of Mavis's tongue poked between her lips as they ruffled. She was enjoying this.

I said, "I want somebody in administration. A boss."

"You think you can pull off the heist if you get inside cooperation? That it?" He unfastened his jacket and inched forward on the seat. Joe was way too invested in this fantasy.

"No robbery. A case." I bit each word.

They didn't need to know I was investigating the murder of Phil Bolden. Mavis knew about my ancient marriage to Phil, of course, but not the recent reboot. This case was private with a capital *P*. I needed to learn about the financial arrangements of Bethel AME Church. I wanted to find a money connection between the church treasurer, Nadine Burriss, and Phil Bolden. Perhaps such a link didn't exist. But my gut grumbled that First National Bank held a key.

Mavis rode to the rescue. "She's detecting, baby. A private eye. You know, like a secret agent." She patted Joe's wrist. "Why don't you call Jackson Peel? Get him to meet her."

Talking about me in the third person stripped my gears. But I could see Joe bending toward Mavis, so I held my gripe. He tapped a stroke on his cell phone; banker Jackson Peel was on direct dial.

That name rang a bell. I remembered how Nadine Burriss described her banking process: *I work with the same banker your mother did. Jackson Peel. Old guy, fruity but sharp as a pickax.* Now I wanted to learn about the other side of those transactions.

As Joe spoke, Mavis unbuttoned her shirt, then shrugged it from her shoulders. Cherry-red bra, nice double Ds. She pulled on a long-sleeved T-shirt, black with the Kings Cross Tavern logo embroidered in green and gold on the chest. Tucked the shirt into black trousers. Mavis was ready for the dinner shift behind her bar.

Joe's conversation with the banker rolled for several minutes. After mentioning me once, he dropped my mother, Alma's, name four times. When the deal was struck, he signed off, moustache bobbing at Mavis.

Joe said, "Jackson's headed to early dinner now. He says meet him in five at the noodle shop across the street."

"How will I know him?" I stuffed the scarf into my collar and rebuttoned my coat.

Mavis instructed: "White and stumpy with curly gray hair. But don't worry about that none. Jackson Peel know'd your mother back in the day. He'll recognize you soon as you stick your face in the door."

"Hurry on," Joe said, whisking long fingers at me. "Jackson hasn't got all night."

I pressed my hands over my heart. "I appreciate you. Both of you."

"Sure," Joe said. "If you finish early with Jackson, drop back here. I'm sampling the house special tonight: fried catfish with three-bean salad." Eyes bright, he turned toward Mavis, wrapping his hands around her waist. I skipped before the curtain-dropping clinch.

I trotted through the tavern to the front door. As I crossed Center Street, I spotted a white man with a ruff of silver curls step into the rush-hour traffic. He held up one hand, the cars halted. As honks escorted him, the man ambled between the vehicles. When he reached the far curb, I swiveled to check for Nadine Burriss's car in the bank parking lot. The Sentra was gone. I watched the man disappear into the noodle shop. My target Jackson Peel for certain.

# CHAPTER **THIRTY-THREE**

Night dropped like a smudged oilcloth when five thirty hit central Queenstown. Traffic clogged street and sidewalk as I hustled against the signal, following the banker Jackson Peel.

I thought I'd moved fast, but by the time I entered the steamy Vietnamese restaurant, my quarry had vanished. I hesitated at the door, panting. Mavis claimed Peel would recognize me on sight, so I snatched the black beret from my head to give him a clear view. After fifteen seconds, a shirt-sleeved arm extended from the farthest booth, beckoning me. I dodged between tables to the rear of the restaurant.

Since returning to Queenstown three years ago, I'd visited the Pho-Get-Me-Not many times. Its location between a children's bookstore and a glorified gyro stand was less than a three-minute walk from my office. If I didn't pack a peanut butter sandwich to eat at my desk, the noodle shop was one of my regular lunch spots. Eating every day at the tavern was too expensive for my freelancer budget. The Pho-Get-Me-Not offered cheap, no-frills meals and spotless service.

Paul, my favorite waiter, waved me toward the largest booth. "Mr. Peel said you'd be joining him."

When I reached his table, the banker stood to offer a damp palm. "Bless your soul, you *are* your mother's spitting image." Molasses smoothed the twang. "Alma's little girl, all grown and filled out."

Peel assessed me as I removed my coat, so I returned the favor. He was short, five-five at most. Jowls hung in pink folds, erasing the jawline. His nickel-colored eyes shone like thumbtacks. Silver curls gave sparse cover to his scalp, but cascaded in ample sideburns next to his ears. His trunk, encased in a brown tweed vest, was solid and round. An oak barrel, bound in iron. Long canine teeth made his smile alarming rather than jolly.

He said, "I'm at a loss to remember the last time I saw you, dear Vandy. You accompanied your mother on her errands every Saturday morning." His eyes grew vague with memories of Alma, me, and wallets fat with cash. "I'm sure it must have been one of those occasions." He held his hand flat beside the tabletop. "You were this high. Pigtails in yellow barrettes. Missing two front teeth."

I made a *yikes* face to avoid rolling my eyes. "I'm sorry I don't remember you, Mr. Peel."

"Oh, please, call me Jackson." He clapped his hands before his chest like a wizard summoning a genie. "Your mother and I were such good friends in those days."

It was tough picturing Alma as he presented her: warm instead of exacting. Cheery rather than exhausted. Encouraged by the ardor of Jackson Peel's welcome, I expanded my goals for our conversation. I wanted to learn about current finances at Bethel AME Church. But I also wanted to find out more about my mother in her prime.

I decided pursuing stories about Alma would soften my informant for the tougher probe. I hoped for new information about Nadine Burriss. But I'd use a roundabout path with Gentleman Jackson. Barging straight ahead could blow my chance. His connection to my mother would work the trick. After Paul took our appetizer orders—spring rolls with pork and shrimp for me, fish balls on skewers for Jackson—I pressed him on my mother's banking chores.

"You said Alma visited First National most Saturdays. Did she make deposits or withdrawals every week?"

"Mostly deposits. She'd arrive with her black pocketbook filled with small bills. She'd upend the handbag and count them out onto my desk." He balanced a porcelain cup between the fingertips of both hands, sipping green tea as he talked. "Some weeks the amounts were small. Thirty, forty dollars. But every once in a while, Alma would flounce in with a great big wad of cash. I remember one day she deposited three hundred dollars. Another time, eight hundred. *Adult money, Jackson.* That's what she'd say when she dropped the big loads on my desk. *I got adult money now.*"

My heart double-thumped. I jutted my jaw. "How in the world did she get money like that?"

His eyes twinkled as steam rose and the Southern accent deepened. That drawl coded *villain* to me, a reflection of my Jersey biases. If his claims about connections to my mother were true, Jackson Peel was more subtle than sinister.

Dishes brimming with appetizers arrived as I asked, "Are you saying Alma's job as a school cafeteria worker paid off big-time?"

He chuckled around a mash of fish ball. "You know your mama ran a nice side business sewing fancy duds for folks around town." When I nodded, he continued, "I expect she kept the size of her income private. Hid it from you and most likely from your daddy, too. But I know for a fact she did all right for herself over the years."

I remembered the weekly allowance my father awarded me when I started middle school. Had that money come from Alma's secret reserve? Had her toil at the sewing machine contributed toward my tuition at Temple? Ancient shame heated my cheeks.

I dug my knife through the filmy wrapper of a spring roll and shifted the subject. "She worked many years as chief usher for Bethel AME. Was she responsible for depositing the church's weekly collection? You must have seen her on the regular in that role as well."

Before he could answer, Paul the waiter grabbed Peel's dish of stripped skewers and deposited a bowl of beef brisket noodle soup. "Your usual, Mr. Jackson."

"Thank you." Without pause, Peel stabbed chopsticks into the bowl like an expert. Noodles and beef chunks flowed into his mouth around his answer to my question. "Yes, Alma deposited the collection every Monday for years. Not giant sums, mind you. But tidy amounts for a small congregation."

I shook off the waiter's inquiry about another course and parked my fork across my plate. "When Nadine Burriss took the treasurer's job, Bethel's intake jumped, right?"

"That's correct." Jackson Peel's pupils narrowed to pin lights. "Is that what you've come to ask me about?" He sighed, folding his fingers across his firm belly. "I've been wondering when Reverend Fields would dig into that."

I jumped to bolster his suspicion. "Yes. Pastor Fields has concerns about the state of finances at the church. He's thinking of engaging a forensic accountant to do the formal inquiry. But he asked me to look into things in advance." Among the many lies I'd slung in the past week, this one hardly registered.

"You being a private investigator and all." Jackson Peel had done his homework. Even if he'd not renewed our contact, he'd tracked my homecoming. Which wasn't hard in a small town with a big appetite for gossip.

"And connected to the church like I am." I spread a thick layer of sentiment to grease the lie.

"Your mother would be proud of your service, Vandy." Jackson lifted the bowl to slurp broth. "She sure loved her church something powerful."

Now I dug for the meat of our conversation. "How much would you say Nadine deposits to the church account each week?"

Jackson raised a pudgy finger. "First off, you must understand there are two church accounts. The one called Bethel, which handles routine transactions: paying salaries, utilities, subscriptions, maintenance, taxes, and the like."

"Just as any business would."

"The second account is a new one Nadine opened three years ago."

"Does it have a name?"

"No. Just a number. But when she and I talk, I call it the Real Estate account. No frills. No confusion."

"That's its sole purpose then?"

"Yes, as far as I can tell, the money in this account is only used to purchase property."

"Property here in Queenstown? In the Flats?"

"You'd think so, wouldn't you? A church investing its resources to uplift the community that shelters its roots would be standard practice. At least that's how I remember arrangements when I was a boy in West Virginia, back when Noah was a youngster." Peel chuckled, his throat shimmying as pink glossed his forehead.

I said, "But Nadine's real estate account was different. How?"

"She didn't invest locally. Instead, she bought existing housing stock in Trenton. Lots of it. Then she poured thousands into renovating those properties."

"Who did she buy from?"

"The only name I saw associated with those transactions was Philmel Enterprises."

I knew this tag. Phil Bolden had blended his name with his wife's to label his Trenton-based operation. I'd heard Tariq sneer as he described his father's business. *Calls his company Philmel Enterprises. Like they got even dibs in it. But Phil Bolden ain't worth shit.* Melinda Terrence had referred to the company, too, when she noted the tax documents kept in her home safe. Now I had the link between Philmel Enterprises and Nadine Burriss.

"Can you give me round numbers on how much was transferred from Bethel to Philmel Enterprises?"

"I'd have to consult my records, of course. But I'd say purchases ranged from sixty to eighty thousand dollars each."

"That's low for property in Trenton." I was guessing, but I sounded wise.

"Trenton's been on a downward slide for decades. These purchases were of derelict buildings in the Sutton Hill section. Drugs, gang violence, rapid turnover of renters. Groceries, restaurants, shops have abandoned the neighborhood since the 1970s. Even the elementary school and Mercy Hospital have closed. You could buy houses in Sutton Hill for a song. And that's what Nadine did."

"Always from Philmel?"

"Yes, only them. I suppose Philmel had bought dozens of square miles in central Trenton. Then resold the Sutton Hill properties to Bethel. The thing was, Philmel Enterprises also held construction contracts for the renovation of those homes. Architects, general contractors, subcontractors, hiring, insurance. Everything went through Philmel."

"A one-stop operation."

"Top to bottom. And when renters started moving into the reno-vated Sutton Hill townhouses, Philmel Enterprises provided com-prehensive management services. Janitorial, landscaping, security, maintenance. Every last bit and bite went through Philmel."

Nadine Burriss's city of paper. Built on collusion with Phil Bolden. Images of the white cardboard structure in her office flashed through my mind. I remembered walking my fingers down its paper streets, past the flimsy façades and empty cutout windows. I'd climbed pretend steps, knocked on a make-believe front door, plucked at a construction-paper tree. Nadine had brought this fantasy neighbor-hood to life through sheer willpower. With help from Phil Bolden. But as he boosted her, he'd been helping himself.

I said, "And the Philmel company took in hundreds of thousands of dollars."

"Every year." A nod, then Jackson drained his soup bowl. As soon as he returned the bowl to the placemat, the waiter swooped it away. In a few seconds a platter mounded with white rice appeared. A grilled pork chop crowned the rice.

My stomach growled. Declining dinner was a rookie mistake. Especially if Jackson Peel was paying. Either he heard my gut or my swimming eyes gave me away. He said, "Order yourself a bowl of noodles, Vandy. I recommend the bean curds in vegetable broth."

Rookie, maybe; stupid, no. I called for the noodles. When Paul delivered the steaming soup, I resumed my questions. "Did you ever ask Nadine where she got that big money to buy the Sutton Hill properties?"

"Once, yes, I did." Jackson sucked on the tepid tea. "Nadine got snippy, like she'd slice my face as soon as look at it." His mouth puckered with sour memories. "I used to get looks like that from neighbors when I was dirt poor and gay as a shoofly in Bluefield." He brushed invisible crumbs from his vest.

Jackson's connection to my mother made sense now. When young Peel had landed in Queenstown he was unmoored, scared.

Alma had offered him kind words and a willing ear when he first needed the support. Like insecure rocker Joe Kidd, Jackson was a drifter saved by Alma's sympathy and insight. I stirred the muddy soup before me until the noodles wrapped around the spoon. If child saving was my mission, maybe I'd inherited it from my mother. I liked imagining Alma and me, united across the years in a league of moms. I wondered if she'd felt she had lost me to my father's influence. No doubt I was Daddy's girl. Was protecting other people's kids her way of making up for my absence? Did that loss sting her as sharply as the wound I experienced when Monica died? I'd never know for sure. But the thought inspired and humbled me now. Wrangling a lone noodle into my mouth, I nodded at Jackson to continue.

He shuddered to ward off bad memories of his early days in Queenstown. "Nadine said the money she deposited in the real estate account came from the congregation of Bethel AME."

"That makes no sense," I snapped.

Jackson's gray eyes widened. "She said donations had jumped."

"Bullshit." I regretted the harsh shot as it burst from my mouth. But if he still fantasized I was Alma, my curse would set him straight. So to speak. "Bethel's people are civil servants, teachers, construction workers, small-business owners. Nobody in the Flats has that kind of big money."

"I know that." He sawed pork from the bone.

"But Nadine's business was good for First National Bank, is that it?"

He bobbed his head. "As long as her deposits stayed below the limit set by federal regulators, we had no problem accepting her money." He stuck the pork chunk into his mouth, chewing with slow strokes.

We weren't going to get any further. I understood the banker didn't know any more than he'd told me. Thanks to Jackson I'd learned the outline of Phil Bolden's money-laundering operation. Now I needed to find the last pieces of the Sutton Hill neighborhood redevelopment puzzle from other sources. I finished my bean curd noodle soup. Jackson cleaned his pork chop and downed half the white rice. When we parted at the front door, we agreed to make a future date for jasmine and matcha bubble milk tea. He pumped my hand then rose on tiptoes to kiss my cheek. Just like that, Jackson Peel won the heart of a second generation of Myrick women.

Wind whipped frosty spikes against my legs as I walked along Center Street toward Kings Cross Tavern. I stopped under the awning to peer through the picture window. Join that boisterous crowd? Bile rose in my throat. I couldn't bear cheery intrusions from Mavis and Joe, either. Jackson Peel had delivered jarring revelations about the way money flowed around Nadine Burriss. And queasy hints about Phil Bolden's role in those transactions. I needed quiet to sort the details. I could scurry home, but the solitude there would overwhelm me with images of my last moments with Phil. Panic beaded sweat on my forehead. A turn around the plaza in front of the library would clear my mind without singeing my heart.

I passed unlit storefronts on Center Street. A new farm-to-table restaurant, the sewing notions shop my mother loved, the offices of the weekly newspaper, the *Queenstown Herald*. Flaunting its old-school origins, the paper's window displayed six ancient typewriters and two boxy computer monitors from the early 1990s.

Knuckles flexing inside my coat pockets, I stared at my reflection hovering above the black carcasses of the old typewriters. Hollow eyes, slack mouth, gray cheeks framed by the turned-up collar of my coat. What did I really know after my interview with Jackson Peel? If I could note the points in order, maybe their meaning would rise from the jumble.

I'd learned Nadine had set up a bank account to handle transactions related to the purchase and rehab of property in Trenton's Sutton Hill neighborhood. Peel believed her real estate account was a secret, which is why he had hoped I was helping Bethel church leaders investigate the matter. How frequent were her deposits? Nadine had told me she carried the regular Sunday collection to the bank each Monday, just as my mother used to do. Did the treasurer then make a separate run with the real estate money? Or did she mix the funds? I'd given her a check to support her Sutton Hill project. And I'd seen Phil hand her a thick wad of cash the night before he was killed. Was my donation blended with Phil's on her next bank run? The idea—poetic and repulsive—roiled my stomach. Legs trembling, I turned from the newspaper office to cross Center Street. I needed to sit with these thoughts. Before I fell.

I walked over the stone bridge that topped a little finger of Lake Trask. The inlet lapped along a grassy bank in front of the Queenstown Public Library. I sat on the wooden bench bolted into the library's stone plaza. Before me, the lake shone like buffed pewter. Cold rising from the dank slats penetrated my coat then my jeans. The lake's icy skin creaked and sighed as it split. I shoved my hands under my arms, chafing my ribs for warmth. My arrival had disturbed a pair of Canada geese nestled in a bare patch on the lake bank. Black and gray like the lake, the birds stalked toward a thicket of bushes, beaks snapping in protest. I returned to the puzzles around Nadine Burriss's money.

I'd given her financial support. Others must have, too. When I first met her, Nadine had led a boastful tour of the church. I'd spotted a photo of Phil Bolden at a committee meeting. Nadine said this group was charged with the Trenton revitalization effort. Was Phil the chief donor to the Sutton Hill project? How much had he transferred over the three years since she opened the account? Where did he get the money he gave Nadine? His wife, Melinda Terrence, claimed she kept her earnings as a college counselor separate from her husband's income. But could that be true? According to Headmaster Charles Dumont, Phil was the bag man who delivered cash to Dumont in exchange for tips about which Rome School families to exploit. Was this corrupt income the bulk of the money Phil gave to Nadine? Jackson Peel seemed confident the Boldens' company, Philmel, was involved in several aspects of the revitalization project. Was he right? Apart from civic pride, what did Phil gain by the transfer of all this money?

More questions than answers. Shadows swallowing light. Phil's murder arose from this stew of dollars and desires. I was sure of that. But how to put the facts together? The congealed mud of this case cracked and sighed like the lake's cold surface, refusing to yield to me.

I stood from the bench, peeling my damp coat from my thighs.

Frigid air *whooshed* under the wool, as if the angry geese were flapping their wings in my direction. I trudged from the library plaza toward the bright lights of the tavern. I'd stop in for a cup of coffee. Maybe neighborhood chatter there would thaw my frozen thoughts.

At the tavern door, my phone buzzed in my pocket. *Zap, shudder. Hum, zap.* I stripped off my gloves to scan the cell's screen.

Messages from Tariq Bolden screamed:

> FIRE AT SPARK
> FIRE NOW GALLERY FIRE
> SHE DIDNT MEAN IT

# CHAPTER **THIRTY-FOUR**

I lost precious seconds on the threshold of Kings Cross Tavern as cold fingers bungled my texts to Tariq. I tapped then deleted gibberish. More numbed junk. At last:

**Call 911 Can come now**

I meant I'd drive to Spark. But if the boy thought I knew fire trucks would reach the gallery faster, okay. I stepped into the bar's warmth to send a more coherent text.

Joe Kidd barreled into me, elbow straight to my gut. I bent at the waist, gasping as my lungs spasmed. He grabbed both shoulders, forcing me upright.

"My truck's heavy," he said. "Your Jeep's faster. Let's go." Voice stretched wire-thin, white surging around dark pupils. His breath draped oil and pepper on my face. I coughed; he shook me. "I drive. Let's go."

Mavis pushed her face around his shoulder. "He got a text from Tariq. There's a fire at the gallery." When I nodded, she said, "Go on, I'll follow with his truck."

Bar noises fluttered around us. Men laughed, glasses clinked, a stool scraped the wood floor. My breathing eased. I croaked, "Okay, but I drive."

I violated a red light and two stop signs before Joe broke our silence to read bulletins from Tariq:

> Flames eat everything
> Workshop gone

We raced around Lake Trask's black mirror toward the outskirts of town. I remembered our motorcycle run to Spark five nights ago. How my face pressed Joe's denim jacket as we careened. How the pocked asphalt spewed dirt on my boots. This time my heavy foot sliced the twenty-minute trip to thirteen. I grunted at skids or jolts, but said nothing. The road captured my focus. Sirens—deep yowls for the fire company, high-pitched wails for the police—guided our passage through town.

Into the dark, Joe's clipped tenor rattled across the dashboard with an update from Tariq:

> Fire trucks now
> Water ice ever where
> She got my murl

Garbled junk? Tariq frantic, confused. Maybe injured? But alive. That's what mattered. Gibberish beat dead.

We tore along the driveway toward the gallery. Forsythia bushes clawed the Jeep's flanks. Bare twigs thrashed glass, their rhythmic beats matched the howl of fire engines behind us. Ahead, I saw the spring shrubs had bloomed out of season. Now branches flowered yellow and orange against the October sky.

We burst through the thicket into the gravel parking lot and stopped. Forsythia-yellow flames leaped twenty feet above the gallery's brick walls.

"Jesus Christ," Joe Kidd shouted. "Fucking hell."

Against my gloved palm I groaned. "Shit, no."

The gallery was on fire. We knew that. The surprise was the horror. I expected flames dancing like a chorus line on the roof. Bright flags waving from windows. But this dreadful energy drilled panic into my skull. I grabbed my scalp with both hands.

Joe screamed at me, then at his gallery. The words evaporated unheard. His spine bent; gulping, he gripped his knees.

Hot air splashed my face. I looked for Tariq. He should have been here. Where was he?

We parked against an overgrown hedge at the end of the lot, two hundred feet from the building. A ladder truck lumbered to a stop, boxing my car and a Mini Cooper near it. Wind amplified the fire's thunder.

My ears ached like I'd thrust my head inside a boom box. I pulled my beret to my jaws, hoping for relief. The roar intensified. Fiery spouts clotted into a red tiara above the gallery's north wing. Flames arched in celebration of victory over our petty hopes. Maybe twenty men swarmed in the orange light, pointing and shouting. Jets of water spit toward the fire, but the crown of flames grew taller.

Leaping over the hoses, Joe ran toward a clutch of firemen near the garage. He waved arms above his head, then thumped his chest. Miming possession, responsibility. His mouth twisted into a tragedy mask, claiming injury, too. He and a helmeted man dodged behind a truck.

I hung back. Watching the blaze engulf the gallery, I felt small, daunted. I stepped across swollen water hoses snaking from the bellies of four fire engines.

I scanned the huddled people. Where was Tariq? He was my job. A Black boy in hoodie and jeans should be easy to find. All the men were white, dressed in the pea-green uniforms of Queenstown's volunteer fire department. No Tariq. No civilians of any kind.

Cops segregated into navy-blue clusters, chattering on radios. I swept my gaze over the courtyard.

Could Tariq have run inside the inferno? On some idiot crusade to save artworks? I shivered despite the heat. I was useless. Or worse, a liability if I got in the way of official effort. I stepped toward the tangled bushes beside the Jeep.

Maybe Tariq had texted. I skimmed my phone. Nothing. I messaged:

Find me in front of garage

The mom-style order worked. Less than a minute later, Tariq scampered to my side. He hugged me, arching until my feet left the ground. He rumbled into my beret, "This is so fucked up."

I said, "I got you, Tariq." We swayed until his trembling subsided.

I angled to look at his face. Soot streaks, bits of paper. No blisters or cuts. Ash clumps in his hair. Checking for damage, I squeezed his arms. "You hurt?"

"Nah, I'm okay." He shook his head. Water welled in his eyes. "But she destroyed my painting. My mural." The gibberish of his texts spewed out loud.

"Who did?"

"My teacher, Laurel. She burned it. On purpose."

# CHAPTER **THIRTY-FIVE**

Fire bellied toward the sky. Flames heaved from every window of the gallery's upper story. Ten seconds pounded my head as Tariq's words landed. What could he mean? Laurel Vaughn caused this hellhole? I shook my head against the impossibility. This crisis must have devoured all logic. Smoke painted my nostrils with scents of burnt grease and charred wood.

When a gust threw sparks on us, I grabbed the collar of Tariq's sweatshirt to jerk him close.

"That's crazy," I growled in his ear. "No way Laurel Vaughn set the gallery on fire."

He pressed his forehead against mine. "She did. I saw her."

"What happened?" I roared over the fire's thunder. "Tell me." I shook him. To drive the fantasies from his brain and to ground us both.

His throat quivered. "When I left school after eighth period today, she was waiting for me in the parking lot. She said she wanted to see my rock star mural. She . . ." Lips clamped shut behind a fist.

"What did she want?"

He frowned. "She had to see it. Now. Said *you* told her how beautiful it was."

"Me?" I croaked.

"Yeah, that's what she said." Defiance tinged the whine. "Is it true? Did you tell her about my painting?"

I remembered my interview with Laurel in her studio a few hours ago. I'd never seen Tariq's mural; my praise was a calculated lie. I'd wanted to jab her heart, provoke a response. I had succeeded. Laurel delivered her rationale then: she revered Tariq's talent; hated its cheapened distortion in the form of his Spark mural. Was this catastrophe the result of my misplay?

I gave the boy a slice of the truth. "Yes, we spoke this afternoon. Of course, I didn't tell her to destroy the gallery. That's insane."

Groaning, Tariq slumped against me. Over his shoulder, I watched water fight fire above the building. Fountains lapped at flame, winning then faltering as the battle surged. When I pulled back, the orange sky framed Tariq's silhouette.

He muttered, "It was her idea. She was excited. Hyped."

"Did she bring you here?"

"Yeah, that's her car." He pointed at the bottle-green Mini Cooper a few yards from my Jeep. "I thought she was for real. Like she wanted to see what I'd been painting all these months. I took her upstairs to the studio." He twisted to stare at the blazing structure.

I grabbed his chin and forced him to look at me. "How did she start the fire?"

"She walked around the workshop for, like, five minutes, ragging about how beautiful the painting was. *Gorgeous. Stunning. Masterpiece.* Shit like that. Then she asked for a glass of water. I went to the kitchen. When I came back, she was kneeling in front of the mural." He pressed fingers to his mouth to block a sob. "I thought she was studying brushstrokes or something. Then I saw yellow leap from her fingers. She'd already touched the cigarette lighter to one corner of the canvas. When she lit the other corner, it went off like a fucking rocket."

Tears streamed from his eyes. I curved my arms around his waist and rubbed his back. I said, "In your first texts to me you wrote, *She didn't mean it.* Why?"

"I wanted to defend Laurel. Pretend this shit was beyond her control. A mistake. Like I'm responsible."

"That's nonsense." I stroked his cheek, smearing stripes of grime from eyelid to jaw. "You didn't do anything to cause this. Nothing."

"I did." His voice was hard. Against my hand his spine stiffened.

"I was the one hooked up with her in the first place." What was he saying? Hooked up? In a relationship? Tariq and Laurel?

I blurted, "No, that's not true. Your dad told me the truth. About him and her."

"Phil told you he had an affair with Laurel?" The son's voice dripped with scorn. He shook his head twice. "And you believed that shit?"

Hot air singed my eyes and gaping mouth. "I—I thought, I mean, if . . ."

Tariq's bark stung my face.

My gut surged then fell. Yes, I had believed the lies shoveled at me.

Phil Bolden claimed the art teacher had made sexual advances on him. Now I understood that lie was designed to shield his son. To cover up the boy's affair with his teacher. Laurel Vaughn had lied to me, too, when she accused Phil of attacking her. Her deceit was meant to protect herself from charges of seducing a minor student. How long had teacher and student been involved? When did the parents find out? Had Laurel's obsession with Tariq pushed her to murder Phil? Not questions I'd put to the boy in this fiery context. I needed to know the truth. But not now. I locked my knees to stop their tremble.

I stepped a pace from Tariq. He stared at me goggle-eyed, waiting for answers. With the separation, chill air battered my coat. I gave him the simplest reply: "Yes, I believed the story your dad told me."

The admission stung. I'd been duped, blind to the deceit playing in front of my eyes. A blast of heat spewed smoke at us. I gagged. Was the bitterness on my tongue fumes or shame? I rubbed my throat. When water sprang to my eyes, Tariq's profile wavered, indistinct in the haze. Behind us, the burning structure raged. The inferno still stormed. But now the fire sounded like mad cackles, mocking me. I wiped my eyes, hoping to clear my vision, sink my guilt.

I saw Joe Kidd dart toward a red sedan marked with the fire chief's seal. He leaned in at the driver's window, then stood to bang the roof. A QPD officer seized Joe's elbow and wrestled him from the car.

Before Tariq could ask another damning question, murmurs hissed from the underbrush close to our position. Words? Or shrubs stirring? Branches rustled. Wind? A fleeing animal?

Tariq's eyes popped. He caught his breath. Twigs snapped in quick sequence. Human steps. Two paces toward us. Crackling leaves marked retreat. I raised my hand waist high. I wanted Tariq to see my gesture, while hiding it from the person behind us.

He watched me point right, then sketch an oblong in the air. I wanted him to enclose our target from the rear. He nodded then glided parallel to the hedge. Teeth gripped his lower lip, nostrils flared. Stepped on the edges of his sneakers to cut noise. I froze, only my eyes moving to follow him. After five paces, Tariq moved toward the bushes. I rotated, arms raised to capture whoever jumped from the hedge.

# CHAPTER **THIRTY-SIX**

With the Spark gallery fire raging behind us, I couldn't hear Tariq's footsteps as he crept beside the bushes next to my Jeep. Calls from firemen scratched in strident chorus; a siren announced the arrival of another pump truck. Tariq thrust a foot, then two arms into the hedge, plunging his body into dark brambles.

A boom thumped the air. Fists of heat pounded from behind me. Strangled shouts arched overhead.

I whipped around to catch the source of the awful racket. A circle of six firemen pointed toward the top of the gallery's north wing. Flames jetted, then vanished as the roof collapsed. Yellow geysers spouted from the open maw, then raced toward second-story windows as if to escape. Fighters had confined the fire, preventing its spread to the south end. The galleries and storage areas in that wing were safe.

Distracted, I missed the body hurtling toward me. Arms pinwheeled, wool flapped in my face and scraped my eyes. I fell, blinded. A mass crushed breath from my lungs. I heard sneakers churn, scattering pebbles beside my head.

Tariq lifted the weight from my chest. Laurel Vaughn writhed in his arms, her boots flailing three inches off the ground.

She'd knocked the wind out of me. I panted to ease the pain, crouching on one knee as Tariq set her on the gravel. I gripped the Jeep's door handle to steady my rise.

He said to Laurel, "Don't move, or I'll deck you." Fists tightened at his flanks.

I stepped closer to them. Laurel's purple cape was dotted with burrs and leaves. Her red hair was crowned by a tangle of twigs; berries festooned the branches. Scratches trailed from both eyebrows, coursing down her cheeks like crimson tears.

Plucking a seed from her mouth, Laurel chuckled. "You're not going to hit me, are you, Tariq?" Soft, creamy tones the way a mistress would indulge her lover. A laugh to rebalance the power between them. "I haven't done anything wrong." As she pulled off purple leather gloves, her lips flushed. She dropped the gloves, grinning at him now, heavy lids smudged with soot.

"Yes, you have," I snarled. "This." I swept my arm in an arc. "You did all this."

She looked past my shoulder. Her eyes widened as if seeing the fire for the first time. "Beautiful," she whispered. Was her sigh satisfaction? She glanced along the corner of her lids at Tariq. "As stunning as you, my love." She crossed her arms under the folds of her cape.

I wanted to break her serenity. "You burned Tariq's painting. Because it offended your sense of artistic perfection."

A smirk lifted her mouth. Red slash against white teeth.

Testing my hideous guess, I shouted, "And you murdered Phil Bolden for the same reason. Control."

Tariq gasped and staggered an arm's length away from Laurel.

She scowled. Her jaw dropped in disgust. With Phil? Or murder? With me for exposing her guilt?

Her hands moved under her cloak. Blue metal flashed between the buttons of the cape. A gun's nose aimed at me.

"Monster," she screamed. Her shrieks flayed the air. "Abomination."

The pistol spit sparks; I dived beside the Jeep. Metal thwapped the car door.

Laurel raced toward the gallery, cape fanned behind her. Tariq pulled me to my feet. We watched her dodge two firemen, startling a third who tumbled to his ass. She ran to the garage and disappeared into smoke plumes billowing from its bay.

"She's heading to the studio," Tariq yelled. "Stop her."

When he lurched toward the building, I grabbed his elbow. I shook my head. "Nothing we can do." I wasn't sure I believed it, but that's what I said.

My left arm felt heavy. My stomach pitched with the soup of pain and disgust. I leaned against the Jeep. My gut steadied and my arm lightened. I fingered the puckered bullet hole in the door panel. Then I touched my coat. Black scorched the cloth above the left elbow. The furrow wasn't wide, maybe half an inch; four inches long. A paltry trench. I flexed my arm, the triceps burned. As if the gallery fire had transferred its fury to my skin.

Tariq peered at me. "You look sick."

Skin around his eyes was gray and swollen. Molten tear tracks gleamed beside his nose.

"Back at ya." I tried to smile but my mouth collapsed. Good thing because vomit surged behind my teeth.

When he grabbed my left arm, I should have moved faster. Pulsing tangoed with stinging in my muscle. I closed my eyes to quell the nausea.

"What's wrong with your arm," he said. "You hit?"

"It's nothing. A crease," I gritted. I pointed at the blackened edges framing the hole in my coat sleeve. "No blood, no worries."

"Let me see."

"My car took all the damage." I tilted my chin toward the puckered hole in the Jeep's door.

He flexed his fingers at me. "Let me see."

"No way, kid."

He needed a task before he overwhelmed me. I wasn't brave or strong. Just practical. And bone-tired. "Here's your job: find some fire guy to move this truck so we can get out of here." I pointed at the engine blocking my car. "Don't say I'm hurt. Just use your charms. We need to move."

"She's dead, isn't she?" He sniffed, gnawing his lip.

I gripped the nape of his neck with my good hand. "Yes. Nothing we can do to change it."

"Did—did she kill my dad?"

I wanted to give him soft words. To rub out the stain. Buff away the hurt. To rinse this flood of lies with truth. Lies his father told. Lies his teacher chose. Lies I'd used. You're never too young to doubt the world adults made for you. Or too old to be an orphan. I'd learned that truth late in life. Now Tariq knew, too.

But I didn't have those clean words. I couldn't give him the truth yet. I didn't know it for sure. But we had one fact in our reach. With my right thumb, I tapped the bullet hole in the car door. "The proof is here. One way or the other, we'll find the truth."

He gulped. When I pushed his chest, he trotted toward a brace of firemen.

Moving the fire truck took ten minutes of backing and hauling until a lane cleared between its bumper and the hedge. We drove through a gauntlet of thrashing branches until we reached the end of the gallery's half-mile driveway. Tariq crouched in the passenger seat, his black hood pulled over his head. I made the Jeep charge toward town, thrilled to escape the Spark inferno.

When we crossed Main Street, I asked Tariq the first of the big questions on my mind: "Home or school?" Where did he want to spend the rest of this horrific night?

"Home. I want to see my mom."

Relief gurgled as a sigh from my raw throat.

As we rolled toward Allentown Road, the familiar streets and sidewalks seemed dingy. Not black, but dull iron, as if the gallery fire had sucked all the light from the town. We passed only one pedestrian, a woman walking her greyhound. They looked like ribbons of asphalt sprung to life in the gloom.

My injured arm bitched as the blocks receded. *Pinch, throb, pinch, thump.* I bit off a moan, then dropped my left hand to my lap. I'd drive one-handed to ease the pain. I had Tylenol stowed in the glove compartment. But if I asked Tariq to retrieve the tablets, he'd know how much the wound hurt. Not happening. I wanted information from him. No way I'd let this pain divert me.

Five minutes of soothing silence bathed us. Then I dived. "When did this thing between you and Laurel start?" *Affair* sounded like a 1940s Joan Crawford movie; *relationship* came straight from a 1970s tearjerker novel. I stuck with *thing* as the best term: plain, vague, unsexy.

Tariq shifted in his seat. Was he willing to talk or would he stonewall until we reached his house? When he flipped the black hood into a cowl framing his face, I knew I was in.

"Just after Thanksgiving last year. That's when it happened. Drawing was the third class I'd taken from her, so we knew each other pretty well. But nothing serious, you know, until December last year."

"She praised your work?" No stretch to imagine the scenario, but I wanted Tariq to tell his own story.

"I showed her my charcoal sketches." I remembered the treasure trove of his beautiful drawings Laurel Vaughn had presented during my first visit to her classroom. The liquid inner corner of an eye; slate depressions beside a gently rounded nose; a noble jaw's mountainous incline. "Laurel liked them a lot. Said I had talent. Even genius, maybe."

"And the more time you spent together, the closer you became?"

"It was easy, being with her. Like that. I mean, student and teacher first, then closer. Laurel saw me, knew me as I could be. The way I wanted to be. My parents never cared about my art, never had time for my creativity." He pulled the cuffs of his sweatshirt over his knuckles. "There was nothing dirty or nasty about what we had. No one can convince me of that. Laurel and me, we were just two ordinary people. And we loved each other."

I hummed as the stabbing pain in my left arm revved. I wouldn't argue with Tariq about power imbalances and exploitation. Or debate consent and naïveté. Nothing I could say now would diminish the effect of the attention and warmth Laurel had given him.

I wanted to know how the affair had ended. "When did your parents find out?"

He growled, "At that fucking Memorial Day party last spring. It was totally my fault. I kept texting Laurel, from the moment she got to our house. I wanted to see her. I must have sent five texts during the first half hour. Finally, she agreed to meet me in the garage. We were holding hands. Nothing serious, no kissing or fooling or anything. Just talking and holding hands is all. But when Dad walked in on us, he went ballistic. I thought he was going to strangle her."

Tariq's hand hovered at his throat, re-creating the scene.

"That must have been scary for both of you." I let the car idle, even as the traffic signal flipped from red to green.

"Yeah, it was." His chest heaved against the black sweatshirt. "My dad is a terrifying man when he lets loose." Present tense seized him. "Me, right then, I'm a punk shitting my diapers. Left them in the garage. I cut and run like my ass's on fire." He gulped. Did the blazing image strike him as crude in the present circumstances? "I told my mom the bare bones when she cornered me in my room. Then she went downstairs to call off the party. Never seen her so pissed before or since."

I stomped the pedal and we plunged through the intersection.

We sailed past the pillowy dark meadows along Allentown Road. The Bolden residence was a mile farther. I had one more question. "You never saw Laurel after that Memorial Day party?"

"No." He tilted his head. "I mean, of course I saw her at school, in the studio or the cafeteria. But not in *that* way. We were never together again." I couldn't see his eyes, but his soft sob floated toward me.

I knew from Ingrid Ramírez's account, Tariq had pursued her during that summer. Post-breakup, but she never realized the context. His eighteenth birthday in July seemed to have been the turning point that confirmed their romance. Now I knew Ingrid was his rebound sweetheart. Though I'd never tell her, the idea curdled my stomach.

For her part, Laurel Vaughn had salved her wounded pride that spring by launching an affair with my friend Keyshawn Sayre, Rome School's head groundskeeper. A second rebound romance. Anger boiled from my chest, pricking my palms with heat. I wiped sweat from my right hand onto my jeans. As I gripped the wheel with my left, the ache in my damaged arm throbbed double time. Ingrid and Key were worth more than emotional ricochet material. They weren't secondhand clothes plucked from a resale shop. My friends deserved to be cherished as rare treasures.

Blinking tears, I swallowed my anger. I hated the situation, not the boy. "Thanks for telling me, Tariq. That can't have been easy."

He nodded. "Then she killed my dad. And herself." His wail was muffled, like a distant wolf howl. "And she called *you* the monster."

Nothing to add. Piling my pain on his would only swell the grief. My boot brick-heavy, I sped the final yards to the pebbled driveway in front of the Bolden residence. All windows were black, the stone elephants flanking the front door cloaked in shadows. I killed the engine and lights to avoid waking Melinda Terrence. She'd learn of the new calamity soon enough.

Tariq pulled his hood around his ears. "Thank you for asking my side. For listening. It helps." His voice faltered, plaintive against his chest. "You think the police will question me?"

"They'll ask about the fire." No use sugarcoating the tough exchanges ahead.

"And the rest?" He meant his affair with Laurel. The possible connection to Phil's murder.

"They'll follow up. When they ask directly, give them the truth." Rich, my urging Tariq to avoid lying to the cops. When I'd devoted so much energy to lying to cover my private missteps. "That's all you owe anybody, Tariq. All you can give."

I watched him lope across the gravel to the entrance. I waited, thinking he might wave from the front door. He slipped across the threshold without a backward glance.

# CHAPTER **THIRTY-SEVEN**

Tuesday morning began at noon when throbbing in my left arm dragged me from flame-singed dreams.

I gobbled two Tylenol caps then stared into the bathroom mirror waiting for the pain to dwindle. The bruise looked dramatic; a three-inch-long racetrack ringed in red. Nasty, but no puncture or broken skin. I touched the tender flesh. Pain snapped its retort. Giddiness washed over me. My skin's message was clear: I was alive, unburned, whole. The horrors I'd seen last night receded. Gladness swelled in me—not foolish or breezy. But lightness sifted through the somber feelings. I'd escaped death before. These buoyant sensations were temporary. I'd embrace them while I could.

I splashed soapy water on my arm, rinsed then dabbed ointment, dangled a gauze pad over the dent, but decide to skip the decoration. Sitting cross-legged in bed, I called Queenstown police to report the shooting and the bullet lodged in my car. Short conversation, three minutes max. The officer recording my statement expressed condolences for damage to the Jeep.

I'd wanted to get to the office, review my case notes, answer police questions, call Tariq Bolden. But Mavis Jenkins blocked my plans. She intercepted me in my kitchen at twelve thirty. Before I'd showered or changed from sweatpants and chenille robe. Before the bagel hopped from the toaster or the coffee finished dripping. With impressive street skills, the bartender used a nail file to jimmy my front door.

When she marched to the kitchen island, Mavis frowned to block my gripe. "For all I know, you was flat in your bed, bled out and dying." She stared at my robe, deploying X-ray vision to assess my injury.

"Who tipped you off I was shot?" I slipped two whole-wheat slices into the toaster; I knew she didn't want bagels.

Mavis dropped her red puffer coat on the dining table. She was wearing the black logo T-shirt and wool slacks from last night's shift at the tavern. "Before you drove him home, Tariq gave the four-one-one to Joe. He said you'd taken a bullet—"

"Not accurate. Just a graze." I clutched the robe to my throat.

"But you could manage the steering wheel. When I arrived to the gallery, Joe filled me in. We were there all night. Morning, too." She poked fingers to the inner corners of both eyes. "I forced Joe into bed about twenty minutes ago and came straight here. I'm beat as a redheaded stepchild." She scrubbed knuckles through her auburn knots.

"When did they put out the fire?" I wanted to work up to asking the question foremost in my mind.

"What fire you could see was gone by four thirty. Smoke, grit, no flames. But they kept flooding the place for another hour. To be sure no embers were still smoldering. Joe wanted to get inside, see the damage for himself. But the fire chief said they needed to check for structural damage before they'd let us civilians in. Cops and firemen got first dibs."

I poured coffee in two mugs and shoved one across the counter to Mavis. "Did they . . . um, find the body?" I guessed she'd heard about Laurel Vaughn.

"Yeah." She exhaled then scraped fingers through her spiky hair. "When cops found her that poor soul wasn't nothing but a pair of boots, a line of ash, and a twisted pistol."

I gagged on the image, covering with a swig of coffee. I scrambled to the refrigerator for cartons of butter, cream cheese, and milk, cradling them all in my right arm.

"You can't lift that left arm higher than your waist, hunh?" Mavis straightened the dairy cartons on the counter. "Let me get a look at you." Without waiting for my okay, she pulled the robe from my shoulder. "Whew, that's more than a notion. You got nicked, and I mean, tagged but good."

"Thank you, Doctor."

"You seen Doc Klein for that?"

"Not planning to. You provided all the diagnosis I need." I wolfed my bagel, swallowed my coffee, and slid toward the stairs. "Help yourself to toast, another cup if you want. I'm taking a shower. Without your assistance, thank you very much."

She harrumphed, then chomped a butter-slathered slice of bread. When I returned to the kitchen twenty minutes later, Mavis was gone.

I wasn't alone for long. As witness or victim of the biggest Q-Town crime since Phil Bolden's murder, I enjoyed plenty of attention all day. Photographer Jeff Heinz slipped a get-well card under my front door; Jackson Peel dropped off a bank-exec-size bouquet of yellow roses in a porcelain vase. The Pho-Get-Me-Not cooks sent a bucket of noodles and a carton of fresh spring rolls.

Less than thirty minutes after I'd toweled my hair and buttoned my denim shirt, Ingrid Ramírez graced me with an actual phone call rather than a text. She'd heard of the Spark fire and my injury from Tariq. Did that mean she'd seen him in school? From her cryptic phrases I couldn't tell how Tariq was handling the aftermath of the blaze. She deflected my question about him with thin platitudes. Prattling like a country-club matron, Ingrid hoped I got lots of rest and felt better soon. She promised to visit me on the weekend.

At two thirty, Belle Ames, my administrative assistant, arrived with greetings and gifts from our office. I peered into the paper sack she deposited on the kitchen island. "You telling me Elissa says to stay home?" That didn't sound like my friend. Her legal business was fueled by her damn-the-torpedoes energy. "Are you sure she didn't say I should come in this evening to make up missed hours?"

Belle snorted at my depiction of her wife. "Yeah, that was her first impulse. But I talked her down." Grinning, she pulled two quart-size plastic containers from the paper bag. 'This is our get-well present. Jollof rice."

I lifted a corner of one container's yellow top. Whiffs of smoky, sweet, and spicy stroked my nose.

I sighed. "Thank you." Tears welled in my eyes. From the spice, no doubt. I brushed them away.

"Elissa's family recipe," Belle said. "My down-home skills. Dig under the rice, you'll find chicken thighs and wings. Elissa said her people call it Party Rice."

I patted the plastic top until it snapped into place. "But this is enough to feed an army."

"Elissa gave strict orders. Don't even think about coming to the office until you bring the containers clean and empty. Three, four days. Understand?"

"Yes, ma'am." I saluted. "Eat, then wash. Got it." I hugged Belle with my good arm, then hustled her to the door before a deluge of tears swamped my hard-boiled PI rep.

Alone again, I pulled the second container from the bag. Taped to the cover was a business card. JUSTINA DIAMOND, FAMILY THERAPIST. My girls never stopped trying to get me to see a shrink. I unstuck the card to study it. Maybe a tear dribbled from my chin onto the embossed name. I stuffed the card under the pile of its sisters in the junk drawer next to the refrigerator. The stack was thick as my thumb now.

Officer Lola Conte rang my doorbell at 5 P.M. I let her in the front door, but didn't invite her farther than the hallway. Skipping greetings, she handed me a square buff-colored envelope. "Found this on your porch," she said.

Looked like a fancy get-well card. I didn't open it. No welfare check for Conte, who got straight to business. "We're here to confiscate that bullet you removed from the scene last night."

"You mean the one that scratched my arm en route to my car?" I patted my left elbow in case she cared to inspect the damaged flesh.

She declined the invitation. "Yeah, that one. You filed a report. We're here to extract the evidence." She jerked a thumb toward the picture window.

I angled to check my driveway. In the gathering dusk, a squad of four uniformed officers surrounded the Jeep. A fifth white man leaned against the passenger-side door, busy with drill and circular saw. The sixth expert waved a forceps in midair, ready to detain the bullet.

"QPD paying for damages?" I asked. The buzz of the drill made my teeth ache.

Conte removed her hat and scrubbed the shock of hair above her brow. Purple-tinged skin around the eyes and chapped lips made her look rough, as if *she* were the one up all night battling fires. A sneer dented the corner of her mouth. "Send a bill to your pal, Chief Sayre. He'll take care of you."

When I grunted rather than rise to that old-boyfriend bait, Conte pouted. She smacked her lips twice, throat quivering as she swallowed hard. Then she shifted her weight from foot to foot. "Can I use your, um, facilities?"

I pointed toward the bathroom beyond the kitchen. "First door after the pantry." When she disappeared, I took a stool and planted elbows on the island. Waiting, I tore open the envelope she'd delivered. The embossed card featured golden clouds on the front and a wish for my quick recovery inside. Signed with loopy flourishes: *Your Brothers and Sisters in Christ of Bethel AME Church.* I recognized the handwriting. In this same scrawl, the pledge *Unstoppable* festooned notecards collected by Nadine Burriss. Was the treasurer fretting over my injury? Or needling me?

Across the kitchen I heard Conte's awful retching; my gut rippled in sympathy. I recognized the clues: thickened waist, insomnia-darkened eye bags, nausea. She was pregnant. I'd been there, scored the T-shirt, won the match. Lost the prize.

I retrieved a carton of crackers from the pantry. When Conte lurched into the kitchen, I dumped a stack of saltines on a saucer and pushed them across the countertop. "Eat these," I said. "Always did the trick for me." Sisterhood? Not yet. Solidarity? Sure. I ran tap water until it cooled and handed Conte a glass then filled another for myself.

I saw protests fizz then sputter as she eyed the crackers. No use trying to playact. She knew I'd scoped the truth. After gobbling three crackers, Conte said, "Barfing is a bitch. Second trimester was easier last time. I'm hoping for a repeat."

I didn't ask about due dates or gender-reveal parties. Not throwing a baby shower. I gulped a third of my glass and plunged to the business between us.

"That bullet your guys are pulling from my car. When do you expect to get the results from ballistics?"

Color feathered into Conte's cheeks as the crackers calmed her stomach. "We'll put an expedite order on it. The Trenton lab should deliver preliminary findings by Saturday."

This was Tuesday. I wanted answers yesterday. "Slow rolling, hunh?" I crunched a cracker for emphasis.

"Not slow. The Bolden case is top priority. But you can't speed science." After a sip, she continued, "What do you figure the bullet will prove?"

"I think Laurel Vaughn shot Phil Bolden. She told me she owned a gun for self-defense. I doubt she owned an arsenal. So the gun she fired at me will be the one she used to kill Bolden. The bullet in my car can clinch the case."

Conte didn't dispute my claim. "Why do you figure she did it? Hate, jealousy, revenge, fear?"

"Yes, those are usually the reasons women kill," I said. I'd investigated cases involving two female murderers during my decade with the New Brunswick police department. Years of domestic abuse motivated one knife attack. The other woman had poisoned her husband to end his string of affairs.

"And for Laurel, what made her pull the trigger?"

I shifted on the stool. "I think it was love."

"Love?"

"The frustrated, distorted kind of love."

"One-sided obsession? Like in movies?"

"Not unrequited so much as blocked." I dented a cracker until it crumbled.

I gave the edited version of what Tariq told me last night. "I don't know exactly how the relationship between Laurel and Tariq Bolden started. She admired him, praised his artistic talent."

"Bolden's kid? She was his teacher at Rome?" Conte's eyes bulged.

"Right. She lavished attention the boy didn't get from either parent. She pushed. He picked up on her signals. She led him over the line; he followed."

Conte snapped, "Nasty bitch should have been fired."

"If the school had found out, I'm sure she would have been. Laurel was the adult. She bore the blame. Period."

"Then what do you figure happened?"

"I think Phil Bolden discovered his son was involved with Laurel. And Phil forced the breakup." No need to spill the sorry tale of the Memorial Day barbecue. Sticking with generalities worked.

"Why didn't the parents tell the school authorities?" Conte was asking the logical questions I had never had a chance to ask Phil.

"I've been trying to figure that out."

I knew Phil and Melinda had invented a story to cover Laurel's relationship with their son. Were they pressured by Laurel to concoct a cover-up? Had she learned about the illicit college placement scam the Boldens were running with help from Rome headmaster Charles Dumont? Had Laurel blackmailed the Boldens into silence? I didn't want to share this speculation with the police. Not until I'd nailed down the evidence. And even then, I'd hold off on revealing everything if I could. I wanted dignity for Phil and Melinda. And protection for Tariq.

I said, "After Phil intervened, Laurel couldn't reignite her affair with Tariq. That was over. The boy had grown up, moved on. She tried to move on, too. Found a new boyfriend."

I thought about Keyshawn Sayre, affectionate and innocent in this soiled business. Laurel Vaughn had used my friend as a diversion. Key was a distraction she hoped would interrupt her feelings for Tariq. A third Black man she'd harmed in the push to salve her ego. Another piece of the puzzle I'd never share with QPD or his brother, police chief Bobby Sayre.

Conte got the picture. "But the distraction didn't work. Laurel was hooked on the kid."

"Yes. And as her obsession grew, so did her anger at Phil Bolden. Phil blocked her true love. Phil frustrated her plans to direct Tariq's future as a great artist. Phil stood in the way of everything she wanted."

"So she killed him." Conte rubbed her mouth and closed her eyes. "As if murder would solve everything."

"Right. Reality clamped hard after the murder. Tariq didn't return to her. He wouldn't abandon the commercial art she hated. When she couldn't achieve what she wanted, Laurel unraveled. She transferred her hatred of Phil to the gallery where Tariq worked, Spark."

"And she lit it up last night." Conte curled then released her fist for the explosion.

I nodded. "When the blaze went off, she had nothing more to gain. Nothing more to lose."

"Her only way out was into the fire."

"Yes, but before she ran, she shot at me."

"Why?" Conte blinked twice, fingers probing her collarbone. "What had you done?"

"I called her a murderer. She called me a monster." The giddiness of the afternoon evaporated. Gloom and horror dripped into the empty cavity in my heart. I stared at gray veins wavering in the marble surface below my glass.

Conte grabbed her water. "You spoke the truth." She wet her mouth, ready to expand on my theory of the case.

Footsteps in the hall interrupted her. A member of her uniformed squad lumbered into view. "We got the bullet, Officer Conte."

He flourished his trophy, a transparent evidence bag. I could see the dark slug trapped in a corner of the packet. The flattened souvenir looked insignificant but my arm pulsed in unhappy remembrance.

"That's my cue," Conte said, taking the prize. "We'll get out of your hair now." She dangled the evidence bag at eye level, turning the bullet as if it were a rare ruby. "I'll have someone call you tomorrow to take your formal statement."

After QPD left, I inspected my Jeep. Perched in the shotgun seat, I saw lamplight peek through the hole in the door. My pinkie finger fit in the tunnel. The gouge was not as deep as a well or as wide as a breadbox. But it served.

Tired, but too early for bed; hungry, but too queasy for food. I lay on the living room sofa playing with the electronic controller of the gas fireplace. I danced flames high, then low. Yellow, then blue. Images from last night's dreams, last night's reality. Despite the fire, my feet grew cold. I pulled the fox-fur throw over my legs. Talk with Conte had reminded me of Keyshawn Sayre. I wanted to reach out to him. I figured he'd learned of Laurel Vaughn's death by now. *Welcome to Tiny Town, where mouths are bigger than brains.* Had he heard about the fire at the laundromat or the drugstore? Had some barbershop clown tipped him to his girlfriend's role in the blaze? Maybe the Wawa clerk had filled in the deets. I wanted to share my angle on the fire, offer consolation if he'd accept it.

Over fifty minutes, I called Key twice, texted him three times. No answer. Was he dodging all calls or just mine? I tried a different approach. During the years he worked as a health aide to my father at the nursing home, Key and I had established a regular game of chess. We played in person in my dad's apartment and exchanged text messages to continue the matches each night. After Key and Laurel became a thing the previous June, we dropped the chess game. I missed the matches for the fun and intellectual challenge. I missed Key for the solid friendship. Maybe I could reach him by resurrecting our match.

I set up the board on my dining table, consulting old messages to position the pieces as we'd left them five months ago. I made my play, a weak feint by the isolated bishop. After sending a photo of the rearranged board, I texted: Your move? Cheeky, perhaps. Disrespectful in the circumstances, maybe. Attention trap, for sure. Waiting for Key's retort, I fell asleep on the sofa, the phone over my heart.

# CHAPTER **THIRTY-EIGHT**

Three sharp raps on the front door startled me from sleep. The cell phone read 11:35. I flung the fur throw from my knees and stumbled to the hall. Under the watery light of my porch lamp, Keyshawn Sayre looked miserable. Eyes bulging within a collar of sunken skin, nose red, lips cracked, hair snarled in ragged tufts. When we hugged, my left arm flinched, but I held the embrace. He needed it, so did I.

We didn't talk much until I'd microwaved two plates of jollof rice and poured out a double dose of bourbon for Keyshawn. He swallowed it straight and asked for a second round on the rocks. Watching him, I picked a few grains from my plate. After he'd bolted a second helping of rice, Key walked to the dining table with the half-full tumbler. He inspected the chessboard, tapping a long finger on the empty square next to my red queen.

"You know that idiot move left her wide open." He pointed at his black castle lined up for the kill strike.

"And you know I did it on purpose." I smiled and shoveled a last spoonful of rice. "Best way I knew to get your attention." I moved toward the table, easy steps, the way I'd go to a wounded dog.

His sigh turned into a sob. Sitting at the table, he pressed both hands around the castle then held them before his face in prayer mode. "This hurts. Like a fucking nail hammered in my eye."

I pressed, my chest to his back, my arms around his shoulders.

"I know, baby. I know." I dropped my face to the top of his head. His hair smelled of grass and smoke, his neck of yesterday's sweat.

We stayed like that until he stopped crying. I brought my glass of club soda to the table and set the Jim Beam bottle next to his right hand. I waited for his questions. They came in dribs between gulps of booze. I kept my answers short; if he wanted elaboration, he asked for more. When he'd learned as much as he could stand about the Spark gallery fire, he asked about my injured arm. And at last, about reasons his girlfriend would have to shoot me.

"I told Laurel I thought she'd murdered Phil Bolden, that's why."

"How could you believe such an awful lie?" Veins on his neck stiffened like rebar.

"I think it's the truth. It fits."

"How in hell do you make it fit?"

I told him the theory of the crime I'd shared with Lola Conte that afternoon. I trimmed the salacious flesh from the story, recounting only the stripped bones: Laurel wanted to continue her affair with Tariq Bolden. Phil stopped her. Laurel wanted to control Tariq's art career. Phil blocked that, too.

"The meddling by Phil grew until she couldn't tolerate the burden," I said. "She gunned him down to remove the interference. And regain control."

Key sipped bourbon as I talked, rolling it on his tongue before swallowing. I told him about police digging from my car the bullet Laurel had fired at me. As the story continued, I expected his eyes to fog with exhaustion and grief. Instead, his gaze sharpened. He focused on my hands, then my mouth, as if tunneling for the truth beneath my account.

At last, Key spoke. "Phil Bolden was killed early Wednesday morning. One week ago, right?" Words spewed through the sieve of his teeth.

"Yes."

"Then Laurel couldn't have done it. I know for a stone-cold fact she didn't do it."

"How can you know that?" Whiny to counter his certainty.

"Because she was with me all night." Simple, plain. Hard muscles in his shoulders rolled. He met my eyes for the first time since entering the house.

"How can you be sure?"

"Because Tuesday was a special day for us. We celebrated being together five months. Laurel fixed a sirloin steak with all the trimmings. And that proves it was a special dinner, 'cause she's a vegetarian. Always tryin' to get me to cut back on the red meat. Hopin' to convert me to bean cakes and tofu and vegetable whatnot." He stopped to wipe a hand across his eyes. Red flared on the crest of his cheekbones, brightening his brown skin. "But that night, she went all out for me. She even got kinda fancy after we went to bed. No way I forget a stand-out good time like that."

I gulped, embarrassed by the intimacy. With no quick answer ready, I reached to the chessboard for a red pawn. I balanced it on my palm, raising the little piece until it was eye level. "We have the bullet. The shot she aimed at me. If it matches the ones pulled from Phil's body, then Laurel is the shooter. I'm sorry, but that's the way it goes." I closed my fist around the pawn.

He pressed my hand to the table and pried open my fingers. Tapping the pawn, he said, "And I'm tellin' you, it won't go that way."

"The bullet's at the lab now." My words droned. "We'll have ballistics analysis in a few days."

"Yeah, Bobby filled me in. He said to keep shut until we got the results back."

So Key had discussed the Bolden murder with his big brother. Not a surprise to learn the police chief would bend official constraints to help his family. Another reason I'd share as little as possible about the case with either Sayre brother.

The fact that Keyshawn and Bobby were collaborating irked me. I wanted my theory confirmed. Annoyance propelled my next question: "How do you know Laurel didn't go out in the middle of the night? Phil was murdered between one forty-five, when a passing driver spotted him walking on Center Street, and six when the body was discovered Wednesday morning."

Keyshawn grunted, disbelief pressing his brows until the glint of his eyes disappeared.

I remembered the lights of my bedside clock as Phil left me that morning: 1:35 blinking red like an infection. The last moments I shared with Phil. No one would ever learn those details. "She could have slipped out of your apartment, done the killing, and returned without you discovering her absence." Sounded stupid as the words tumbled out. I expected Key to strike back.

"You think I don't know when my woman's coming and going from my own bed? What kind of fool you take me for?" Veins like tree roots bulged along his neck.

I inhaled to dull the throb beating in my left arm. Then I gobbled a slug of soda. The cool soothed my throat. This wasn't an argument either of us could win. I wanted to stop our fight before it escalated. The more we scrapped the worse we'd end. Each of us had lost our precious person. Their deaths had blurred our lives into tedium and despair. I didn't want to lose Keyshawn, too.

Closing my eyes, I said, "I'm tired. I don't want to fight you. Not now. Not ever."

"Same here, Vandy. Believe and trust, you're my people." He stood from the table. Reaching for the chessboard, he rearranged the pieces. I watched a new formation arise under his fingers. Black magic for real. Key erased my bonehead move, rescuing the queen from the castle attack. "You get some sleep," he said, gaze down, no smile. "I'll catch you tomorrow."

After he left, I wrestled with my bedsheets for three hours. Keyshawn's testimony wrecked my neat solution to Phil's murder. I believed Key: Laurel Vaughn couldn't have committed the crime. She had plenty of motive; nothing he said had disrupted my understanding of her desire to eliminate Phil. And I knew firsthand she had a weapon and the will to fire it. But what about opportunity? Her affectionate night with Keyshawn had erased her opening to commit the murder. Now I wanted to find new pieces to fix this puzzle.

I rolled my head, scrubbed grit in my eyes. The jigsaw pieces were out there and so was Phil Bolden's killer. The motive question prickled. If Laurel hadn't shot him, then someone with similar frustration had pulled the trigger. The cause rang true, even if I'd assigned it to the wrong perp. I watched the crimson lights of my bedside clock flicker from 3:29 to 3:30.

What did I know about Phil Bolden? His character and talents lay at the core of this case; start there. He was both villain and victim in this case. Whoever killed him had been wronged by him. Phil was a seductive persuader. I'd learned that costly truth at an early age. He could paint gorgeous fantasies. Bright vistas of uplift and renaissance spilled from his mouth. Conviction was his superpower. I'd seen Phil's skills on display at the Rome School homecoming banquet two weeks ago. His drunken speech had won the alumni crowd to his cause. With a few sentences, he'd made them want to fund his vision of a new library project. He'd convinced them to follow him anywhere. It's what he did; what he always did. Phil hadn't lived long enough to abandon the glorious schemes he'd launched that night. He'd died before he could crush those dreams with neglect. Or rejection. The way he'd done me.

Damp creases on my pillow pressed hot against my cheek. I sat, crossed my legs, stared at moonlight lapping curtains by the window. Phil's pattern was clear: seduce, inspire, convince; then abandon, undermine, and thwart. I'd been his test run, an early exercise of his power. Phil had persuaded me I could be more than the lonely child of a small-town cop. Through Phil, I converted my awkwardness into grace, my intellect into achievement. My unlovely name, Evander, sounded sweet in his mouth. I thought I could find purpose through Phil. Until his attention shifted and he moved on to other women, other worlds. Maybe my father was right to block Phil's involvement in our daughter's life. If Phil had been around during those years, I might have murdered him myself. I squeezed arms around my waist; heat pulsed from my damaged arm through my torso. Hot tears dribbled on my breastbone.

Phil had worked the same enchantment on his second wife, Melinda Terrence. Proposing to weave straw into gold, he'd convinced Melinda to channel her ill-gotten money into rehabbing a destitute Trenton neighborhood. With Phil casting the spell, I'm sure the offer was thrilling. Melinda had bought the simple virtue of the scheme. Until Phil switched gears and turned the plan into a money-laundering system that enriched his own company. When Melinda wanted out, he blocked her. Had this frustration—betrayal, really—prompted her to kill him?

I dabbed a corner of my quilt to smear the wet between my breasts. How many others had Phil led on? Had he convinced Rome headmaster Charles Dumont to join the college placement scam with promises of personal wealth? But in addition to greed, Dumont was motivated by ambition. Dumont had expected Phil to lead the school's capital campaign. When Phil upended those multimillion-dollar plans, had frustration pushed Dumont to desperate violence? Phil was selfish and beguiling. Had he manipulated Nadine Burriss into misusing her position as church treasurer? Had he convinced her she could spin her dreams for community improvement into reality?

And what about Phil's son, Tariq? I knew his artistic dreams had clashed with his father's material ambitions. Phil had had plans for his only son. He expected Tariq to concentrate on academics, perhaps on a career in business. My gut bunched until I gripped my knees to corral the pain. I didn't like the direction these thoughts were leading me. The kid was innocent, had to be. I rolled from under the sheets, hoping the night air would chill my legs. When that didn't work, I walked to the bathroom for cool tiles and a glass of water.

I splashed my wrists and neck. The drops evaporated; the heat fled. Running hands through my hair lifted the scent of baby shampoo. I remembered how this same sweetness mixed with tarry smoke had wafted from Tariq's halo of black curls when I squeezed him in my arms as the Spark gallery fire raged. He'd hoped sports achievements would bring acceptance from his father. Instead, he won Phil's scorn. Then the boy found a champion in his art teacher, Laurel Vaughn.

Stalking to bed, I slipped under the covers. Cool sheets lapped against my thighs. What a contrast between these two adults in Tariq's life: his father withdrew attention and denied approval. Laurel's affection boosted Tariq's ego and inspired his self-expression. Phil Bolden thwarted the boy's emotional attachment to his teacher. Was the resulting frustration enough to push Tariq to murder his father? I pulled the quilt to my chin, then clamped teeth to its padded hem. I wanted a different chapter for Tariq's story, a happier ending. As the clock's bloodshot numbers flipped to a new hour, I shivered.

# CHAPTER **THIRTY-NINE**

I didn't remember setting the clock for six thirty, but the damn alarm jolted me awake anyway.

I pinched the left sleeve of my T-shirt. The crease on my arm had turned maroon. Gaudy as a Mardi Gras float. But the ache's beat was slow and regular, like the thump of a receding parade. Manageable. Beyond my bedroom window, Wednesday's fog loomed above my neighbor's roof, gray and thick as a widow's shawl. I took a long shower, hotter than usual. But when I toweled off, my skin was still cold from last night's speculation. Tariq Bolden was on my mind, so I texted him. Early for a teen, but so what. I wanted to catch him. Hear from him direct. No joy. The block hurt almost as much as my wounded arm.

I waited a decent hour before contacting Ingrid Ramírez. She could fill in the gaps on Tariq. No more texts, I went direct. Phoning was still bad manners; adulting gone wild. So I braced for Ingrid's reprimand. Instead, her voice lifted in relief.

"Good, it's you," she said. "I wanted to call you. Wasn't sure you'd be awake at this hour."

"I'm up. I'm looking for Tariq. You seen him?"

"Not this morning. He's dealing with his own shit in his own way. But here's what I wanted to tell you. You remember my friend Morgan Gaylord?"

"Yes. What about her?"

"First, about her parents. I saw Mr. and Mrs. Gaylord before first period this morning. In the hall. Going into the headmaster's office. And Morgan wasn't with them."

"Strange."

"No shit. It spooked me. I mean, nobody wants to see nobody's parents going in for a conference with the big man. Especially if the kid's not included. Total bad news."

"Did you speak with the Gaylords?"

"Are you shitting me? Of course not. I ducked into the girls' bathroom when I clocked them. They never saw me."

"What am I supposed to do about it?" I remembered my tense conversation with Charles Dumont two days ago. I'd hit him on the college placement scam; he had hinted retaliation against my student friends. When I left his office, he was summoning Morgan Gaylord for a conference. I wouldn't tell Ingrid about my exchange with Dumont. Or my worry about his threats to her and her friend.

"Nothing you can do about that," she said. "Who knows what Dr. Doom said to the Gaylords? But here's what you can do."

"Yeah?"

"About five minutes ago, I get this weird-ass call from Morgan. Freaked me out."

"What did she say?"

"She told me she was sorry."

"Why?"

"That's what I asked. She goes, 'I'm sorry,' two more times. Then she sobs, lots of gurgling. Then she says, 'I'm sorry,' again. Her voice all creepy and weak, like she's underwater or something. Bubbling, like hitting bottom in a lake."

"Where is she?"

"She says at home. But I could hear the wind real loud, so maybe she's outside somewhere."

"You call Morgan, keep her on the line. I'll drive to her house. I'll find her."

"Thank you. I knew you'd help."

I had Hugh Gaylord's business card with his scribbled address, the one he'd given me after I dented his car in the Boldens' driveway last weekend. As I dug the card from my wallet, Ingrid gushed worries about her friend. She needed to do something, anything, to feel useful. Giving her a concrete job, I asked her to confirm the address. After she repeated the digits, I told her to dodge the Gaylords and stay clear of the headmaster's office. He had his sights fixed on her. I didn't want Ingrid playing junior detective. As I hurried to the Jeep, we signed off. I didn't promise to call back and she didn't ask.


The Gaylords' house was on Allentown Road, several acres and a higher tax bracket beyond the Boldens' place. I drove onto the sandstone pavers in front of the mansion ten minutes after my call with Ingrid. I guessed the architect had been going for Versailles-style palace trumps Tudor-style castle. An arcade of glass panes stretching two stories above the front façade reflected the sodden clouds as I jumped from my car. The Gaylords' golden-beige BMW was gone, but a sky-blue Triumph ragtop was angled near gates leading to a giant pasture. I remembered seeing Morgan drive this nifty convertible when we met at the Forum Sandwich Shop. If the car was here, so was the girl.

I pounded on the front door; no servants, no answer. Racing beside a bed of dormant azaleas, I circled the building looking for passage to the rear. A wooden gate blocked the brick path between the house and garage; I busted it open with a kick. The backyard was as wide as a football field, Olympic-size pool covered in black plastic; an arcade of yew trees led to a tennis court on the far horizon. Near the sliding back doors, two black wrought-iron tables perched on a circular patio. Umbrellas protruded through each table, their canvas canopies folded like dead grasshopper wings.

Morgan Gaylord slumped in a chair at one table. Her head lolled to the left; blond hair draped over the hood of her white parka. When I reached her side, I saw her hands were folded over her stomach. Her bare legs stretched under the table, ankles crossed, coral-lacquered toes naked. As if she'd dozed off while sunbathing in the frigid morning air. She wore pink panties with red hearts and a matching bra. Her eyes were closed. Under the spray of pimples, her skin was silvery as fish scales.

I shook Morgan's shoulder; nothing. A tap, then a shove. She grumbled but didn't open her eyes. I slapped one cheek. She frowned, eyeballs rolling under blue-flecked lids. When I struck again, her gray lips pursed. I peeled the right eyelid. Pin-dot pupil unresponsive to light. Five times I'd seen kids like this at Rutgers. I saved three of them. I phoned 911 to report the drug overdose. Possible suicide attempt. Emergency medics were five minutes out. They could get here to deliver lifesaving treatment faster than I could drive to the hospital in Princeton.

I hauled Morgan to my Jeep, where I laid her across the back seat. After I fired the engine, I piled a blanket over her legs to warm her until the ambulance arrived. She moaned when I worked the lapels of her jacket to close them over her chest. Her breathing was even but shallow. Her heart under my fingertips beat steady. I saw an envelope stuffed in her pink bra. Lavender-tinted paper. Addressed to *DADDY & MOMMY.* Unsealed, so I opened it. Morgan's block print sprawled across the page within a border of lilac blossoms.

> *Daddy, I'm so sorry I let you down. I couldn't make college happen the way you wanted. I know I could have done better. Mommy, I'm sorry I disappointed you. Now, you won't have to worry about me ever again. I love you, Morgan*

I refolded the note and slipped the sheet into its envelope. Wetting a finger, I dabbed the gum to close the seal. Morgan's parents deserved the fiction that they were the only ones to read their daughter's farewell message.

QPD arrived four minutes later followed by a screaming ambulance. I trailed the convoy for thirty minutes to Princeton-Plainsboro Hospital. I wanted to see Morgan into safety. And I wanted to confront her parents for answers about the college placement scheme that had pushed this child to the brink of destruction.

# CHAPTER **FORTY**

Wednesday afternoon I phoned Ingrid twice from Princeton-Plainsboro Hospital. At 12:15, I reported I was in the waiting hall of the emergency department. Morgan was alive, that's all I knew. Yes, her parents had rushed over. No, I would not bring Ingrid to the hospital; there was nothing she could do here. My second call, at three thirty, was from a sofa in the seventh-floor visitors' lounge across the hall from Morgan's room. I told Ingrid her friend was out of danger, resting comfortably. The nurses were great, the doctors attentive. Both parents were guarding her bed. I said Ingrid had saved Morgan's life. She hung up, still sobbing.

As I extinguished the phone, a shadow crossed its shiny surface. "You were being kind, Ms. Myrick." Hugh Gaylord's voice was tight, his eyes glazed with tears. "All blessings go to you. *You* saved Morgan's life."

"I'm glad I got to her in time, Mr. Gaylord." I shifted right, hoping he'd sit. He did. My hurt arm squealed when he bumped me, but I bit my lip. My pain was small potatoes compared to his.

The love seat wasn't made for two adult strangers. Our bodies touched at thigh and hip. In this forced intimacy, I could feel tremors rack his torso as he bent over his knees. Gaylord was wearing a navy blazer over charcoal slacks. The power-casual uniform he'd chosen for his conference that morning with Rome headmaster Charles Dumont. Gaylord's Adam's apple jogged at the sweat-stained collar of his shirt.

Subduing a moan, he straightened. "I don't know how to thank you." He dragged fingers over his lips. "We'd be lost without Morgan. Devastated."

I wanted him talking, so I reversed earlier intentions and lobbed a tough shot. "I read Morgan's note." He gasped, but I offered no apology. "What do you think she meant by 'I couldn't make college happen the way you wanted'?"

He stuttered, "I-I don't know. I mean, not really . . ." White glittered around his pupils as he dragged his gaze from my face.

"Not true, Mr. Gaylord. You *do* know what your daughter was referring to."

His sob was rough. I studied his profile: long nose and chin, heavy lids over hazel pupils like Morgan's. A single tear dangled from the corner of his mouth. His tongue darted to catch the drop.

"Yes, of course I know." He scraped blond strings from his hairline until they clumped in ridges. "It was the pressure to get into a good college."

"Lots of kids feel that. Especially in a hyper-competitive school like Rome." I leaned into his ribs. "Tell me what happened to Morgan."

He sagged against my body. "You're right about Rome. The place is a pressure cooker. Like the old joke goes, at Rome, every student is above average." No eye contact, no laugh.

"How did Morgan get onto Melinda Terrence's List?"

"You know about that?" His heart raced next to my injured arm. Throb against throb; wound against wound.

"Yes. Contacts filled me in." I wouldn't spill what I'd learned from Ingrid or Morgan. Let him imagine I had a vast network of confidential informants.

He said, "Melinda called us about fourteen months ago. She'd already had a meeting with Morgan at school. Just as she did in the spring with every second-year student."

"Did she tell you Morgan was unusual, deserving of special attention?" I coated my voice with phony sugar.

Gaylord's face flushed. "Of course, that was the tactic. Flatter the parents, underline the singular talents of their child."

"You knew Morgan's GPA wasn't strong, but you bought the glossy promises Melinda pitched anyway."

"She told us what we wanted to hear, yes. But we only wanted the best possible outcome for Morgan. We thought we could guarantee that."

"With cash, right?"

"Yes." His voice dipped to a whisper. "A lot of money." He sighed, then blew on the steepled tips of his fingers as if they were scorched. "Are you a parent, Ms. Myrick?"

"Yes." No need to correct his question with a past-tense answer. I was still a parent. *Forever*.

"Then you know you'd do anything to guarantee your child's success. Anything."

*For Monica, yes, everything*. I grazed the necklace at my throat. Her scrolled initial felt cool against my heated skin. *But everything wasn't enough*. I choked back the sob that wanted to spurt from my gorge. Not falling into the diversion, I pushed. "How much did this 'anything' cost?"

His fingers became objects of fascination. Was he adding the sum in his head? "We agreed to pay Melinda Terrence two hundred and twenty-five thousand dollars for her services."

I tried to sound cool; sure, I knew plenty of folks who tossed their money like Mardi Gras beads. "Her services included what?"

"Tutoring for the PSATs and SATs. Completing college applications. Drafting the essays. Rehearsing interviews with recruiters. Arranging and escorting private campus tours. Consulting with admissions officers at the schools we targeted."

"Did Melinda bribe those admissions officers to place your daughter in their universities?"

Gaylord hesitated. He fiddled with the hidden tie in his jacket pocket. A careful answer: "Not to my knowledge."

I snapped, "You're not under oath here. I want to get the facts, not convict you."

His lashes fluttered like beige moths. "Okay, yes, I'm pretty sure money transferred hands."

"And the payments you gave Melinda, were they in checks or cash?" I knew the answer but I wanted it confirmed.

"Cash, always. She insisted. Or, rather, she said her husband insisted."

"Why did Phil Bolden want your payments in cash?" Heat jumped in a knot between my shoulder blades. Would Phil always have this effect on me? I shifted, hoping the telltale warmth hadn't transferred from my thigh to Gaylord's. Was this story going to hurt more than I could bear?

He blew a long breath, oblivious to my discomfort. "I don't know. But I'm sure he did. I remember one time I came to their house short of the usual amount. I gave Melinda what I had on me—seven hundred dollars. I handed her a check to cover the difference."

"Was she okay with the check?"

"No. She said, 'We need it in cash.' When she glanced at a photo of him on her desk, I figured the 'we' included her husband. Then she said not to bother. When she pushed the check across the desk to me, her face twisted into a weird smile. She said, 'No worries, God will cover the difference this week.'"

"What do you think she meant?"

"I don't know. She'd mentioned church a few times before. Asked my wife about our own church and said she'd like to visit some Sunday. Of course, we said she'd be welcome to join us at Grace Episcopal anytime she wanted."

"Did she?"

"No. I got the impression Phil was quite involved in one of those churches in the Flats. You probably know them. I guess he felt more comfortable attending a church that catered to his own people, you know how it is." Eyebrows hiked, Gaylord shrugged. Speculating about the segregation of religious practice in America wasn't his bag. "Maybe Melinda wanted to worship somewhere closer to her own roots."

Or maybe Melinda chafed against seeing her money siphoned by Phil Bolden to Bethel AME Church. I coughed, suppressing my guess.

But Gaylord seemed to pick up my doubts. He shifted until he faced me. Maybe his raw feelings heightened his perceptions. Or perhaps the near death of his daughter had pressed religious thoughts to the front of his mind.

"We invited Melinda to come to church with us a few times. She never accepted. But maybe now . . . Now, with what's happened to Morgan . . . Our faith has been tested. We've been found wanting. Eve and I need to renew our connections through prayer . . ." His jaw sagged with mumbled expressions of virtue.

I wanted to slap the piety off his horse face. He'd almost lost his only child. These nods toward prayer chafed me. I wanted to scream: *This is ass–covering, not soul–baring. You know what real horror is? It's losing your daughter and then her father. And not being able to bring either of them back no matter how hard you work. It's feeling your life sucked out of your body every time you see your baby's photo. Or you hear your husband's name.* That *is desolation, you entitled asshole.*

Before the rant exploded from my mouth, I turned my questions inside out. "Mr. Gaylord, did you ever deliver any payments directly to Melinda's husband, Phil Bolden?"

He reared against the back of the sofa, surprised by my vehemence. Then his haystack eyebrows shifted. "I never did meet Phil. Only heard about him around the school." Thinking made his nose quiver, then his chin. "A few months ago, we invited the Boldens for dinner. Melinda accepted, then two days later called to cancel. She wouldn't say, but I got the impression she and Phil had had a falling-out. About something major. Several months ago, she told us she wanted to stop working with her List of special students." Big teeth gnawed flakes from his lower lip. "She said she wanted to go back to helping all Rome students on an equal basis."

This was important information. The plan to drop such a lucrative side business couldn't have pleased Phil. He was transferring hundreds of thousands to Bethel. According to banker Jackson Peel, the Bethel money deposited by church treasurer Nadine Burriss was spent buying property and services from Phil Bolden's company.

Phil was laundering his wife's shady cash into legitimate money. How could he tolerate her dismantling the system he'd established?

I asked, "Did Melinda mention when she wanted to quit her side business?"

"She told Eve she would work with the current group of students. See them through to acceptance in college next spring. Then she would stop the List. Eve said Melinda sounded exhausted. Maybe discouraged, too. That's when Eve repeated our invitation to come to church with us. We felt sorry for Melinda."

Hugh Gaylord craned his neck to look toward the corridor beyond the visitors' alcove. I followed his gaze. Through the glass walls of her room, I could see Morgan swaddled in a cocoon of sheets and blankets. Eve Gaylord perched on the edge of a chair near the bed, one hand poised on the girl's knee. Her blond ponytail tipped to the right, the mother seemed to be listening. But Morgan's face was turned to the ceiling, her eyes and mouth closed.

Gaylord said, "I need to get back to them." He shifted his weight as if to rise.

"I understand, Mr. Gaylord. Your priority is in that room." I touched his knee, mimicking the mother/daughter scene. When I squeezed, I felt him relax into the sofa. "But I want to know what you learned this morning from Charles Dumont."

Sharp breath in, sputter out. "How do you know about that?"

"I know your daughter met with Dr. Dumont recently in his office. I don't know what he told her. My guess is the message was dire. I think Dumont's interview with Morgan set her on the path toward her suicide attempt."

Gaylord cringed at the blunt words. Wrinkles pleated between his eyes. He stroked his right brow, smoothing the pain.

My heart panged as I saw the heartbreak on his face. But I had more to deliver: "And I think when she learned you and your wife had a conference scheduled with Dumont this morning, that news pushed her over the edge."

"Oh, God, forgive us," he groaned. "We didn't know. We didn't see." He held his head in both hands, driving fingernails into his scalp.

I leaned to angle my face toward his. I pressed my shoulder against him, hoping he'd absorb my sympathy with the contact.

I repeated my question. "What did Dumont tell you?"

"He—he said Morgan was failing all her courses this semester. Even with help from Melinda Terrence, he doubted Morgan could get into any prestigious university with this GPA."

"Did he have a solution?"

Gaylord's eyes bugged. "How could you possibly guess that?" He raked his gaze from my hair to my throat, searching for signs of witchcraft.

I owned no magic, only gut instinct. I said, "Dumont is shrewd and self-serving. Transactional. He looks for personal-gain opportunities in every problem. He saw one in yours."

"Yes, it's true." Hands trembling, Gaylord continued, "Dumont told us he could save Morgan's fall semester grades. He said he could talk with her teachers, encourage them to look again at her midterm marks."

"For a price?"

Nodding, he rushed the damning story: "Yes. He wanted ten thousand dollars. In check form. To support a new building fund, he said. Five thousand today. Another five thousand next month. The school plans to construct a new wing of the library. Name it in honor of Philip Bolden. Dr. Dumont said our money would go to that fund."

My stomach churned. Dumont had exploited Phil's death. Why was I surprised? The man was a vampire, sucking blood from any victims he could trap. I closed my eyes against the nausea. When I opened them, Gaylord was studying my reaction. He didn't know I was the first wife; my response seemed exaggerated. Or maybe he assumed I was sickened by Dumont's extortion scheme. Both, but I wasn't telling.

"And you made out a check to that fund?" I asked.

"No, Dumont said the school's finance department hadn't completed the paperwork to set up the library fund. At present there is no established mechanism for receiving money directly into the new account. So he told me to make the check in his name. He'd transfer the money to the new fund when he was able."

"You saw through Dumont's ploy, right?" Naked subterfuge for personal gain was easy to spot.

Gaylord nodded. "We knew what he meant to do."

"You wrote the check as he asked?" The answer was obvious, but I wanted to hear it anyway.

"Yes, of course. Our daughter's future was at stake. How could I do otherwise?"

My voice cracking, I used the present tense to offer comfort. "I have a daughter, too, Mr. Gaylord. I'd do the same as you."

If writing checks could restore my child to life, I'd have filled my house with a hundred Monicas by now. Instead, I had her necklace and my golden memories. With my thumb I polished circles over the M dangling at my throat. Then I pressed until the initial's edges pricked my skin, masking sorrow with gentle pain.

Perhaps blending my anguish with his own, Gaylord loosed a raspy sob. He fished his tie from his pocket. Rolling it into a ball, he dabbed both eyes then his nose. We stood from the sofa, swaying as we separated. Gaylord shook my hand, then loped across the hall toward his daughter's bedside.

I took five minutes to calm my outrage. About the Gaylords, about Phil, about all the lost and hurt people in this case. The muscles of my back and arms were stiff with bottled grief. Standing, the tension jetted through every limb.

I angled toward a picture window overlooking the hospital parking lot. The seventh floor provided a panoramic view of the woods and streets between Princeton to the west and Queenstown to the east. A dense quilt of trees alternating brown and ochre covered the puny homes below. Highways ran like stitching between the clumps of foliage. At the edge of the parking lot, I saw a traffic circle, red and white lights turning in the gloom.

Phil's murder case involved a circle, too, with money greasing the rotation of the wheel. Armed with Hugh Gaylord's painful testimony I now knew how that money flowed. Dumont funneled Rome parents to Melinda Terrence. These snobs paid Melinda to buy seats in prestigious universities for their children. Was it Phil who first demanded that payment for his wife's counseling services be in cash? I'd never know for sure. Certainly, Phil's was the inventive mind that saw a way to shuffle Melinda's money into the urban revitalization project of Bethel AME Church. Had he joined the church committee before or after he began transferring cash to treasurer Nadine Burriss? Not that it mattered. Nadine was obsessed with rebuilding her old neighborhood. Persuasive homeboy Phil Bolden provided her with a fire hose of cash. Nadine enlisted banker Jackson Peel's help in opening a special account for these donations. With this money, Nadine purchased derelict Trenton houses owned by Phil Bolden. As Peel told me, she also bought construction and maintenance services for her rehabbed community. Services provided by Phil's company. Over time, millions of dollars of Melinda's illicit cash returned to Phil's pockets as legitimate earnings.

I could hear Phil's excited narration of this marvelous plan: *Everybody wins, babe. Rome kids get into top schools. Sutton Hill kids get new homes where they can grow up healthy and happy. I can build a comfortable life for our son, give him everything I never had. Even that vulture headmaster gets money for his fancy clothes. No losers, babe. Only winners.* If he'd told the story to me that way, with his honey voice and soft eyes, I'd have bought it, no question.

Through the window frame, I watched gold-tipped clouds wheel across the bright sky. Staring at their foamy whiteness made my eyes ache. I rubbed my lids, then focused on dark splotches spreading across the landscape below. This afternoon, I'd learned from Hugh Gaylord about shadows that had disrupted Phil's happy scheme. Gaylord's story supported the report from Dumont: at some point in the past year, Melinda decided to jump off the money wheel. According to Dumont, she had told Phil she wanted out. They argued, according to Gaylord. Paradise wrecked. I figured Melinda's rebellion was the act that precipitated Phil's death. Everyone in the scheme was injured by the rupture. Nadine, Dumont, Melinda. No one escaped undamaged. Who'd been harmed the most? Who had murdered Phil?

I turned from the alcove, stepping past the sofa as my eyes adjusted from sunset embers to the hospital's antiseptic glare. My fists still ached with pent-up fury. When I reached the hallway, I spotted a target for my anger.

Charles Dumont exited the elevator at the far end of the corridor. He halted to study the room numbers and arrows on the wall. Head down, he walked toward me. Did he intend to offer his best wishes for a speedy recovery to the fallen Rome student, Morgan Gaylord, and her parents? Repulsive ghoul. His black hair was slicked into a helmet, strands forming stiff points above his white collar. He wore his uniform of black-on-black suit and green striped tie. Undertaker drag. Not a good look for a visit to a stricken girl. A vulnerable teen he'd hounded into a suicide attempt. Not happening, not on my watch.

I ran to intercept Dumont, blocking his access to Morgan's room. I squared my shoulders and jutted my head.

Recognition lit his eyes above a tiny smile. Then both receded, replaced by a scowl. "Ms. Myrick, such a surprise to find you here. Do you know the Gaylords?" Cute icebreaker. He extended a hand as if we were chums at a cocktail party.

In reply, I threw a left jab to Dumont's chin. My injured arm yelped, but seeing him stagger to one knee erased the ache. Pain transferred from my body to his. *Fair trade, vampire.*

His eyes boggled, jaw working left and right. When he tried to stand, I clubbed a short right to his nose. Cartilage cracked like kindling. Another punch to the same spot. Blood spurted past his mouth, the deluge covering his shirt buttons in red. He squeaked, more shock than pain.

As an educator, he'd want knowledge, so I dropped some. "Here's why I hit you: you hounded that poor girl. You extorted money from her parents."

He mumbled through the blood and tried to rise to one knee.

With my left hand, I pressed his shoulder until he sat hard. I dabbed my right fist to his cheek. "You cheated the school." Knuckles tapped bone. "You exploited Phil Bolden's memory." Tap-tap.

"There's more, asshole, but time's up." I flattened my palm against the red splotch on his cheekbone. "Understand?" I shoved.

He tipped like a bowling pin. Mewling, he curled on the tile, knees tucked to chest.

I heard a shout behind me, then thudding shoes. Dumont was on a hospital ward; instant help was at hand. He was in no danger of bleeding to death here. Caregivers gonna care, even if I didn't.

I walked to the elevator and punched the down button. As the car neared the first floor, I swiped my fists on both pantlegs to remove the headmaster's blood. The lobby was crammed with people, all ignoring me. Good. I inhaled. If I had to, I'd accept the penalty for my attack on Dumont. But if I could leave the building unnoticed, I'd prefer that. Responsible, sure. Remorseful, no way. The bastard deserved more beatdown than I'd delivered.

The best way to convey innocence was to stroll. So I ambled toward the revolving doors at the entrance, arms swinging.

Over the crowd, a high-pitched voice rang my name. "Myrick, stop. I need to talk with you."

Lola Conte waved her hat and trotted toward me. Her face was pale and shiny; behind her ears, perspiration curled her brown hair. Had word of my assault on Dumont raced to the hospital lobby already? QPD was faster on the uptake than I'd figured. No point in fleeing. I prepared to surrender and take my legal licks.

When she reached my side, I tried to smooth jitters from my voice. "Officer Conte, can I help you?" Under her puffer coat, her uniform blouse escaped from her belt. Her black tie was twisted, the knot jerked loose.

She countered with another question: "How'd you hear the report so fast?"

"The report?"

"You monitoring QPD radio frequencies?"

We were speaking at cross-purposes. Like dingbats in a vaudeville routine. Hoping to end the bullshit, I said, "What report?" I refused to spill about Dumont unless she demanded it. "Why are you here?"

"You don't know?" Eyes spinning, Conte scanned my brow for holes. I wanted to strangle the cop for her nonresponsive answer.

I shook my head. "Know what?"

Her mouth sagged around gray teeth. "Melinda Bolden was transported here an hour ago. She was attacked in her home. Blunt-force trauma to the head. She's in surgery now."

# CITY OF PAPER

## CHAPTER **FORTY-ONE**

The crowd in the hospital lobby swirled around us, grumbling as Lola Conte and I blocked the exit. Conte's horrific news didn't sink in right away. Melinda Terrence attacked? How? When? Nothing made sense. A shoulder jostled my back. A blond man in scrubs swabbed nicotine breath across my neck. I grabbed Conte's elbow and drew her toward a rack of brochures near the reception desk.

I pinched the bruised knuckles on my right hand until the pain cleared my mind. The battered face of Charles Dumont slithered from my mind, replaced by Melinda Terrence. She'd been assaulted. Bludgeoned in her own home. Was Tariq injured, too? I blinked, then stepped closer to Lola Conte. She retreated, eyes on my fists. Maybe she feared I'd slug her. She wasn't far off base.

"Tell it to me slow," I said. Gritted teeth trapped my request. "From the top."

Conte whispered, "The maid—Olivia something or other— arrived at the Bolden home at twelve thirty this afternoon. She said she had washed breakfast dishes in the kitchen like usual. Then she looked to see if Mrs. Bolden wanted a fresh cup of coffee. She said she found Mrs. Bolden in her office, slumped over the desk. Unconscious. Lots of blood on the back of the head. The maid called in the report at one-ten."

I remembered Olivia the housekeeper who had served coffee during my condolence visit to the Bolden home after Phil's death. Had the shock of discovering her employer's battered body delayed the 911 call? How much tidying had Olivia done before going to the home office today? I didn't suspect Olivia of anything, but questions flew like hornets through my mind.

"And the son, Tariq? Where's he?"

"My partner and I were first on the scene. We arrived when the ambulance did. We searched the house. No kid."

"Maybe he's in his dorm at Rome." Hoping for the best made me stutter. "D-did you call there?"

"Baker tried the kid's cell. No answer. I sent him to the campus to check the residence hall. The boy deserves to hear about his mom from an official source. Not the campus gossip squad."

I imagined her arrogant partner, Baker, seething when Conte handed him the rookie assignment. I wiped a smirk and asked the obvious: "Did you see the Boldens' car in the driveway?"

"A brown Infiniti, yeah."

"And what about the Mustang? White, convertible."

"Sure, it was nose to nose with the Infiniti. What of it?"

My stomach sank. "The Mustang is Tariq's ride. If it's at the house, he should have been, too."

"Maybe someone gave him a lift to school. Last night." Lola shrugged. "Or this morning. Before the attack on his mom."

"Maybe." I didn't buy the scenario. Too neat. "Call your partner. See if he's found Tariq at school."

Lola grunted, then tapped the speed dial for Baker. I dragged four deep breaths. I wanted to calm my nerves, disperse my racing fears. Tariq had to be safe, deep in a snap quiz in seventh-period econ. Or playing hooky with delinquent friends, trolling the mall for townie girls. I didn't want to phone Ingrid. Not yet. She'd already been stressed today. Rescuing a friend from a suicide attempt was trauma enough. I wanted to save her from new alarm about Tariq unless absolutely required. I'd wait to contact Ingrid when I found him. Bringing him home wasn't her responsibility. Tariq's safety was my job.

I listened to Conte's end of the conversation with Baker. Tariq wasn't in his dorm room. A quick consult with the registrar yielded his class schedule. At this hour, he should have been in World History

Since 1989. According to the teacher, he hadn't joined the class. Conte told her partner to check the library, gym, cafeteria, nurse's office, and playing fields. Baker's anger singed my eyelashes through the phone.

Conte stuffed the device into her coat pocket. She gazed for so long at benches flanking the exit, I guessed she wanted to sit. Murky green colored her cheeks. Brutal assault on the mom, vanished son. Absorbing tough news was hard on anyone, even a cop. Especially a pregnant one.

We took the bench. After a moment, Conte pushed wet strands from her hairline. Straightening, she said, "You think he's on the lam?" She glared at me as if I'd uttered a sacrilege. "You make the kid for the perp?"

"I don't." I sounded firm, like I'd assessed all the angles. Like I wasn't drowning in hopes and fears, not facts. "They had tensions, sure. Maybe more than most moms and kids. And the murder of Phil Bolden didn't bring them closer. Maybe even drove a new wedge between them."

I wasn't going to admit to Conte my part in poisoning relationships in the Bolden family. I wasn't sure how much Melinda and Tariq knew. If I had to confess, I would. But not yet. Not ever, if I could fix it before those ugly truths emerged.

I continued, "I don't think tensions were wound tight enough to drive Tariq to attempt to kill his mother. Despite their differences, he needed her. He loves her." I'd bank all my money on that.

Conte nodded. "Yeah, that's how I figure it, too. The boy's not our prime suspect." She lifted her chin and glanced around the lobby. No one paid attention to our little confab. We weren't sick, we weren't doctors. She went on. "We sent the maid to headquarters for further questioning. We'll get her story straight or break it before nightfall. We'll check her background, her family. Run the names through immigration. Where she came from. How long she's been in the country. Dig up her relatives, boyfriends. Known associates. Check the fingerprints. Any priors on file."

As Conte riffed, her eyes brightened and her mouth puckered around a smile. Police work's rough discipline brought her joy.

"Maybe this Olivia's got partners who pulled a burglary and clobbered the lady when they botched the operation."

I said, "Your theory is this gang of burglars took the son?"

"Yeah, could've happened."

I sputtered, "So, as you see it, this band of nitwits compounded the burglary with murderous assault and kidnapping? And they left Olivia the housekeeper behind to take the fall?" I shook my head. "Not a chance."

"You got a better scenario?"

*Not really.* Images snaked across my mind; a hodgepodge of guesses and fractured memories. My heart competed with my brain to win the flip-and-fumble contest.

Before I could respond to Conte, raised voices drew our attention to the reception desk. A man dressed in a tweed coat and black driving cap pounded on the chest-high counter.

The clerk stood from her swivel chair, two hands extended in a soothing gesture. "Sir, if you'll give me a minute, I'll direct you to the proper department."

The man brandished his wallet. "I'm ready to pay, I tell you." He waved the leather under the receptionist's nose, then smacked the counter. "Credit card, check? PayPal? Venmo? What do you want?" Red-faced, he peeled a stack of bills from the wallet. "I got the money. See?" He thumped the cash against the walnut surface.

Money. My face stung as if I'd been slapped with that wad of cash. Phil Bolden's money. That was the filthy heart of this case. I stroked the vein pulsing at my temple. Yes, that had to be it. As simple and deadly as money. The attack on his wife, the disappearance of his son, even his murder. All were connected to an obsessive desire to control Phil's money. To make it flow. Melinda Terrence benefited from that cash flow but she wouldn't have staged her own beating. Charles Dumont craved the money, but I'd left him upstairs bleeding and innocent of the assault on Melinda. Only one suspect remained unaccounted for: Nadine Burriss. The church treasurer obsessed by gold. I needed to move fast to prevent this cascade of disasters from claiming another victim.

I turned toward Conte, ready to enlist her in my desperate effort to save Tariq. I needed the backup and the witness. I saw Conte's hand hover near her service weapon. Yes, I needed the gun, too. But her mind was on halting the fracas at the reception desk. When Conte stepped toward the shouting man, I slid to block her. I wanted her with me, not breaking up this petty brawl. When a hospital security guard hustled into view, I grunted in relief. The uniformed woman—five feet three in all dimensions—pointed at the distressed man, mouthed a few syllables, then jerked her thumb toward a side corridor. Problem pacified.

I grabbed Conte's wrist, steering her toward the exit. "I know who attacked Melinda and kidnapped Tariq Bolden." My heart pounded, elation mixing with dread in a wild tattoo.

Her eyes bulged, unblinking as saucers. When a bubble of protest flickered on her lower lip, I dug fingernails into her flesh. "I need you, Lola. Come with me now. I'll explain as we drive."

She flinched, but followed my lead. "Where?"

"Move. Now." I dragged her to the door. "Tariq Bolden's at Bethel AME Church. If we delay, he'll be murdered."

## CHAPTER **FORTY-TWO**

Navigating my Jeep through the parking lot of Princeton-Plainsboro Hospital demanded high-level concentration. Lola Conte waited until we'd reached an intersection before launching a volley of questions.

"What makes you think Tariq Bolden is at Bethel?"

"The church is connected to the money his mother and father were channeling."

"You mean laundering?"

"Yes." I zoomed left across two lanes clogged with delivery vans and taxis.

Conte shifted under the seat belt until she could look at me square. "Who at the church? The pastor? Some deacon or assistant minister?"

"The church treasurer. Nadine Burriss."

"Dangerous?"

"Desperate, yes. And she has a gun." I punched my horn to force a path around a dawdling SUV. Webs of graying twilight draped over rush-hour mobs, increasing the street snarl as we neared Q-Town center. We had to cross the tangled roads of Abbott's Landing, then the commercial district. Beyond there, Bethel AME was on Quincy Street, five blocks into the heart of the Flats. Ten minutes from here. Fifteen if we were unlucky.

Conte pulled her phone and raised it to her face. "Then we need backup. I'm calling in our current location and destination."

"Stop." Anxiety shrilled my voice. "Not yet. Let me handle this. Nadine knows me. I can talk to her." As I steered, the raw skin on my left arm crackled with new pain.

"She a friend?"

"No. But our connections run deep. Through the church. Back to my mother." I didn't mention how Phil Bolden linked me to Nadine. Keeping my private life out of this equation remained a priority. "I can de-escalate this situation faster without QPD swarming in, guns blazing."

When we jolted over a pothole, Conte's words spurted toward the dashboard. "What makes you so sure there is a situation?"

"Nadine Burriss got money from Phil Bolden. Millions over the past three years."

Conte whistled. "Now you're talking serious money."

"For sure. When sums hiked past the nickel-and-dime stage, my mother used to call it 'adult money.'"

As we dipped through a pool of lamplight, I swerved to avoid another pothole. I could see Conte's mouth flatten as her eyes closed. "You figure this Nadine lined her purse under the table? Lots of Gucci and Louis Vuitton?" Clichés of ghetto queens danced in her head.

"No, she used the funds to support urban redevelopment in Sutton Hill, one of the most blighted neighborhoods in Trenton."

"Some kind of bleeding heart?" Conte raised three fingers to her mouth, covering a burp. "A snowflake do-gooder, hunh?" Another belch, then a hiccup.

Did contempt make the cop nauseous? I wanted to defend Nadine Burriss against the sneer. To paint her crimes with softer shades. I understood Nadine's obsession, though I'd never condone her actions.

"She grew up in Sutton Hill and wanted to give back."

"You know this how?"

"We talked." I remembered our two meetings in Nadine's basement office. How dank shadows hovered over the scale model of the redevelopment project sprawled on her table. How that white cardboard cityscape shone like a dream, pure but within reach. Not a ghetto girl's fantasy. An attainable goal. Solid as timber, real as brick. If only Phil's money kept flowing.

Conte's retort broke my reverie. "And now you think this woman has grabbed the Bolden boy? Why?"

"To coerce his mother to continue supplying the funds Phil Bolden promised."

"You figure Nadine'll hurt the kid?"

"Maybe. If you force her. Or scare her." I raised my voice over the traffic's blare. "That's why you can't call in the troops. Not yet. Give me time with Nadine. Let me talk to her first."

"What makes you think she's run to the church?"

"It's her safe space." I remembered my mother's description of the old church: *Bethel remained our rock, our solace, and our refuge. Why would we move anywhere else?* I added, "Under pressure, Nadine will run to comfort. And that means Bethel."

Conte cradled the phone against her waist, then returned it to her coat pocket. "Okay. For now." When she withdrew her hand, I saw two cellophane-wrapped packets of saltines. "But why you hafta hit every fucking pothole from here to the Flats? You got my stomach marching double time."

Using her teeth, Conte ripped a corner from one packet. "You better hope these crackers work." A burp around the first crunch. "Or I'm barfing all over your fancy ride."

"You puke and I'm coming for your paycheck." I bared my gums so she could see the grin in the dark. "Every last dollar."

"Knocked up is a bitch, man." She gobbled the next saltine and tore into the second packet.

No lies detected. Pregnancy wasn't for the fainthearted. I pumped the brakes to ease around a corner opposite the First National Bank. With luck, we were four minutes from Bethel AME.

Listening to Conte smack her saltines, my mind drifted toward the woman we'd confront at the church. I remembered the changes in Nadine's appearance during our several talks. The thick waist, the popped belly button under her sleek dresses. Not fat, a firm, protruding stomach. She wore rings during our first visit. They vanished later. Had she removed them to accommodate pregnancy-swollen fingers? The last time I saw her she'd switched from high heels to flats to accommodate the shift in her center of gravity. I remembered noting her swollen ankles and puffy cheeks. Could Nadine Burriss be pregnant? A baby fit the physical evidence I'd seen. And an affair with Phil Bolden made sense. Awkward, humiliating, but possible. A romance, blighted yet fertile, would have pushed Nadine past the brink. I wanted to test my guess without provoking her to desperate violence. How many lives hung in the balance, dependent on my delicacy and diplomacy?

At the stone Civil War monument that marked the informal gateway to the Flats, Conte's phone buzzed. Her partner, Baker, had returned to the hospital. He reported Melinda Terrence was out of surgery. She remained sedated but doctors were optimistic. The surgical team had stopped the bleeding that had threatened her brain. With time and physical therapy, they expected her to make a full recovery. Conte instructed Baker to stay near the stricken woman to take a statement as soon as she regained consciousness.

I wasn't the praying kind; I'd experienced too much anguish to resort to futile conversations with the big bearded guy now. Why had he taken a flyer when I needed him most? But as we crept into the shadow of the church, I pitched a silent appeal toward the sky. Melinda was safe; now I wanted to bring her son home.

Near the iron gate of Bethel Cemetery, I doused the headlights. I cut the engine and slid the Jeep against a pile of damp leaves at the gutter. Conte jerked the door handle, eager to storm the church.

Before she jumped to the pavement, I grabbed her wrist. "You follow the sidewalk along the parking lot." I pointed toward the new two-story wing of the church. "Nadine's office is in the basement. Last room in the back. There's a side door to her office. Always propped open. You wait in the stairwell. No noise. Listen for my signal."

"What about you?"

"I'll enter the church through the main door. Approach Nadine's office from the corridor. I'll make noise so she won't be surprised when I enter. I don't want her spooked. She might hurt the boy if she's scared. The more she feels in charge of the situation, the better for all of us."

"Got it." Conte gulped, not nausea this time, enthusiasm. "I'll give you ten minutes. Then I'm calling backup."

"See you on the other side, Lola." When I raised my hand, it shook. Excitement, yes, but fear, too. I clasped her neck to curb the tremors. "I want everyone to come out of this alive."

# CHAPTER **FORTY-THREE**

When I stomped into Nadine Burriss's office, the blaze of overhead lights dazzled.

I stood blinking, then raised a hand to shield my eyes. Wet panting filled the air. Spurts from Nadine; deep gasps from the boy she held captive. Tariq Bolden trembled in a straight chair, his wrists cuffed together with plastic zip ties. At my entrance, Nadine jammed a gun into the flesh under his jaw. I saw his Adam's apple jog beside the metal probe. A tear slid from his right eye, matching one crawling down my cheek. We were both afraid.

Nadine's face was stiff. With anger or fear? Hard to read. She waved a cell phone with her left hand, drawing a circle like a magic wand. "Get back," she said.

I halted. She might have the gun, but I wanted to control the room. I stepped two paces. "Nadine, I'm not here to harm you. And you're not going to hurt Tariq."

"I told you, get back, bitch." The folds of her dress stretched across her torso when she leveled the gun at me. "I can finish you, then get on with my business."

"What business is that?"

"This boy's mama has my money. I want it." With her thumb, she tapped the face of the phone, then raised it to her ear. "Why don't she answer? Don't she want to know I got her child?"

I saw my opening. The way to break Nadine's plan and maybe save our lives. "You trying to negotiate with Melinda?"

Her lips pursed in exasperation, like a teacher with a dull student. "Yes, what you think I mean?"

"I don't know what to think." My thick tongue clubbed the words. I sounded as stupid as Nadine always suspected I was. I could turn my fear into strategy if I worked it right. "You attacked Melinda this morning." Dense and slow. "Now you want her to help you? Make me understand."

Though Nadine's knees relaxed, tension stiffened her shoulders. I saw rolls of flesh bulge above her ballet flats as she squared on me. The ankle swelling looked painful.

If she thought I was an easy mark, maybe I could defuse the standoff. I said, "I'm unarmed." Truth rolled queasy desire in my gut: I wanted to smash my promise to Monica. I longed for my gun. To block Nadine's view of my thumping heart, I raised both palms in front of my chest. "I got no beef with you if you release him." I tipped my chin toward the boy. "Untie him. Let him go."

Eyes narrow. Shock. Doubt. Then a barking laugh. "Bitch, you lying. You think I'm stupid, hunh? Just like all of them." She pointed the gun at Tariq. "He goes free after she transfers all his daddy's money to me."

"What did you tell Melinda this morning?" I wanted to air the story, let Nadine feel she was dictating terms. "Did you ask her to hand over the cash in her safe?"

"Yeah, the nasty cow let me into her place, nose in the air, sniffing like I was some no-account trash. Like she hardly knew me and couldn't care less. Offered me a cup of coffee when we got to her office." Another laugh. Twisting her mouth to spew toward Tariq. "Your mama brought me coffee with her own lily-white hands. Sat the cup on the desk and had the nerve to ask what I wanted. Said she was busy."

Tariq moaned and shifted in his chair. His hands writhed over his lap. I could see weeping red lines on his wrists where the plastic cut the skin.

Nadine continued, "I told her I was busy, too. I said she needed to hand me the cash in her safe. And she had to keep on with the payments to Bethel, just the way Phil used to do."

I said, "But she didn't agree. She wanted to stop the arrangement."

Nadine glanced toward the conference table behind Tariq's chair. There the cardboard mock-up of the Sutton Hill neighborhood gleamed like a white wonderland. Her ivory city of paper. Since I'd last seen it, Nadine had inserted stiff figures of men and women. I could see puppet children with dogs playing on the cardboard sidewalks. Two profiles had distended bellies. These tiny cutouts confirmed my guess. She'd fashioned miniature figures to replicate her own pregnancy. She'd created a new generation of happy residents for her old community.

Her focus deflected, I fiddled the cell phone in my pocket. I wanted to record this standoff.

Nadine swung her gaze to me. "White bitch laughed in my face." Voice rising to imitate the mocking tones. "She said she'd never give me one more red cent. That's when I dropped the truth."

"Which truth?" She could have launched so many darts: Phil's betrayals, his disdain for his own wife and son? His reunion with me? Which poison had Nadine chosen to tip her arrow?

"I said her precious husband wanted his money to go to *our* project, in *our* city." Nadine smiled for the first time. "I told her Phil was in love with me and the Sutton Hill project was our baby."

Nadine's fingers flexed as she switched her grip on the gun. Grasping the barrel, she swung the handle in an arc above Tariq's head. Enacting how she'd struck his mother. "Poor thing dropped like a sack of potatoes."

The boy cringed; I did, too. Twelve feet away. Too far to reach her with a lunge. I held tight, thigh muscles trembling with tension.

Grinning, Nadine halted the weapon's flight, then drew the handle along Tariq's jaw. She cooed, "I'm not going to hurt you, baby. Not yet."

I wanted her focused on me. I aimed my best shot. "But Sutton Hill wasn't your only baby, right?" I pointed at her taut stomach.

Nadine gasped, left hand grabbing cloth at her belly button. She squawked, "Shut up, devil. You can't know that."

Tariq's feet kicked as if jolted by electricity. Gray stained his lips as he pressed tethered fists to his forehead.

"But it's true, Nadine. I *do* know it." Sweat dripped between my breasts. I stared at her stomach, my gut churning with hers. Another lie; I didn't know for sure. Playing my instincts: all signs pointed toward pregnancy. Her thick waist, swollen feet and fingers, even changes in her dress and shoe styles. But I was still guessing.

Until she gave in. She whispered to Tariq: "I didn't tell your mother about my baby." Nadine's gaze ricocheted around the room, garish paintings to desk lamp. Fluorescent lights to rug underfoot. "I didn't mean for you to know."

She sounded tender; the hand holding her cell hovered over his shoulder. She wanted to comfort him, but refused to drop the phone. It was her lifeline, her last hope for getting the money she craved.

The boy sagged, chin pressed against his T-shirt, elbows dangling over the chair's arms. His eyes were closed, his chest jerking. Had he fainted? I wanted him looking at me. On my team, following my lead. Withdrawal now endangered us both.

I pleaded, "Tariq, stay with me. I got you." A stretch, but not as big as the lie I planned to lob next.

"Yeah, I'm okay," he mumbled. His eyes rolled, then the lids peeled open. Glaze over his pupils made bile rise in my throat.

Nadine advanced on me. "You got nothing, bitch. Except your jealous mind and filthy mouth." She pointed the gun at my chin. "Use your phone, call Melinda. She won't take my calls, but she'll talk to you. You tell her I want that money. I got her son. And I'll hurt him if she doesn't deliver."

I shook my head, slowly, because my neck ached. "Nadine, it won't work."

"You better hope it works." She leveled the weapon with my nose in her sights.

"It can't. Melinda's dead. You killed her." I blinked with each word, careful and heavy. I needed both of them to believe this lie. "Driving here I got word from the hospital. She died in surgery. You killed her, Nadine."

Tariq's scream shattered the room. He slumped to the floor, dragging the cityscape from the table. Mouth pressed to the carpet, he moaned, "No, no, no." I clamped my jaw to block my own cry.

Nadine yelped, "That can't be. I—I didn't hit her that hard." Frantic, urgent. The phone fell from her grip, then the gun *thunked* on the rug, abandoned in her panic. Mouth wide, screeching: "No, no. She can't be dead, too."

New math: too equals two. Two deaths—Melinda and Phil—a twin killing. My heart pounded double time. I looked at Tariq, curled on the floor. In his agony, did he hear Nadine's words? I risked a glance toward the cracked door. Was my cop ally within earshot for phase one of Nadine's confession? No sign, no certainty.

Nadine knelt to rescue her cardboard paradise, crooning solace to the crumpled buildings and beheaded paper dolls.

Below her cries, I caught rummaging outside the rear door. Lola Conte, a fox mincing through underbrush. Had the others heard her? I glanced at Tariq and Nadine. Introspection curtained their eyes; they registered only their own troubles. On their knees facing each other but seeing no one, the boy and the woman remained gripped by their lost worlds.

Only I heard the cop's approach. Cool air from the stairwell brushed my forehead. The door cracked, but Conte held hidden. I'd told her to wait for my mark. She was following orders. Could we escape this deal with no deaths?

Nadine's weapon glinted with oily menace on the rug. Dark paisley whorls camouflaged the gun. Grab it, this standoff ends now. Neat package: Conte the champ, Myrick the muscle. I stepped onto the rug, my spine bent for the snatch.

I grazed the pistol's butt. Nadine clasped my left ankle with both fists. She howled, "Fuck you."

She jerked, leveraging her weight to upend me. I twisted left, knees in the air. Face cradled by the crook of my elbow. I slammed to the floor, left shoulder point taking the brunt of the fall. Collarbone snapped like a firecracker. Sinews in my shoulder stretched then gave, *pop-pop*. No screaming; breath wheezed from shocked lungs.

Left eye planted in the carpet, I saw Tariq grab the gun. His movements were herky-jerky. Back straight, elbows jutted, head reared, pupils tight as a drill bit. He stood, squaring his hips. With finger coiled on the gun handle, he aimed at Nadine's brow.

"You killed my mother. And my father." He motioned for her to stand. "Now you die, too."

On my knees, I extended the good right arm toward Tariq. "No, don't."

He looked at me as if I were a worm, wiped a palm against his shirt, then refocused on Nadine.

Her eyes pinwheeled in her head.

Pain translated into nausea spurted through my stomach. I doubled over to curb the bile. My lies—all of them—bore deadly fruit now. I hadn't told the truth about my relationship with Phil, hoping I could cover my recklessness with misdirection. I'd lied about Melinda, casting blame for a fake death on Nadine Burriss. My careless actions had yielded a harvest that might sentence this boy to death.

Wobbling, I stood. I slipped my injured arm between buttons on my jacket. Maybe the improvised sling would ease the strain on my shoulder. My breath expelling in whistles, I tried a short command, "Let her go, Tariq." Each gasp stabbed my left side. "She can't hurt anyone now." If I'd had more breath or less pain, I'd have given the longer explanation.

"She killed my father and mother. She talks now." Tariq's voice was cool, rumbling from deep in his chest. He tightened his finger on the trigger. "I want to know why."

His gun, his show. I looked a plea toward Nadine. Could she replace mulish resistance with cooperation? She didn't have to be charming. But to get us out of this alive, I wanted Nadine to ditch her resentment. Warm her anger with a wash of sympathy for the battered boy.

No such luck. But she did talk.

"I followed Phil and you," she said, glaring at me. "That night when you visited the cemetery."

The intimate walk to our daughter's graveside. Phil's confession about the stuffed toy. The sunset flicking gold streaks into his eyes. His warm hand in mine. His skin scented mossy green. I remembered that evening: my last good hours.

"He spoke with you on the church steps," I said. "Donated money, too."

"Yes, he said you were a college pal. An *old* friend." Nadine drawled to underline my decrepitude. "The envelope contained two-thirds of what he owed me that week. Phil said that was all he had. He said the donations were over. We were done."

"Contributions and affair? Both finished?" Breathing stung, but I wanted to wound her so I kept poking.

Strike. Nadine's nose and cheeks reddened. She said, "Yeah, he tried to do me that way. Throw me over like some snaggletoothed side piece. So I told him about the baby. Our baby."

"What did he say?" Tariq growled. His father's character was in the spotlight. Attention sparked, he lowered the gun.

Nadine, bruised but smug again. "He said, no worries. I was a smart girl. An ambitious girl. He was sure I'd take care of it the right way."

I remembered watching Phil bend over Nadine that evening to drop a dry kiss on her cheek. By her account, he'd just instructed her to abort their baby. I recalled how he'd trotted down the church steps and across the street to join me in the Jeep. Phil's tone then was brisk, relaxed. Like he'd bid farewell to a casual pal from round the way. *Sure, I know her. Nadine and me go way back. To Trenton. Always try to boost my home girl when I can.*

My stomach galloped under aching ribs. "You followed us to my house?"

"Yes. I figured Phil would be a minute, then I could catch him for a longer talk. About the money and the baby. Change his mind."

"But he stayed." I wanted to be the one to say this in front of Tariq. Maybe the straight pitch now would start a healing process. Make things solid between us going forward. I wanted that future, with Tariq in my life.

Nadine didn't care about my future with Tariq. About anything at all except telling the story of her abused trust. She said, "Yeah, he stayed until all hours. With you. And I waited him out."

My breathing broke into hiccups. Hard, painful sips of air. Had I been as duped as Nadine? As flat-out stupid? Or just delusional. That night I'd taken Phil to my bed. My idea, my lead. No force, no ca-joling. He'd joined me happily. Like our reunion was the fulfillment of a dream deferred. A long-desired homecoming. Now I knew he'd just learned of Nadine's pregnancy. He had cheated on his wife with Nadine. And on both of them with me.

I coughed, jolting pain from my elbow to my damaged shoulder. "When he left my place, you followed him." As if wounding her would salve my conscience. Didn't work. The guilt clung, putrid and sour.

Nadine bristled, her knees twitching. "I followed him, yes. But only to speak with him again. When he reached the parking lot, I jumped out of my car. I had the gun in my coat pocket. I didn't plan to use it. Only frighten him. Make him see I was serious."

She rubbed her belly, for consolation, I guess. Then she barreled on. "I wanted him to think about our Sutton Hill project. And about our baby. We'd started both. I said we ought to see them through together."

I wondered how close she'd gotten to Phil that night. Near enough to smell my jasmine scent on his clothing? On his skin? She wasn't naïve. She knew he'd betrayed her. But could she smell me, too? Was that final confirmation, in droplets of sweat and perfume, the revelation that caused her to pull the trigger?

I asked, "What did Phil tell you?" I kept my eyes on Nadine.

To my right, I heard Tariq's labored breathing swell and fall as the story unfolded. We were going to get out of this together, he and I. Damaged, maybe, but whole and safe. That was my silent pledge. I straightened my good arm along my flank. I hoped Tariq could read my intention in the rigidness of my neck and the stillness of my fingers.

Nadine sniffed. "He laughed. Even when I pulled the gun from my pocket Phil laughed. Like he didn't believe me. Or wasn't afraid. Or didn't care. You know how he goes. Big balloons of laughter, like we're on a picnic with a basket of fried chicken. That's how he sounded. Like I was a fool and a half. So I shot him."

Tariq keened, high-pitched like a wolf howl. I wanted to touch his neck, soothe his anguish with soft fingers. When I flinched, tremors sent pain snapping across my body. I fluttered my lids to scatter the hurt.

The boy raised his weapon toward Nadine. Concentrating, he poked the tip of his tongue between his lips. She stood flat-footed, her forehead smooth.

Sirens bayed in the parking lot. Conte had called in the troops. My heart thrummed with hope; this standoff could break without blood.

Tariq and Nadine lifted their eyes toward the narrow bank of windows near the ceiling. I saw surprise, rage, fear jitter across their faces. Emotions toggling as if linked by a fine wire. Then both jaws clenched. They didn't care; the police were a distant threat or a never-never promise. The only future either of them knew was right now, right here.

I inhaled. Too much breath; the agony shot from clavicle to sternum, then straight for my navel. No matter, I sucked a bigger breath. I shouted, "Conte, now."

Lola burst into the office, arms extended, sweeping her pistol in an arc encompassing the three of us. Her hat was pulled low; I couldn't read her eyes below the bill, only the tight line of her mouth. Muscles beside her ears clutched as if she was chewing gristle.

I said, "Conte, easy. No shooters here." Not exactly true. But I didn't want her killing Tariq, then asking questions later. "The boy is with me."

I pivoted toward him. "Tariq, look at me." When he did, I continued, "You don't want to shoot Nadine. You don't want to kill her or her baby. Your brother. Or your sister. You don't want to hurt them."

Conte grunted. Disbelief, horror. Sickness. I could feel ripples of energy roll from the cop's torso. Her pistol bobbed. She wanted to move. Now. I had to act before she did.

I said, "Tariq, here's how this ends. No noise. No shooting. No danger." Too much talking cost me another jolt through the lungs. My shoulder was on fire.

He nodded, listening to me, eyes and pistol on Nadine.

"Put the gun down," I said. "Easy. Don't throw it. Set it on the rug. Easy." I hoped repetition would relieve the ache in my arm. Didn't work. The throb kept pounding.

The boy did as I asked. He laid the gun at his sneaker. Black metal against white canvas and rubber.

"Now nudge it to me, gentle," I said. "No kicks. Just a shove."

Tariq toed the gun once. It didn't budge. A second bump. The weapon slid over the carpet. I stooped, good arm extended for the catch.

Nadine was faster. She grabbed the gun, a smirk plastered on her face. Rising from the crouch she fired toward Lola Conte. A bullet thwacked the rear door, denting its metal surface. Was Nadine's squeal laughter or a squawk of disappointment?

She lowered her hands for a second shot. This time she struck true. The bullet hit Conte in the right shoulder; a red hole spouted below the collar of her uniform. As the cop stumbled, her weapon leaped across the rug toward me. I reached to seize it. The handle was still warm when my palm curved around its ridges.

I shouted "No!" just as Nadine did, our voices blending in a choral surge. *No.* My index finger slipped into place against the trigger.

Nadine spun in a half circle, momentum driving her to one knee. She fired at me, but her crouch sent the shot zipping toward the high window. Glass shards clattered down the cement block wall onto the cop's hat. Sprawled, Conte didn't move.

I fired one bullet. Straight through the heart. Nadine slumped on her side, eyes fixed on the overhead lamp, a fond smile bending her lips. A corsage blossomed through the pleated fabric on her breast. Scarlet petals lapping over royal blue. She exhaled once, then died.

I rushed to Tariq, enfolding him with my busted arm. He ducked his head, driving the bony forehead into my damaged shoulder. I screamed, but only on the inside.

I let the gun slide down my right thigh. My hand uncurled, fingers licked by flame. The gun seared my palm. Could this stench be my burning flesh? I wanted to drop the dead weight, release my guilt. I'd vowed to never fire a weapon at another person. I'd used Monica's memory to bind the pledge; keeping guns at a safe distance was my way to hold her close. Now I'd broken that promise.

I dropped the heated weapon. Metal plunked on carpet. My whole body still hummed with the gun's retort. Vibrated with a promise violated. I'd wasted two lives, Nadine's and her baby's. Maybe I'd saved two lives, the kid's and the cop's. That balance would matter someday. But now, all I knew was I'd extinguished two. That horror scorched my empty gun hand. I squeezed Tariq tighter as we crab-walked backward from the crimson pool spreading below Nadine's limp body.

Flashing lights of squad cars cast red-and-blue bolts onto the office ceiling. Conte rose to her knees, clutching her shoulder. With blood streaming over her knuckles, she grumbled orders as her fellow officers flooded the room. Sweat slicked her tight face, hollows under her cheeks glowed green. Standing, she removed her hat to brush glass from its top. Then she pressed the hat to her chest before crouching to study the corpse of the woman I'd shot. Lola tipped the hat toward me and raised her chin in salute.

I pulled Tariq as far from the tidal wave of blue uniforms as I could. I knew we couldn't leave the scene. Not until statements had been collected and Lola's account was verified by the eyewitnesses.

But I wanted to tell Tariq one new truth. With my right arm still wrapped around his waist, I whispered, "This is important. Hear me. I lied just now." Panting brushed my words toward his face. "Your mother is okay. She came out of surgery this afternoon. She will recover."

He jolted. "She's alive?"

"Yes. I lied to make sure you came out alive, too." My wheezing was part agony, part joy.

He wept, bouncing his chin into my collarbone. "She's not dead. Not dead." His hair smelled of desperate sweat and baby shampoo. "Not dead."

I inhaled, my head muzzy with pain. "Yes. That's right. As soon as we're done here, I'll take you to the hospital to see her."

Tariq locked both arms around me, squeezing tight. Air jetted from my aching lungs, releasing gusts of rancid guilt. I coughed to cover the groan. I felt better than I had in almost three years.

# T FOR TULIPS

# CHAPTER **FORTY-FOUR**

Transformation of my backyard was overdue. The inside of my home looked like a spread in *House Beautiful*. The garden like an episode of *Scrapheap Reno*. Bald patches, gopher mounds, pockets of crabgrass, moss blankets dotted with toadstools. I couldn't do much for the space until spring, but I could make use of fall bulb planting season to start the beautification journey. Tulips were the canvas. And Tariq Bolden was the artist to undertake the work.

His father had been dead for seven weeks; his art teacher for six. Nadine Burriss, shot by my hand, died a month ago. A lot for a kid to shoulder. I hoped replanting my garden would deliver the boy solace as his world tilted on its axis. I didn't care if my motives were obvious; sometimes clumsy worked best. If the contact also thrashed out my guilt, good on me.

The quirky autumn weather cooperated with my horticultural therapy plans. After Halloween, a freak warm spell seized Q-Town. For two weeks, temperatures never dipped below fifty degrees. With the soil in my backyard still soft and swollen, mid-November provided the perfect weekend for late bulb planting. I enlisted Tariq Bolden for the job.

I decided on a tulip garden because I'd promised to bring those flowers to Mavis Jenkins's wedding. Mavis planned to marry Joe Kidd at the beginning of May. Tulips—hundreds of them in her favorite colors—would be my contribution to the wedding décor. Joe vowed to complete restoration of his art gallery by the chosen date. Fire marshals had wanted to condemn the structure. But Joe was persuasive and passionate. The gallery would be ready to make a splendid venue for their wedding. He swore it; Mavis believed him. Didn't matter what I thought. The ceremony was set for the first Saturday in May. Planting my tulips now meant they'd be up and ready to stun by that date.

But before Tariq started work, I needed a master plan for the garden. I called on Keyshawn Sayre, Rome School's head groundskeeper. And my friend, if I could still call him that. I needed Key to craft a new design for my yard. And I hoped to repair my relationship with him. We hadn't spoken in weeks and our chess game languished, untouched. I wanted to ease Key back into my life, if I could.

I phoned him on Wednesday, a week and a day before Thanksgiving. The next afternoon, Key drove his brown utility van into the alley behind my house. I scrambled down the porch stairs when I heard the clank of iron latches and the squeak of hinges.

"Come on and help me with this," Key shouted, his hip braced against the gate's wooden slats. "No excuses." He looked robust in his green corduroy barn jacket. A burgundy cloth cap pulled over his forehead left his ears exposed to the nippy weather of late afternoon.

I trundled over the grassy expanse toward the garage. "You know I can't do nothing trussed up like this." I pointed at the black cloth sling supporting my left arm. I'd managed to wrestle my damaged limb into the navy puffer coat and slip yellow knit gloves on both hands. A matching yellow felt beret warmed my head.

When I hopped over an exposed tree root, my shoulder protested the wrenching move. The arm was still out of commission. No cast for the fractured clavicle, Doc Klein said when I made my only visit to his office. Complete immobility of the arm was required. Fat chance. But I smiled and grabbed the prescription for Vicodin. Good for restless nights and rainy weekends when nightmares invaded my sleep. In those dreams, flames bloomed into red corsages and flares burst through the navels of distended bellies. No faces, no arms, only bonfires, and a steel gun scorching my fingers. Vicodin helped. Its smothering blanket provided relief and distraction. Better than booze, the pills gave me foggy nights at home, blurred hours in the office. I swallowed guilt with each pill, doling my horde in dribs. If I ached longer, maybe my killings would recede to a faint throb.

Keyshawn squinted at my sling. Then he pointed at the good right arm. "You still got one wing to fly with. So buck up, quit squawking, and hold the gate open so I can drag this thing inside."

I leaned against the gate. Then bolted upright. What the hell was Key carrying? With deceptive ease, he hauled a park bench from the rear of his van. Not an aluminum lawn chair or plastic stool. A whole-ass bench. I scrubbed my eyes like a kid on Christmas morning catching Santa in the act. The bench was a grand three-seater with scrolled black iron arms and feet. Wooden slats painted forest green formed the seat and back. Key dragged the bench to a spot beneath the three-hundred-year-old oak tree near the back wall of my yard. Grinning, he caressed the top rail. "Go on. Take it for a test drive."

I sat, swinging my legs like a toddler. Key tramped over the lawn, stamping divots he'd dislodged as he dragged the bench. "How you like your bench?"

"I love it, Key." I patted the seat, urging him to sit on my right. "But I don't understand. Where did you find this? And why?"

"I always thought a big lawn like yours deserved a pretty park bench." He stretched his arms along the back rail. "And I know how much you like the seat on the plaza in front of the library. So I figured you'd enjoy a bench of your own."

"I do. It's perfect." I shook my head in wonder. "Where'd you get it?"

He shrugged, smiles warming his handsome face. "Rome School has a warehouse full of old things. Furniture, machines, tools, equipment. They're always dumping the old, installing the new over there. Those Rome people got more money than God so they can afford to switch and scrap on the regular. When I saw this bench collecting dust in the warehouse, I figured nobody would miss it. I gave it a fresh coat of paint and knocked the rust off the scrollwork."

He stroked a finger over the curlicued armrest. "I knew I had to bring it to you."

"I love it, Key." Repetition was my safe move.

"Glad to hear it."

My heart pounded under the broken collarbone. The dance caused pain to swell, but I didn't care. "You're always looking out for me."

"It's my aim."

For ten minutes we sat on that bench, watching light play through the oak's bare branches. Gusts swirled dry leaves, making them prance over the lawn. I described my tulip hopes and my plan to enlist Tariq Bolden in planting the bulbs. Key grabbed a stout branch from between the oak tree's protruding roots. He drew a serpentine stripe along the fence as a boundary for the tulip beds. More etching in the earth around the oak then around its smaller partner, a sycamore. He dragged his stick beside the long fence leading to my back porch. The flower bed Key envisioned was massive. He insisted I plant at least one thousand bulbs.

When I objected to the size of the project, Key said, "Tariq Bolden is a youngblood. Grown and ready. Strong as a bull. He can handle the work. Let him do it. Let him help you." Key resumed his place beside me. "That's what he needs now. To be of help."

He meant more than that. Himself, me, we all needed to be of help. I settled my shoulder against his. Now was my opportunity to speak. While we were in this good place, warm and strong. Now was the time.

I said, "I want to tell you something. Something important to me."

Gazing at the dark house, he murmured, "Say what you need to, Vandy. I've always got time to hear it."

"These past weeks, I've been lying to everybody."

"For good reasons or bad?"

"Some good. To protect other people. Some bad, to protect myself."

"It's not bad to protect yourself. Never."

"Maybe. But I'm tired of it. I don't want to lie to you anymore."

"Say what you got to say, then."

"Phil Bolden. I slept with him. Last month. The night before he was killed. I wanted him and I did it. Maybe I hoped I'd restore my marriage. Or dreamed I'd remake our family. Maybe I missed the old days. Lots of reasons. None of them good. Then I lied to cover my selfishness."

I thought Keyshawn would withdraw his shoulder from mine. But he didn't. The weight of my confession seemed to press our bodies closer. Over his silence I heard the beat of heavy wings. The barn owl who lived in my oak tree had lifted from her nest to launch her night's travel.

Key took my right hand and pulled at the knit glove. When my skin was bare, he squeezed my knuckles, then flattened the hand between his two palms. "Thank you for telling me." No surge of surprise, no hitch or stammer. Had he known my secret all along? "You keep telling. I'll keep listening. Always."

The warmth of his hands reminded me how cold the night had become. I said, "Come back to the house. Have some coffee to knock off this chill."

He squeezed my hand. "Mark me for a rain check on that. I'm due at Bobby's house for Thanksgiving dinner tonight."

I craned to stare at him. "Thanksgiving's not for another week. Has your brother completely lost his mind?"

"Maybe, but don't tell him I said so." Key's rich laughter filled the air between us. "Actually, the shindig tonight is Celeste's idea. She's trying out new recipes for her Thanksgiving dinner and I'm her guinea pig."

Celeste was Bobby Sayre's wife and the mother of their three children. I recognized this was a switch in long-standing tradition. "Bobby's hosting your family get-together this year?"

Key nodded. "We got folks from three states driving in next week for the festivities. Twenty-two people." He whistled at the size of the event. "Celeste is flapping like a chicken with her head cut off. Double crazy now she's expecting again."

The pregnancy news hit hard. More babies, bigger futures. My chest ached. Not the broken collarbone. Inside, where I clasped my dreams. I gulped, then covered with a snicker. "And Uncle Key's the taste tester for her new menu?" I kept my voice bouncy. Frothy as meringue. I wanted him to invite me to the Sayre family party. I wanted a taste of their normality, to be included in the fun of Thanksgiving within their embrace.

"Yep, that's me." Standing, Keyshawn chuckled. "Hard head, cast-iron stomach." He patted his middle and slipped on his gloves.

No invitation. Not yet. Maybe another year. One without missteps or murders or lies or confessions. I stood from the bench. "Better get a move on then. Tell Bobby and Celeste I said hey."

"I will." He leaned to squeeze my right arm then expanded the embrace to a full-body hug. "Take care of yourself, Vandy."

I adjusted the beret on my head and watched Key turn for the garden gate. I felt clear, lighter than I had in months. This good man was right: telling was everything.

Two days later, Tariq Bolden and I filled the back seat and trunk of his Mustang with bags of tulip bulbs, potting soil, and mulch from Walmart's garden store. Keyshawn had specified one thousand bulbs. We bought two hundred more than that.

As Tariq backed his convertible onto the gravel path beside the garage at the bottom of my yard, I studied the colorful pencil sketches he'd drawn for our project. In his romantic rendition, the tulips would convert my strip of Q-Town into a little corner of old Holland. I'd specified flowers in orange, red, and pink. Watching him draw my ideas into reality, Tariq's sketches gave me hope. If we pulled together, this could work.

I watched Tariq hoist two sacks of red tulip bulbs on his shoulders.

Pleading age and infirmity, I toted one trowel and a thermos of hot chocolate. When I dropped to my knees, ready for digging, I asked, "How far apart?"

Tariq knelt beside me. "Give 'em room to grow, maybe two inches between bulbs." He planted three bulbs to demonstrate. He patted the soil with gloved fingers and reached to sink two more bulbs.

"*Oui, oui,* chef." I saluted and plunged my tool into the soft earth. Sun on my neck felt good, like a blessing. I kept my eyes on the ground, careful to preserve a distance between my shoulder and Tariq's as we worked. Like the flowers, he needed room to grow.

We toiled for twenty minutes before he spoke. "Do you think we could save a few of these bulbs. The flowers're going to be beautiful." He held one in the sunlight, turning his hand as if admiring a jewel. He peeled flaking skin from the bulb's belly.

I thought he wanted to say more. I asked, "You thinking of planting these somewhere else?"

"Yeah, maybe we could sneak them into the ground near the headstone at my father's grave. It looks basic right now. Naked. Like nobody cares."

I hadn't visited Phil's grave in Trenton yet. Couldn't bear the grief. Or the rage. Phil had done so much harm to so many people. But I'd go if Tariq wanted my help. "I think that's a fine idea." I hoped the lilt in my voice covered the doubt.

"You think it's against the law or something? Planting like that instead of leaving a vase of cut flowers."

I shrugged. "Maybe. People who run cemeteries don't always have the interests of the families top of their minds when they fix the rules. Insurance, city ordinances. That's what they worry about. Not feelings or hopes."

Tariq grunted and bowed his head. In the weeks since I killed Nadine Burriss, he'd let his hair grow. Curls framed his face and his neck like black petals. Despite the denim jacket and sagging sweatpants, he looked like a classical Greek statue sprung to life in my garden.

I continued, "But that's where people like us take the lead. We can sneak in after dark, stick tulip bulbs where we want them, and those crypt-keepers won't be any the wiser. You up for a raid?" I wriggled my eyebrows.

"You *know* it." Tariq's eyes snapped with excitement. "We'll be the Masked Planters. Like Batman or Zorro. No capes, only tulips." He wedged a bulb in the ground to demonstrate our disruptive technique.

I dropped another bulb into its hole. "What color tulips do you want to bring your father?"

"I'm thinking red and orange. He liked bold colors. I guess he'd like these."

"For sure. The louder the better. Orange and red would be perfect."

Tariq murmured, his face bent toward the ground, "Do you think we could plant tulips for Monica, too?"

I leaned until our shoulders touched. "Yes, I'd love that. I know Monica would love these tulips, too." I hadn't shown Tariq his sister's grave in Bethel Cemetery yet. Too raw, too soon. But this planting project would be a perfect chance to unite them. He deserved the connection; so did I.

"Let's add pink ones to the mix," Tariq said, his voice vibrant. "We'll scatter the bulbs. Random like. It'll be a surprise when they bloom next spring."

"Yes, a fine surprise." I sniffed, then scrubbed my gloved finger beside my nose to catch a falling tear. "I love the idea."

We resumed our work, speeding along the rear fence. Two hundred bulbs, three hundred, then five hundred disappeared into our trenches during the next two hours.

"Time out," I called after thirty minutes more. We'd reached the bed surrounding the sycamore tree. "Bio break. Bathroom, food, nap."

"Okay, sure. Whatever. I'm hungry. I know you got lentil soup in the fridge."

"Because you put it there." I laughed. If the kid had inherited his father's cooking skills along with the dimple, who was I to argue with genetics?

He said, "Right. Let's eat. My stomach's about to climb up my throat."

We brought bowls of hot soup and baguettes to the sunroom at the rear of the house. The space was nestled beside the screened porch overlooking the backyard. I could see the bench Keyshawn had installed for me under the oak. My own private niche of dreams. With the sun's light a faint crease on the horizon, I cranked the heat so the glassed-in room would feel as toasty as the kitchen.

Tariq and I sat side by side on a rattan sofa I'd saved from my parents' home. Matching armchairs flanked the couch and shared its green canvas upholstery. I left the floor lamps unlit. We could see well enough to eat in the gathering dusk.

The soup was chunky and salty, heaven in a bowl. I slurped to match the kid's gulps. Twice he hummed, like he wanted to start a new conversation, but then he swallowed the idea with another swig of lentils. Darkness enclosed the sunroom. But in the wisps of twilight, we could see the outlines of three deer as they inspected our gardening. Two does and a fawn shedding its spots for a first-winter's coat.

Maybe the little family inspired Tariq. Or perhaps the shadows over our faces gave him enough cover for his questions. "Will my mom do hard time? I mean, real prison, like, federal. Not a county jail?"

"I don't know." I shook my head, though I figured he could only hear the rustle of my hair against the cushion. "She's pleading guilty, so that should trim her sentence."

After three weeks in the hospital, Melinda Terrence had been transferred to a rehabilitation clinic in Hunterdon County for an extensive therapy program to restore full speech and movement on the right side of her body. I knew from Tariq that she was expected to remain in the residential facility for several months. Though her speech was impaired and she was temporarily confined to a wheel-chair, Melinda had begun cooperating with state and local law enforcement from her hospital bed. She pleaded guilty to counts of conspiracy to commit racketeering and money laundering. Charges of tax evasion were still pending. According to Elissa Adesanya's informal estimate, Melinda could face up to three years in prison. With time off for good behavior and continued cooperation, she might be out in twelve months. She'd get supervised release, a pile of community service hours, and a stiff fine. Cheap exchange for her life, I figured.

Tariq brought the case to a new direction. "Do you think my mom's testimony against Mr. Dumont will lighten her sentence?"

"Cooperation like that could help."

"Why you think he's pleading not guilty?"

"Who knows why smart people do dumb things?"

"Like he thinks he's better than everybody else?"

"If he can convince people the whole scheme was cooked up by your father and mother, maybe he believes he'll save his reputation."

"Stuck-up bastard." Tariq blew a raspberry across the surface of his soup.

"For real." I broke crust and stuffed my cheek with bread.

Tariq added, "But I heard some parents are dropping truth bombs on him."

"Oh yeah? Who?" Student networking was stronger than my intel game.

"I know Morgan Gaylord's folks are squealing. She said her dad spent two days in his lawyer's office, spilling everything about the college admissions scheme. Money, dates, emails. Morgan said her dad wants to nail Dumont to the wall."

"Good." I turned my face so Tariq could see my teeth flash in the gloom. "Couldn't happen to a bigger asshole."

I'd read newspaper accounts of emergency meetings of the Rome School board of trustees. The trustees had voted to suspend Dumont from headmaster duties pending the internal school investigation and the court trial. He was done-zo at Rome. I figured Dumont wasn't reviving his academic career unless Queenstown Middle School hired him as a janitor.

Now that Tariq had raised the subject, I followed with another question. "How's Morgan doing these days?"

He sighed. "She's okay, I guess." He glanced at the black lawn beyond the windows. The deer had vanished. "I mean, how can you be all right after something like that?"

I could ask the same of him. Had he contemplated suicide in the troubled weeks just past? I let it stew unsaid.

I asked, "Is she back at school now?"

"No, she said she hasn't got the stomach to face the kids." His breath rippled warm over my cheek when he turned his head. "Like me, sorta."

"You don't want to go back to Rome?" I knew he wasn't attending classes yet. I was glad he'd raised the subject.

"Not yet. I hear from Ingrid how the kids are talking. About

Morgan. About me. I guess we're celebrity freaks now." My barn owl's hoot punctuated his mournful comment. We listened to the bird's wings thrash the night air as she rose from the oak tree. Her evening's hunt had begun.

I stifled the urge to press Tariq to return to class. Not my call, but I wanted to push. Give him a lecture about getting back in the saddle. Facing your worst fears as the best way to overcome them. All that bullshit adults love to sling at defenseless kids. I knew badgering was an ugly kind of assault. But my tongue thickened with the mother's urge to nag.

Instead, I asked, "What do you want to do?"

Throttling that impulse was my finest moment in a season of mistakes. Maybe I'd get a handle on this adulting thing yet.

I heard relief whistle from him before he answered. "I could go back next semester. I know Mom and Dad paid tuition for the whole year. And my room's paid, too."

"Okay." Agreement was enough now that he was talking.

"And I know my mom wants me to finish the year. Graduate on time next spring."

"I bet she'd like that."

"Getting my diploma might be something I could do for her, you know. Maybe help her with rehab and everything. You think?"

"I'm sure it would help." I squeezed his knee. He'd arrived where I hoped he would go without my bludgeoning. Wins all around.

He cleared his throat. Change of subject. "I heard through the vine, your cop pal Conte got suspended after the shooting."

Tariq was more plugged into Q-Town rumbles and rumors than I was. Maybe a career as a newspaperman was in his future. Or—plot twist—a private eye. Over my dead body.

"Lola Conte's not my pal. But yeah, that happened. Routine after a police-related incident like that." I felt squeamish adopting that dodge of official lingo. Like I was part of the problem, not the solution.

"How long a suspension?"

"I don't know for sure. Most likely Conte will ride a desk for the time it takes QPD to complete their investigation of her. And me. Then they'll decide what to do." Did Tariq know Lola was pregnant?

If not, I wasn't spilling. She'd told me her baby was fine. Untouched by the bullet to the shoulder. And a boy. I owed a present now.

"Will they fire her?"

"Doubt it."

"But they have our testimony. Two for-real eyewitnesses."

"True." I'd spent many unpleasant hours with police interrogators getting my account of the shooting of Nadine Burriss into memo form. They had grilled me like I was a suspect, instead of a shooter in a defensive battle. I figured they'd done the same to Tariq.

"Doesn't seem fair," Tariq groused. "I mean. You saved our lives."

"That's how I see it, too. Nadine opened fire. I didn't have any option but to shoot back. My phone recording helped seal the case." The audio of those moments was muffled by my jeans pocket. But clear enough to exonerate Lola and me of wrongdoing.

At first, Black Q-Town had mourned the killing of respected church staffer Nadine Burriss. *Such a gifted young light. Called to glory too soon. Why they always have to kill our best and brightest?* But as more information emerged the complaints evaporated. Nadine Burriss's death was on its way to becoming a tragic legend in the Flats. Another painful chapter of our community lore: recited, revised, memorialized. A distorted object lesson for the young. Never erased; passed down the generations like a griot's tale. I'd read a *Trenton Times* article showcasing two families scheduled to move into new townhouses in Sutton Hill after Christmas. I remembered the paper figures of Nadine's dream city. These giddy families were her cutouts brought to life. She was gone, but her fierce obsession would bear fruit. The *Times* article heaped praise on Philmel Enterprises for spearheading the Sutton Hill renovation scheme. The loss of civic leader Philip Bolden was mourned by several neighborhood sources. No one mentioned Nadine Burriss.

Now Tariq wanted more information about Lola Conte's treatment by QPD. "Why'd they dump Conte on a desk job? Isn't that some sort of demotion?"

"More of a safety measure. Until she can get her mind back in the game. She needs the time and the inside work."

I knew from Lola's complaint that she felt the administrative assignment was indeed a punishment. After telling me the ballistic report on the bullet dug from my car proved Laurel Vaughn had not shot Phil Bolden, Lola griped, "I closed this case. And I closed it right." Over tea and graham crackers in my kitchen, I'd told her to take the cool-off period as a protective move, an arrangement benefiting herself as well as the department.

Tariq was running on the same rail. "Inside work? You mean inside an office? Or inside her head?" Smart kid.

"Both," I said.

Lola had grumbled, then showed me the business card of a psychologist. JUSTINA DIAMOND, FAMILY THERAPIST. QPD regs mandated six sessions on the couch and a formal clearance before Lola could return to active duty. "You figure this shrink is part of QPD protection, too?" she had asked. I recognized the name on the card. Four months after I returned to Queenstown, Justina Diamond's card had been pressed into my hand, too. At the time, I'd thanked my friend Elissa for the good intentions and stuffed the token into the junk drawer next to my fridge. My collection of those cards now rose an inch thick.

Tariq interrupted my memories. On a tangent, but not entirely off planet. Damaged friends were on his mind, too. "You know, talking about Morgan, I think there is something we could do for her." He nudged my right shoulder as he reached for a chocolate crunch bar.

"Whatcha got?"

"Her folks are going ahead with the family Thanksgiving dinner this week. Despite everything that's gone down."

"Ugh. That's kinda rough, isn't it?"

"I know, right?" His munching reminded me of the nosy deer. "But Morgan invited Ingrid to come to dinner. You know, like, for support."

"Nice plan," I said, wondering where this daisy chain was leading.

Tariq got us there quickly. "And Ingrid invited me to come with."

"Her plus-one?"

"Right." He paused, eyes flashing toward me.

"You going?"

"Sure. I got Ingrid's back. Always. She's my bestie."

So now they were sailing from hookup cove into the friends zone? News I could use to avoid awkward blunders with both kids. The ripple of laughter that accompanied his declaration sounded genuine. But I didn't buy the shift. For my money, desire was a forever itch. I was exhibit number one. But arguing the point was foolish. They'd work it out minus me.

Thanksgiving still on his mind, Tariq tossed another laugh. "And now I'm inviting you."

"Me?" I squawked like a plucked turkey. "How do I fit into this scheme?"

"You're my guest. I know Morgan would love to see you."

I let my sarcasm fly. "Her parents, not so much."

I recalled my conversation with Hugh Gaylord in the hospital lounge as we waited for his daughter to regain consciousness. How he'd tipped me to the details of the Boldens' college scam.

Tariq didn't know about that fraught exchange. He spoke to the practical side of the dinner arrangements. "The Gaylords got millions, billions. They can afford another place at the table."

"Thin the soup and add more cornbread to the stuffing, hunh?"

"Why not? You'd balance out the guest list."

"You think the Gaylords would make me eat at the adult table?"

"Not if you griped." He chuckled then tore the wrapper on a second chocolate bar.

"Thank you for the invite. I'll go with you." Not the Thanksgiving invitation I'd wanted certainly. But maybe the one I needed.

Now was the time to rip off a scab I'd been picking at for a month. Lies were core to my business model, the top tool in my private-eye kit. But the lie about the phony death of Tariq's mother still rankled. I wanted to get it into the open. See if he harbored any resentment.

"I want to apologize for lying to you about something."

"About my mom dying?" The kid was deep and smart. Gave me the creeps and made me feel proud at the same time.

"Yeah, I should have figured out a different way to handle that. Something else I could have said or done to throw Nadine off track. And not shock you."

"You tricked her. It worked." Not forgiveness exactly, but close. He sniffed, a whimper from the gut.

"Yeah, sure—but . . ."

He twisted his mouth to one side. "Lots of lies going around my family, in case you hadn't noticed. It's kind of the Bolden family code. Lie 'til you get caught. Then lie some more. You fit right in, Vandy."

"Because I lied?"

"Yeah."

"That's harsh. On everybody."

"But true. None of that shit happened. Not one fucking thing. All of them lied to cover for me."

"To protect you."

"With lies and attacks on each other." He choked down a cry. "Makes my skin crawl to think I pushed them into that. Like I failed."

"No, Tariq, you got it backwards. You're not to blame." I twisted my sore arm from the sling to squeeze his wrist. "We were the adults. Not you. Your parents, your teacher. Me. We had the responsibility to help you. Adults failed you, not the other way around."

"That simple?" He sniffed. "Some seriously fucked-up shit there."

"That simple, yes. And that complicated."

"Protect, maybe. Teach, for sure. That's what Laurel said." His voice hitched over a gulp. "When she drove me to the gallery, she said she wanted to teach me to burn down the world."

A lesson written in flames. "You couldn't know she meant for real."

I stood from the couch, rearranging my sling as I straightened. Guilt darted through my chest. Its edge was dulled and mottled like an old knife now. Still there, but sheathed. I could manage it.

Tariq followed me into the kitchen. The flare of overhead lights dazzled our eyes. At least, I decided that was the cause of the tear I swiped from my cheek.

After he stacked the empty soup bowls in the sink, Tariq patted puffy crescents under each eye with a dish towel.

"I've got ice cream in the fridge." I jerked open the door to the freezer side. "Vanilla, pistachio, or rocky road?"

"Nah, thanks, I'm okay." After scraping remnants of lentils from the bottom of the stockpot, he squirted dishwashing liquid and turned the spigot. Plumes of steam rose from the pot. He dunked the soup bowls, spoons, and the thermos bottle into the water where they disappeared under mounds of suds.

I leaned against the refrigerator, watching him roll his sleeves over sinewy forearms. I thought of the batteries, paper clips, coupons, rubber bands, and postage stamps layered in that junk drawer next to the fridge. The stack of psychologist Justina Diamond's business cards was still buried under that pile. Was this the moment to dig out the mangled card? Maybe Tariq could use a shrink's help. Me too, if I was honest. Did the shrink offer group rates? I could afford a family plan if the kid and I doubled up. Yes, we could make this work. We had to. For Phil. For Monica. Yes. For us.

Tariq plunged his fingers into the soapy water. I tugged open the drawer and scrabbled through the layers of junk with both hands.

# ACKNOWLEDGMENTS

Once more with feeling: Profoundest appreciation to my agent, Josh Getzler, who steered me and this book through a rough year with formidable grace and resilience. The team at HG Literary, especially Jonathan Cobb and Jillian Schelzi, brought their top game of smart readings and diligent insight to the push to make *Death of an Ex* a success. I can't thank you enough for your support.

I am eternally grateful to my editor, Madeline Houpt, for once again providing the creative leadership that helped Vandy Myrick flourish in these pages. Maddie's careful eye and ear corrected many shortcomings that plagued early versions of this book. Over the long haul of crafting *Death of an Ex*, the author and the fictional detective both benefited from Maddie's deft touch and patience. Many thanks also to the deep bench of talent at Minotaur Books. These stars of publicity, copyediting, promotion, and design delivered marvelous work. Huge appreciation as well to the experts at Macmillan Audio, who put together the fantastic audiobook. I feel privileged to collaborate with this dream team of book people.

To the readers who dived into these stories of Vandy Myrick, I am bursting with gratitude for your support. Vandy is messy in so many ways, which makes following her choices both challenging and, I hope, rewarding. I love writing about this tough, flawed, and vulnerable buzz saw of a character. I'm delighted that Vandy has found her people and been embraced by so many readers and fans.

A special shout-out to two remarkable organizations, Sisters in

Crime and Crime Writers of Color. With their diversity, generosity, and full-throated advocacy, these groups exemplify what is meant by community with heart. I am privileged to belong to the creative enclaves of SinC and CWoC. Finally, thank you to my family and friends, who support and celebrate my writing journey by keeping me hopeful, present, grounded, and grateful. To my children—Nick and Adam—Rachel, Matt, my brother, Steven, and most of all, John—every moment has been joy-filled because of you.

# ABOUT **THE AUTHOR**

STEVEN C. PITTS

**Delia Pitts** worked as a journalist before earning a Ph.D. in history from the University of Chicago. After careers as a U.S. diplomat and university administrator, she left academia to begin writing fiction. Delia is the author of the Vandy Myrick Mysteries, featuring a Black private investigator in New Jersey. She is also the author of the Ross Agency Mysteries, about a Harlem detective firm, and several short stories. She's a member of Sisters in Crime, Mystery Writers of America, and Crime Writers of Color. Learn more about Delia at www.deliapitts.com.